A CAGED AND RESTLESS MAGIC

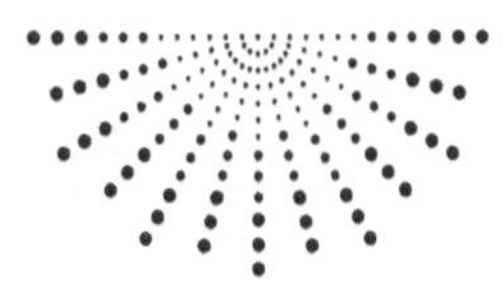

EMMIE CHRISTIE

A TERRIFYING HUNGER

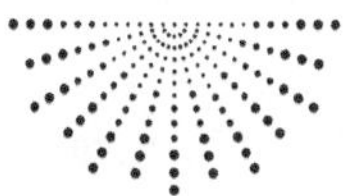

The air smelled of impending lightning.

Saida prowled up the foothill in her foxan form, spreading the pads on her paws wide to keep pebbles from shifting under them. Red fur covered her except for where she'd grown pockets instead, and of course, where the human hair in her tail refused to transform to fur. The sky over the nearby mountain grumbled with the beginnings of a winter storm.

Saida sniffed, following the magic scent of deep sleep, of a creature breathing so slow she counted them like the seconds before thunder. She tracked a full-grown swanseize. She'd only glimpsed yearlings before this.

The cave mouth opened in the side of the path. Saida flattened against the outside of it, panting a little from the surprise.

"Now, hold on," Tricksy Stone said. "When I said you need to focus, I didn't mean on something that could slice you to pieces!"

Saida slid the small, round rock out of her pocket. She flicked her ears back. The swanseize wouldn't hear their voice, but it might hear her if she answered out loud. She thought to them, *It's hibernating, so I'll be fine. And it's not a carnivore.*

Tricksy Stone stretched, rearranging themself into a long oval so their long end seemed to curve around her hand in an optical illusion. "But this isn't the magic you teleported to find. You should just ignore it."

"Even Tricksy's worried, see?" Goosefeather said from inside her left pocket.

You both worry too much. Saida shifted partway to human, standing on her hind legs. Her front and back paws changed to human hands and feet, and her fur retreated, revealing smooth, reddish-brown skin, the hue of riverbank clay after a rain. She grew clothing out of her skin like she grew fur: short red trousers, keeping the pockets where they were, and a cropped red shirt, more out of habit than anything else. Humans tended to get very strange if they saw the rounded parts of her bare-skinned. Her tail had morphed into a long red braid that swung down to her calves. She'd grown a few feet, too, but not to her full human height. She needed to remain small, but to gain dexterity. She slipped Tricksy Stone back into their safe place. Then she reached past Goosefeather and drew out one of three thin objects, each swaddled in rags. With nimble fingers, she unwrapped a tiny, empty glass tube with a cork, then sidled around the edge of the cave to the inside on two legs.

Even open to the outside, the temperature warmed. The interior opened to a higher area.

Bundles of bone and fur the size of adult male humans lay in random spots. A magic scent drifted, emanating decay, bile, and dried blood. Her nose pinpointed it with the same accuracy as if she could see it.

Oh no.

Its magic had overgrown and twisted its nature so much that it had attacked humans.

Saida crept along the wall away from the cloud, not wanting to immerse herself in the smell of death. The breathing grew louder, and the cavern heightened further.

She turned a corner and stopped. A giant snowdrift seemed to have piled up in here.

No. Not snow.

The swanseize had a long, graceful neck, and talons the size of her forearm. A shaft of light from an opening in the cave above streamed down, and the beast's white feathery wings glimmered like an aurora in a winter sky.

Saida's lips parted in wonder.

And then it yawned.

It unhinged its mouth at the end of its serpentine neck, revealing the raptor teeth meant for tearing tough plants by the roots lining the inside of its beak. A magical overgrowth of musty dreams and hibernation breath wafted out. Powerful enough to produce a transplant, for sure.

Maybe she hadn't teleported here for this specific magic, but it would work just as well. Besides, this swanseize had hunted and eaten humans, and if she left it alone, it would kill more and more as its magic twisted further. She'd found a few other overgrowths that had warped in such ways, always violent and hungry. Sometimes they would attack her, but she had to at least try to help.

She wiggled the tube's cork out, careful not to make any sound, and waited for the magic to drift closer.

It didn't.

"Don't," whispered Goosefeather, the more cautious of the two friends she carried.

Maybe she should fear it, but the stockpile of magic in the beast's breath enthralled her more than anything else. She inched off the wall towards it, a stronger and more concentrated scent than the one emanating from the balls of regurgitated human bones.

The swanseize rolled to its other side. Winter would end soon on Scent, but not yet. She held out the tube and let it fill with the magic, stoppered it, then tip-pawed back to the edge of the cave.

She slunk outside, gulped in a deep breath, and exulted. She had found magic that would work as a transplant, after a month of searching! She'd needed a transplant soon for Vision to meet her yearly goal.

Vision. She hadn't gone back to that world, since—

Saida shook herself and slipped the tube into her pocket. She needed to distance herself from the swanseize's cave. A yawn did come before a sleeper was about to awaken.

She jogged down the foothill's other side, towards the mountain. After about an hour, she'd reached the valley. Scent magic blanketed the area, created by the hundreds of squat aliberry bushes. She stopped to eat some, hungry after the thrill of encountering the swanseize. The fruit hinted at sweetness but left the term open for interpretation. She ate a handful, just to get more of the taste. Her stomach stretched uncomfortably.

"A smart foxan woman stocks up when she can." She patted her stomach. "Make room in there."

She popped three more aliberries in her mouth and twirled in the Scent magic. It roiled around her level with her waist, and she imagined the small foothill nearby as a mountain, and she as something huge next to it. Maybe a giant tree growing on its slope, or, if she opened her mouth wide, as one of its yawning caverns. She spun so the scent of aliberries whirled with her, until she ended up falling over from dizziness and a little bit of nausea, laughing at herself. She laid in a patch of open ground and the fog enveloped her nose, though Scent's rumbling, overcast sky remained visible to her physical eyes.

"You need to focus," Tricksy Stone said, jabbing her in the thigh.

Saida levered herself up and slid them out of her pocket. The rock fit round in her palm, innocent and smooth as a newborn baby. She pursed her lips. "I can hear you just fine. You don't need to be a literal prick."

"You told me to remind you. Your exact words were, 'Get my ass up if I get distracted for too long. It's important to help the worlds.' I'm just doing what you said to do."

Saida rolled her eyes, but she appreciated Tricksy Stone's warning. To her, it felt like a mere few minutes had passed since she entered the valley, but the sun lay low on the horizon, now. She had found the swanseize in the morning.

She didn't *forget* about time passing. She just got sidetracked sometimes.

Saida sniffed, checking the strength of the Scent magic the aliberries had created. Though large, it couldn't generate a transplant. The nearby wildlife ate the subtle fruit often enough, so that the magic the berries produced had enough room to stay in the same place.

The other overgrowth called to her, and she could pinpoint it better now, the closer she was to the mountain. Maybe she could snag two transplants in one visit to Scent. Such luck! Their nearness to each other had helped her find them on the same day.

It was the same day, right?

"Yes," Tricksy Stone said. "Though it's getting later."

An electric scent of lightning sizzled down nearby in a premonition of power, as if deciding where to strike. The smell dissipated.

At the edge of the valley, she found a little path that mice and their hunters used and crept upwards through the brush, laden with a few inches of snowfall. She chose her steps with care, avoiding the harder edges of crusted snow so it did not crunch underfoot. She shivered but grew her fur thicker under her clothing, shifting back to her full foxan form, and the cold didn't reach her anymore.

The snow smelled like dead leaves, as much of it had melted and mixed with the soil. The aroma filled both her nose and mouth, but with no more potency than on any other world. It produced no magical scent as the aliberries had.

A few years ago, by this very mountain, she'd had to hold a cloth over her face just to slog in melting snow because of the intensity, as if she had stuck her face straight into the slush. Now she could just breathe through her mouth.

As a foxan child, she'd found magic everywhere. Everything had seemed brighter, and stronger, and more intense back then—though, human children seemed to experience that, too. Regardless, it did seem like the worlds had lost some of their power.

I need to trim more transplants.

She didn't have trouble finding enough overgrowths. Not yet at least. She usually sensed at least one on the world she visited. Their magic rippled outwards, triggering her foxan senses even from across worlds, leading her to them like a bee to honey.

But the worlds expanded far past what she could explore as one person, and sometimes she couldn't focus. She could easily roam for two months without direction, purpose, or even a conscious mind.

She pondered her goal to avoid further distractions. Tricksy Stone's reminders helped, but she didn't want to just rely on them. *Each world needs at least one transplant a year, to keep their magic from fading. To keep them from drifting too far apart.*

She couldn't let another slip-up happen like when she had stayed in the world of Vision for three years. Vision had strayed farther from the other worlds after that; now it took a minute or so for her to teleport there, instead of in an instant, and sometimes, the portal didn't connect at all. She hated to imagine what would happen if the world floated even farther.

The sun slanted lower in the sky, shining on a small town nestled a little way up the mountain trail. She gave it a wide birth in case they had woodcutters or hunters or whatever else on their outskirts.

For a moment, the smell of pastries wafted to her, and laughter drifted up to where she paused on an overlook above the town. Small clusters of figures swayed in time to music.

Humans in the Scent world tended to distrust her kind, who they called fox-people, though that wasn't quite what she was. She avoided them as a rule so they wouldn't throw rocks at her, or worse. She'd visited that village a few times. A drunk man had mistaken her for a wandering prostitute once, as her human form's round parts seemed to tell him. He hadn't enjoyed the reveal of fur and sharp teeth when she had shifted to escape. She hadn't gone back since.

She climbed further up the mountain, and the bitter winter wind cut through her foxan fur. A sizzling, electric magic brimmed near the top of the mountain, ready for trimming.

"You could portal back, now," Goosefeather said. "You have a transplant already."

"But I could get *another*."

They seemed to shift in her pocket. "You're just procrastinating going back to Vision."

She had no answer to that. She shifted to her most human form, taller—with their long strides, they made better time.

The gray sky opened, and rain and sleet slicked the mountain path. Her teeth chattered. She couldn't hike much further in this storm; she might march right off the edge of the trail. She dug into a snowdrift nearby and tried to wait out the sleet.

After a half hour, a loud roar sounded further down the mountain. The swanseize!

She peered outside her little dugout. The sleet had thickened to clumps of white drifting down. The overcast sky, still gray with unfallen snow, lit up with flashes here and there: the magic of the sky itself. Brimming. Overflowing.

She had to journey on, or she wouldn't reach the mountain top when she needed to. Some overgrowths appeared at specific times— when their magics reached a peak. Besides, she didn't want to wait around if the swanseize might be headed her way. Shivering, she started back up the path.

She fought through the deepening snow even with her long human legs. She reached a plateau.

Lightning struck a nearby tree.

"I think you've gone far enough," Tricksy said.

"You might have an argument there," Saida said. She slipped her hand into her pocket and stroked Goosefeather's softness to calm herself. Grabbing her last tube, she uncorked it, swallowed hard, and thrust it up into the air.

She could almost imagine Goosefeather's worried intake of breath —if they had had breath.

"It'll be alright," she said. "The magic knows."

Another flash of lightning. Snow lightning — a freak winter storm, the sign of magic needing trimming.

The swanseize roared again, much closer, close enough that Saida jumped. In that moment, the lightning flashed near her feet, charring a part of the mountain stone, and magic exploded around her, the prickling scent of sparks and sweet electric light. It filled up her tube and she coughed, corking it, and dropping it into her pocket.

Something slammed into her, a scaly foot covering her whole body. She gasped, the breath knocked out of her, her vision sprouting colors.

A huge beak, snuffing at her pockets. Where she had her tubes. It wanted its yawning magic back, and it would rip her apart to find it!

She shifted to her smallest foxan form, trying to wiggle out from beneath it, but it only clamped its foot down harder.

Portal time. She opened her senses to the shifting fissures, those roaming chinks in space. She sensed one under the snow a few feet to her left, puttering like a mouse under the crust.

She couldn't teleport with the swanseize on top of her. It would fall through with her.

Saida snuck her paw in the pocket and pulled out the tube with the beast's yawn, then tossed it to her left. *C'mon, go after it! Forget about me!*

It snatched the tube midair with one claw, not letting her up. The swanseize regarded her with regal eyes, so high up on its snake-like neck.

It opened its beak, revealing those sharp teeth lining the back of its throat. It had just woken up, and it looked hungry.

The giant creature screamed and toppled off her. It flapped its wings, swiveling towards something, and blood spurted from a wound in its side.

Saida gasped, able to breathe again. What could have injured a swanseize? Her vision blurred and refocused.

A human, yet not human, stood there. At six feet, he seemed too thin, and his arms draped too long, all the way to his knees. He didn't have skin, or even bones. His form consisted of smoke, or smog, and tattered bits of him wafted up like smoke from a fire. He cradled a black box in one arm, with strange, snake-like designs on all sides.

Insubstantial as he looked, his oversized hands tapered into claws and dripped with the swanseize's blood, and from him emanated a sense of unbearable hunger, a grasping, reaching need to consume.

The monster she had accidentally let loose on the world of Vision.

He stepped forward, and the swanseize screamed again, and backed away, stumbling, then spread its giant wings and leapt off the mountain plateau.

The not-human rotated, not his whole body, just his smoking neck towards Saida. "WATTHE," he said.

She swallowed. Back when she had first seen him, she had said, "What the—?" in consternation. He had repeated it, over and over, as he'd hunted her.

"WATTHE." He strode towards her.

"Now! Teleport now!" Tricksy Stone said.

She told the portal where she wanted to travel, bolted towards it, and pounced through the snow.

* * *

SHE EMERGED from a snowdrift on the other side, gasping for breath, ice crystals clinging to her. She clambered out of the drift as fast as she could and twisted to look back.

Had he followed her?

The portal closed seconds later. She waited.

Nothing. No horrific gray humanoid with claws for hands. She shuddered and shook herself, raining ice all around, speckling the blanket of snow. Her whole body trembled like a rabbit frozen in the eye of danger, and she panted with her tongue out. She couldn't sweat in her foxan form, so she shifted to more human, with two long legs.

How had Watthe—for that was the only thing she could call him, now—journeyed to Scent? He shouldn't be able to do that. She'd left him on Vision.

Best not to think about it. She would just go on with her day and thank the Senses she had escaped.

She tried to slow her heartbeat. She had teleported to where the twelve or so Scent portals stayed in Between, a region with some brush and small hills. The portals roamed the area like a herd of animals. The winter here reflected the winter in Scent, though nothing generated magics in Between, so the snow did not smell any frostier than a normal winter.

After a minute or so, she trotted down one of the hills, guessing at the snow-laden path that led out of Scent's portal area. She needed to check on her den.

In her pocket, Goosefeather hummed a little tune. "Home, almost home, almost home with friends."

Two foxans, both shifted to their full foxan form, loped nearby through the snowy brush. "Father!" She called.

Darrow, her father, had a graying coat and four reddish-brown stripes along both cheeks. He stopped and panted, his tongue lolling out. "Saida, my little autumn leaf! How—how long have you been . . . gone?"

"Three days," Tricksy Stone said.

"Three days," Saida repeated.

Her father twitched his ears. "Huh."

Pell, the other foxan, stopped and circled back around. Gray speckled his brown coat except for the left side of his forehead, where just chapped brown skin, thin and papery, remained. Besides Saida, the three remaining foxans on Between had all aged well into their seventh century.

Pell blinked and licked his paw, then rubbed his bald forehead. "How are . . . the worlds? Did you find . . . my Genma? She lives on . . ." his brow furrowed. "Sound."

Saida swallowed a lump in her throat. Pell's daughter had died hundreds of years before Saida had been born. "Pell, the humans don't live as long, anymore, remember?" She paused. "I have looked for Genma's descendants, though."

"Gemna's gone?" Pell's shoulders slumped. "I . . . guess she is. How could I forget?" He raised his paw to rub at his forehead.

"Pell, you're doing it again." She shook her finger at him. He stopped and looked sheepish.

Saida sighed. The holes in the older foxans' memories changed and moved like the portals in the ground. Sometimes they told her stories of how permanent portals had once connected the worlds, and how humans from Vision could visit Scent, or Taste, whenever they wanted. Other times they struggled to remember Saida's name.

If she didn't remind them, who would? If she didn't help them, maybe their minds would fade along with the worlds' magic. None of them had shifted to their human forms since Saida could remember.

"Once I find your descendent, will you come with me to visit them? On Sound?"

Pell ducked his head. "Can't leave. Can't. The Hunger. The box." He shivered.

The Hunger: the one thing the old foxans seemed to remember with any clarity. They'd told her about it over and over, a powerful entity from over 800 years ago that wanted to eat their magic. She'd thought of their stories as melodramatic memories of humans, but now, she couldn't help but match their stories to the stark image of Watthe striding towards her with blood-red claws, a strange box in his arms.

Her father flattened his ears and dropped to his belly, whining like a dog at the mere mention of "The Hunger."

Saida bowed her head to hide the tears burning in her eyes. She waved goodbye. The snowy path wound around the hills on a slight decline, and the uneven road began showing through as she left Scent's winter portal area.

Goosefeather brushed her leg. "It's hard, we know."

"Isn't it cruel for me to remind them of their descendants?" Saida wiped the tears away.

"You can gauge when to try, and when to leave them be," Tricksy Stone said. "It's good that you try to get them to come with you. Though I don't think they will."

"I wish they could hear you, too. You could help them, like you've helped me."

"Everyone's help looks different," Goosefeather said. "You're distracted and forgetful for other reasons—"

She stopped listening. After about ten minutes, the temperature warmed, and she entered a forest.

Between was not large. Saida could traverse it in an hour, less if she shifted to human. She couldn't understand the other foxans, who hadn't left the tiny world for seven hundred years or so—if she believed their stories.

Saida had counted every tree in the forest once—3,124—had roamed every little hill and swum the lake hundreds of times. Nothing ever changed there. The lake water remained pure, the birds and rabbits and other small animals repopulated at the same rate, and the trees never grew or died. The Between didn't have any sensory-based magic, but it did seem to be fed with the magic from the other worlds, so that it remained a tiny, perpetual utopia. Compared to the rest of the five other worlds, however, all just a portal's length away, it made Saida feel cramped and trapped if she stayed there too long.

"Saida!"

Falrie trotted out of the woods. Saida grinned. "Hey, Mom."

"You have been gone for . . . three days!"

Falrie was a lanky, handsome foxan, the lines on her snout accentuating her cheekbones as if they refused to show her age. She always remembered things a little better than Pell or Saida's father. "There is a terrifying appetite out there, Saida. A thing that . . . wants to consume us!"

Saida wiggled at an aliberry seed stuck in her teeth, trying to feign ignorance. The too-thin smoke humanoid loomed in her thoughts. The foxans couldn't find out about Watthe, or their fear might take over completely.

"Mom, you tell me this every time I come back. But I can't stay here."

Falrie reached out and laid a hand on Saida's half-shifted paw. "I know you're restless. Believe me, I remember being a new adult!" Her gaze softened. "Just—try to check in a little more often . . . okay? I worry about you."

Saida curled her claws over Falrie's. "I'm sorry. I'll try and be better."

The older foxan bowed her head. Just like the others, she never shifted to human form. Saida didn't know if any of them could, anymore.

Falrie's gaze drifted to the sky, her eyes glazing over.

"Mom?"

Falrie didn't respond, and Saida drooped. She half-shifted, shrinking, and her long braid morphed into her tail, tucking between her legs.

When the other foxans went into their trancelike state, they could do it for hours at a time, or even days. Falrie and Darrow were Saida's parents, and Saida was born three centuries ago, the sole foxan born after the Severing of the Worlds. Apparently, stable portals used to connect all the worlds so even the humans could travel among them—but the Severing, a vague event that none of them could remember—had cut them off from each other except through the foxans' ability to teleport.

It did help Saida to check in more often, and they always seemed happy to see her, so maybe it helped them, too. It also served as a routine of sorts, so she didn't lose track of time and stay on one world for months on end.

"*I* tried to get you to come home sooner," Tricksy Stone said.

She jiggled them in her pocket. "Congrats, you've won the self-righteousness prize. It's shiny and golden and isn't at all shaped like an ass."

Goosefeather cackled. "It definitely is, though."

Saida jogged towards her den in earnest. The forest's familiar trees flashed by, and the hill where she had dug out her den. Her safe place. Her home.

She sailed through the short, round opening, just tall enough for her half-shifted form, and inhaled deep.

"Welcome home!" Jar of Sky said, up on the little makeshift mantle, in their dreamy, breathy voice.

"About time!" Crinkle Leaf Pile said.

A cacophony of voices flooded the den from the thirty or so magic trimmings she had collected. She laughed and spoke to each in turn, admiring them all according to how they preferred. She swirled Rosewater in their tube. She held Jar of Sky up above her head and oohed and ahhed at the pinpricks of stars they displayed. She jumped in Crinkle Leaf Pile and rolled around on them, joyous in the fact that they never flattened but remained the perfect dried and crunchy texture.

"What do you want to be called?" She asked the Scent magic.

She pulled out the tube of lightning. They zipped around in their container, still frazzled, unsure. The whole den stilled, and some trimmings gave little gasps.

"I am—called Winter Lightning," they said in a sparking, electric voice. "I was—so angry. I wanted more. Here—it is different. Here—I am not angry. But—" They raised their voice and sparked inside the tube. "I still want more."

"I know," Saida said. "You're big enough to transplant to another world. I'll take you there soon." She sighed, patting the now-emptiness of her pockets. "Remind me, Tricksy Stone, to check on the swanseize next winter. If it survives its injury, I'll still need to trim its magic."

She might not like humans, but she didn't wish them harm. The swanseize would kill and eat more of them before she could trim the overgrowth that drove it to do so.

"Winter Lightning's a good name," Tricksy Stone said. The pattern on their smooth surface shifted, showing an optical illusion. "Now, who wants to hear the story of how our gardener almost got eaten by a swanseize?"

"Maybe tomorrow," Goosefeather said. "She's exhausted. Look, she's already closing her eyes on Leaf Pile."

Saida yawned. "Go ahead and tell stories. I'm just going to take a little nap."

2

TO LOVELY, GREATER HEIGHTS

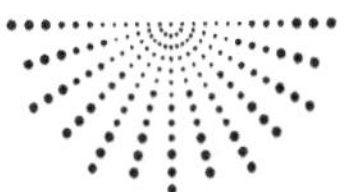

Alesio practiced holding his breath.

As a security guard for St. Rina's cathedral, he had to stand still for hours on end—no shifting his weight or scratching an itch. In the pews, people crowded shoulder to shoulder for the morning service, yet no one fidgeted. Everything echoed inside the cathedral; the vaulted ceiling amplified every voice, every crescendo, every note, and the parishioners did not wish disrespect with careless noise.

Alesio didn't just work at the cathedral for the money, though it did pay well. When he held his breath, keeping even his internal sound at the lowest possible level, the acoustics of the place, the silence itself, reverberated through the bottom of his boots, and even a little bit through his half-deaf left ear.

The reverend Lasrial ascended the stage on the right, his crimped golden robes trailing several feet behind him, symbolizing the god of Sound. He promenaded past the line of bowls on the altar, filled with all different kinds of food from the parishioners, and the spoons they had tapped three times for their offerings of sound. Aromas wafted from the bowls, and Alesio's nose twitched with appreciation.

Lasrial lifted his arms, his wide sleeves just brushing the marbled floor. "Do you hear me, worshippers?"

The congregation replied in unison to the rote question, their voices reverberating upwards, all around, loud, bright, and swift. "We hear you."

"We are blessed to have the Cadenza's own bellringer, Hestafon Jaffrey, here today." He gestured to the performer already on stage.

Hestafon bowed in front of a table where he'd arranged his bells. Purple bows lined the collar and lapels of his silk jacket, matching the purple bows the performer had tied to each of his bell handles.

Would I need a fancy outfit like that to perform at the Cadenza?

He hoped not. It looked expensive. And stupid.

Of course, Alesio's guard uniform seemed a bit much to him already, with its golden shoulder pads and how the crimped sleeves and trousers matched the Sound statue waves.

"I'm honored you have come to listen to me today." Hestafon plucked one of the mid-sized bells from the table in front of him.

Alesio rolled his eyes. The bellringer had added the words, "to me" to the rote phrase, a not-so-subtle boast that the congregation had gathered to listen to him as much as worship the Sound. Hestafon had performed at St. Rina's twice while Alesio had worked there, and each time, the man's arrogance seemed to multiply.

Though, many of the people packed in today *had* come to listen to him. Everyone leaned forward and murmured: "We're honored to witness your worship."

Hestafon raised the bell, holding the clapper down with his other hand to keep the instrument silent. Alesio had held his breath for the last five minutes, and his lungs stayed strong. The congregation seemed to hold its breath as well, heads tilting up in reverence to the statue of the Sound, that god of the ear that rose to the highest part of the vaulted ceiling.

A thick sheet of gold rising from a stone base seemed to ripple upward like waves on a golden sea. The depiction of the god of Sound always caught the air in Alesio's chest and squeezed it.

Hestafon rang the first clear, crisp note. Alesio released his breath, closed his eyes, and matched the note with his voice, keeping it aligned with the pitch and the tenor, so no one noticed his addition.

Hestafon picked up a second bell and played a quick, angelic song, a composition worthy of the Cadenza's name.

That's a new piece. Irritation roiled in Alesio's stomach like a bad piece of hotrat. As much as he disliked Hestafon, talent did not always bless the most honorable of people. The bellringer belonged on that stage.

A cough. An older lady in the fifth row covered her mouth with a handkerchief. Her pew mates stole side glances at her and straitened their postures, angling their shoulders away in that universal sign of disapproval.

Alesio swallowed, hoping she could control it, but another cough rang out, this time in between bell notes. Hestafon shot her a side glare as he swept his arms in a grandiose way, striving to keep the audience's attention.

The lady had seated herself on the left side of the congregation, Alesio's side. He strode out of the shadows and waited at the end of the fifth pew, his gaze forward, his arm held out as if for a dancing partner. The old lady sidled past her crowded pew mates with a shamed face and rested her hand on his arm. He escorted her to the outside to St. Rina's garden—sound-proofed by the line of dense bushes surrounding it.

"I'm so sorry." She wrung her handkerchief like a dishcloth. "I thought the cough was gone this morning. I just missed service so much. I couldn't miss Hesty!"

"Don't worry about it." He tried to keep the accent from the straits out of his voice and his lips from quirking at the ridiculous nickname. "Happens to everyone."

The lady hadn't used Sound magic or done anything beyond making a noise she couldn't control. Nothing ever happened at St. Rina's that warranted real security. The worst thing an attendee had done was shout in excitement while worshipping the god of Sound. No sign of sharp-edged voice blades or arrows whispered from afar. No one would dare try such things on the piper side of town, where no one even plugged their ears for safety when they slept. He turned to leave the sound-proofed garden.

"Clef wants to talk to you," the old lady whispered from behind him, near his right ear. His good ear.

"What?" He wheeled, his jaw tensing.

She folded her handkerchief and slid it into a pocket. She'd stopped coughing, and her voice had shifted to the more jagged accent of the straits. "He wants you back. Says he has a match-up for you, an out of towner. Big money."

Alesio gritted his teeth. "Tell Clef I'm not interested. I paid my debts."

She raised manicured eyebrows. "Making it alright here, I see. Maybe I should apply to be part of security. Keep myself secure."

"Maybe you should. You're older. It's hard to stay sharp out there."

"Young man." She stepped forward, and her voice warned that she could sing blades. "Age is a whetstone of experience. It only sharpens. Dullness comes when you take yourself out of the game."

He licked his lips. "It's not a game if it's my life that I'm playing with."

"You seemed to enjoy it enough back at the cages, with everyone shouting your name." She paused. "Requ—"

"I'm going to have to ask you to leave."

"With the same answer?"

He opened the door to the cathedral's garden and gestured for her to leave first. She tsked and sailed out, then waved to him with her handkerchief as she left.

It's been two years. Feels like yesterday.

He'd made Clef so much money on cage matches, over a hundred whole notes each time at least, but the strait's leader hadn't counted most of it towards his debts. "That's your room and board's worth," Clef had said. "And I sponsor your fights. You can leave when you make your own money." He had finally named an actual price after Alesio had asked for two years.

Alesio had scrimped and performed in the street for years, then had shoved the 45 whole notes at Clef. The leader had kept control of his face except for the corners of his lips, which had wrinkled with fury like a snarling dog.

Clef must really miss the money I earned him if he's stooped to begging me to come back.

He began holding his breath again, strode back inside the cathedral, and took up his post again in the shadows off to the side of the pews. He could try and beat his record of five minutes and 36 seconds. He had control over that, at least, regardless of where he worked, or what he did, and it helped quell the anger roiling in his gut.

Hestafon finished his performance and bowed. The service ended with a few more call and response phrases from the reverend Lasrial and the congregation.

The parishioners gathered up their offerings of food they had and filed out of the cathedral, and Alesio tensed. If Clef had sent someone to attack the famous bellringer to make a point to Alesio, they'd do so now, when people were distracted.

But, of course, nothing happened. Clef didn't mess with the piper side. He ruled the straits with an iron fist; the other straiter factions in the past decade had fizzled out after he'd infiltrated them all. He knew his place and dominated it. *Dullness comes when you take yourself out of the game.*

Once the parishioners had all left, Lasrial swept back in from bidding goodbye to the crowd and closed himself in his side office. This signaled the start of their short break. Alesio relaxed his stance and scratched the itch that had crawled up his left elbow, though he still held his breath. He strolled over to the offerings of food left at the altar, rubbing his hands together in anticipation.

The god of Sound did not eat, of course, and had no need for food, but Lasrial encouraged the practice, so the church didn't have to feed their staff. But free food was free food. He picked up a bowl of sticky rice and clinked the side of it three times with a spoon, as tradition dictated.

The other security guard, Tak, strode over to the altar as well and clapped Alesio on the shoulder. "You seem out of sorts, kid. That old lady trumpet at you for forcing her out of the service?"

Tak was a well-built, mustachioed man in his forties who enjoyed playing the harmonica in his free time. He didn't need the money, but he worked at St. Rina's because he enjoyed the services. A true worshipper of the Sound.

"Not exactly." Alesio spooned rice into his mouth. "She just wouldn't stop talking about other things."

"Ah. Yes, well, some older people are like that."

"You would know, I suppose." Alesio grinned and pointed with his chin at Tak's salt and pepper mustache.

Tak tweaked the stiff ends of his facial hair. "That I do. That I do. Estro likes it, though, and his opinion counts the most. He says it makes me look distinguished." He raised his eyebrows and waggled them.

Alesio laughed and handed him another bowl of sticky rice, the most common food offering. "I'm just going to ignore that. How is Estro? You two decide when to get married yet?"

"He's just a little worried about the house we picked out." Tak shrugged and clinked the bowl three times. "Says it's too close to the middle of the city. I told him it'll be alright. The middle's not what you have to worry about, you know."

Alesio nodded, a strange little lump in the back of his throat. Tak didn't know Alesio's background, and Alesio planned on keeping it that way.

A crinkling from up on the stage made them turn. Hestafon had plopped into a chair on the stage, opened a candy from its wrapper, and bit into it. The candy burst open and drizzled honey on the table.

Alesio gritted his teeth. He'd have to clean the table later or Lasrial would trumpet at him. And did Hestafon care about his instruments at all? What if he dripped honey inside the bells?

Of course, the Cadenza performer could just buy a whole new set if he wanted. Alesio had saved for so long to buy his antique mandolin, but he kept it tuned and inside its case.

Hestafon harrumphed. "Security."

Alesio and Tak eyed each other. Tak swallowed a bite of rice he'd just taken.

The performer crooked his finger to summon them. They set their rice bowls down and moseyed over.

"Yes, sir?" Tak asked.

Hestafon flitted his fingers, holding out the wrapper to Alesio. "Throw this away for me, one of you."

Alesio gritted his teeth but grabbed the sticky wrapper and transported it to the trash bin off to the side.

This is just until I get my big break. Working at the cathedral paid the bills, so he could perform in the evenings and catch the ear of someone at the Cadenza.

He had to believe that he'd make it, or he'd find himself somewhere else, somewhere even lower, where he definitely didn't want to be.

MONA HAD GIVEN Alesio the prime 10:00 time slot at the Drinks De Capo, when everyone was just sloshed enough to throw money in his donation jar, but not sloshed enough to shout drunkenly in the middle of a song. He began his set with a medium tempo number, "Miss My Berry-Lipped Lady," and about a fourth of the pub joined in, raising their drinks on the chorus. He'd learned the mandolin to accompany himself, as he didn't want to split the performance money. His average playing functioned as a chip to convey the cheese.

He loved to sing.

Magic flowed out of him and engulfed the place. The reverberations of his voice tingled up through his feet, a little like when he had sung the one note at St. Rina's. He couldn't see the magic, but he *could* see its effects. People smiled and swayed with the beat, their eyes dreamy, caught in their own fantasies of their berry-lipped ladies or berry-lipped men, those maybe lovers they passed on the street and who might say yes, if the singer just worked up the courage to speak.

He had a few fans. The same four or five women had frequented the pub every week or so for the past couple months, and they always shot him winks and smiles. His berry-lipped ladies. He found himself grinning and wondered if he might ask for a dance with one, maybe the girl with the chestnut hair and the soprano laugh. They might like his looks and not just his singing, but at least they tipped well. He might break past a note and a half tonight.

He finished the first song and bowed to scattered applause. He waited while more beer flowed, more donations fell in his jar, and drank some water to keep his voice up. He tilted it back to mimic a shot of alcohol to remind the customers to keep drinking, too. A little bit of the water spilled on his shirt, his nicer performance shirt of higher-end cotton, an ivory color to accent his dark brown skin. Good thing he hadn't spilled actual wine or some other spirited drink on it.

The crowd waited, buzzing, now, heads turned his way, faces inviting and smiles wide. The five girls' conversation near the front floated up to him.

"I told you!" The one with the soprano laugh said to a girl from another table. "He's good, isn't he? 'Alesio.' No last name. I wonder if that's his stage name."

"We have to come next week and remember to invite . . ." he lost the rest in the loudness of the room.

If only his father could see him here, doing well, climbing up in the world. People respected him here. People knew his name.

Well. Someone *did* want to listen to him. Someone important. Mona had told him that a few days before, a piper with the Cadenza insignia on their lapel had shown up, asking the days when Alesio performed. A talent scout.

He grinned and raised his cup and shouted, "Drinks!"

"De Capo!" The pub roared back. The chant encouraged people to drink 'from the beginning', to buy drinks all over again.

"Drinks!"

"De Capo!"

With a dramatic flourish, he began the next song, the second fastest in his set: "Strings of Fate" which had a quick and jerky rhythm, like a puppet on a string.

> *Do you know the one above us,*
> *They who pull the strings?*
> *They make us dance and set us up*
> *And like birds, we all take wing!*
>
> *Oh, our strings of fate are heavy,*
> *Though they give feathers for to fly,*
> *Do you dare to cut them, do you?*
> *Do you have the strength to try?*
>
> *Do you know the ones below us,*
> *Those ones who flew so well,*
> *Who defied the one above us,*
> *The puppeteer, I've heard them tell*
>
> *Do you know the ones around us*
> *Who cut their strings just right,*
> *Those who use their feathers*
> *To soar to lovely, greater heights?*

He finished the song with a rousing chorus of "Do you have the strength to try?" And repeated the De Capo ritual. Most of the bar seemed to enjoy his rendition, but the people at one table all crossed their arms and jutted out their chins, most of who wore silken clothing. Pipers.

He sang "Strings of Fate" for those who disliked living in the shadows when the golden light of the Cadenza shone just a few streets over. Mona's pub split the two sides of town. She brought in the curious few pipers who gambled to visit the 'dangerous' side, and those from the straits who dared to visit the 'golden' side. He'd need a different song in his set for when the scout visited.

"Plum cream wine?" Mona said to the next in line at the bar, a man dressed in his factory uniform, a rough fabric that had faded to a greenish gray from many washings. "Coming right up." She reached behind her to her fancier bottles, priced much lower than a few blocks over. The factory worker waited with a quiet eagerness. The man couldn't have bought such a beverage anywhere else. Mona slid the drink along the bar-top with an ease that would've seemed reckless if her movements had not also spoken of the practiced dexterity of many years.

Mona managed the Drinks De Capo with a smart mind for business: she hired only the best performers of the lower end of the city, inciting the curiosity of the pipers and the pride of the straiters. Alesio wouldn't have had a chance to attract a Cadenza talent scout at all without her hiring practices. No other bar in Anthem brought in the unique blend of customers hers did. Though sometimes it made pleasing everyone a little difficult.

More donations in his jar. He'd guess he was up to about a quarter note or so. Some customers pulled out personal cloths and wrapped them around their heads to mute their hearing between songs, so their ears wouldn't begin to hurt with all the noise. A few ran up and grabbed some complementary cloths that Mona kept on the edge of the bar. People used cloths both for sensory overload and protection against more sinister sounds, depending on where they lived.

Raucous cries rang out for another rendition of Strings of Fate, but he didn't want the energy to peak too soon. He brought his arm down slow and let his voice tremble a little. "This one is for holding hands, so hold someone near and dear and sing along. You all know the words: this is "Dear Flute, Dear Love.""

He sang the tragic ballad of a woman cursed to live inside a flute, who fell in love with the man who played her, though she could never tell him because she did not have lips. The crowd sang along to the sad tale. A few straiters in their factory uniforms, now immersed in their drink, cried on their tables. One shouted, "I hear you, my flute! I do love you!"

Alesio let the last measure ring out, and it shivered through him. His five fans stuffed a few sixteenth notes in his jar, wiping tears. The pipers seemed to have liked that one, but now a few guys near the front fidgeted. They'd come for partying songs.

What would his father have liked to listen to?

Who was he kidding? His father wouldn't have taken the rags from out of his ears, citing his mantra, "You can't be too careful! You never know who might try and cut you with a sharp whisper!"

Alesio licked his lips, shouted, "Drinks!" and played a party song, the fastest he had in his repertoire, and ended up dancing with the soprano-laughter girl—though, when drunk, she seemed more interested in kissing her friend.

After his hour-long slot, he packed his mandolin back in its case and counted a note and a quarter in the jar. Not a bad night. He left a half note with Mona to put towards his discounted room above the bar, then hid the rest under the floorboards behind his nightstand. Then he traipsed out into the night along the brick road.

A few people passed him, and their footsteps fashioned a rhythm, a beat in his mind, and the wind sang a melody along with it, a light, subtle piece, like a bird about to fly. A song of hope. Music flowed everywhere if people listened for it.

He picked up his pace, climbing a staircase that led up to a higher street, then to the landing that overlooked the piper side.

The sky shone a velvet black with few stars. The lantern lights of Anthem sparkled in comparison, and the Cadenza glittered the brightest of all, that building with the giant pipe organ gleaming high and golden against the night. The people on the piper side seemed to play in a different time signature, exchanging whole notes like half notes, and half notes like quarter notes. The sound of the city in the evening—thousands of people below talking, singing, and playing guitars, some washing their face or brushing their hair or kissing their lovers—all of it rose around him like the drumming of rain on bricks, the individual sounds mixing and merging into the singular, distant roar of life. He breathed in deep, and held it in his lungs, that breath filled with the noise of the golden side, and the Cadenza over it all like a giant statue of the god of Sound.

Many people worshipped whatever they imagined the Sound

looked like. Most worshipped the golden, rippling wave, like the one depicted at St. Rina's. Some worshipped the Cadenza itself, and that seemed the closest to godhood he could imagine. He wondered what performing would be like in that place, how a high note might ring with a clarity he'd never known, or a low note might boom with enough resonance to bring him to his knees. How silence itself might speak with more wisdom and clamor for more attention.

Even though some might call him unworthy, or out of place, or say he should use his voice as a weapon—someday, he would perform there. Someday, the whole world would listen to him, and know his name.

3

THE SOUND OF SWEETEST SILVER

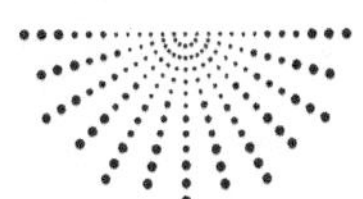

Venturing into the world of Sound was noisy, of course. Venturing into the city of Anthem was like walking into a trumpet.

Music spilled out of every third building, which usually displayed a bar sign. Corner singers repeated the same song all day to update citizens on news, advertisements, and idle gossip. Most everyone on the wealthier side wore silk scarves tied around their ears to diminish the general volume.

Saida passed a corner singer that mimicked an upbeat flute solo, their tongue curling and flicking, their throat bobbing up and down, though the sound had a slight tinny ring to it. The sign on the shop read "The Flutist Ravina" and someone had arranged toy flutes in the shop window all signed by Ravina. Down the street, another corner singer imitated a guitar a little better than the one for the famous flutist, even pretending they played one of the guitars from the shop, though the sound resonated from their mouths. In the shop window, someone had arrayed toy guitars, the traditional recyclable mugs and bowls meant for offering food to the Sound, and the small statues of the golden wave representing the Sound itself.

Saida skulked along the edge of the street, keeping an eye out for any fox-people, the descendants of her fellow foxans, though they tended to hide even from her. She was hunting the overgrowth she could sense somewhere in the city. She hadn't pinpointed its source yet, though she sensed the overgrowth on the wealthy side. The tendrils of its magic reached out to her as if asking for help, like a silver set of bells ringing in a sweet, yet desperate, alarm. Her ears tracked the sound just like her nose could on Scent, or her eyes on Vision.

She could also sense a transplant, one that she had already placed into Sound, somewhere off in the straits. She did not remember doing that.

"Want me to remind you?" Tricksy Stone asked.

"I can't get distracted right now." She paused. She should check in on the transplant at some point. She'd like to ask how they felt in their new world. "Remind me later, though."

She tried to blend in. She had grown a hood and a high collar to conceal her un-shiftable sharp, foxan chin, transformed the fur on her legs into silk pants, and changed her back paws into soft boots. She'd tucked her long braid behind the hood.

One corner singer pointed at Saida and sang:

> *Have you heard about our violins*
> *Shaped like two hearts entwined?*
> *Come buy them at the Bow and Heart*
> *And see your love align!*

Saida pulled the hood further over her face and turned from the singer, only to have another on her opposite side sing:

> *The noble pianist, Lotes,*
> *Says of our chocolate,*
> *'The sweetest drops of half notes*
> *That you will ever get!'*

Each human harnessed the raw magic of their world and produced an altered version of it. They used it in unique ways, and some could harness it better than others. In the largest city on Sound, with so many humans in one place, it made everything very loud, especially in the first few hours before she'd adjusted to the volume. These corner singers were not helping.

She didn't like to mess with human magic. It was never potent enough to create a transplant, and to trim it, she'd have to get much too close.

The two corner singers both vied for her attention, now, with louder and louder renditions of the same verse, inching closer. She quickened her pace and dodged into a clean nearby alley behind the chocolate store, her fingers trembling.

"So, you'd rather be near a deadly beast than human merchants?" Tricksy Stone shifted in her pocket. "What are we going to do with you?"

"Rude," Saida said. "The swanseize was sleeping. The humans could try to keep me in a cage."

"Well," Goosefeather said. "At least you'd have chocolate. And you could just teleport away the next day."

"I could try to change into a giant gem for a few seconds," Tricksy Stone said. "That would get their attention. And you could sneak back and grab me later."

They had pulled a trick like that together once, back on Taste. They'd managed to snag a long, thin wafer called an olo, flavored with cinnamon and chocolate. She hadn't even handed Tricksy over; the store person had just stared at their gleaming ruby surface while she'd pilfered the treat under their nose. Of course, then she'd had to run.

But later, Tricksy Stone had had trouble changing back to regular size. They hadn't fit into the largest pocket she could grow, and she had had to find somewhere she could lug a giant gem around in her arms. And she'd known that, if she had tried to teleport while they'd been stuck in that shape, they couldn't have teleported with her.

"We're not doing that again," Saida said. "You can't do it unless you're on Vision, or you might stay like that. You might transplant."

"You know I wouldn't, though," Tricksy Stone said. "I won't unless I have no other choice."

Sound had the largest population out of the all the five worlds with its two cities, and Anthem was the larger city of the two. To venture inside a store on the pipe organ side, or "piper" side, as the wealthy called themselves? She may as well ask them to cage her up right then and there.

While the rich wore head scarves to denote their status, everyone had to show their ears when entering piper stores to prove that they didn't have rags stuffed inside their ears, as people from the straits did. The poor deafened themselves to keep safe from sound knives, rather than for comfort from the loudness of the world.

Shifting to her human form did not change her *all* the way to human, just like she couldn't transform all the way into a traditional fox. As a human, she always had more angular cheeks and chin, and pointed ears that never changed, no matter how she tried, and sometimes her eyes refused to switch from vertical black slits to human ones. When in her full foxan form, sometimes she couldn't change her back left foot or front right all the way, and her tail always had strands of human hair in it.

Saida peeked around the alley corner, gritting her human teeth. Anthem was one of the worst places she could've sensed another overgrowth. She'd much prefer to have detected it at least in Sound's countryside, which stretched far beyond what she'd even begun to explore or link the portals to, just like the other worlds. She'd even have taken going to the ancient ruins on Sound instead. At least it would have been empty of living humans.

"You don't like anything unless it's the wilderness," Tricksy Stone said. "And why aren't you taking Winter Lightning to Vision? You already have a transplant. Why chase down another one in a city? You hate all cities!"

"It's efficient to find more than one at a time."

The corner-singers had switched their attention to other passers-by. She bolted past, listening for that luring, calling sound, that magic that had caught her ear even in Between. She couldn't tell its source, yet, but she had gotten closer. It didn't emanate from the giant pipe organ building, the Cadenza, thank the Senses. That place had way too many humans ready to pounce, guarding it like a den. Only the most respected and wealthy people performed there, and she didn't know that part of Anthem well enough to escape if someone discovered her. Well, maybe she used to know it, but she'd forgotten it by now. Why did she have to remember the things she wanted to forget, but forget the things that could've helped her?

There! The cathedral top appeared around another corner, high in the distance. Somewhere in there, it had a . . . bell. Its magic rang clear to her now, powerful, and sweet.

"You can't avoid Vision forever." Tricksy Stone bumped her in the thigh. "Just because that's where you found Watthe, doesn't mean you can pretend the whole world vanished! It needs a transplant!"

"She is acquiring transplants quicker, this way," Goosefeather said. "Fear of one thing means she just focuses on another."

"Hey," Saida said. "I'm right here!"

Tricksy Stone flipped in her pocket, their way of throwing up their hands. "This is just like when she doesn't want to go to Touch. Took her four months this time around to go there. She's gonna run out of worlds at this rate—"

Saida slid Tricksy out of her pocket, grasping them in both palms so their shine didn't attract any nosy human. Their smooth surface modified in small optical illusions; the top right half that should have led to the bottom angled back up in an impossible way. They could move a little, but not as much as they could've on Vision. "I'll take you back there after this one, okay? I know you miss it. Thank you for staying with me."

Tricksy Stone shifted their angles in a semblance of a paradoxical smile. "You know I want to stay. You don't have to thank me."

"Excuse me, miss?" A bright-eyed young woman with a red head scarf around her ears appeared in front of her before Saida could lower her head, holding out a sample tray of chocolates shaped like the Sound wave from the store down the block. She stared at Saida, and whatever lyric she had prepared to sing, however, died on her lips. She narrowed her eyes.

Saida shot away, weaving in between people along the sides of storefronts so she did not cause a scene in the middle of the street. *Have to escape.* Sweat beads popped up on her arms. *Cannot get caught.*

She ended up panting near a bunch of morning drunkards, too confused to notice their own feet, let alone the strangeness of a random woman's face.

The cathedral rose nearby, just a few streets over.

Gonna find the overgrowth and get out of here. No distractions. No lingering. Teleporting to Vision did sound better at this point than navigating a town full of people. Watthe had somehow traveled to Scent, after all. He wasn't on Vision any longer.

She squinted up at the huge building. The windows arched up like eyebrows on a disapproving store owner. Too high for her to jump to. And she couldn't very well waltz through the massive front door; they'd check her ears for sure in such a swanky place.

"You'd think," she said to her two friends, "That having portal magic would get me anywhere I want. But no. Having energy to teleport once a day just lands me in trouble."

"*I* think you manage to find trouble just fine on your own," Tricksy Stone said. "Like with the swanseize."

"That wasn't trouble. That was fun." She prowled around to the other side. A small door nestled there, big enough for people without giant egos. She tried the knob. Locked.

"You can't go in there," a raspy voice said.

Saida whirled and crouched. The voice had come from inside a line of thick shrubs a few yards away. She peered closer and a v-shaped chin took shape in the semi-darkness. She sucked in a sharp breath.

"The church is guarded," the fox-person said. "You should leave now."

"Why are you here if it's so dangerous? Why are you on the piper side at all?"

The eyes flashed in the semi-darkness of the bush like two tiny full moons. "Some of us know the way in and out. I'll take you, but we must go now. If someone sees you, I can't help you."

She hadn't had luck finding fox-people in Anthem before now. A tell-tale angular chin or glinting eye had caught her attention once or twice, always scampering away, not even daring to stay in the alleys for too long, not daring to beg. Afraid, even, of each other.

Saida stepped closer to the line of bushes. The fox-person wore a nondescript, faded brown cloak, and their cheek sported faint yellow stripes. If she could just make out the pattern, she could maybe figure out which foxan they descended from. "I can't right now. Where are you staying? I can meet—"

The v-shaped chin pulled back. "Nowhere."

"Please. I'm from out of town. I'm trying to find—"

"No one knows each other's safe places. If a human found one of us, it ends there. If we break, and we know where someone else is? They find another, and another." A pause, and a rustling. "Are you coming or not?"

Saida sighed. "I have to get into the cathedral."

The eyes narrowed, then flashed again. "Are you trying to steal the magic in there?"

Fox-people could sense magic, but they didn't have the ability to trim them like foxans did. She'd tried to explain the process before to the few fox-people she'd met, but none hadn't believed her. She doubted this one would either.

"No. Never. I—I just want to be close to it."

A growl. "Better not. It's dangerous enough for us, you know, without rumors of magic-stealers flying around to fuel superstition."

"I promise I won't. I should go in, before someone sees me."

She turned back to the cathedral, feeling those eyes on her from within the bushes. She *really* hoped she could do this without causing a scene. Creeping back towards the side door, she pulled out Goosefeather. "Can you help me?"

"Are you doubting my abilities?"

She slid them into the lock, twisting them in her fingers, listening.

A little click sounded, and the door slid open. She pocketed Goosefeather and crept inside.

Find the bell. Avoid the people.

She tiptoed through the room, a small washroom, and couldn't help but touch the soft washcloths and towels. An urge to curl up on one of the towels as a foxan swept over her, but she suppressed it. She had to focus. She couldn't just play around inside a human town like she could out in the wild. Even though humans did make some of the softest towels ever.

Another door. She listened, waiting, with her ear against it, just in case. No sound came from the other side—nothing, except for the increasing sound she hunted, ringing in her ears. She twisted the knob, and the door slid open without any noise. The humans kept the hinges well-oiled, here, in this place of worship. That made sense. Any sound made here was supposed to be the on-purpose, showing off kind. She peeked around the corner.

The room opened into a gigantic inner hall, as large as the swanseize's lair. The emptiness seemed to echo, and Sound magic surrounded the huge wave statue up at the front: a representation of what the people imagined the god of Sound looked like.

Saida tilted her head, considering it. Maybe they did look like that.

The humans on each world worshipped their specific magical sense. She didn't know if any of their gods were real. If they were, would they leave the worlds so empty? As much as she disliked humans and their towns, not many remained. Vision had just one tiny village.

Regardless, the golden Sound statue didn't produce the overgrowth she looked for. People visited here all the time, and bits of its magic clung to them when they left, so it didn't hold much excess. She swung her head from side to side, hunting for the sound that rang and rang and rang in her ears, louder now than in the small washing room.

Up on the dais, near the statue? She shifted, shrinking, using her soft footpads to dampen any sound she might make on the marbled stone floor. The magic of the bell emanated from there, mixed in with the Sound statue. She skulked up the steps.

An instrument case lay on the stage, and inside nested several bells in velvet-lined divots. A sweet, yet strong, magic hovered over one of the bells. Not enough to make a transplant, but more than enough for her to trim.

She had overestimated its potency. It happened sometimes—magic was hard to gauge from across worlds.

She slumped. She hadn't *needed* a transplant from Sound. Not really. She'd just wanted more time before she visited Vision.

Why was it so hard to do the things she knew she should do? She wanted to help the worlds and keep the magic from fading, she did, but at the same time, her brain did not always agree with her legs.

"Hey!"

The shout rang out like the sound of a silver bell. She jolted. Had she stepped on the bell and rung it by accident?

A stocky human in a dark-blue and gold uniform appeared from out of the shadows on the side.

She slammed the case shut, grabbed the handle in her mouth, and dashed down the steps. *Shit! Shit!*

"Stop! Hey, stop, uh, fox?"

He leapt to cut her off, quicker than she'd expected. She skittered to his left, ducked under his arm, and bolted through the open washroom door. The case banged against the side of the doorframe, and she hoped she hadn't damaged the bell.

Focus, Saida, Focus!

She loped through the washroom, the guard shouting behind her. A punch of Sound magic thudded against the door to the outside, flinging it shut. She shifted her legs just tall enough to reach the doorknob and her front paws into human hands to twist it, still holding the case in her teeth.

"What? How did you—did anyone else see that?"

Saida yanked the door back open and shot outside, panting with panic.

She couldn't teleport yet. She could only do it once every sunrise.

"Stop, thief!" The guard chased her in the side alley. No flash of reflective eyes greeted her from the line of bushes, and she hoped that the fox-person had left. If they witnessed this fiasco, she would never gain their trust. Maybe she should have tried later.

Too late for that now.

She couldn't barrel into the bushes and reveal the fox-person's secret, safe path, not with the guard in full view. She pulled the case out of her mouth and gripped it, whirling in a blind guess towards a street. The people passing there jerked their heads up.

Hide. She had to hide! A small hole in a brick wall caught her attention, and she shifted down again, shoving the instrument case through, and then squirming after, to the gasps of the people behind her. She loped along the wall as a foxan, gripping the handle in her mouth, her heart hammering.

People yelped. "A half-beast!"

One woman shouted at her, "Fur-mix!"

She flinched. The same slur popped up in the different worlds with a frustrating regularity.

I hate cities.

She came to a break in the wall, and the guard waited for her there, his gold-shouldered uniform easy to spot. She skidded to a stop and dodged his grasp, though this time he grabbed onto the case. She shifted back into a half-human—a full transformation took a few seconds—and in his surprise, she yanked it back.

"Stop, or I'll use force!"

"That wasn't force?" She sprinted towards a side alley, leapt onto a dumpster, and jumped over a wooden fence. With the guard out of sight, she darted through someone's back yard. She jumped another fence, dashed through a grittier alley, and huddled down between two houses, gasping, trying to control her breathing. The guard shouted a few side streets over but didn't seem to close the distance.

She had to do this quick.

Saida shifted to full human in case she needed to sprint down the alley, then set down the case and popped it open.

The bells remained untouched in their expensive lined and inset molds. She slid out the seashell she had brought from her right pocket and pulled the bell from its velvet protection, listening.

A tickling, puttering sound came from within.

Curious, she peered inside, careful to keep the clapper from ringing. A swarm of ants trundled around inside the bell, feasting on something sweet and sticky spilled on the inside. The unique sound had created the magic, coursing through the bell so that the instrument quivered in frustration, wanting to pour out into the world with louder and louder ringing, unsatisfied with silence.

Saida smiled and held out the seashell so the magic of the ants' movements and eating trickled into the container.

"You promised!"

Saida tensed and almost dropped the clapper but held it back just in time. She didn't want to startle the insects inside.

The fox-person hissed at her from a nearby shed, wreathed in the shadow and their brown, featureless cloak. "How dare you show yourself to humans? Give the magic back!"

"I swear on the Senses, I'm trying to help. I'm just trimming it." The shadow of the shed just allowed her to make out the stripe pattern on the fox-person's face. Three faint orange stripes marked both their cheeks, and two more down their chin. Not any pattern she recognized from Pell or her parents.

"You!"

The guard darted around the corner of the house. Saida set the bell back down in its case with care, then slipped the seashell in her pocket. The human slowed and held his palms up, as if to show that he had nothing to hide.

A quick side glance told her that the fox-person had disappeared.

The guard inched closer. She flattened her ears under her cloaked hood and growled. He stopped, but too close, close enough to grab her by the scruff.

Carn's voice echoed in her mind. *Why don't you want to stay? Why do you want to leave me?*

No, no, no! She couldn't think about him!

"I don't want to hurt you, fox, uh, lady," the guard said. "Just give the bells back. This doesn't have to be difficult."

Wait. Now that she had contained the sound of the insects, the tenor tones of his voice rang clear.

The guard possessed the overgrown magic!

She hadn't realized it in the cathedral because of how he'd startled her, but the sound of sweetest silver poured from his lips like a freshwater spring in the mountains. The overgrowth she had sensed from Between.

Once she heard it, she couldn't help but also notice his neat and trimmed beard and how it outlined a strong jaw. His dark-brown skin brought out a chocolate in his eyes.

Saida blinked. She couldn't trim a transplant from a human, and not this one for sure. His quickness and strength alarmed her, and those large hands could shove her into a cage.

I have the small trimming from the bell. That's enough. I need to leave.

Saida still couldn't teleport. She had to hide somewhere till sunrise, away from prying eyes. She backed away from the open case of bells, then took off, chancing one backward glance.

He had dashed over to the case, then stared after her with a furrowed brow. He did not give chase.

After a few minutes of furtive ducking around fences and darting through back alleys, her heart quieted a bit, and she found a space under a porch.

"His voice is pretty," Tricksy Stone said.

"Yes, I know."

"And his arms."

"His *arms* are pretty?"

"Don't deny it," Goosefeather said.

She scoffed, but fiddled with the seashell, focusing on the sound echoing within. The sound of tickling inside a bell, the sound of happy insect feet. A unique sound.

But not as unique, and not near as powerful, as the guard's voice.

"It's time I took that transplant to Vision." She'd rather travel to the world she'd avoided than be lured by the beauty of such a sound and get caught.

4

THEY WHO PULL THE STRINGS

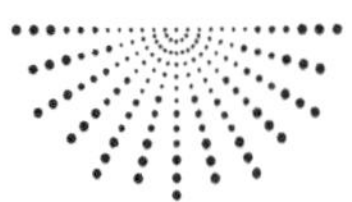

"Do you have any idea what this looks like?"

Alesio and Tak stood at attention, their eyes forward. Reverend Lasrial paced in front of them, his crimped golden robes fluttering along the thick carpet. The bell case lay open on the desk in the reverend's office.

"A theft in the middle of the day! From a—a fox-person! A creature from corner-singer songs!"

Alesio held his breath to keep himself from saying anything. He didn't want to incur further wrath. He held his breath for a lot of reasons.

"Hestafon will talk about this for months!"

Tak winced and almost covered his ears but stopped himself. The soundproofed office protected anyone in the main worship hall from hearing Lasrial's ranting.

In times like these, Alesio was grateful for his partial deafness. It made up for the other times when it made things more difficult. Times like when he'd cried, trying to listen to the street musicians' harmonies, trying to pluck out the exact notes and match them with his voice, but his defective ear blocked the sound. With his left ear angled towards the reverend, Lasrial's voice seemed farther away, like a harsh chord played across the street.

You're a natural, kid, Clef had said. *That ear of yours gives you a natural shield. You wanna make some money for me? Just for a couple fights. Keep you and your dad in enough notes so you can eat.*

"—we to persuade future Cadenza performers to perform here if any filthy, homeless half-beast can snatch their beloved instruments?" Lasrial swept his silken long-sleeves wide.

"With all due respect," Tak said, "The fox-woman didn't end up with it—"

"I didn't say you could speak in this room," Lasrial said.

Tak shifted his weight, his white-flecked handlebar mustache twitching. As a piper, the older man probably wasn't used to such dressing-downs, where the purpose was not to inform, but to humiliate. Alesio kept his chin tilted down to show proper shame and a submissive posture.

It didn't seem to matter how far up Alesio climbed or what job he worked; people still treated him the same. Lesser.

Lasrial pointed at Alesio. "You will clean out the bells and write a personal apology to Hestafon."

"Yes, sir."

"We will send out a notice regarding the thief. Probably rabid."

When he'd seen the fox-woman at first, in the cathedral, he'd thought a small dog had wandered in, but then she'd shifted into an adult woman in mere moments. Her tail had changed into a long braid, and he could've sworn that her clothes had *grown* from her. Her bright red fur had rescinded on her face, limbs, and midriff, revealing smooth, reddish-brown skin underneath.

He'd heard the corner singers' songs regarding fox-people, of course. Performers from the straits tended to sing older ballads, which sometimes mentioned the strange creatures. Alesio had never even considered that they existed.

She'd had such glimmering, galaxy eyes that locked onto him when he spoke.

"How dare it come inside the cathedral? It's almost like it was daring us to catch it." Lasrial paced in front of Alesio, then back to Tak. "Why, if the songs are to be believed, she could have stolen Hestafon's magic!"

Once Alesio had caught up with her, he could've sworn that she'd pocketed a seashell, of all things, and had left the bells.

"It doesn't belong on our streets! It should stay in the countryside with the other wildlife. And why would it vandalize an instrument just to abandon it?"

"Sir," Alesio said, before he could stop himself, releasing his held breath. "She didn't spill the honey. Hestafon eats honey candies, and he dropped honey on the table near the bells. He must have dripped it in the bell as well."

Lasrial stopped pacing in front of Alesio.

Damn it.

"That reminds me," Lasrial said. "You're on half pay for the week."

Alesio bit his tongue. Breathed in deep. Gave a short nod.

He'd forgotten his main job, here. Silence. Taking the beating. Holding an impassive face like it didn't hurt, working so near his dream on the golden side of town, and keeping his voice down to calm the anger of the powerful.

I need to impress the scout for the Cadenza. He couldn't stay here much longer.

THE TRANSITION FROM ST. Rina's cathedral to the straits always held Alesio in a kind of trance.

Bright red rooftops and tidy roads led to grime on the side of cramped buildings, the edges of streets lined with trash. The people near the middle of town power-walked to places and more of them wore hoods over their ears, to hide whether they had earplugs in or not. And yet, those may as well have lived on the golden side when compared to the straits.

Cramped buildings led to dirt roofs caved in, with makeshift straw and wire holding up each family's sky. The trash edging the roads led to piles in the center of the streets, people lighting them as the afternoon chilled into the evening. Shouts rang out like alarm bells, always ringing, ringing, ringing, triggering the fight or flight instinct, till the body either wore down or tuned it out. Alesio's 'natural shield,' as Clef had always put it, trained him for the latter.

He strode along in the shadows, ducking between the burning trash piles where the men clustered in their greenish-gray factory uniforms, the shreds of rags stuffed in their ears. Many small factions worked the straits, but Clef had infiltrated and ran them all under the umbrella of his. Alesio did not want another conversation with one of his lackeys, sent to bring him back into the fold. He'd changed out of his cathedral uniform to his straits clothing: a factory worker pants and shirt that he'd purchased at one of the straiter shops.

The screams of a cage match echoed from farther off in the heart of the straits like a dissonant melody, the part of a composition created to make the listener suffer along with the singer. The men around the nearby street fire didn't even flinch, the rags in their ears softening the sound. One of their shoulders bore the marks of their wins, another sported them on their cheek.

Alesio didn't use rags or plugs for his good right ear. Even with the danger of a sound knife in the dark, he'd rather try to listen for the steps of a possible assassin than to shield himself further from their blade. Other sound weapons could be made but knives were the quickest and easiest to fashion with the breath.

Of course, he'd have no chance if they had an amplifier. New rumors from Flock, the city a few days' journey away, told of groups there having silver devices that fit inside the mouth. They could pierce a sound shield, or even Alesio's natural deafness, amplifying and sharpening their blades of magic to impossible levels.

The spire of the instrument factory loomed out of the darkness ahead. His father had worked there for the past twenty-six years and where Alesio would have worked too, if he hadn't found the job at St. Rina's.

One lone corner-singer, shivering by a dive bar, sang to potential customers with the enthusiasm of a melancholy parrot:

> *Sit on down, down, down*
> *At the Eighth Rest,*
> *We'll help you find your god of Sound.*
>
> *Drink your found, found, found*
> *At the Eighth Rest,*
> *No pews here, but we got good ground.*
>
> *Get on found, found, found*
> *At the Eighth Rest,*
> *Yeah, there's plenty 'nough to go 'round.*

Passing the Eighth Rest, he arrived at the hostel where his father spent his few non-working moments. Among its more attractive attributes, the building featured one broken stained-glass window and a dirty sign that read, 'One Bag Policy.'

Alesio trudged up the steps and opened the door. It squealed and slid partway, then ground to a stop. He had to sidle sideways to fit through.

"Just visiting," he told the woman at the front, a wizened, wiry cage match fighter by the thin sound-scars running along her jawline. She wore a tattered jacket which she'd sewn seven crooked tally marks onto, displaying the number of wins she had on her record.

She squinted at him, then her mouth dropped open. "Requiem?" Her whisper almost didn't register.

Shit.

"Not anymore." He slipped her a quarter note. "Not to anyone."

His father had just changed hostels for this reason. Alesio would hate for another incident where a horde of sweaty, desperate, admiring, jealous men mobbed him. His father would hate it even more.

The woman smacked her lips. "One time there was, I saw this . . .

'Requiem' fight." She kept her voice low, but Alesio still flinched on the inside at his old alias uttered out loud. "He caused quite the upset at the betting booth. Made his sponsor rich as a rat in a piper dumpster, he did." She cleared her throat. "There's some who'd pay good money to know where he is, now."

Alesio gritted his teeth but added an eighth note to her outstretched hand. She tucked the money in her sleeve, then smacked her lips again and shrugged. "Ten minutes to visit, or you pay for the night."

Inside the hostel, men slept in stacks of thin beds and one sheet. Flashes of sleeping in such places as a child made his shoulders tense up, and he shivered and cracked his neck.

"Alesio!" His father swung his legs off one of the middle bunks and faltered his way down the ladder. Alesio offered his hand to help, but his father shook his head. "I can do it. I can do it." He reached the bottom after much hesitation on the last step, as if the ground wavered underneath him.

His vision has gotten worse.

His father smiled up at him and patted his shoulder. His thin frame spoke of the long, hard years working at the instrument factory, and parts of his eyes had whitened to a milky color. He wore rags in his ears. "It's good to see you, my boy."

"Let's talk outside." Alesio flicked his gaze around the room of 25 or so sleeping men, many of them snoring fit to wake the god of Sound themself.

"Yes, yes." His father trundled ahead, and Alesio followed him past the cage fighter at the front and back through the broken door.

He dug in his coat pocket for the little bit extra he had earned at the pub the other night. "Here." He slipped the notes to his father's hand in a quick, stealthy motion. "For this week."

His father didn't glance down at the notes, as was standard good practice when transferring money in the straits, but he brushed his fingers over them, and frowned. "This feels like more than usual."

"Been doing alright."

"They give you a raise at that fancy church?"

They both spoke in undertones. Alesio shifted his weight and angled his good ear towards his father to hear him better. "I have a few fans at the pub, now."

"Sssk!" His father slapped Alesio's shoulder. "I told you to quit that weeks ago. You shouldn't spend time anywhere near the straits when you could work full time at the church!"

Alesio cut his gaze to the street. One man shambling past had jolted at the sound of rebuke, but he hurried on. He turned back to his father.

"I'm close. There's a scout coming by tonight. From the *Cadenza*. I have a chance to make it for both of us."

"You're already making it plenty. You could be living a piper's life. But you're going to throw it all away on this dream, eh? You're staying close to the straits cause you like being near the cage matches?"

"You know that's not true." Alesio fought to retain control, holding his breath in between sentences. He didn't say anything about the woman Clef had sent to the cathedral the day before, and the message underneath. That Clef wanted him back.

He couldn't mention such a thing without his father perceiving what he had tried to quell in front of that old woman: that he *did* miss the cheers of the crowd. At least there, he had had actual recognition.

Alesio shook his head. "It took seven years to pay Clef off and get out. I'm doing better things. Bigger things."

"You're doing good, son. You are." His father slipped something into Alesio's pocket. The extra thirty-second note Alesio had given him in addition to his normal five. *Him and his sounddamned paranoia.*

"This isn't from fighting," Alesio said. "I earned it fair."

"I just want you to make the right choices."

Alesio ground his teeth. "You know Clef owns the people behind the factory, too, so really, you still work for him." His throat felt raw. He swallowed.

"Not officially. I don't have my name on any of his pieces of paper." His father straightened and crossed his arms. "He doesn't have any leverage on me, so he can't force me to do things that might hurt you."

Alesio raised his chin and crossed his arms, then uncrossed them.

He didn't want to mirror his father's motions. "Why can't you just let me take care of you? I can do that, now."

His father's milky eyes flickered. "Stay out of the cage matches, son. That's all I want. Not anything else." He turned back to the hostel and shuffled inside.

ALESIO'S HANDS shook as he ascended the stage at the Drinks De Capo.

He'd played for almost two years at the pub. He hadn't had nerves this bad since the first time he'd performed. His left ear rang, as it sometimes did. It seemed like, if it couldn't translate the waves of sound, it just created its own. His throat still felt a little raw from when he'd talked to his father and he sipped some water.

Who is it? Which of these pipers is the Cadenza scout?

The crowd tonight seemed more of a mix than usual: a few tables of pipers, marked by their silk clothes and silk features, made possible through the soft luxury of daily baths, and not trudging through dumpster fires. Straiters filled tables, too, with their gray-green factory clothes and grime on their faces. One or two of them had a sound-scar peeping out of their sleeves or collars.

Alesio tuned his mandolin, trying to hide the tremors in his hands. He'd worn his good cream shirt again and his nicer trousers without the holes, having washed them the night before.

"Let's have "Strings of Fate!" One of the straiters called out. Everything seemed loud today. He sucked in some deep breaths, then held the last.

"My Flute, My Love!" His five loyal fans shouted all at once, in the front, then giggled and waved.

Alesio bowed to the crowd. He could do this. He'd managed audiences long enough that his instinct to control the energy in the place zipped through him, steadying his hands and his ready smile. "I thank you for joining me tonight! I have something I think we will all enjoy."

He plucked a complicated riff on the strings; a whirlwind of notes meant to stun and quiet a room. It worked.

He paused, letting the last bits of sound ring in their ears, then he began the infamously difficult song: "Gossamer God," which required a light touch accompanied by an intricate and blurring-fast tempo.

I have heard the echo
Of a billion phantom stars,
A silhouette of harmony
Far away, a world apart

Have you heard this starlight?
Can you make out its silver chords?
What a graceful, gossamer god
This bright Sound we adore.

The footpaths of the foxes,
That constellation path,
Their lights resound through us all,
Harmonizing with the past.

I have caught the tempo
Of a night sky's speed of thought,
I cannot stop this rhythm
This song the stars have wrought—

—On me, the effects do echo
And ripple out in waves
This starlight a cappello
This phantom sky falsetto
This Sound I'll always crave.

The crowd cheered at his rendition, banging on the tables. He'd risked some credibility performing such a notorious, strenuous song, but high risk won high eyebrows, and the pipers shouted with the rest of the pub in appreciation. The sound bounced off the walls, resounding through the bar, through the floor, through his boots. So loud. And yet, somehow, not loud enough.

Alesio sipped in quick breaths and flexed his hand to keep his fingers nimble. All his practice with enlarging his lungs had allowed him to perform the song without breathing once through the entire thing.

The cheering died out, and he swept his gaze over the crowd to find the cause. Someone new had sat at one of the straits tables: a burly guy in a dark purple sleeveless vest, displaying sound-scars all up his arms and up his neck and face. Even the other straiters seemed nervous around him, hunching their shoulders, and not facing him.

A cage fighter.

Shit. A cage fighter.

Mona glared at the man from where she stood behind the bar, shoving a rag into a poor, poor mug, as if readying makeshift brass knuckles. Alesio masked his nerves with a broad smile and launched into his next piece.

Why had a cage fighter come? They didn't leave the straits.

The guy met his eyes and jerked his head, showing the side of his neck. There he had tattooed a bird with a gray color. The sign of the shrike.

This guy wasn't from Anthem. The old woman at the cathedral's words echoed in Alesio's mind: *He has a match-up for you, an out of towner. Big money.*

A cage fighter from Flock. The people from the other city imitated bird calls to create magic, instead of singing or playing music. A faction there called themselves shrikers and were known for the brutal way they killed.

Clef must have told the shriker where Alesio performed, and the out-of-towner had decided to scope out his potential competition. On the same night someone evaluated Alesio for the Cadenza.

Damn you, Clef. The strait's leader must have known somehow about the Cadenza scout and had wanted to sabotage Alesio's chance with intimidation. He clenched his teeth. He'd spent a little too long between songs, just a few seconds, but on stage, a few seconds stretched like hours. The crowd shuffled in the awkward silence. His breathing shortened. His throat felt raw again, all of a sudden. He forced a smile. "Alright. Drinks!"

"De Capo!" The bar shouted back.

"Who's ready for some 'Berry Lipped Ladies'?"

His fans up front shouted, and the rest of the crowd followed in lumbering appreciation, hesitant now with the shriker in their midst. He began the number, but he couldn't stop oscillating his gaze over to the shriker, then away. The magic of his voice must have wavered as well, as many people did not sing along or sway with the beat. In desperation, he began one of the songs often performed at the Cadenza or higher end bars, called "Waves of Gold," but the pipers did not seem enthused at this. Perhaps they heard it a little too often. The rest of the pub quieted as the lyrics spouted about the blessings of those who worshipped the Sound. Blessings they didn't have.

Murmurs had begun in the middle of the song, and once it ended, a few shouts rang out from the straiters' side. "Strings of Fate!"

Alesio swallowed. He didn't want to perform that one, but the balance of energy in the room could explode at any moment. Mona posted herself in front of the bar, ready to escort the rowdies out, but Alesio knew he had to placate the straiters, or he might find himself with a sound-knife in his back later. He played the anti-piper song with a resigned kind of flair, and at the end of it, half the silken-clothed clients had left.

The night had started off so well, and now . . .

Mona gestured for him to clear off the stage a little early. The musician for the 11 o'clock time slot waited on the side. Alesio swallowed, bowed, and exited, zipping up his mandolin case.

Some of the straiters moved to intercept him, and the shriker stood up. The rest of the pub silenced.

Shit. Shit.

Mona gestured Alesio towards the door. As part of their agreement for his discounted room, he also worked security at the Drinks De Capo.

He grimaced. Such an arrangement didn't always make sense to him, as he often would have liked some security for his performances. But he didn't want to jeopardize his good standing with Mona. She did always give him the best time slot.

"How's it going, gentlemen?" Alesio slung his mandolin on his back, inhaling deep. Should this devolve to a fight, he wanted all the breath he could muster. "What do you say to getting some fresh air outside?"

"We don't want trouble," one of the straiters said.

The other patrons stared down at their tables. A few snuck hands into pockets and pulled out small cloths to stuff in their ears.

The shriker shambled through the path between tables, joining the straiters. The shrike bird, the shriker's inspiration in both name and behavior, impaled its victims on the nearest sharp object. Alesio found himself scanning the bar for anything somewhat sharp. The edges of tables. The meat skewers on peoples' plates.

Course, anything could be considered sharp if someone pushed hard enough.

The shriker grinned, running his tongue along his teeth, a gap showing on his bottom left. "19." He raised his eyebrows and waited.

Alesio kept his mouth shut—not just because he'd won a lower 16 matches, but also because it would mean confessing to the whole bar that he had participated in cage matches.

Alesio tipped an imaginary hat. "That's a funny way to say how many thirty-second notes you're donating, but I appreciate it nonetheless. Just leave them in the jar and thank you very much."

The shriker threw back his head and guffawed, giving the whole bar a view of the bird tattoo on his neck. He ran his tongue over his missing tooth again. "Your warble is kind of cute, singer. We should try a duet sometime."

He shouldered past Alesio and out the door. The straiters followed.

The people seemed to breathe again at their tables. Mona wiped her forehead with a cleaning cloth at the bar. Alesio's breath seeped out of him like a punctured balloon, and he sagged into a chair near the back.

The shriker had assessed him and judged that he could beat Alesio in a match—and Alesio couldn't blame him after such a wreck of a performance.

The strings of fate pulled at him, yanking him down, down, down.

5

AN AGONY OF HUMANS

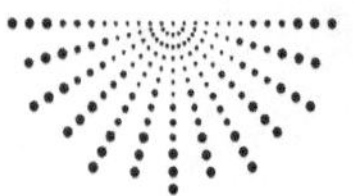

Things in Vision moved in ways that the eye disagreed with.

If one looked beyond the beauty of the lavender dawn—that type of morning where it almost made Saida blush, the way the sun romanced the sky—the ruins that it illuminated seemed to shift their angles or change the curvatures of their broken arches. Of course, the gears and pulleys that could've relocated their balconies and bridges and roofs didn't work any longer. The eye tried to adjust them to fit rational order, so that the side of buildings did not become ceilings of others, or their trees did not grow along the roads like ivy clinging to houses, but the structures *themselves* did not move. The magics needed to power them had jammed long ago, half-working, half-not, locked in place.

The little road she followed decried logic as well, winding in one direction, then up into the sky, then rotating to the west. She trotted along it, shivering as the gravity changed when she took the first step upwards, and then she trekked towards that intensive purple sunrise with nothing but a road under her feet.

"How does this feel?" She asked Winter Lightning, holding their tube out and trailing them through a low-hanging cloud like a torch.

Winter Lightning sparked in their container for a moment, then stopped. "Not here. It's too warm. Too languid."

Saida sighed. "It's summer here. Everything's languid." Indeed, she'd kept her shorts and shirt short, letting her brownish-red human arms and legs breathe, and grew a thick sole of a shoe that curved around her feet just enough to protect them bumping into rocks. Sweat slicked the short fur on her neck that had refused to shift into her long braid.

The road ended a few paces ahead, where it should have bent back to the ground or switched the gravity so she could walk to that road above her. But it didn't.

She paused, staring at some city ruins in the distance. From up in the sky, she had a good view of the crumbling buildings, the jagged bridges, the roads that led nowhere. All the worlds had ancient cities, remnants of the humans and what they had built so long ago. Many such ancient cities existed on Vision, and all the worlds, remnants of the humans here and what they had built in this world of surreal orientation.

When she first started out exploring, the portals had delivered her to random places. She'd had no way of directing them somewhere specific if she hadn't been there before. Now, she could guide them to deposit her in the places she had traveled.

Though she'd visited each world many times, (Vision and Touch less than others, these past few decades), they extended far beyond the fifty or so portals that linked them. Even Sound, the world with the most humans she'd ever encountered, consisted of sweeping landscapes that stretched for thousands of miles, interspersed by ruins. Anthem was the largest city she had discovered anywhere, and its inhabitants seemed to know of just one other city in their entire world. On Vision, she'd found one small, non-ruin village after all her years of exploration.

The unknown both excited and scared her. It excited her because she loved experiencing the new, the strange, the different—but it scared her because it also meant she had no idea whether more dangers awaited. Dangers like what she had found underneath Vision.

Is that the ruin where I found Watthe?

The large humanoid of smoke and elongated hand-claws had haunted her steps for a year now. She hadn't meant to set something like him loose while digging in the rubble of a ruin. She hadn't meant to fall into that—that *other* place, that space of negative energy that hadn't been Vision at all.

She'd splashed into a strange kind of swamp; more the partial absence of substance and ground rather than a thick ooze, a deterioration of what made dirt dirt, and mud mud, as if something had eaten through the materials and what remained could not support her. She floated half in, half out of the ground. Smoke seemed to waft from all over, but she did not smell smoke. She could not sense much of anything, except an ominous clinging of the smoke to her skin and how it seemed to reach for her. If she stayed in any one place for longer than a few hours, a fatigue overwhelmed her. Her eyelids drooped, and she struggled to stay upright.

After perhaps a few days, or weeks, the truth revealed itself to her in a moment of clarity. The smoke, and the swamp—everything there—was an overgrowth.

"Saida," Goosefeather said. "Saida, come back to us."

She blinked and swallowed. She teetered on the edge of the road in the sky, just holding Winter Lightning up. The wind ruffled her braid, drying the sweat that ran into the short fur underneath. She lowered her arm and backed away from the edge. "Sorry," she said. "Sorry."

"What about there?" Winter Lightning sparked towards the east, though no magic leaked from the tube. As with any magic outside their source world, their power did not work until they transplanted. "It's bright in that direction."

Saida glanced east. "Oh. That's where the village is. You're probably sensing human magic."

Winter Lightning flared up. "That sounds exciting!"

More humans. Saida bit her lip. *I guess there's only so many things I can avoid at a time.*

THE OVERGROWTH HAD TAKEN up the entire space. Without a foxan to trim it, it had fermented, breaking the magic down into something else, or another kind of magic altogether, leaving holes in the ground and the physical space behind. As if waking from a long hibernation, it seemed to sense her and her magic and grasped at her with a slow, desperate hunger, draining her energy.

She'd slogged through the swamp, parts of it bowing deeper than others like a crater, parts of it giving way under her so she had to scramble to grab anything she could to not fall further down, and down, into the place that was not a place, but more of a suspension of a place, a hollow shell. Smoking trees and bushes and undergrowth did grow out of the decaying ground-that-was-not-ground, but in a twisted, wrap-around way, ending with their tops back down like a wilderness of arches.

Saida woke with a start, her heart pounding fast, and jolted upright. She had to keep moving. Every moment she idled, her memories reminded her of that horrible, other place, where she had fallen through Vision.

She had to make some concessions, however, journeying a few days to find the village instead of teleporting. She preferred to approach humans with as much caution and scouting as possible. She also wanted to try and convince Winter Lightning to transplant before they arrived.

"Here?" She asked, waving the tube next to a wild field of purple potatoes, some of them growing upside down, their roots blowing in the wind like muddy hair. The grasses and plants in Vision were usually lavender, or light pink, or some other pastel color.

"Seems a little . . . close to the ground," Winter Lightning said.

"I thought you might say that. Had to try."

A broken-down stone road led into the sky here, but underneath it, the air flickered like a wavering mirage, signaling that the gravity did not match. She checked it with her arm, and it pulled her sideways. If she had tried stepping onto the sky road, she would have fallen into the wind who knew for how long.

Saida shivered. Vision's unique gravity and angle magic seemed to fade faster than the other worlds. Even teleporting here took longer than it should have; about fifty seconds. She couldn't hold her breath for much longer than that.

Should I bring more than one transplant here this year? Would that strengthen the magic?

When she'd slipped up for three years and hadn't completed any transplants, each of the worlds had seemed to drift farther apart, not just Vision, and the magics had weakened. Yet, when she did fulfill the quota she'd set for herself, nothing seemed to change for the better.

She'd wandered through that place like a lost child, wide-eyed, and terrified, for how long she did not know, except that the days strung together, and she forgot things like her name, and what she could do, and that she could teleport at all. At times, the void-swamp yanked her down, threatening to swallow her up and keep her hanging there suspended, floating, and she struggled to yank her legs free.

And then, part of that ground had risen and underneath it, something cracked like a baby bird chipping at the inside of an egg, and that—that thing had formed in front of her.

She had said, "What the—!"

Saida shook herself. She grabbed one of the purple potatoes and bit into it, and it grounded her.

The flavor would have shocked her on Taste. She liked to world-hop for that reason too, beyond doing the transplants. If all the intensity of one sense started to wear on her, she just teleported to a place that focused on another.

Saida pocketed another potato for later and slipped out Tricksy Stone. "Are you enjoying your visit to your old world, friend?" *Keep talking. Distract me,* she thought, even though they could hear her thoughts just as well.

They revolved as if stretching. The little angles of them that slanted upside down and back up again without reason moved in disorienting ways, growing larger, then smaller, then large again. They could do more things on their source world than anywhere else. "Oh, yes. Very much so. I can turn here and change like I used to. At least, where the magic is working."

"Do you miss being here?" She swallowed a lump in her throat.

Tricksy Stone ceased shifting. "Of course. But I would miss you more."

Winter Lightning sparked back and forth in their tube, as if watching this conversation. "Why did you not transplant?" They asked Tricksy Stone. "You are strong, strong enough to thrive in other places. Yet you stay with her. Do you not become restless?"

Tricksy Stone smiled their paradoxical smile, the lines of their surface curving. "My home is with her. She is the world I prefer."

"Oh." Winter Lightning still sounded confused. But they did not press for more, and Saida gripped Tricksy close, as well as Goosefeather, who brushed her hand from inside her pocket.

The magic trimmings she brought back to her den, and her friends Tricksy Stone and Goosefeather most of all, understood her. They joked with her. They traveled with her. They grounded her when she might have drifted into the sky.

She traveled on, nearing the village. She'd visited there once before, to transplant the softest flower petals from Touch she'd ever found. An endless, shallow sea covered most of Touch, but some high places sprouted vegetation. The petals had also wanted to place themselves near the humans on Vision. Most of the magic in the countryside was broken, but not in the village. Vision magic powered the structures in the village; the roads and parts of the buildings and angles of tree branches could still change locations, reaching where otherwise would be impossible. In the same place that the humans lived.

Probably because *the humans live there*. She'd long assumed a connection between world magic, and what humans did with world magic just by existing.

Vision's unexpected twists and turns and crazy angles reminded her how much she loved surprises, of traveling to such strange and different places, and how on each trip she found somewhere new.

If the worlds closed . . . if the skies she loved drifted too far for her to reach, she'd have to stay in one of them forever, or just in Between. And once that happened, once she was trapped, she would lose Falrie, Darrow, and Pell.

The houses appeared first. They displayed the same illogical arrangement as the ruins. Saida held Winter Lightning out in one hand just in case they liked any patch of grass or something before she stepped into the human settlement.

No such luck.

Shifting down as small as she could, the size of a large cat, she crept closer, checking for farmers out in their fields. Rows of grain waved in the wind, some curving up as if against an invisible wall. The road wound about, circling a few treetops, before it slanted down and met the rooftops. She stole across the first home, hoping her footsteps did not alert anyone below. The road twisted down to the other side, to the ground. She could have walked along the ground, but the roads led to places that the ground did not.

No one strolled the road, however, along the rooftops or otherwise. No one had worked the fields, either. *Strange.*

She kept an eye out for fox-people. The one she'd met on Sound had been the first in many, many years. She'd met two on Vision, an ancient couple living out in the wild . . . fifty years ago? They lay buried somewhere far away, somewhere she had long forgotten. Maybe the remaining few had hidden in the cities and larger villages, the places she tried to avoid—

His mouth, forming as she watched, had opened, and split, so the jaw unhinged much too far and his lips crept far too wide, and he had repeated her word in a thunderous, "WATTHE," and tilted his head at her. Smoke poured off him, then lessened a little, defining his features and his humanoid shape, like a woodcarver uncovering a statue in a block of wood. He cradled a small black box that seemed more solid than him.

"You want her magic?" His voice modulated down to a lower level and something in his throat rippled, as if his vocal cords developed as she watched. He'd looked down at the box, then back up at her. "Eat her?"

And from him, or from the box, perhaps, emanated a formidable, more sentient Hunger. An all-consuming craving for her magic. Patterns on its surface seemed to move, to writhe.

"—aida!" Goosefeather said. Then, to Tricksy Stone: "I don't know what to do! She's worse here. Just like how she was on Touch."

"I'm back." She gripped Winter Lightning in her paw. "I'm back."

She'd fled. She'd teleported in a moment of terrified clarity. She hadn't returned to Vision since, hoping to all the senses that she would never, ever come across him again.

But he must have followed her through the portal that day because now he'd shown up on Scent, hunting her. Hungry. A broken off piece of that fermented void magic, given life.

Falrie's words echoed in her mind: *There is a hunger that wants to consume us.*

The street passed under another street, dipping into the ground, then up again, twisting like a ribbon. The gravitational direction switched, so that she strode up the side of someone's house, then up into the air. A gear stuck out on the roof, and she rotated it, shifting her paw to a hand for a moment. It creaked, and the road rumbled as it moved to connect instead with the earlier street she had passed under. The sound made her nervous. Gravity shifted again.

"This is wild!" Winter Lightning said. They seemed to understand that she valued distraction and pitched their voice higher. "The angles here! The magic makes them zip like lightning, in unexpected ways!"

Saida stopped. "Here, then?"

"Not—not quite," Winter Lightning said.

She was rushing things a little with the poor Scent magic. A transplant could take at least a week to settle down. Sometimes longer, considering she herself liked to stop and smell the swanseize. Or she would lose her way, her mind wandering down a maze of thoughts.

"A foxan!"

A woman with a sickle and an empty bag had stepped out on her front porch, watching Saida tread by on the overpass street.

Saida tensed.

"Dear foxan, save us!" The woman let the sickle clatter to the ground and prostrated herself.

Saida bolted along the road, making it to the other side, then leapt off the path onto a nearby roof. The woman did not give chase, but her exclamation seemed to have alerted someone else in another house, who ran out as well. "A foxan! We are saved!"

More doors opened, up and down, and sideways and below. Their words echoed, and she kept trying to dodge the next door. She had left the road, though, and they knew their town and how it worked, and they seemed to herd her somewhere. "This way!" One called. "Please come!"

She dashed for the outskirts. The village had a hundred or so houses in all, and it wouldn't have taken long to traverse the whole place, except that the road and the gravity twisted in on itself! She panted, her long foxan tongue hanging out.

Out of the two reactions humans had to foxans, she much preferred hatred. At least with hatred, they didn't try to cage her and expect love in return.

Why is it that, the more worlds I travel to, the fewer places I feel safe?

One of the humans tried to reach for her with widespread arms. She couldn't let any humans touch her! They would tie her up and never let her free! She pulled Tricksy Stone out of her pocket, held them up with both hands, and shouted, "Change!"

Her friend transformed, growing to a stone the size of a large melon, their red color swirling in a mesmerizing way, around, and around. The human blinked and rubbed at their eyes.

Tricksy Stone shrank back down, and she tucked them in her pocket, then ducked underneath the human's outstretched hands, dashed along a balcony, then leapt down onto the ground near a fountain.

Wait. She knew this place. The flower petals from Touch had transplanted here, mixing with the magic it had liked in the fountain, a continual flow of water from the air to the ground. But the water had vanished, the flower petals had disappeared, and the shifting magic of Vision—that disorienting perception of the eye—did not work around the fountain. The gravity pushed Saida towards the ground, like on every other world, when it should push up at the sky.

She stopped, confused. *Where is it?*

"The magic you gave us has gone." One old woman tottered

forward and prostrated herself before Saida, the same one that had first called out to her.

Saida flattened her ears and went low to the ground, scanning for exits.

"Our world is dying. *We* are dying. Can you help us, foxan? Can you bring the magic back?"

Other humans gathered around the fountain. Saida twitched, but Winter Lightning sparked and zipped in the tube. "Here," they said. "Here, I can thrive."

Saida's tail-braid had puffed out, and she panted, unable to sweat in foxan form, but when a transplant felt ready, she'd learned to listen. If she didn't, getting them to transplant somewhere else could take months.

Trying to calm her nerves, Saida shifted her paw to a hand, uncorked the container, and emptied Winter Lightning into the fountain. The Scent magic wafted, spreading outwards, then shot in random lines, frosted and electric.

The people, of course, could not see or smell the magic, but it affected their mood. They laughed and smiled as Winter Lightning zipped around the fountain in a joyous dance. The deadening around the fountain revived: the angles re-impossibled themselves and gravity switched, so Saida held onto the lip of the fountain to keep herself from floating upwards.

Murmuring from the people rose. "She has saved us!"

The old woman toddled towards her, floating into the air and hooking herself with her cane on the lip of the fountain. Saida tensed but allowed the old woman closer.

"It is not enough," the old woman said. "It will disappear, and fizzle out again, if it is alone."

"I've always tried to place one transplant here a year," Saida said. "I don't know—it's hard to do more than that."

The old woman gazed out at the small crowd surrounding them, and Saida did, too. The children's ribs stuck out through their clothing, and the skin draped over the adults' cheekbones like thin sheets on chairs, showing the hollows under their eyes and next to their mouths. Their magics flickered like weak flames in their chests.

"Our world is dying, young foxan," the old woman said. "It has been dying for centuries. It needs more magic, or it cannot sustain us. Are you prepared to guide all of us to the afterlife?"

Saida cringed. The humans on Vision and Taste, not understanding the foxans' power of teleportation, had deified it long ago, believing that foxans guided humans after death to their new lives. The humans here had passed the folktale down from hundreds, or thousands, of years. She didn't want to tell them the lie their religion rested on.

But she *had* wondered why Vision seemed so empty compared to the other worlds. She'd come to the same explanation as this woman; that the lack of magic seemed correlated to the lack of humans. Saida had even had trouble finding overgrowths from Vision to transplant to other worlds. Tricksy Stone was one of the rare ones she'd trimmed that was strong enough, but they hadn't wanted to transplant.

One of the other humans switched a gear on the side of a house and the gravity shifted from up to back down in a slow, drifting way. Saida and the old lady floated back down.

The other humans gathered around the fountain. Close. They reached for her, murmuring adoring words. Some of them clasped small carvings of foxans.

"Save us, foxan."

"Save us."

One little boy reached his hand and touched her, and she willed herself to stay still. This small child wouldn't hurt her, or yank on her tail, or try to lock her in a cage. The hollows of his little cheeks sucked in as he smiled. The shining devotion in his small human eyes, that light of Winter Lightning that only she could see reflected, made her twitch.

Adoration and love expected. It *caged.* Two of the five worlds, Touch and Vision, adored fox-people, the descendants of the foxans. Carn had tied her to a post in the cave and expected love in return.

I already know of another overgrowth that would produce a strong transplant. The man's voice from Sound.

"I will do this." She held her paws out in a stop motion. The little boy reached for her again, and she flinched back. "I will try to bring more magic. One from each world. That should help bring it back, that much, all of them different and unique."

The small crowd nodded and murmured.

"Just, please," Saida said. "Let me leave now."

The trap of humans opened, and she dashed along the irrational road towards freedom.

———

WATTHE HUNG in the secrecy of the chocolate shop eaves' shadows, his thin shape arching around the globule of light the lamp cast by the back door. He hung also between the old and young parts of himself, a pendulum swinging back and forth between what his original substance knew, that of mindless growth, of twisting upwards, then downwards, of smoke and hollow ground—and what that substance had had to adjust to, having just landed on this new world of loudness. He hung, waiting.

The foxan had come this way.

Passers-by in the open streets had whispered about it in daylight. The Hunger had told him to hide in the shadows of the city, not to show himself to large groups. The humans had talked about something called a fur-mix, and had tossed their heads, and held cupped palms over their mouths. One seemed to know more than others and talked about it the most. The 'humans,' as The Hunger told him they were called, did not have fur, or pointed ears as the foxan did, and he had calculated that a fur-mix and a foxan meant the same thing, here.

He'd followed the woman who'd whispered the most, had found this shop where she lived and worked. Now, in the burgeoning shadows of the night—so like the smoke from the Primal Plane, shadows seemed, like his smoke, yet they held more substance in the Sensory Plane—he waited, hanging over the eaves like a spider.

The Hunger perched in Watthe's arms as if ready to leap, as if it had limbs. It had raised metal designs on all four sides, designs that squirmed like a tangle of thick worms if he stared long enough, writhing to its inside and back out again to one of the other sides. He stared for a long time, waiting for the woman to come back.

He'd picked it up in the Primal Plane and the world had gained solidity around him. He'd been waiting in that Plane for so long, as just a section of its shadow-ground. He hadn't felt anything except a shapeless, formless hunger, for he himself had not had a shape or substance at all, or even a concept of himself as separate from the ground. But when he'd picked up The Hunger, it had spoken to him, and it had given him a shape. A direction for his craving, the same direction and craving that it possessed.

The foxan's magic.

He had been so close to her on Scent. Her power, her teleportation, had emanated from her like a delicious ray of light. He craved it along with The Hunger: the ability to move freely, to go wherever he wished! He'd found a workaround, to follow her across the worlds, but it wasn't as convenient or reliable as hers seemed to be. Finding her transplants had required a certain amount of time.

She had smelled crisp and bright, like the stars overhead in these new, fascinating worlds—

The box pricked him with one of its strange, raised metal designs, a sharp edge coming from somewhere in that worming mass. "Imbecile!" The Hunger said. "She is coming!"

The woman in the red head scarf returned from some other place, her arms swinging back and forth like her legs as she hurried in the dangerous dusk, going to the back door, and digging out a ring of keys from her bag. He waited till she fumbled with her keys, then he dropped.

He covered her scream with the void of his form, holding her suspended inside his chest. Waiting. He waited till she would not have breath to scream, then released her mouth.

"Do a . . . no speak." He laid a finger on his lips. He had learned human speech by listening to it and mimicking it to himself for the past year on Vision, hanging around the one village he had discovered.

Her eyes squeezed shut. He thumbed them back open, holding them so she had to pay attention. She opened her mouth to scream, and he covered it again, not letting her breathe. Her eyes bulged, and she tried to squirm inside his chest, inside the hunger of himself. He waited till she stopped struggling, then released her again, and she dragged in some air.

He once again held his finger to his lips. She nodded. Sound aired all around them, from the various bars all down the main road, so even if she had screamed, nothing probably would have come of it. But he was careful. He could not show himself yet.

"I am a look," he said.

She frowned, not seeming to understand.

He tried again. "I am . . . looking . . . for a fur-mix." Her mouth opened in an 'o.' "You have speaked of this. Tell me."

She waited, watching him, as if frozen, until he nudged her with his clawed hand against her throat. She swallowed. "I—did see one." She panted a little, not getting enough breath. "She had reflective eyes. Like the songs say."

"As I heard you already speak." He lowered his face towards hers, opened his jaw wider. She almost screamed, then, but did not have enough breath to manage more than a squeak. "More. Where did she go?"

"I don't know! She went down the main road, this one, near my shop! Then she vanished!"

The Hunger spoke. "She's hiding something."

The woman's eyes widened at the voice reverberating from the box in the other half of Watthe's arms.

The Hunger knew things, things Watthe did not. "Not for a long." Watthe curled his sharpened fingers around the human's neck.

"I swear! I never saw anything! Just a red flash in the face, and then nothing—"

Watthe sighed in the loudness of the Sound world at night. All around, chaos unfolded from the various bars and merchant stalls. "The sad is, no one hears you scream."

"No, please, please! I'll do anything you want! Maybe the clef leader knows. He's important, he—he might know about the creature you want! I swear, I'll talk to him!"

Watthe considered. He waited for The Hunger to give him an order which way, but no voice spoke from the box.

"Take me to this . . . Clef."

6

A SILHOUETTE OF HARMONY

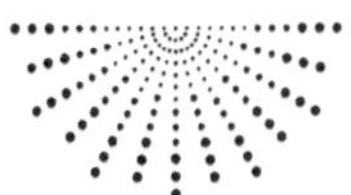

Saida tried to direct the portal to the cathedral as close as she could and ended up teleporting inside the bushes that lined the nearby garden.

She froze, her gaze flicking down the line of greenery, hoping the fox-person who had reproached her the last time would appear.

The world of Sound blared in her ears; the early morning risers walking the street, the bushes rustling in the wind, the wind itself, even the silence buzzed. It always took a while to adjust enough not to flinch at someone speaking at a normal level.

But no skittering or other noise indicated a startled someone running away from her.

She released her breath and hung her head. She'd come here for the overgrowth from the human's voice, but she'd also hoped to find the fox-person here again. Or any fox-person.

They had said that this trail was a secret way. Maybe it would lead her to them.

She squinted at the cathedral. No one guarded the front main doors, but someone she didn't recognize stood posted outside its garden down the line of shrubs.

She shrank down to full foxan and trotted along the other way under the bushes, away from the guard.

"Where are you going?" Goosefeather asked.

"Guards can't stay in the same place all day. It'd be easier to get close to him if he's not inside a giant echo box. If he were outside."

The sunlight filtered through the dense bushes like golden bell-bugs. The route wound around the garden, and a small wooden ring on the ground clued her in. She lifted it and a trapdoor eased up. She slid into the hole in the ground and followed a tunnel wide enough for a thin human. It was dark, but she didn't need to see in the world of Sound to know where to place her feet.

After a few minutes, the tunnel ended. She fumbled around and her hand brushed against another little metal ring, which she tugged on. It opened, letting in a sliver of light, and she squinted at the brightness of it, letting her eyes adjust. She peeked out. The tunnel led into a back alley of a bar with gold trim along its eaves.

She marked it to find later. These secret ways would help her conceal herself. "Tricksy Stone, if I forget about this when I'm in Sound again, remind me."

"Put another on my tab," they said.

She squirmed out of the tunnel and dropped to the alleyway. With no one chasing her or hunting her, she scanned for more secret ways in a focused manner. If more than a few fox-people lived in Anthem, they must have a path winding through the whole city. All with their own isolated dens, their personal Betweens where they felt safe.

She would hate to frighten one by stumbling across such a private area. But she did need to know a better way to traverse the city to have a chance to trim that human's overgrown magic. She didn't need a repeat of the last time, running pell-mell through the open streets with people shouting things at her. That was a great way to get caught.

There! The bar's golden-plated sign glinted off a ladder, leading up to the roof. She checked to ensure that no humans watched her, then climbed the ladder by just shifting to her human hands and feet, then ducked behind a line of large pots along a ledge. She changed back to full foxan and sidled along it, keeping below the pots. Someone sang below in the bar, a beautiful voice with a moderate magic. No need for trimming.

She peeked down. Next to the bar, another building's roof jutted close by, and she leapt onto it. The path led across the top of the city like that for a few more minutes, until she had learned enough of the area to satisfy herself.

Behind her, the cathedral had shrunk, and the morning waned. She should get back to check if the guards had changed shifts yet.

"I haven't given up, Pell," she whispered. "If you have any descendants left, I'll find them. But first, I need to get a man to talk to me. Or maybe even sing."

***

"Sure you want the garden shift?" Tak peered at Alesio, tweaking the ends of his stiff handlebar mustache. "You look like you could use the good food this morning."

Alesio rubbed at his eyes. "I'd rather listen to the street than another performance, right now."

"Suit yourself." The older man shrugged and headed off with a happy bounce towards the cathedral's main doors, and Alesio let his breath out in relief. He didn't want to hold his breath today or try anything difficult at all. He would've preferred to wallow in his room at the Drinks De Capo for a month. His raw throat needed the break. But, of course, he couldn't afford such pitying pursuits.

His reputation had taken a huge hit at the bar last night. *Thank the Sound my father didn't come.* He didn't know if he was ready for his father to see him succeed—let alone fail so spectacularly.

The cathedral's garden spanned its west side, a small haven for quiet reflection in the loudness of the city. Tall bushes muted the outside bustle of passers-by, and some of the wealthy parishioners paid for time slots to pray there as well as inside the cathedral. Alesio had been stationed at the garden's entrance for around fifty minutes when the fox-woman peeked around the corner.

She resembled a large fox this time, like when he had first seen her in the cathedral. Her clothes fit her like someone had tailored them for her, a little red shirt tucked into a matching pair of red trousers, which had a place for her tail to stick out.

He clenched his teeth. *Not today. I can't deal with this today.*

Why had she returned? If Tak or, the Sound forbid, Lasrial saw her, he had no control over what happened.

She padded a little closer, soundless on furred paws, weaving under the shadows of the bushes walling off the garden. People strolled by her, chatting to others, and she stayed near enough that her shortness let her stay out of their periphery, but far enough away that they couldn't have grabbed at her. A difficult line to walk; and she did it with such grace, using her low stature as an advantage, as invisibility. Alesio could appreciate that skill.

The fox-woman paused under one bush as a larger cluster of people wandered past and had to remain there for several minutes as the lunch rush began at high noon. When the street emptied, she crept along the side towards him, towards the garden's entrance.

Don't show yourself, he wanted to tell her. People prayed in the garden and would see her through the metal gate.

She locked eyes with him, then lowered herself under the bushes, her tail puffing up a little, her ears lying flat. If he hadn't known she could transform, he would have mistaken her once again for an actual fox or small dog.

He couldn't say anything. He had to remain still and silent when working. His rotation here would end in another ten minutes or so, and the people inside the garden would leave as well.

Should I report her? She might steal something.

He shook that thought away. People said a lot of things about those they never met, but he didn't want to think like they did.

He tilted his palm out while keeping it low to mean 'wait,' then, at the pace of a languishing and legato music composition, he lowered one finger. Four minutes till the hour switch. He hoped she would understand the warning; he dared not whisper. His job description forbade any speaking unless some crisis occurred, and if the people walking by heard him, some of them might complain about 'that guard that spoke' at the cathedral.

Her gaze flicked to his hand, and she shrank back under the nearest overhanging bush.

At the three-minute mark, he lowered the next finger. She continued to wait.

At the shift change, Tak marched out to the garden. Alesio pointed at the ground, which meant he wanted to stay outside for the next hour as well. Tak raised an eyebrow but shrugged and traipsed back inside the cathedral.

Two people filed out of the garden, their slippers swish-swishing on the marbled walkway, that aural decadence that the wealthy so loved. He bowed as they left, and the fox-person cocked her head, her nose twitching. She must've smelled the food offerings the people had left.

Well, no one had reserved the garden for the next hour.

Alesio opened the gate, leaving it open just long enough for her to dart inside. He kept himself straight and upright, as if nothing had happened, and the fox-person wove towards the food at the end of the garden like a professional shadow.

A mid-size statue of the Sound wave rose at the far end. The parishioners had left two offering bowls, one of sticky rice, and one of smooth, melty candies. The fox-woman side-swept some of the rice into her mouth without moving her gaze from him (and, he suspected, the gate he had left a little ajar).

Her eyes widened and she stuck her snout in the bowl and snapped up the rest of the rice in two bites.

He stepped towards her, and her head jerked up, the food still in her mouth. He waited, then stepped once again, in a pattern, a predictable rhythm with no sudden movements. He stopped a respectable distance away, then pointed at the spoon, and tapped his hand three times. He put no great stock in the god of Sound, but he did like some of the little traditions.

She tilted her head, then curled her claws around the instrument and tapped her other paw with it three times, mimicking his motion.

Well, that was adorable.

A smile almost cracked his face, but he gave her a grave nod.

What was he doing? He couldn't let her stay here any longer. What if the next parishioners on the schedule arrived early and caught him feeding offerings to who had almost stolen from the cathedral?

Lasrial's voice echoed in his mind: *It doesn't belong on our streets!*

That's what everyone said about people from the straits.

He'd just wanted to give her food. Was that so bad? If someone had extended mercy after he had messed up last night—if the scout had approached him and talked to him at all—his whole life could've changed. Maybe he could have begged for a second chance. Maybe the scout would have focused on the well-done first half of his set instead of the jumbled mess of the second. He wanted to do the same for someone else, another outcast. Another professional shadow.

The fox-woman inched forward a half-step, then another, not towards him, but around him, heading towards the garden gate. Good.

She stared at his lips, as if hoping he'd speak, then stole back out and disappeared under the bushes again.

He took up his post at the garden entrance and closed the gate behind him.

SAIDA HAD HOVERED around the human the whole day, hoping to snag the magic wafting from his voice, but he never spoke. After several hours, he left and traipsed across town, and she had followed him. He'd entered a pub with his head down, as if he half expected them to throw him back out.

She didn't dare follow him inside, of course. In such a busy place, even with her ears covered and shifted to human, someone would notice her non-human features before long. She stayed outside in the alley by a window, shifted to human, hood up. Better to exist as a mysterious, vague shape than a fox-person, here.

She explored the area nearby and discovered another secret way:

under the dumpster in the back alley, a small hole led down and under the street.

A lone homeless woman in the corner had a fortress of crates towards the back. She scuttled over to Saida, dirt plastered on her cheeks, her body covered in little more than the tatters of an old shirt and a pair of trousers full of holes. "This is my alley tonight. Shove off."

"I just want to hear the music. Please." He'd refused to even say anything to her all day. Here, maybe he would perform. "I can pay you."

"What with?" The woman jutted out her chin.

Saida held out a gooey mass of one of the melty candies she had stuffed in her pocket. The woman sniffed it, scooped the goop, and retreated to the crates, where she'd stacked them so she could hide under them if it rained.

The rice and the chocolate he'd let her eat had filled her up more than since she'd teleported here, and it didn't churn in her stomach like the stuff she scavenged from dumpsters in cities.

She hadn't meant for him to see her. She'd smelled food and crept into that garden, not thinking about how he could have trapped her in there without much fuss. But she hadn't eaten after staying in her den for a few days, and hunger had overtaken caution.

She usually remembered events in random order, but her memory seemed more connected these past few days, like a fence linking fenceposts in a predictable line, and her promise to the people in Vision lingered in her ears: *I will try to bring more magic. One from each world.* She had wanted to back out, to back away from all those grasping hands and hearts.

But their world was dying.

She would hate to lose the magic of such a gorgeous world as Vision, with its pastel sunrises and gravitational chaos. She didn't know what would happen if all magic faded in one world, but it couldn't be good. What if it affected the other worlds? She couldn't let such a thing happen. The instinct that had driven her to create transplants and cross-cultivate magic in other places now told her she must save Vision.

"You could have gone back to the swanseize first," Tricksy Stone said. "But you chose the muscle-bound hunk man. Interesting."

"The muscle-bound hunk man with magic," she corrected under her breath. "And the swanseize is out of hibernation so I couldn't get close enough to it anyway."

"You remembered," Tricksy Stone said. "Goosefeather, you were right. She is getting better."

"I'm always right," Goosefeather said.

"Shh. I think he's going to sing or something."

A speedy music cut through the raucous din, silencing it. Saida cocked her head, interested. And then—

When he sang!

She had expected a baritone from his lower speaking voice and his stocky build, yet a shimmering tenor trickled through the window, invisible except to her foxan ears, which let her sense the magic just like she could sense magic smells on Scent. She reached out with a seashell.

She lowered it before it snagged the scraps of magic, though. Those wouldn't create a transplant. She needed a good catch.

But how could she grab an overgrowth straight from someone's mouth? She'd trimmed the swanseize's yawn near its jaws, but it had been in hibernation at the time.

Maybe she could get the human to sing inside the cathedral?

The song had a fast beat, and the human played the verses twice. The second time the words caught her attention:

> *The footpaths of the foxes,*
> *That constellation path,*
> *Their lights resound through us all,*
> *Harmonizing with the past.*

She lived a strange life, visiting the different worlds when the people in them had no knowledge of places beyond. But sometimes it seemed the worlds almost fathomed each other, as if they could hear echoes of people speaking from another room.

She sensed that awareness of the other side, that knowledge that just a thin, filmy veil separated them from the phantom stars of another world. One that had fox-people in it.

Of course, humans had no way of knowing how important the lyrics were in their old songs. But the stronger the magic of the worlds, the more connected and aware the humans seemed to become of something else beyond, like some sort of sixth sense.

She would find a way to trim this human's magic, one way or another.

7

HIS SILVER VOICE

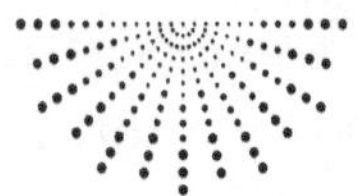

She waited outside the pub for several hours, past the time when most everyone had left. The singer did not, so he must sleep there. She prowled around the whole pub, trying to memorize the secret ways and routes if someone tried to chase her, then dozed off under the dumpster next to the trapdoor.

The human trudged outside before dawn, heading in the direction of the cathedral, wearing his uniform with the crimped gold-shoulders. She skulked behind him, hoping that he might hum a little ditty on the way to his silent job. But he stood at attention outside the cathedral's main doors, his face impassive and his lips unmoving.

Drat. Why could he sing in one place and not another? What was so great about silence and standing still?

She'd have to figure out something that would tempt him.

Leaving the human for the first time since she had heard him sing, she crept through the city, using the secret ways of the fox-people as much as she could. When she couldn't, she tied her hair over her pointed ears, flattening them on top of her head. That way, she appeared more human at a passing glance.

She snuck past a rat trap on the side of a flute shop; a small metal cage with an offensive amount of three-day old bugrat viscera heaped

76

inside. She gagged and hurried on, searching for another secret way. Many of the main streets had them, and the more she looked, the more she found.

She rummaged behind instrument shops, uncovered an old, rusted banjo, and toted it back towards the cathedral.

A nearby child sang a tune under her breath, skipping along, her mother's hand in hers. Her little voice wavered, but she produced a potent little magic of forced happiness, a learned mask. Saida cocked her head and fell into step behind the two.

Humans wove magic into whatever they did: baking, fighting, dancing, and more. She couldn't do that, as a foxan. She didn't need to trim this child's magic, but it still fascinated her. What lifestyle had the child undergone to harden her young face so? On the piper side, wealth and extravagance echoed through the streets, but, not always, it seemed, did freedom follow. The way that the mother gripped her daughter's hand . . . Saida kept herself from growling at the caged look of the girl's fingers. This thing called love trapped so many humans, and they never seemed to notice. The Senses knew how long it had taken her to learn such things.

Saida. Goosefeather brushed their feathers against her fingers. *Saida, you are safe. You escaped Carn.*

She swung away from the mother and daughter, panting in a side street, her pinned ears slipping out of her hair. She shoved them back under.

This is so hard, focusing all the time. She played around a lot in the different worlds, romping and frolicking through the extensive, far-reaching wilds. She trimmed five transplants a year, one for each world. If she sensed one, she'd find it at her own pace. Hunting them down with such purpose, with such urgency—and in cities, no less— wore on her. She needed to figure out how to trick the human into singing, so she could leave this place.

With renewed motivation, she skulked back to the cathedral. The silver-toned singer did not guard either the front main doors, or the garden entrance.

She had to wait.

<hr>

ALESIO HAD HAD a long night at the pub.

Neither Clef nor the shriker had showed up, thank the Sound, but he'd had to stay long again to repair the damage to his reputation from the previous disastrous night. He'd stayed till 2am to do so, and had had to drink what seemed a whole keg of tea with honey to keep his raw throat happy, but the patrons loved him again and Mona had given him his prime slot back at 10 o'clock. Now he just had to endure another day of silence and immobility.

Would the fox-woman show up again? He *had* directed her straight to the food offerings in the garden. That might have been a mistake. What if she kept coming back?

People crowded the pews, but not as much as the day Hestafon had performed. This day featured Oppia Yaden, not Cadenza level, but a respectable flutist dancer who played at high end piper clubs. She did not play the flute in the traditional way, but wore many layers of clothing designed with holes, so that when she danced, the air whistled through them much like a flute.

"Do you hear me, worshippers?" Lasrial boomed out.

The congregation replied, "We hear you."

The Drinks De Capo mantra worked much the same way: to keep patrons interactive so they'd more likely buy what was being sold. Alesio had introduced the idea of call and response to Mona when he'd started working at the bar, playing off the name, and the fact that many of her customers had gone to church services.

Lasrial introduced the performer, then added, "We will have a new performer next week, one that I think you will all enjoy listening to. You are invited as well, Miss Oppia."

The flute dancer bowed, though her lips pressed together in a thin line, and she did not start her piece for an uncomfortable minute or so.

Odd, Alesio thought. Mentioning another performer's high profile before the current one had even played? Lasrial never made such gaffes; he always showed deference to the rich and talented.

Alesio didn't have the energy to puzzle out Lasrial's unconventional behavior. He watched the proceedings with an exhaustion not just of one night's little sleep, but of years of waiting.

I will not give up. He'd had setbacks before. Clef could not intimidate him into returning to the same place he had scrabbled to escape from. Though his fists wanted to tremble, and his breath sharpened inside his throat where it already ached, he stilled himself and stared at the eastern windows.

He managed the violence in his mind this way. When his thoughts crept through dark alleys and his lungs wanted to burst with a cudgel of sound at Clef's neck, he stared out of one of the cathedral's stained-glass windows, at the shape of the Cadenza in the distance. He had his sights set on something grander than blood and knives.

At four years old, he'd gotten lost on the piper end of town. A practicing singer's voice had surprised him out of tears as if someone had reached out to hold his hand. Their voice sent him soaring, and dreaming, and had opened for him a new way of thinking. He remembered thinking, "It's just like when I took my first steps!" He didn't remember that earlier memory of walking anymore, but he remembered *remembering* it, how it felt, that experience of a new perspective.

He'd kept that memory of a memory close, through everything. Through Clef's machinations and grooming of anger. Through the years of locking his dream of singing away so he could survive. Through everything, he'd kept it. He'd survived so that memory could live, too, so he could become that person singing that had so changed him as a child.

No, he couldn't give up now.

Lasrial ended the morning service, and Alesio stood sentinel as the parishioners filed out.

<hr>

THE GUARD ROTATIONS changed every hour. After two of these, again around midday, the singer took up his post outside the garden entrance. Saida waited till he escorted the parishioners in the garden out and snuck through behind his back.

The dense line of bushes surrounding the garden soundproofed it. She shifted to human, slung the rusty banjo off her back, and plucked a few strings.

He spun around, his eyes flicking over to her. He slipped inside the garden and shut the gate after himself, giving her one sharp shake of his head.

When the gate snicked shut, she tensed.

It's alright. Goosefeather could pick that lock in a second or two.

She plucked another string with her human hands, which jangled out into the peaceful garden like a startled duck.

She frowned. That wouldn't make him want to sing along. She'd hoped he would sing within a few moments so she could snag the magic and hightail it out of there. Maybe fiddling with the little knobs on the end would help? She spun those around a few times and gave it another go.

The sound *worsened* into a horrible, discordant whine. She slapped her hand over the strings in alarm.

The human rubbed at a spot between his eyes, then at his left ear. "What. Are. You. Doing?"

Maybe if she sang. She cleared her throat and tried to imitate that song he'd sung the last night about the stars, trying to imitate the up and down-ness of music, and the strung-together words.

He stopped at her halting sound, and the tightness eased in his jaw. He covered his mouth with one hand, but his eyes twinkled, betraying him. "Are you—are you trying to sing "Gossamer God?"

She nodded. "The song you sang last night. It was very pretty."

The corners of his mouth curved up, then he pursed his lips as if trying to contain the grin. "So, you followed me, to the bar? Why?"

The silvery hum of magic from his mouth echoed the power she had witnessed the night before, not at the same intensity, though. Just like Winter Lightning and the swanseize's yawn, the overgrowth he produced seemed strongest at specific times, with specific parameters.

The quiet of the garden rang in her ears. Outside, the city still bustled on, but next to the altar, among all that waving greenery, it was like none but the two of them existed in that moment.

He shook his head. "You shouldn't be here. It's not safe. People could catch you and—and hurt you—"

"Kill me, you mean."

"If you know that, why are you here? I gave you food the other day because you looked hungry, but this can't be a habitual thing—"

"Don't you want to sing?" She stepped a little closer, then proffered the banjo to him. "You're so good at singing. I just want to hear your voice."

He blushed and shifted his weight, staring at her. Her heart pounded. She was so close to him. Close enough to touch. She clutched the seashell in her fist.

SHE WAS HUMAN AGAIN. Her bright red braid swung down to her calves, reminiscent of the tail it had changed into before, and her sharp, v-shaped chin and slitted pupils echoed her fox side. She stood just a half-head shorter than he, and her half-smile revealed human teeth, not fangs. Her clothing, once again, seemed to fit her as if someone had tailored them for her shifting ability, her shirt and trousers almost matching her red hair and blending into her reddish-brown skin at the edges of her legs and arms so that he couldn't quite tell where her clothing stopped, and her skin began.

A beam of sunlight pierced the clouds and streamed into the garden. The fox-woman's eyes reflected it, and in that moment, she seemed like a section cut out of a red-dawn sky. His left ear rang with a sudden brightness as if the sun itself sang to him, and he gasped and just stopped himself from dropping to his knees.

Those shining eyes blinked. She stepped forward a tiny bit. "Are you alright?"

It didn't *hurt,* but it was unsettling. Her words reverberated up through his boots, up to his chest. Her single step chimed in his head like an eighth note followed by a rest.

He heard music in lots of things. The wind, the complaining of an unsatisfied crowd, the pattern of peoples' steps in the market. But he didn't just hear it. The notes of her words rippled towards him like wavelets in the air he could see, and when she moved her foot forward, the fragrance of something fresh like mint and vast like the horizon flowed from her. A longing engulfed him that he didn't understand, a yearning for whatever reflected in those eyes, to see what she had seen.

The glow in her eyes vanished. The music, the ripples in the air, and the incredible smell dissipated. She'd left the beam of sunlight.

He stared at her, openmouthed.

She stayed still with one foot forward, as if waiting for him to do something. Had he imagined it all?

He blinked, shaking his head.

POSTED OUTSIDE LASRIAL'S OFFICE, Tak squinted at the slender man striding through the cathedral hall in what seemed a nice gray cotton shirt and black trousers. His face pinched in, and he did not glance at Tak for permission to enter. His eyes gleamed a strange, polished gray that unsettled him for some reason.

Tak didn't recognize the man from their regular parishioners, but who was he to keep new devotees from worshipping? Long as they were . . .

"Halt," Tak said. "Let me see your papers." The man's likeness had appeared on posters in many piper shops. They'd all read, 'Stay Away at All Costs,' and 'Dangerous!'

The man's eyes flicked behind Tak.

Lasrial spoke from behind him. "Thank you, Tak. You may leave us."

"Yes, sir." Tak swung to the side, and the slender man glided past with a wry smile. Tak fought to keep from hissing a warning to Lasrial.

The leader of the clefs wouldn't waltz up to St. Rina's in broad daylight, would he?

He sweated outside Lasrial's office, wishing he could just go home to his husband and drink today. Estro had asked him once why he wanted to work when he didn't have to—Estro worked security for the Cadenza and made enough for them both—but Tak liked basking in the hushed echoes of the cathedral.

Right now, though, he might just up and quit—

"Tak," Lasrial's voice called.

He straightened. Maybe thirty seconds had passed, but he'd sweated through his uniform. He swung open the door.

The slender man perched on the edge of a seat, while Lasrial sat behind his desk. "Please come in," Lasrial said. "Shut the door."

Tak swallowed and did so. Maybe he'd been wrong. The man didn't have any sound-scars. The strait's leader would have sound-scars, right? His clothing covered much of his skin, except for his hands and his face.

"Tak," Lasrial said, "This gentleman has informed me that the thief that broke in last week is something of a . . . mutual interest we have."

"Sir?"

"Did you happen to see the fur-mix after Alesio chased it away?"

Tak's thoughts spiraled. "I—I don't—"

"Keep in mind," Lasrial said, "That the Sound is always listening, and knows if we tell lies."

Had Lasrial always had gray eyes? The same color as this other man's eyes?

The slender man watched him with head cocked. If the rumors about Clef were true, he knew when people lied. Lasrial had just given him a subtle warning. Tak licked his lips. "I've seen her."

"And you didn't tell me?" Lasrial bolted to his feet, his face reddening.

"Where?" The slender man asked, in a quiet, commanding tone.

"I—I didn't think it was worth it. She wasn't inside the cathedral." He also hadn't wanted to get Alesio in trouble. The young man had a bit of an edge sometimes, but what kid didn't? "I saw her in the garden the other day. When I was posted outside the main doors. Had to do a double take, because I hadn't thought they were real, you know?" He hesitated.

"And?" Lasrial folded his arms.

"Alesio fed her some of the parishioner's offerings."

Lasrial used a word that Tak hadn't known reverends used.

"Now," the reverend said. "There are going to be some changes around here. A new, higher power is coming, and I need to know I can trust you."

"Yes," Tak said. "I'm sorry." He paused. Why would the reverend talk to a vicious leader from the straits—someone he despised? The incredulity and confusion started his tongue up again, though his brain told him to shut up. "Is it someone from the Cadenza? Is it Hestafon?"

Lasrial barked out a sharp laugh. "Hestafon! That fraud?" He leaned forward. "You know he uses an amplifier, right?"

Tak's jaw dropped.

"That's why he uses bells, of course, so the bells pick up the amplifier, and no one's the wiser because he doesn't open his mouth to sing." Lasrial shrugged. "Most of the performers at the Cadenza use one. They're all fakes."

Tak didn't know where to look. This was almost heresy, an assault on those who harnessed the magic of Sound. Had the reverend meant to be so forthright, so blatant?

Tak flicked his gaze over to Clef, then away again. "So, who is coming?"

"Someone who will give us a greater understanding of the Sound." Lasrial's face had brightened out of its sneer, and he tilted his face up at the ceiling as if he could see something they could not.

"As for the fur-mix," Clef said, "I have an idea."

Lasrial lowered his head and sniffed. "I'll have some traps set. That should do the trick."

"No, no," Clef said. "She can teleport, but just once a day, once every sunrise. So, we would need to double the trap somehow."

Tak blinked. *Teleport? What are they talking about?*

They seemed to have forgotten about his presence. He cleared his throat.

Clef glanced at him and cradled his chin in his hand, gazing with an unblinking quietness in those gray, polished eyes. "Tak, was it? Why would the fur-mix risk exposure? Did it seem like it cared for your co-guard?"

Tak shrugged. "I thought maybe she just wanted food."

"Perhaps." Clef tapped his chin, then swiveled his seat on the desk back to Lasrial. "Now, about your employee."

"I'll fire him, of course. He'll run back to you and do your filthy match."

What is going on? Why are they working together?

"No," Clef said. "I have just the thing that will convince him. You just be ready to summon Watthe when the delivery comes." He inclined his head to the left and side-eyed Tak. "I trust you will keep this conversation . . . under wraps." He tapped his ear. "The Sound is always listening, as the reverend said. Wouldn't want dear Estro to get caught on the wrong side of Anthem, now, would we?"

Tak stiffened. Clef smiled back.

"Do you understand?" Lasrial asked.

Tak locked his jaw. "Yes."

SAIDA'S LIPS had dried out. She licked them, staring into the human's eyes. *Sing! Sing! I can't stay so close for much longer!*

The human lifted the banjo from her outstretched arms, his hands wrapping around the long end of the instrument. With quick, deft movements, he unwound the broken strings from the thicker end, stretched them, the muscles in his dark brown arms rippling, then retied them. A small furrow appeared on his brow, and he twisted the little knobs that she had messed with, plucking the strings as he did. The harsh sound wavered, then steadied into a pleasant one. His eyelashes fluttered back up, and his chocolate eyes stared at her. She stood just a little away, a half step.

His lips opened, and he sang a small tune:

I sing to you from inside
This flute, my dear, my love

She whipped the seashell up next to his lips, and he paused, mouth agape.

The magic had grown in potency as it had back in the bar. It swirled around the seashell but did not enter it.

Why isn't it working? Is it because it's human magic? She'd never trimmed human magic before, let alone tried to prune one at a transplant level. *Maybe he needs to sing something specific?*

The magic bumped up against the shell with more urgency, but still, something unseen seemed to block it. It wanted to leave this world, just like every other overgrowth. But for some reason it couldn't.

Maybe she hadn't tried at the optimal time. The storm that had generated Winter Lightning had brewed in the sky over Scent for several days.

Yet, the accrual of the magic had damaged him. She caught flickers of injury in the mournful lilt of the song he'd sung, and in the controlled way he held his breath like a dam holding back an angry sea.

Still, though, his magic seemed unable to create a transplant.

She waited so close to him, up on her tiptoes, holding the seashell to his lips. How long had she stood there?

He stared back at her, also unmoving.

SHE STOOD SO CLOSE.

All sound ceased around him, and just her shallow breaths filled his ears. He breathed in deep for the first time since his colossal failure of impressing either of the people sent to scout his abilities. His throat seemed less raw, somehow. Her long braid laid over her shoulder tickled his arm, and she smelled like a sweet kind of foreign berry. She held a seashell, of all things, up to his lips.

She shrank away and shifted to less human. He kept still. She had a wildness about her; a tensed, coiled thing in her eyes. Any movement from him could scare her off.

"Your voice . . . it sounds like it's suffering."

He blinked. "Well, it's a sad song."

"No." She stared, still, at his lips. "Your *voice*."

What had she tried to do with the seashell? She'd focused on his face. Did she like him, or did she perhaps have stalker-like tendencies?

Wait. She'd had a seashell with her when she'd snatched Hestafon's bell case. What did that mean? According to some of the old ballads, fox-people stole magic. They crept close enough and breathed on you —or stabbed you, different songs detailed different things—and then you lost the ability to use magic. He'd never heard mention of a seashell, though.

He shook the thought away. He knew better than to listen to such narrow-minded prejudice. "What's your name?" he asked. *What was that vision just now? Did I imagine it?*

She started, then backed away. "I've got to go. I've—I can't be here."

He'd just told her that exact thing, but now he wanted to know more about her. "My name's Alesio," he said, as a way to edge closer without physically doing so. She stepped back towards the garden entrance.

"Saida," she said.

Through the gate's metal latticework, Alesio spotted someone striding out of the cathedral's doors.

He shifted to a slight crouch.

Why is Clef here?

WHY BY ALL THE Senses had she told him her name? *Stupid, stupid!*

She realized that his gaze had shifted away from her, and his stance reminded her of a corkscrew, all wound up. She backed away, flattening her ears. Why had he tensed up? Would he lunge for her?

She chanced a quick backwards glance to where he was looking. Someone stalked away from St. Rina's, away from the garden, and down the street.

"Stay here till he leaves," the guard named Alesio hissed. "He's dangerous. It would be bad if he saw you."

Everything in her warned her to run.

"Please," he said. "That's the leader from the straits. He—he might try and use you for his fights."

And Senses take her, but she did stay. Not because of his explanation, but because of the draw of his silver voice, luring her so she wanted to reach and touch his lips.

I'm in trouble.

8

SECRET PRAYERS

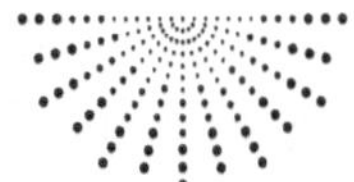

Saida did not visit the pub that night.

She wandered the secret ways of the fox-people, winding along the rooftops, slinking in the shadows of the bar signs swinging in the wind, roaming through the small, underground tunnels—dug not by hammer and shovel, but by claw and fang. She could not think about humans anymore today. She could not trust the human part of herself that wanted to listen to the guard, even though doing so would not gain her a transplant. She needed to interact with anyone but him—and herself.

"Hello?" She tested her voice in the silence of one tunnel. "Anyone?"

Nothing.

"We're still here," Goosefeather said. "You can talk to us."

She smoothed their feathers in her pocket with her paw. "I know. I know. I just think—maybe I need a face to talk to today, you know?"

"I can make myself *into* a face." Tricksy Stone shifted, morphing, stretching out the folds in her clothes. Saida rolled her eyes.

Scuttling sounded ahead. She sucked in a breath.

A bugrat stuck its nose out of the side of the tunnel and squeaked. She sighed. "Hey, little guy. You seen any fox-people around?"

"You're not one of us." The voice came from ahead in the tunnel. The darkness hid any form or shadow the voice's owner had.

Saida stilled. The bugrat sniffled and trundled back into its burrowing hole. "What makes you think that?"

A rasp of cloth, and footsteps, coming closer. An inhaled breath from maybe five feet away. "Because you did something to the bell magic. Something different."

"I trimmed it."

"And you walked out of the wall. The wall opened and you stepped out of it. Behind you was . . . a different place. The sky was different, for a half second." A pause. "What *are* you? Where did you come from?"

"I'm so glad to properly meet one of you." Saida swallowed. "I'm a foxan. I am—" how had she explained it to the fox-person couple she'd met years back? She never knew how to explain. Or maybe she'd figured out what to say before but didn't remember. "I'm from another place, and I can sense magic, just like you. But I don't steal it, not in the way that you think."

"In what way *do* you steal it, then?" In the complete darkness, the sound of the fox-person's voice gave it shape, and she could imagine their tense shoulders, their clenched fists. The bugrat scuffled along in its own miniature tunnel, leaving those with sharp teeth behind. "Are you like how the songs say? The ones that give us a bad name?"

She could explain so much easier if they would travel with her to another world and see through her eyes. The other ones she'd asked had cowered when she'd opened a portal, and run away from her, calling her a magic thief. She didn't want this one to run.

"I am a gardener," Saida said. "Magic is like a plant in some ways. It needs tending, pruning, to keep it healthy. I just trim the excess."

"What are your intentions for the trimmed part?"

"I plant them somewhere new. Somewhere they want to go."

Another pause.

"Please. I need to know something." She gathered her tail in her paws. "I have family. They are very old. Ancient, according to your time, because they live so long. And they have descendants."

A rustling of cloth. They had backed up a step.

Saida spoke quickly. "Your ancestors were, or are, foxans. My people. They are searching for their great, great, great grandchildren." She released her tail. "I know this is kind of strange to ask, but please. I need to know. Do you know your grandmother's name? Or even your great grandmother?"

"My parents orphaned me when I was too young to know them. The Sound knows who birthed *them*." More rustling. Another step back. Their voice drifted from farther away. "Leave the fox-people alone. We don't want anyone to know us, and we don't need to know anybody."

"Wait—please!"

They scampered back down the passage. After a few moments, just the sound of the bugrat remained, trundling in its miniature tunnel like it couldn't decide which way to dig.

"By the Senses!" Saida braced her clenched paw against the dirt wall, trying to quell the quivering in her chest. *Pell. I'm sorry.*

She trailed along the passage, where it angled upwards. It opened out of the side of a building next to a broken wire fence. A bonfire blazed in the dirt street. She'd traveled all the way to the straits. She tucked the new secret way in the back of her mind, adding it to the map in her head of the city, and she didn't have to ask Tricksy Stone to do it for her.

What was she supposed to do now?

I should leave. I should just try my luck on another world. Find another overgrowth on Scent. Or Taste.

Her promise to the people in that tiny village on Vision hovered in her mind. She needed as many strong transplants as she could find, and she'd never found anything so strong as that human's voice. But it seemed unable to break free, perhaps unable to let go of its origin world. Was she just wasting her time trying to trim it? Was this human's magic trapping *her*, like a candle attracting a moth?

Down the dirt road a little way, an ancient brick overpass drew her attention. A shower of plinking sounds, like small hail, echoed from within. Half-dressed, mud-spattered children ran in and out of the overpass, their faces upturned, their tongues out, laughing.

The place emanated strong Taste and Sound magic, mixed. A transplant. It had drawn her here unawares in the distraction of her own thoughts.

She'd planted them many, many years before, in the dawn of her first outing away from Between. Maybe a hundred and seventy years ago? A hundred and eighty? Before she'd found Goosefeather, or Tricksy Stone. Before . . . before Carn when she'd had no fear of people and cities. She'd brought her first transplant from Taste here, because they had wanted to rain salt down where no one would expect.

"You remembered," Tricksy Stone said. "I hoped you would. I didn't remind you, because I hoped you would, all on your own."

"Saltfall." She whispered their name, edging closer to the underpass. She hadn't named them before for some reason.

They paused, and the pitter-pattering of the salt hitting the ground stopped, too.

The children waited; their faces tilted up to the shadowed patch where she'd stuck the salted paper. Taste's magic, mixed with Sound, had connected the worlds so that a shower of salt filtered through the paper.

"Saida!" Saltfall let loose a torrent of salt, and the children squealed in delight, skipping in and out of the deluge. "Saida, it's so good to see you! You can hear me, now? I talked to you before, but you never answered!"

Saida tried to talk, but Saltfall continued. "Look how much the children love me! I give them good doses of salt! They were all malnourished, before. And when the adults come, I just don't fall, so they never believe the children and I don't have to worry about them taking me down! Isn't it wonderful?"

Saida smiled. "It is. It's wonderful. You're doing a lovely job."

The deluge stopped, and the children ceased running. Their shoulders slumped. "Guess it's done for today."

"Aw. You didn't let me get a turn."

"Sssk! I did to!"

Squabbling, but laughing again, the pack of small humans dashed off, passing Saida without a glance.

"Guess I got a little carried away, there." Saltfall sighed. "I can't connect to Taste for as long as I used to. I used to rain like that for hours. Now it's just seconds."

"I'm trying to help with that," Saida said. "But magics are weakening everywhere, and humans are too. I'm trying. I'm concentrating harder than I ever have before. But it's not enough."

Saltfall seemed to consider that. "So, the other foxans still can't help?"

Saida shook her head.

"But what is important is that you keep doing what you're doing," Goosefeather said. "Without you, the worlds would already have drifted far, far apart."

"That's right." Saida forced a smile. "Sorry, Saltfall. Didn't mean to worry you. I promise everything will work out."

"You put a lot of pressure on yourself," Saltfall said. "But you're not alone. I'm sure the other transplants are trying to help, too!"

Saida nodded and waved, not trusting her voice. *You're not alone. You're not alone.*

I began hearing the voices in magics after . . . after what happened on Touch . . .

That stray thought pushed itself through like a needle, pricking her. She didn't want to think the next thing, but she did. *None of these voices are real. They're all just shattered parts of me, talking to myself.*

She covered her mouth and blanked her mind. *Forget. Forget that. I am not alone.*

"Don't be a stranger," Saltfall called after her.

———

THE NEXT DAY, her legs walked her back to the cathedral, back to the garden, under the safety of the dense bushes. Alesio waited there in his ostentatious yet also dashing blue and gold uniform. His gaze flickered to her, and his lips curved up.

I have no reason to just talk to him!

She pivoted towards the side door of the cathedral and picked the lock with Goosefeather, not thinking, just escaping, shifting to her human form, and trying to act pious, puckering her face like a sweet old lady pondering the sound of sadness in the world.

Maybe he would follow her in.

Maybe he wouldn't.

She tucked her ears flatter under the hood she had grown, inched open the door to the main hall, and peeked around it. A few worshippers knelt in the pews, praying to the giant golden statue, the wave of Sound. Everything echoed.

Her legs carried her to the back pew, where she knelt and bowed her head.

I don't think you're real, she said to the Sound statue. *Well, not in the way these people think.*

Probably not the best way to start a conversation with a deity.

She peeked behind her. Had Alesio followed her in? No sign of him. Did she want to escape him, or escape this feeling of not wanting to escape?

She turned back to the statue. It loomed above her, its Sound magic resonating most of the way through the pews. She blinked. Hadn't it seeped through the whole room the last time she'd snuck in here? Or had that been all because of the guard's magic?

Saltfall's words echoed back to her. *I can't connect to Taste for as long as I used to.*

Had the transplant said something else important? Saida frowned.

"Saida," Goosefeather said. "You know that—"

Focus, Saida. Focus.

If magic faded even here, in the biggest city full of the most humans she'd ever found, she didn't know if she could stop the worlds from drifting apart. It seemed like it took a little longer to teleport every so often, not just to Vision. What if she had to choose a world to stay on, forever? What if she couldn't even teleport to Between, and she lost her mother, father, and Pell?

She had to stop that from happening. She had to keep the worlds together, to tie them to each other like lifeboats in a stormy sea. The cries of the people on Vision wrenched at her. They depended on her.

Yet for all her desperate attempts, the ropes frayed, and the crests of the waves curled over her.

She couldn't do this by herself! She couldn't shoulder this growing weight. Maybe for one world, but not all five! And the one overgrowth from the human that could've helped the most seemed blocked!

If you are real, in some way, she prayed to the Sound god, *could you help me? The worlds are in danger, and I'm trying to help. But the magic isn't working like it should.* She paused. *And I'm not working like I should.*

No resonant, all-knowing voice spoke. What had she hoped for, anyway? A higher power to obey, to just follow direction without worry or wavering?

Something moved in her periphery. The reverend, with his golden, crimped robes symbolizing the Sound, swept into a side room opposite the washroom.

Curious, she left the pew and slunk after him. The other guard, posted at the main door, faced outward, so she shifted straight to foxan, shrinking into her creature half that crept and padded, instead of jouncing around on two feet. She slipped into the door after the reverend, hunkering under a chair. A kind of reckless restlessness had overtaken her.

The reverend closed the door behind him and straightened some papers on his desk.

"What are you doing?" Tricksy Stone asked, and she wanted to shush him, except that the reverend would hear her.

The human crossed the room and hummed a little tune. Part of the wall opened, and he stepped through it!

She peeked around the chair to see better. The secret wall opened just enough to fit the average-sized human.

Footsteps outside the door. Had Alesio followed her?

Why does it matter? Don't I want him to stay away?

She skulked forward a bit to see more of the secret room. The light from the office streamed into the dark space, revealing a human-sized shape, but not human.

Gray. Giant hands. Too-long fingers that tapered to claws, holding a box.

Saida pressed herself to the floor, ears flat, tail between her legs. The figure remained still. It was a statue.

A statue of Watthe.

Terror shot through her. *What is happening? How is this possible? Why would this human even have this?* She tried to make sense of what she saw, but thinking felt like she was trying to walk through the sludge shadows of the Primal Plane.

The reverend knelt in front of the likeness. He murmured, "I live to serve you, god of the Planes. I am your humble servant."

Her thoughts kicked forward a little. This human knew of the other worlds.

Watthe must have told him!

How had Watthe followed her? She'd left him on Scent! Had he somehow figured out how to teleport on his own?

Saida backed away under the chair, fumbling for the door. She needed to get out. She'd stayed in Sound too long. Still, she did not want to teleport here, so near this crazy Watthe-worshipper.

"Fur-mix!" The reverend barreled out of the secret side room, hands reaching for her.

Her claws scrabbled at the handle without purchase, so she shifted just her fingers to save time and yanked the door open.

Alesio stood there. His eyes widened and his mouth dropped open. She bolted past him.

The reverend chased her. "Alesio! Do your sounddamned job and catch the thing!"

She dashed through the main doors.

"Why aren't we teleporting?" Goosefeather asked.

She didn't have breath to explain. She didn't understand it herself, except for the vague notion that she had to tell Alesio about the terrifying statue and the reverend's secret room, so he stopped working there. If she teleported now, she didn't know if she could force herself to return to Sound.

"Not right now, though, right?" Tricksy Stone said.

"Not right now." She dashed around to the escape route she had scoped out, that little hole in the foundation of the building next door. She wiggled through and dashed along the zig-zag access path between the buildings.

Footsteps behind her. Alesio, or the other guard?

"Why does it matter?" Tricksy Stone asked.

"It doesn't matter!"

She would tell him goodbye at the pub that night.

9

ANOTHER KIND OF SAFETY

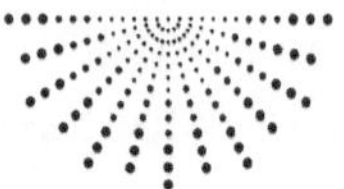

Saida waited outside the pub that night, crowding herself on the edge of the windowsill and peeking around the frame. She wanted to slip inside the bar with her ears plastered down, to weave through the tables and the patrons and whisper a goodbye as he sang. She wanted to lounge and listen to the silver in his voice, not through a pane of glass, and listen how his magic threaded through the room and made the customers sway. She could've swayed along with them. She wanted—

She wanted—

She could not want such things.

Such a clever trap. This world had crafted the perfect cage to try and lure her in, one with pretty arms and kind, chocolate eyes. She hated to leave without figuring out how to trim the magic for him. She wanted to help save Vision, but also, she wanted to ease the suffering in his gorgeous voice.

Besides, she couldn't leave without warning Alesio about the reverend and how he worshipped an entity that seemed obsessed with stalking and eating her. But she couldn't warn him here. She couldn't go inside. What had she been thinking?

Well, she hadn't been thinking. She'd panicked, and run, and made promises to herself she couldn't keep. She was such a scatterbrained, restless sieve of a person, with all the commitment of a wave on a shore.

"You can't spend too long, deciding," Goosefeather said. "That monster will find you if you stay in one place."

She would tell Alesio tomorrow. She would find him after his shift at the cathedral. First, she needed to throw her hunter off her trail, to ensure he would not find her before then.

SAIDA SPENT the morning and late afternoon scouting the hidden ways to enter and exit the straits. Her thoughts circled on themselves like one of Vision's illogical buildings.

Am I really going to do this?

"I'd try to talk you out of it," Goosefeather said. "But that's not what you want, is it?"

"I want to warn Alesio. But first, I need to know for sure that Watthe won't find me while I'm talking to him. To keep him safe."

Towards the evening, Saida traveled to the outskirts of Anthem in the straits using the fox-people's secret ways, leaping across rooftops, darting through hidden alleyways, and weaving among strategically placed piles of broken crates, to the farthest distance she could manage from the Drinks De Capo on the straits side.

Another bonfire raged on this street, ringed by men in faded green-gray factory clothes, some of them holding bottles. A block away, the factory itself loomed like a grimy mockery of the Cadenza, tall and smoky gray, disappearing into the surrounding, low-hanging smog. A bar across the street blared a cacophony of something that resembled music.

Inhaling deep, she stepped out onto the street, in plain view of one side of the bonfire.

One of the men shouted and pointed. The whole circle of straiters rotated towards her.

She shifted her snout to more foxan, shrank her body, and landed on all fours. She flicked her braid as it transformed into her tail.

"What is—is that what I think it is?"

"I saw it first!"

"Shut it, I need the money. My kid's coughing up a storm!"

The group lunged for her like one organism. She lingered long enough for them to get a good look, then hurtled across the street, dodging their grasping hands.

"Sound take you!"

"Crazy fur-mix!"

A bottle smashed by her feet. She gasped and ran faster, skidding behind the bar and jumping up to the thin ledge. From there, she clambered up to the roof.

"There it is! Up there!"

She flicked her tail, standing tall on the peak of the roof. A clamor below informed her they tried to climb up after her. Another bottle sailed her way, which she dodged.

"Stop that, you drunk idiot! It'll sell for more alive!"

Saida hunkered down, skittering to the other side of the roof, then leapt off and onto a barrel, then down to the ground.

"Where'd it go?"

"The other side! The other side!"

She darted to the next building over, an abandoned hovel without a roof. On the other side of the wall, she scrabbled her claws on the metal latch in the floor. She hooked it and lifted the trap door up.

"It must have jumped down! Look around!"

Panting, she ducked down into the tunnel, lowering the trapdoor shut behind her without letting it slam. Footsteps close by, then someone ran overhead. She bolted along the tunnel in a panic, her tongue lolling out.

Then she hightailed it back to the pub, huddling under the dumpster where the secret entrance was, trembling for a long time.

ALESIO CLAIMED the garden shift first thing. He hoped the fox-woman —Saida, she'd said her name was—visited again, and at the same time, he hoped she wouldn't.

He couldn't get her out of his head.

The brightness of her outline, silhouetted like the dawn, gleaming like the composition of a sunrise, had echoed the feeling of listening to the Cadenza performer as a kid. For a moment, it was like someone had pulled back a giant curtain in the sky and revealed a different sky behind it.

Another image rolled around in his head, however, that he couldn't ignore: Clef waltzing out of St. Rina's.

Alesio shook out his legs and rolled his shoulders, taking deep breaths. His shift would start in a few minutes.

What had Clef done in there? What if he'd planted an explosive or dangerous item in the cathedral? Maybe he wanted to blow up St. Rina's to make Alesio come back.

No, no. That seemed extreme and out of character. Clef kept to the shadows. He cared about making money on his terms, nothing else. He and the rich pipers seemed to have an agreement: though they technically owned the factories, Clef controlled them through the factions he ran in the straits, and in return, he wouldn't mess with the piper side.

Something seemed to be closing in, something Alesio didn't understand. It was all crumbling. The reverend had seen Saida and shouted. She'd fled. Would she return?

You're so good at singing. I just want to hear your voice.

His cheeks heated.

He'd just met her. He knew next to nothing about her, but he wanted to know more. Something about her pointed chin, red hair, and mischievous smile as she struggled to play a rusty, half-stringed banjo made him feel as smitten as a kid with his first crush.

He wanted to go somewhere with her. Somewhere new.

What am I even thinking right now? That doesn't make any sense!

Tak ambled past on his way to his post at the front doors and said something. Alesio angled his good ear towards him. "What did you say?"

"Lasrial is out in force today."

"When is he not?"

Tak leaned against the wall. "Yesterday, he said something odd." He lowered his voice. "He—he said that most of the Cadenza performers use amplifiers. That that's why they're so good." He snorted and shook his head. "You ever hear such a thing? Now, I wouldn't put it past Hestafon, but all of them?"

Alesio raised his eyebrows. "That's a bold claim. It's not like Lasrial to badmouth a pip—I mean, a Cadenza performer."

"He seems off, lately."

"Besides that, did you notice anything weird yesterday?" Alesio asked. "I have this feeling that someone bad's about." That sounded vague, even to him. But how he could broach the topic of a murderous leader of the straits with an old, rich piper who worked because he wanted to, not because he had to?

Tak licked his lips. "You mean besides the uh, the fur-mix?"

Alesio clenched his jaw. "She didn't steal Hestafon's bells."

"But she snuck inside the cathedral again! In Lasrial's office!" Tak shook his head. "She'll pinch something when you're not paying attention. Maybe even your magic. My cousin told me that his friend had a fox-person grab his guitar and after that, he couldn't play any instrument well."

Alesio rolled his eyes. "Your cousin's friend? Are you sure it wasn't your cousin's friend's wife's next-door neighbor?"

"If those old songs are true, it's because of those like her that we work here, Alesio. Fox-people, and those others from the straits." The older man patted the harmonica in his pocket. "I'm just saying. Keep your instruments close." He bobbed his head and strode to his post at the front main door.

Those others from the straits.

Alesio clenched his fists. Should he keep himself out, as well? *People should stop saying things they don't know anything about.*

THE AFTERNOON WORE on to evening. She needed to get up to meet Alesio on the road before he went inside the pub where she could not follow.

But her legs wouldn't obey her mind. Her limbs shook. A roaring in her ears blocked everything else, even Tricksy Stone or Goosefeather.

Grasping hands. Angry shouts.

Who knew if Watthe, or any of the citizens, had found out where she'd gone? What if they waited for her right now to squirm out of her hiding place?

She panted, her tongue lolling out. Goosefeather brushed against her, trying to soothe her. She couldn't hear them.

The homeless woman in the alley peeked under the dumpster, holding something in her hand. Her lips moved, but Saida didn't hear her, she heard nothing except a dull roar.

She was cut off. Alone. How long had she huddled here? How could she know without Tricksy Stone to tell her? How much would she forget without their voice to guide her?

"Foxan."

Saida blinked. The word pierced through the silent roar in her mind.

The homeless woman rubbed at the dirt on her face. Stripes showed where none had before, and her eyes flashed in the shadows of the growing evening. The same fox-person that had confronted Saida at the cathedral garden stood there. She tossed a small bit of fried cheese that a bar customer must have tossed on the ground the night before.

"Eat. Hurry, or I'll eat it for you."

Saida crawled out and snapped up the bit of cheese, and that little movement seemed to help, slipping out of the trap of her own thoughts.

The roaring faded.

"—are you okay?" Goosefeather said. "Can you hear me? Don't be afraid. I'm here. I'm here. Tricksy Stone's here. Can you hear me?"

"I'm alright."

Saida peered at the fox-woman out of the corner of her eye, not wanting to scare her away. "Why?" She whispered. "Why help me? You said—"

"I've watched you." The fox-woman rubbed dirt from the ground back onto her cheeks, concealing her stripes once more. "I see how you pine for that human and his magic."

"I don't—*pine*—!"

"Lots of us listen, all on different nights. This alley always has a beggar. He has quite the following, among us who can hear the silver waves he creates." She paused. "Out of everyone in this city, even on the golden side, none has his strength of magic, yet the other humans only listen to where he comes from."

Saida's mouth hung open, then she swallowed the last bit of fried cheese. She feared to say anything, lest the fox-woman regain her wariness and run away again.

"I thought about what you said. About how you prune a small part of the magic, so it grows healthier. I checked on the bell case, where the fancy bellringer lives, and you were right. The bell sounds clearer and more beautiful." She laid a light, furred hand on Saida's shoulder. "We want you to do that for the human singer. We want you to help him. He is in pain, for all his magic. We have heard it in his voice."

"I've tried." Saida hung her head. "Believe me, I've tried. But his magic is stuck, for some reason, I can't trim it. I don't know why."

The fox-woman patted her shoulder, then backed away. She seemed as averse to touch as Saida. "It would mean much to us for you to try again."

If I figure out how to do it, maybe she'll tell me where to find the others.

"I—I can try again, I suppose." Saida licked her lips. She could try once more before she left.

"You should know something," Saida said. "There is a bad . . . person in the city. Like a shadow, but he can hurt you. He is hunting me. I need to leave so he can't find me. But you and the rest of the fox-people must stay away from him."

The fox-woman nodded. "We have seen him. We stay away, just like we stay away from everyone. It is no different."

It's a little different, Saida thought, but she didn't have time to explain. She needed to meet Alesio.

"Thank you for helping me."

"Fear paralyzes us all. The trick is to not let it keep hold of you. You escape by moving a little at a time." She jerked her chin toward the street. "Go. Meet him."

Saida crept along the secret ways, towards the route he used. She hadn't gone more than a few blocks before Alesio appeared, rambling towards the pub. Saida's heart pounded and her cheeks grew warm.

This. This feeling is what I fear the most. It leads to cages and lies and breaking all apart.

I will not let it keep hold of me.

ALESIO FINISHED his shift at the cathedral without Saida showing up at all.

Maybe Tak was right, and he should never have encouraged her in the first place. She didn't belong there.

It's because of people like her that we work here.

Why did Tak's words bother him so much? Many around him had uttered worse things.

He trudged back to the pub, watching the casual smiles change to furtive glances, listening to the *swish-swish* of silk change to the *rasp-rasp* of rough cotton. Why did this trance come over him when leaving the piper side, as if he were fascinated by the withering of a flower? The anger slashed inside him, wanting out, wanting to cut through the air.

He tried to play the memory in his head that he clung to, of listening to that performer at four years old, to push the anger away and replace his rage with glimmering gold.

It didn't work.

His throat felt raw again and he wished he had some tea with honey. He'd had a sore throat a few months ago, as well. Maybe he needed to do more vocal warm-ups before performances.

It's because of others from the straits.

He'd worked with Tak for two years now, had joked with him and bantered back and forth. The older man and his husband seemed like good folk. And yet for all that, Tak still couldn't see past his preconceptions of what a 'straiter' was.

His words hurt far worse than any of Lasrial's rants. They had deflated Alesio more than any jibe from an audience member or heckle from someone in a rowdy crowd. Tak had said his piece with all the casualness of someone mentioning the indisputable fact that it was raining.

The piper side would never allow Alesio to perform at the Cadenza.

He'd dreamed of it for so long, but it was, as his father had told him over and over, 'a piper's dream.' He saw the ridiculousness of it now; as if he'd lived in a house without mirrors all his life, and then saw himself for the first time.

At least at the cage matches, he had had recognition. People had screamed his name, had gotten excited when he fought. Why did he fight so hard not to fight when his left ear provided a natural shield? Why did he want to perform, to sing, for someone to *hear* him, when his own body seemed to say he might as well try to push through a brick wall?

The anger swirled like a bucket of knives in his chest, and he watched the transition of gold to grime on the streets with a strange, masochistic pleasure; the grim happiness of witnessing the ruination of something he couldn't have.

His body shook, and he laughed in the street. Singing for a bunch of sounddamned pipers? A whole room of people that had pushed him down his whole life? Why had he wanted such a thing?

His father would tell him to fight for a better life. A better future. He could almost hear him now, shouting at him. "Stop! Don't!"

Wait—

That *was* his father's voice.

Out of the shadows several feet away, three figures struggled in dark clothing, two of them holding the other. "Run!" Alesio's father screamed. "Run away!"

Alesio tensed and sucked in a deep breath. He'd send a blunt wave of sound to throw them off their feet.

"Shut up!" One of the others said, and the air wavered like a heat mirage, coalescing into an object next to his father's throat. Sound-knife.

His father stopped struggling, and Alesio's breath shuddered in his chest. He would take his chances with a sound-knife, but his father didn't have his natural shield. He could sing a knife into existence to combat that one, but who knew if they had other knives, both real and sound-based?

Clef slunk out from behind the three figures, along with someone else . . . no, some*thing* else, unfolding into a higher shadow, almost nine feet tall.

What is happening? Everything seemed to slow down, even his thoughts.

It glided towards Alesio, the light from a nearby pub window illuminating something impossible, a smoky, gray-skinned giant with hands like massive claws, the fingers narrowing into sharp points. Smoke seemed to drift off it as if it burned in a fire. It cradled a black box in one of those hands.

A monster...!

"Where is the foxan?"

Its voice rang in his good ear like a jagged chord, harsh and off-key. Alesio winced.

"I'd answer him," Clef said from behind it.

Alesio's thoughts stuttered into words. "What—what's a foxan?"

The monster loomed closer, then bent its head to stare at the box in its arms. "Does he not the word know, oh god of the Planes? Or does he not his situation know?"

"He means the fur-mix you're so partial to, Alesio," Clef said. "Where is she?"

Alesio swallowed. Had they hurt his father? What could he do against something so huge? How did Clef know about Saida?

"I don't know." Clef had an uncanny awareness of when people lied, so Alesio was glad of the truth that rose to his lips. "She doesn't tell me where she goes."

The creature twisted its head to Clef without moving its body. Clef nodded, then inclined his head lower like a slight bow.

The creature revolved its head back to stare at Alesio, unblinking.

Why does it want her? Why is Clef working with this thing?

The other two faction members kept their eyes down, their bodies bowed towards the monster. The strait's leader had always scoffed at the god of Sound. But now, he reminded Alesio of how Lasrial gazed at the wave statue in St. Rina's. Full of awe and deference.

What insane terror had Saida gotten herself into?

The monster spoke to the box it held, holding the container out. It had a strange, raised pattern of worms on the outside, which somehow seemed to move. "Oh, god of Planes, what would do have me? It seems this one is an end. Shall I eat him? He has magic. Oh, yes."

Alesio's thoughts froze again. His father shouted and struggled against the two clefs that held him.

"Oh, Great Watthe." Clef kept his head down. "If I could remind you of our deal. The bigger things we are looking to do together." He shifted his weight from one leg to the other.

Watthe, as Clef had called it, seemed to consider Alesio as someone would consider a box of chocolates. "Take him, then." It flowed to the side.

"Alesio." Clef gestured to his minions restraining Alesio's father. "I need your word that you will give me a good match. Like the old days."

"No! Don't do it, son!" His father ripped away from one of the men.

"Sound take you!" The clef member shrieked a sound knife into his father's shoulder. He dropped to the ground.

WATTHE WAS HERE.

Saida huddled in a ball in the dark. One of the humans had sung a sound knife into the older man, who had fallen, a circle of dark red blooming in his shoulder.

Watthe worked with a group of straiters, too? With that man that Alesio had said was their leader?

I should help!

"What can you do?" Goosefeather asked. "He'll just eat you if you show yourself!"

"FATHER!" Alesio surged forward, and Watthe enveloped him. He stumbled, not knowing which way was up or down. Something tugged and grasped at him, at his mouth.

"You much magic have in your throat," that jagged voice said. "If only I didn't you need. I should like to taste."

Then Alesio was back out, falling to his knees.

Watthe murmured to Clef, "I must a sighting check on the outskirts of town." The monster melded back into the darkness.

The strait's leader squatted in front of Alesio, his eyes glinting. "Do we have a deal?"

"Yes! Yes, just let him go!"

Clef gestured, and the faction members left his father lying there and strode over to Alesio, strong-arming him away. "Dad! Can you hear me?" Alesio sobbed. "Dad?" One of them stuffed a rag in his mouth, and then something hard hit him in the face, then the head, and he blacked out.

SHE COULD HAVE DONE SOMETHING. Anything. Maybe she could have stopped them from dragging him away. Maybe they wouldn't have hurt Alesio's father.

His father lay on the ground, wheezing. It didn't seem like a good sound.

Had Watthe left? No shadows stirred in the alley.

Maybe Watthe had gone to investigate the trail she'd planted earlier. Maybe not. He'd known that she'd hung around Alesio; perhaps he'd also figured out she watched and waited for her to emerge.

Alesio's father coughed, then seemed to breathe a little slower, his wheezing a little quieter. A few humans plodding by crossed to the other side of the street.

Just a little motion. Just a small movement.

She shifted her paw into a foot, then worked on her hands, and grew into a proper human-ish woman. Swallowing the ball of fear in her throat, she took a step towards the man, then another, and another, and she dashed the rest of the way.

"Human?" She fluttered over the dark redness at his shoulder seeping through his faded shirt. His eyes had closed. "Father of Alesio!"

His eyes flickered open. His lips moved, but he didn't seem to have much strength. She didn't know anything about human health or medicine.

"Goosefeather, what do I do? Tricksy?"

The feather ruffled in her pocket. "Seems like the bleeding is the bad thing, right? Maybe try to stop that?"

She had an idea. She ran inside a nearby bar and asked the closest patron, "Do you have sound cloths?"

They blinked at her, then pointed at the stack of folded cloths that almost every bar had, for those leaving who wanted a clean bit of ear protection or to dampen sound in between songs. She snatched a whole handful and sprinted back out to Alesio's father. She ripped the coarse cloth of his shirt with a shifted claw, then pressed down with several of the bar cloths to try and stem the bleeding. Blood soaked through seven or eight of them, then the next few seemed less bloody even after she held them for a minute or so. She knotted three together and tied them around his shoulder in a makeshift bandage.

"Who are you?" He murmured, his breathing shallow. "Is Alesio alright?"

"Um. I'm—I'm Saida. And I don't know." She paused and decided to just tie the cloth around his shoulder to keep pressure there. "They took him away."

"Damn it. They'll make him fight a cage match." The man sat up and groaned. The cloth wrapped around his shoulder soaked a little more with blood, but he couldn't just lie in the street. She went and grabbed some more cloths from the bar just to have some extras.

Cage matches. Brutal fights with Sound magic.

She helped the human to his feet, supporting him with his good arm around her shoulder. He was a thin man, besides which he'd lost a lot of blood.

"There was a creature with them. Something huge and shadowy and . . . I don't know what, but even Clef seemed to obey it. Or did I imagine all that?"

She winced. "We should get out of here. They could come back."

He grunted in what sounded like assent, and they staggered down the street following his directions. His slight frame weighed heavier as time passed, and his wheezing worsened if they quickened their pace. People averted their eyes from them, pushing the rags in their ears further.

He led them down another street, and another. Saida checked behind them for tall shadows.

"These cage matches," Saida said. "How deadly are they?"

He tightened his grip on her shoulder. "You from the piper side of town?"

"I'm—I'm from another city."

He squinted at her, then narrowed his eyes. "You're the fur-mix they're looking for!" He shoved her. "What trouble have you gotten my son mixed up in?"

She shrank away. "I'm sorry. I didn't mean to. I just like his singing at the pub." She hung her head. "The . . . shadow creature, um followed me from my old city."

He stood there, one arm hanging down with the other hand

pressed against his bad shoulder. The urge to run flashed through her like she imagined how touching Winter Lightning would feel.

"I know what it is to have something chase you," the man said. "Always looming. You try to outrun it, but it always knows where you'll be next. You try to keep safe in the ways you know how." He shook his head. "Sounddamn it! I knew that dream of his would get him hurt! That bar is too close to the straits. Look what happened tonight!"

She waited, unmoving. She wanted to help. She did. She'd take care of Alesio's father, even if he hated her. "Keep pressure on the wound."

He sucked in a breath but pressed down on the bloody rag. "He should just work as a wealthy guard and stay safe on the piper side! Sssk! Sounddamn it all!"

She inched closer and offered her shoulder again. They continued down the street. She thought about her mother and father, and how Falrie wanted to protect her by keeping her in Between.

After a few minutes, Saida said, "If he loves something, that's another way to keep him safe, though, right? In his own mind? If you lock his voice up, that could do something worse to him on the inside."

They trudged on for a while longer in silence, through the streets burning with trash. They stopped in front of a larger building. "This is where I stay," he said. "Are you going where I think you're going?"

"He's fighting tonight?"

He grimaced and nodded, pressing the cloth to his shoulder. "But you'd be in danger there too. That horrible creature asked after you."

The momentum of helping this human had helped her make the decision. "I'm used to unkindness. I'm used to being scared. But I'm not used to being scared for someone else. He's so kind, and his voice is so sweet. He deserves more than death in a cage."

"Do you love him?"

She blinked, then laughed. "Love? I don't love. I just don't want him to die."

He snorted. "Try not to get yourself killed."

10

A REQUIEM OF HOPE

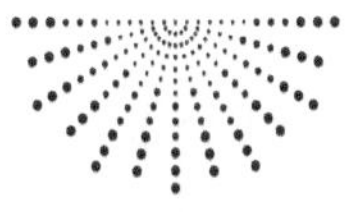

LEAVE

Alesio timed his breaths with the drip and the drop of the water falling from the low ceiling. He'd woken an hour ago, bound and gagged, crumpled on the floor of the tiny stone room. The crowd roared above him: the masses of the straits gathered for a night of blood and anger. His head pounded with pain, his left eye felt like it wanted to close, and he had a bloody lip. His bad left ear rang nonstop and his sore throat had gotten worse.

Is my father alive?

"—was a nasty one," Clef's smooth voice resounded, someone else enhancing his voice to speak above the crowd. "Have you all been enjoying yourselves?"

The crowd shrieked in assent. Clef waited a few moments before he spoke again. "Our final match is a special treat. One I've prepared for a long time, and that you've all been asking for . . ."

A chant started somewhere, and the rest of the crowd picked it up. "Requiem! Requiem!"

"That's right, Requiem has graced us tonight for another performance!"

Roaring, banging, screaming from above.

So strange. Strange how it's so loud up there, and yet so quiet down here.

He worked the gag off little by little, working his chin and jaw side to side till the rag fell to his neck.

How long had he laid here? Was it the same night? Or had a whole day passed? Clef scheduled cage matches for late nights.

A water droplet fell towards the floor, out of synch with the pattern. Alesio formed his lips into an "o" and curled his tongue, sharpening the sound. His one song note zinged through the air, spearing the drop of falling water.

Requiem. He'd tried so hard to bury that name. But the thrill of vivacious excitement still sparked through him.

He'd missed the recognition, yes. But now his father could be bleeding out on the street, and that made him also miss the wrath of the cages, the freedom to strike. The lack of restraint.

"Tonight, Requiem will face the notorious shriker from Flock City. You've heard of him, you fear him, now you'll see his sound in action —you might want to put those rags in your ears now—Brezeek!"

Alternating cheering and boos from above. Some visitors from Flock must have journeyed to watch Brezeek fight, but not too many. Another testament to Clef's influence over factions even in Flock: he set the tone for the cage matches, and everyone else followed his lead. He feared no one.

Except for that creature, that monstrous thing that had shown up out of the night along with Clef's goons. What had Clef said? Something about a deal between the two of them?

It had enveloped Alesio like a sponge and drained his energy. *You have magic in your throat.*

He clutched his head and shuddered. Was Clef planning to keep Alesio on a leash, using that thing as a guard dog to force him to fight? Maybe, even now, it lingered over his father. Maybe it would always be there, watching . . .

Is my father alive?

The crowd banged on the ground, and the water drops in Alesio's stone room fell quicker. One, two, three, one-two-one-two, one-one-one-one-one-

He sent five daggers of sound, piercing the quick drops before they hit the ground. Requiem. Song for the dead.

He'd picked the name to intimidate his enemies. Fighters didn't have to kill each other, though many died from injuries. But now he would fight not knowing if he sang a requiem for his father, who hadn't wanted this for him. His father would've preferred to starve in the street rather than pledge his or his son's life to the strait's leader. His father always looked to the future, as if that would help him survive in the present. Alesio had kept them both alive.

Is my father alive?

Anger rose inside him. He had tried to escape it for so long, to replace the fights with a floating golden place, where he didn't use his voice for violence. His throat tightened and he coughed.

But his father had been right. That dream wasn't real.

A door opened. He sang a blade towards the man who opened it, but the man had rags in his ears, so the sound-knife hit but did not pierce him. The clef grunted in surprise, but retied Alesio's gag and dragged him out of the room, up a flight of steps, and out onto the stage, all lit up with lights so the crowd could watch the fight. He opened the door to the cube-shaped metal grate, big enough for a boxing match, hauling Alesio inside. The crowd roared.

The shriker who had showed up at the Drinks De Capo waited at the other end of the metal cage, arms crossed, also gagged. The shriker's handler waited beside him for the countdown.

Is the shriker also here by force? Or did he choose this life?

The clef untied Alesio's hands. Alesio rubbed at the lines from them biting into his wrist.

Does it matter? It's not a real choice when you grow up in it. When that's all you know how to be.

Alesio held his breath.

"Three!"

He opened the way to his lungs, to that storage of air he'd held onto.

"Two!"

Breezeek crouched, flexing his hands into fists.

"One!"

Their handlers ripped their gags off and sprinted through the doors.

SAIDA HAD BEEN to the straits of Anthem a few years back, hunting an overgrowth that had ended up being the sound of a puppy jumping into a mud puddle. A tiny magic, but more powerful in its pure joy than the pulsing neon beats and raucous shouts from bars on both sides of the road. She'd left after collecting it, avoiding the calculated stares of passerby.

Now, she padded through the street, just her feet shifted to paws to create as little sound as possible, sidling along the shadows of buildings and darting past burning piles of trash, as the humans gathered round them could not spot her because of the light in their eyes, and couldn't hear her because of the rags stuffed in their ears.

The echoing alleys seemed empty until a silhouette moved, and a voice whispered, "Hey there, whatcha got, whatcha got?"

She sprang away, zigzagging. Winter Lightning had zipped with an electric heat, and she tried to mirror their speed and alacrity. She flashed out of the way before a sound-knife hit her neck, hurtling across the street and down another, panting and letting her tongue hang out a little, even though she hadn't shifted to her long foxan tongue.

The silhouette didn't chase her, or at least, the voice didn't. Most humans in the straits had joined a faction for protection. The way some of their members prowled around reminded her of the Palates, a roving, predatory group from Taste that ate other humans.

She shuddered, glad that she had escaped, and followed the sound of screaming and shouting. The sound of a whole forest full of people, all in the same place. She guessed at least five hundred humans.

She found it: a massive stadium, the rows of seats built downward into a natural crater, the ground shaking under the force of human stamping. All the humans harnessed the raw magic of Sound and created a massive blanket of it. Not good for a transplant, though. Like the other human magics she'd found, even this huge one didn't want to leave. Maybe since so few humans remained, the worlds needed as much of their magic as they could produce.

How, then, had Alesio's magic grown so strong? Why did it want to leave Sound and mix with other worlds?

The questions swirled in her head like awakened voices in the night. She should have wondered those things before, but she hadn't. She'd treated Alesio as just another overgrowth, but his magic was more powerful than that, and she had no idea why.

She shook her head, bringing herself back to the present. *Find Alesio. Keep him alive.*

The descending rows of seats encircled a platform far, far down, where a large metal grate, shaped like a cube, rested. A giant cage. Two figures faced each other inside, too far away to tell who. Was Alesio already fighting?

She had hoped to find where they kept him before the fight and help him escape, but if Alesio already fought down there, he could die in the next few minutes!

She snuck underneath the first row of seats and peoples' feet.

BREZEEK LAUNCHED a sharp bird call towards him: *bree-bree-zeek-zeek!*

Alesio released a small amount of the air he had stored in his lungs at a steady pace on his right side with a wave of continuous sound, invisible except for that telling ripple, that vacillation of vision. He didn't need it for his left, of course. The blade bounced off his sound shield and vanished.

Brezeek dashed in a line along the back of the cage. He trilled a high sound at the cage itself, slicing part of it open, and he reached and bent some of the cut wire mesh down, so that they pointed at Alesio. The shriker grinned.

Well. Gotta avoid those.

Alesio curled his tongue, preparing blades in his throat while keeping up the pulse of steady sound waves for his defense. The raw pain in his throat grew, however, and he wondered how long he could keep it up without coughing. He let loose two blades in quick succession, but Brezeek dropped to the ground flat, avoiding them. The larger man was fast, faster than Alesio, and his sound rang sharper and higher.

The shriker twirled his feet and hands under him and emitted a long, thin screech, and the sound sliced along the ground vertically, cutting through the stone and the top of the cage. Too strong for Alesio's sound defense.

Alesio angled his left bad ear towards the attack, and the steep slice disappeared as it hit him, as if bouncing off a sound shield.

The crowd roared, a dull ache in the back of his mind.

"And there it is! Requiem's ultimate defense!" Clef's voice rang out in smug possessiveness. *You're mine,* he seemed to say. *You'll never escape this. You* need *this.*

Alesio dashed along the side of the cage. Brezeek followed his own attack, leaping through the air and chasing him around to the other side.

Maneuvering him. Forcing him back towards the metal spike. Alesio braced himself.

SAIDA WOUND through the long shadows of seats, lamps set at the ends of the rows, so people had dim lighting in the dark. People had thrown an underbrush of garbage under their seats. Drips of sauce and bits of meat stuck to the ground. She snatched a bit of non-stinky meat and chewed it. Not bad for the straits.

She waited under the twelfth row, trying to gauge when the lady with a sleeve of loud, clanking bracelets in the seat nearby her would stop staring at the man whose seat she hid under. She'd tried to dart out once already, and the lady had jerked her head in her direction.

"—don't know, though." The lady slid her hand up to frame her face so that her bracelets jangled down her arm. "I really like Lotes over Hestafon. Something about the voice. Not that I've listened to the real thing, o' course."

"The corner singer imitators are no good," the man on her other side whined, inching forward. The lady didn't glance at him. "They're always off. I'm telling you, the bell-ringer's music, I heard it once!"

"Like you ever were on the piper side, Kino," the other man said.

"I'm telling you—"

"Get your hotrats! Get 'em while they're fresh!" A vendor shouted down the line of people. From her vantage point she couldn't see much except that the seller wore a kind of strap around their neck attached to a box. They waved a hotrat in a folded bread. "Only a sixty-fourth note! Get 'em now!"

The lady raised her hand, and the sleeve of bracelets clanked once more like cheap instruments. Saida took the chance and slipped down to the next row, squirming her smallest shifted self underneath the wooden plank, and tucking her tail around her paws.

She crept about halfway down the stadium seats before she made out who was who.

Alesio fought someone even stockier than him, a big, sound-scarred human with a bird tattooed on his neck. They ducked and dodged inside a giant metal cage, aiming shots of sharpened sound at each other.

His magic sounded harsher, and violent, mimicking the sound knives he created. Hurting him on the inside. She wished she could trim his magic, not just so she could use the trimming, but to stop the violence in his voice. The pain.

How could she help him? She couldn't teleport to him; she'd trap herself in that horrible place—with everyone watching!

Trapped. Just like she'd been trapped on Touch.

Carn had kissed her back on Touch, pushing his mouth on hers. She'd tried to escape, but he'd snatched her by the tail and shoved her into a cage, one just a little too small so that it cut into even her smallest foxan form.

"I love you," he'd said. *"I'm doing this for you. For us. I have to know that you'll stay. I have to know that you love me back, or I don't know what I'll do."*

"If this is what love is," she'd said, *"I don't want it!"*

"Saida," Goosefeather said. "Come back. Come back to us! Don't you have a plan?"

She trembled, grounding herself by brushing Goosefeather in her pocket. She had escaped Carn. She had made sure he'd died.

She hadn't found Alesio in time to rescue him before the fight. Now she had to watch and just hope he stayed safe, doing nothing. Just like she'd watched in the alley.

BREZEEK BLASTED a series of staccato chattering at him, many sound darts peppering him on all sides, trying to pierce his sound shield, to force him backwards—but Alesio's shield held true.

He'd practiced holding his breath up to seven minutes with light motion, three minutes with exercise, enlarging his lung capacity as much as possible. That meant he could do more with his breath. He felt stronger than when he'd earned his reputation as Requiem. The crowd chanted his name, and he hated how much he missed it the sound of it. How much it resonated in his ear, and up through his boots.

The shriker grinned, though. He'd never stopped grinning.

A shiver ran through Alesio's spine. He glanced down.

The darts that had bounced off his shield had cut through the floor's metal grating, creating bent and twisted wires. He could impale his feet if he wasn't careful.

The darts shouldn't have kept their potency after touching his shield. Sound magic didn't work like that!

Unless . . .

Alesio jerked his gaze to the still grinning Brezeek, searching for the glint of silver in his mouth. Alesio had to squint, as his left eye still wanted to close from when Clef's man had punched him in the face.

There. It capped one of his teeth in the back. An amplifier. Illegal, of course, though the cage matches themselves were illegal, so such rules didn't apply.

Alesio had had an advantage, though, so this evened things out. Amplifiers meant big money. Tak's words echoed in his ears: *All the performers at the Cadenza have them.*

The roar of the crowd returned to him. They chanted the shriker's name. Brezeek wove too close to Alesio considering the speed of sound, and how a knife could appear faster than he could react.

Alesio closed the rest of the distance in a sudden lunge. Keeping his center of gravity low, he grabbed the shriker's arm, pulling him off balance, and used the momentum to throw him onto his back. He aimed the man's fall away from the sharpened points on the floor that Brezeek himself had made, though for a second, he considered doing the opposite. What was the point of trying to be a good person, when the people around him didn't believe it?

Shame overcame him for that thought. The scraped feeling in his throat built to an unbearable point, and he stopped the pulses of sound to swallow, losing his shield for a moment.

"And once again, Requiem shows his skills with not just sound, but with body! He's a deadly fighter, that one! Oh, but what's this?"

Brezeek had seemed to use the grunt from hitting the ground to send more darts. Alesio tried to keep his left side leaning towards the shriker while he got his sound shield back, but a dart slipped through and grazed his right thigh. He lost concentration on the rhythm of the pulse, and another dart would have stabbed him in the stomach, but he danced out of the way, avoiding the many spikes sticking out of the ground. He panted on his knees.

Is Clef trying to throw the match?

The strait's leader must have bet big money on the shriker. That's why he had wanted Alesio to return, knowing the crowd would back the infamous Requiem, he'd ensured a win for Brezeek and a huge payout for himself.

Dullness comes when you take yourself out of the game.

The straiter woman who had snuck into St. Rina's cathedral may have had a point. Had he lost his edge?

Brezeek launched another series of darts. Alesio released more stored sound to fend them off—which just created more spikes all around.

Shit.

ALESIO WAS TRAPPED.

Saida had reached the seventeenth row, just a few rows from the front of the stadium. Alesio had a ring of protruding, jagged metal surrounding him, and the other fighter tried to push him into them. She had to help.

"This is your one portal a day!" Tricksy Stone said. "What if Watthe comes back?"

She *had* to help. She'd curled in a ball while the human had hurt Alesio's father, and when they'd taken Alesio. She had to do something now or she would never forgive herself. If she teleported him out of the cage, they'd probably just stuff him back in—but she *could* teleport him away from those spikes.

Fear paralyzes us all. You escape by moving a little at a time.

She concentrated on finding all nearby portals. There, one in the ring, chittering and sliding around in the cracks of space. It slipped under Alesio, obeying her direction. Alesio disappeared as if falling into a sinkhole and reappeared on the other side of the spikes.

"Whoa, what's this?" The man with the echoing voice boomed out over the screaming crowd. "Seems like someone has a new ability he's never used before!"

Saida slumped. She used more energy to open a portal from a distance.

Alesio and the other fighter stared at where the hole in their world had yawned open, then closed again. Neither of them moved.

The lights on the ends of the rows glowed brighter, as if signaling the end of the match.

"Everyone, please!" The booming voice said. "Check under your seats! We are looking for a fur-mix! We'll give a note and a half reward to whoever catches her!"

What?

No! No!

The person on the seat she hid under bent down. Their eyes widened.

Saida scrambled up to the next row, but the whole line of people had bent to look under their seats, and four of them pointed at her.

"Here!"

"It's here! It's real! Over here!"

She ducked grasping hands, dodged sweeping arms, and bolted down the row of seats, leaping over legs and spring boarding off laps. One of the vendors blocked her way, and she skittered around them, but someone grasped her tail and yanked her back. She snatched one of the hotrats with her claws and flung it at them, and they screeched and released her.

She rounded the seat row and tried climbing the steps, but several people had flooded them, now, blocking her way. Saida dashed to the next row on the other side of the steps and tried squirming underneath to hide, but a scrawny, wiry woman grabbed the fur on her neck and squeezed. Saida sagged, the instinct of a foxan cub overcoming her.

NO NO NO! She pawed at the air with sluggish movements.

"Use us!" Goosefeather said.

She landed a scratch on the woman's arm, but other hands reached out to hold her down. Then someone shoved and jammed her inside a small cage. She bit and clawed and screamed.

This isn't happening, this isn't happening! No! Not again! NO! NO!

She tried to shift to more human, trying to break the cage with larger limbs. Those holding the cage jumped back at that—but the metal sliced into her skin, and she collapsed, trembling and bleeding, back to her smallest foxan form.

Someone carried her up the auditorium steps. The bars blurred in her terror and tears.

A few people stuck their fingers in the bars, poking at her fur. She snapped at them, and they drew back, cursing and laughing. She growled.

"Just like an animal."

"Filthy fur-mix!"

"Don't let it close to you! It could steal your magic!"

"Now, now," the booming voice said over the crowd. "We've found it, we've found it. Thank you for your help, folks! And the fight is back on! Look at that dodge!"

"Use us!" Tricksy Stone said. "One of us, at least! Use me!"

"You'll die," Saida whimpered. "I can't. I can't do it. I can't lose you."

This is what comes of getting too close to humans!

ALESIO'S EARS RANG, and he staggered, holding his head.

Everything had muted for a few seconds, and his ears popped, as if he had gone deep underwater. He'd . . . sunk . . .? into the ground, and then come up on the other side of all the spikes.

Brezeek had stopped attacking for a half-second, confused, but when Clef had commented on the strange location switch, the shriker sprang back into action. Alesio let his shield drop, not wanting to create another trap around himself from the reverberation of the darts and evaded a set of them that Brezeek shot at him.

He didn't have time to understand what had just happened, but it had given him an opportunity. He squinted and let loose the full force of his lung capacity, the whole of his stored air that he'd kept in his lungs. His throat felt like it started to bleed.

He caught Brezeek off guard and pushed him backwards into two of his own spikes, stabbing him in his shoulder and leg.

Not enough to kill, thank the Sound. Alesio didn't want that on his conscience. He'd killed three men in the matches, all from when he had had to protect himself from dying. He didn't want to sing any more requiems.

Brezeek screamed and waved his arms, signaling that he forfeited the match.

How do you like that, Clef? Alesio flopped against the back of the cage, heaving for breath. *For once, your gamble didn't pay off. You backed the wrong man.*

The crowd cheered for the win, and for the blood. It reverberated around Alesio's head. Would Clef let him leave after this? Or would he threaten his father again, unless he joined back up and did more fights?

Did any of it matter if he couldn't reach the Cadenza? When he'd never had a chance in the first place?

Up the steps. Through a door.

Maybe they'd put her in a cage match. Pit her against dogs so humans could bet who would win. How had they known she had hidden under the humans' seats?

Up another round of steps. Through a hallway, then a door. Her tongue lolled as she tried to cool herself down.

A man stepped up to the cage, just far enough away that she couldn't slice at him with her claws. He wore a nice gray shirt and black pants. She recognized him as the man Alesio had pointed out to her in the garden, the very same one that had worked with Watthe in the alley.

"Well, well," he said, in the voice that had boomed over the crowd. "Looks like we caught ourselves a foxan."

She jolted. No human on Sound should know that term. They should only know 'fox-person.'

He smiled at her. His eyes gleamed a disturbing gray color like a rock polished by the flow of a stream. "I figured you'd be here. Figured you couldn't help yourself from saving someone you cared about. I have a sense for these kinds of things." He spread his arms, indicating the arena of hundreds of people. "I've been successful so far, don't you think?"

"You're a soggy piece of week old hotrat." She spit in his face.

He straightened and wiped the spit off. "Take her to St. Rina's. Our benefactor knows to find her there."

Her panic solidified into a cold, paralyzing terror.

11

WHAT WE ARE MADE TO DO

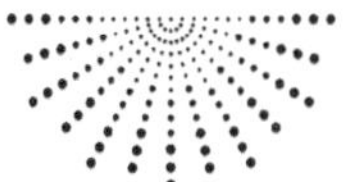

Alesio held his right thigh where Brezeek had grazed him with a sound dart. One of the guards had tossed him a rag once they marched him out of the cage, and he'd tied it around his leg. He'd also vomited anything substantial in his stomach after the match, and the vomit had had streaks of blood from his throat.

Across the room, Clef leaned against a desk, drawing on a piece of paper, ignoring Alesio. Four other guards stood at the corners of the room; their lips pursed to shriek sound knives should he try anything. He'd waited for a few minutes now, and the adrenaline from the fight had dissipated, leaving him drained and aching. His left eye had half closed, leaving him limited vision.

He still didn't know if it was even the same night he'd been taken. His brain hurt.

Clef had to have bet against him, knowing that Brezeek had had an amplifier. In defeating Brezeek, he'd bested Clef's machinations. The strait's leader must have just lost a lot of money. Alesio knew from experience of previous times he had disappointed Clef that, when the silence broke, the guards would start to pummel him. Then he'd owe another bullshit debt.

The room was silent, save for the scratching of Clef's pen as he drew.

Alesio folded his arms. He didn't have time for fear. His father waited for him out there, hurt, almost blind, and so frail. *Let's get this over with.*

"I won for you," Alesio said, his voice scratchy. It hurt to speak. "You told me, 'Just like old times.' If you would have told me to throw the fight—"

"Quiet." Clef didn't look up from his paper. "You're not my concern right now."

Alesio rocked back on his heels. His throat closed with the pressure of old memories, old beatings, scars of violence etched into his psyche. The cut on his leg seeped a little blood through the sound cloth from his tightened muscles.

"Just do it," Alesio said. "Beat me and send me away. Do it. Just let me get to my father."

Clef paused his drawing, then, but still didn't raise his head. "You're asking for it?" He chuckled. "Oh, my. I guess I did mess you up."

Alesio stepped forward and caught a glimpse of the paper.

Clef had spattered it with random patterns of black ink, framing a gray, thin humanoid figure with arms that hung down to its ankles. Oversized hands with claws large enough to crush a man's skull.

That same creature that had enveloped him in the street. He'd put it out of his mind until now. He'd hoped it was a dream.

"What—what *is* that thing?"

Clef's head snapped up. The pupils of his eyes were dilated, matching the darkness of the drawing, yet they gleamed like a polished gray stone. He used to have brown eyes. "You'd do well to join us."

Shivers rippled down Alesio's spine.

A knock at the door behind Alesio. Clef glanced at it. "Come in."

Two clef members stepped through, one of them hanging back. The other approached Clef and handed him a small slip of paper. Clef perused it and smiled.

He opened a door in the desk and grabbed a small drawstring bag the size of his fist. A few eighth notes fluttered out. He tossed it to Alesio, who caught it more out of reflex than anything else. "Your cut of the winnings." He began drawing again on the paper. "Don't say I never took care of you."

"What?" Alesio stared at the bag in his hands. It had to have five or six notes in there, at least.

So, Clef *had* bet on him—and had won a lot. He'd never given Alesio a cut before.

"Get him out of here." Clef waved his fingers, and the guards crowded Alesio towards the door. He left in a state of shock, his legs moving without him directing them to do so. In no time at all, he found himself outside the building that served as Clef's headquarters. The moon rode low in the dark sky.

My father! I have to find him!

He stumbled in his haste, running through the straits, dodging the dying bonfires, and the drunken bodies outside the bars, not stopping for those still awake in the dark hours of the morning who called to him in fatigued challenge. He dashed to the place where he'd last seen his father, close to the Drinks De Capo. He searched the streets and found a scrape of blood on the brick. A few drops led away, and he followed them. They stopped after a few yards, and he bit his lip, adrenaline pumping through him. Where had his father gone? Had someone taken him? Or had he stumbled away on his own? If so, he'd have tried to seek shelter at the hostel.

Alesio dashed back to the straits. Sweat trickled into his now mostly closed eye and into the cloth around his leg, stinging the cut. The night continued around him like a never-ending nightmare. The taste of coppery blood remained in his throat.

He staggered to the hostel, bulled his way past the old cage fighter who managed the hostel and into the room of sleeping men. She followed him in, glaring.

There lay his father on one of the bottom bunks, murmuring as he slept. Someone had wrapped some standard bar cloths around his shoulder to stop the bleeding. He rushed over, but stopped short, not wanting to wake his father, and breathing in short, controlled bursts, forcing himself to inhale and exhale in silence.

He's alive.

"Hey!" The hostel owner whisper yelled behind him.

He turned. She had her palm out. She didn't seem to want to wake the group of sleeping men, either. He pulled out the bag of money that Clef had given him, snatched four eighth notes, and stuffed them in her upturned palm. She gaped at the money, but he spun back to his father, inspecting the wound in his shoulder.

The sound-knife hadn't gone as deep as he'd feared. The blood had soaked through the cloths, but the wound itself had clotted. He didn't know if he should let his father sleep or if he should change the makeshift bandage, but at least the injury had stopped bleeding. *I should probably let him sleep.*

The woman eyed his bag of money. He motioned back to the front desk so they could talk and handed her four more eighth notes.

"This is for someone to dress his wound—carefully—once he wakes up, and to carry him to the Drinks De Capo on a stretcher. Ask for the owner, Mona." He shook the bag of money. "A half note will be there for you once you do."

She nodded. Half notes were unheard of in the straits, but he didn't want to haggle, and he wanted her to treat his father with care. He strode out before she could ask for more, which, in his state, he probably would have handed over.

He trudged back to the bar, now hiding the bulging money bag under his cloak. He informed a sleepy and irritated Mona that his father would stay in his room, and he would pay the difference. He also asked her for someone to clean and dress the wound every day and to not let him leave for at least three days. She'd argued with him until he'd shoved the entire bag of notes at her, minus the fee that he'd promised the hostel owner.

In his room, he changed out of the cream-colored performance shirt Clef and his subordinates had captured him in the night before—now caked in sweat and ripped under his arms and in the side—and into his security guard uniform. The cut in his thigh had clotted, at least. He cleaned the blood that had caked onto his chin from his bloodied lip, but he could do nothing about his black eye, now completely shut.

His adrenaline gone, he limped his way to St. Rina's, his ribs smarting. The night had waned, and the sky lightened as the sun yawned on the horizon, ready to rise. He stopped at the street just before St. Rina's to gather himself in the empty street. With his black eye, he didn't look the part of a security guard. He looked like someone who would attack a security guard.

Just another day. Act like it's just another day. That's how you get through it.

Why am I even here?

He would never perform at the Cadenza. The dream lay dead in his mind, but he couldn't quite bury it. Not yet.

He had a story rehearsed. It might not convince Lasrial, but he couldn't work today. The fatigue of the fight, and his injury, and the terror over his father's stabbing would overcome him soon.

"Whoa." Tak whistled. "Did a jeweler get a hold of you? You have yourself quite a shiner."

"You should see the jeweler." Alesio forced a grin. He paused on the main steps. "It wasn't too bad earlier. How is it now?"

Tak guffawed. "I don't want to know what your definition of bad is. It's like a slab of meat left out and turning purple. And your voice sounds pretty bad." He shifted his weight and stretched his legs and arms. They both did that a lot, before their shifts started. "Did, uh, some trouble find you last night?"

Alesio gritted his teeth and barked a short, bitter laugh. He kept his words clipped so he didn't have to talk as much. "Something like that. Bar fight at my other job. Had to keep the patrons from rioting. I need to take today off. Just coming to tell Lasrial."

Tak glanced toward the inside of the cathedral. "Just saying," he said in a lower voice, "You might want to—"

"Alesio."

Lasrial appeared in the main doorway, his arms folded. He had a scratch on his cheek which he dabbed at with a cloth. "Your services are not needed any longer."

"What?" Alesio started, his body tensing. "Sir, I wasn't—"

"I am aware of your . . . other pursuits in the straits." Lasrial's lip curled. "As you well know, using your voice for violence is against the law and we do not tolerate it here. You must leave the premises immediately, or I will be forced to call the authorities."

Alesio felt as if he had fallen from a high place and hit brick. He couldn't inhale.

Had someone recognized him at the match?

He wanted to punch someone in the face. Lasrial's could have worked, but Alesio stilled himself and his trembling hand that wanted to clench into a fist. His throat tightened even more.

Tak's mouth hung open, his eyes flicking back and forth between them. Lasrial said something else, but Alesio didn't hear it. He'd wanted to leave, but not like this. He had the cut of the winnings from Clef, which should allow his father to stay at Mona's pub for a few months, but after that, he couldn't perform any longer on the whims of people throwing a few thirty-second notes in the donation jar.

He should've never reached for something so high as the Cadenza. He couldn't even afford to perform in a middle-class bar.

Unless he fought in the cages again.

The money Clef had tossed him burned in his mind. He couldn't escape his old life no matter how he tried. The strings of fate pulled on him, yanked him down, down, down.

It's like I was made for the cages. I'm no good at anything else.

Alesio shoved his hands in his pockets and left before either of them saw the tears drop from his eyes.

SAIDA HADN'T SLEPT. Who could sleep inside a trap? How could anyone let down their guard in the most dangerous place of all, to allow themselves to become blind, deaf, and mute, unable to feel or smell anything? She spun in the cage, right to left, left to right, grasping the metal mesh, trying to bend it.

The reverend had stashed her inside the secret room, next to that statue of Watthe. She'd scratched his face when he got too close. He'd cursed at her, kicked her cage, and closed the wall, leaving her in the dark.

Trapped.

She was trapped.

She felt like her younger foxan self once more, shifted in age to when she'd trotted up to the first human she'd seen, head cocked, ears flickering with stupid interest. *Humans! How fascinating*, she had thought.

She hadn't sensed the rope coming, or that he would yank her down a stone stairway. She hadn't sensed the twisted malice, how he and the others he brought to his homemade altar would pet her fur for hours, no matter how she begged them to stop. Trapped for months in that place, in that dark underground cave. At the altar of what worship meant to some. She hadn't—she hadn't been able to leave—

"Let us help," Goosefeather said. "Please. We can get you out of here!"

Saida clutched them against her chest. "It's almost sunrise. I can almost teleport again."

Fear paralyzes us all, the fox-person's voice echoed in her mind, but she couldn't move forward an inch on this. What would she do without Tricksy's wisdom? Or Goosefeather's warm, soothing words? She loved them with a strange kind of love that trusted without question, that cared but did not cut; the kind of love that proved false with anyone else. Though she faced all the terror in the worlds, she could not give them up.

"Saida," Tricksy Stone said. "You know that we're not—"

"Shh!" She spun in her cage again. "Do you hear that?"

"You must listen to us!" Goosefeather said. "You must listen to yourself! We *are* you—!"

The secret wall slid open, and Watthe loomed inside. He had to hunch even after he stepped in. The reverend, Lasrial, followed, gazing at the giant humanoid with a fascinated awe.

Carn had looked at her like that. She pretended to retch.

Lasrial rattled the cage with a long cane, staying out of reach of her claws. "Quiet!"

"Foxan." Watthe crouched in front of the cage. "Finally. Found you." He glanced down at the box that he cradled in his right arm. The pattern on its surface writhed like a mass of worms, ever shifting on the box's four sides. "Do I must eat her now? I have questions."

A pause. Watthe inclined his ear to the box. Lasrial knelt next to the gray monster, though he didn't have much room to do so. Saida swallowed bile in the back of her throat.

"I know," Watthe said. "A minute, just."

When is sunrise? She couldn't sense any portals yet. The energy she used to do so hadn't returned yet, and even then, summoning them underneath her cage would require precision and focus she didn't know if she had. She had to stall.

"I have some questions for you!" Saida tried to inject confidence into her voice, but it came out as a whimper. "How are you traveling around the worlds? What *are* you? What is that box?"

"Foxan," that harsh, grating voice said. "I ask questions." He leaned closer, and she shrank to the back of the cage. Something about him seemed different. His form seemed more substantial and distinct, less like smoke. A gleaming, grayish skin covered his body. "Where the rest of your kind are? Where they are hiding?"

Her lungs refused to inflate. She swallowed. *Just don't say anything.* She waited, shivering, and after a few seconds, he extended one of those abnormal finger-claws, growing it as she watched, poking through the wires, and aiming at her throat. She pressed against the back of the cage, wishing for the sunrise, wishing for anything but this moment.

He shook his head as if to clear it. "No! Not yet! We need more to know!"

"Who are you talking to?" Saida asked, her voice a thin sliver of sound.

Lasrial slapped the cage with the stick again, tumbling her so that Watthe's claw scratched her collarbone. A thin line of blood ran down her fur. "Don't speak to god unless he asks you to, fur-mix!"

"God?" Watthe rotated just his head to Lasrial, leaving the front part of his body still facing Saida. "What do you think when use this word you?"

"Oh, Watthe." Lasrial prostrated lower. "Forgive my impudence. You have not yet told us of your true status. But I know. I know you are god, the manifestation of our dreams, the avatar of the golden wave, oh Watthe, the god of Sound!" He raised trembling hands to the gray being.

Watthe cocked his head. "You are a mistaken. I am a god not. This is." He placed the unsettling box on the ground in front of Lasrial's outstretched arms. "The Planes god. The god of Sensory and Primal. I made serve to it was, it is what we made are all to do." He swiveled his head back to Saida. "Now, tell me. I will not a third time ask. Where are the other foxans? I know more there are."

Saida bared her fangs. "Why should I tell you when you'll just eat me?"

With a sweep of his claw, Watthe sheered the cage top off. Saida screamed and tried to bolt away, but the monster snatched her and held her up to his face. Where he touched her, her body drooped and became unresponsive. "Because I give a quick death instead of your fingers I eat by ones, your legs I break many, many times, and the marrow of them I suck out as you watch!"

She shifted her arm to human, but not her paw, so she could reach his face. She raked her claws over his shiny new skin, drawing blood. He shouted and dropped her, grabbing at his face, and she darted over to the secret wall. The reverend, still prostrate, tried to snatch her, but she leapt over him and scrabbled at the door. Watthe swung his massive claws but she dropped flat enough to avoid them. She slid the wall open just enough for her small foxan body to squirm through.

Behind her, Watthe roared.

Sunrise. Is it sunrise yet?

"Not yet!" Tricky Stone said. "Run! RUN!"

It rained as Alesio trudged away from St. Rina's.

Of course, it's raining. Wet, cold clothes go perfect with this sounddamned day.

An inhuman roar erupted from the cathedral. Alesio swiveled back around, the hair on his arms standing on end.

Saida shot through the main doors, a blur of red and black streaking down the steps. Tak jumped back. "Whoa there! You're not—"

The tall gray monster appeared in the doorway, seeming bigger somehow in the light of day.

"Holy Sound!" Tak fell backwards on his rear to avoid touching the thing. It sprinted after Saida.

What is happening?

"Get out of the way!" The fox-woman shouted. She dashed straight at him, which meant that that *thing* dashed at him too.

"W-what?"

He stared at the oncoming monster, at how its jaw unhinged, at the dark gray skin, and how its form wavered in the air like smoke on a hot day. He remembered how it had enveloped him in a void of gravity and space, what horrible things it had whispered.

"*Move!* You're in my portal!" The rain had slicked her fur and she'd trailed blood in her mad dash. He tried to dodge aside, but it seemed too late, as she leapt up and pounced *into* the street. The ground under them both gave way like water.

"Hold your breath!" Saida screamed.

The opening in the world closed just as the monster's face snarled above them.

And they fell.

1 2

IN BETWEEN

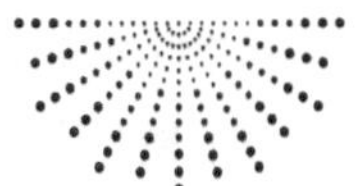

Alesio tumbled into mud, feeling as if his stomach had taken a detour into his lungs. He retched onto the ground, but only a small amount of bile came up, still streaked with blood. He'd already thrown up everything else after the cage match. He dragged in long breaths. He hadn't been able to breathe that whole time he'd sunk into the ground and kept falling through a kind of space he hadn't felt before, more than just an absence of touching something, but an absence of air, of light, of *anything*. He didn't usually have trouble holding his breath, but the strangeness had unnerved him, and he'd almost given in to the temptation to suck in air right before they'd landed back onto solid ground.

Wiping his mouth and bracing his hands on his knees, he peered above him, watching for that — that thing. The monster.

Nothing but trees met his gaze.

He straightened, listening for anything that might jump out, watching for waves of sharpened sound. Birds chirped and leaves rustled, and through the trees, a few clouds scudded across a placid blue sky with no sun. Something seemed off in his right ear, his good ear, almost like he'd stuffed a sound cloth in to dampen noise. He rubbed at it to try and dislodge the blockage without success.

137

"Where are we?" Alesio asked, spinning in a circle, his voice still coming out growly and rough. "Where did the city go?"

Saida panted next to him in a heap, a tangle of arms, paws, and tail, her chin and teeth too pointed to pass for human, her body too large to pass for fox. She rolled to her stomach, groaning. A thin red crisscross pattern marred the red fur on her shoulders, hard to see because of the color.

"You weren't supposed to come." She shifted her paw to a hand and rubbed at her eyes. "Why didn't you jump out of the way?"

"Well, excuse me for not realizing you were going to—to—*bury* me in the ground—"

She pushed herself up, shifting to her full human form, clothes growing out of her skin like fur, a shirt, and pair of short trousers. His face warmed, and he stared at the forest floor of small plants and dead leaves.

Blood dripped on the ground, and he glanced back up. A long scratch on her collarbone trickled red. She swayed, her eyes unfocused, and he moved to catch her.

She hissed at him, and he set her down on the ground and backed away. "Sorry, I—I just didn't want you to fall."

She winced and craned her neck to examine the raised red lines on her shoulders. She picked up a leaf and pressed it on her shoulder, hissing again and closing her eyes. "You're fine," she said through clenched teeth. "Just hurts."

The monster that had chased her flashed through his mind. He cringed. "What was that? Some kind of—of cave creature from the north?"

She gave a half chuckle, half hiss, pressing another leaf on the collarbone scratch. "You're adorable. He's from another world."

He blinked. "What?"

"Saida!"

He whirled at the sound of another voice. Another fox-person, shifted to their smallest, most fox-like form, had stepped out from behind a tree and stared up at Alesio, their tail puffed up, ears flat. "A human!" He couldn't tell if they presented male or female. "A human is . . . here!"

They scampered into a nearby bush.

"Well," Saida said. "Now it's just a matter of time till my mother gets here." She sighed, adjusting her shirt so that it didn't rub against the injuries on her shoulder. "C'mon. Let's go inside." She shuffled past him, waving him to follow.

Inside? Inside where? He picked his way through the underbrush after her, stepping over a long-dead log rotting halfway into the forest loam.

Memories flooded him. The cage fight. Lasrial firing him. Finding his father sleeping. That monster showing up, not once, but twice.

Saida seemed about to wriggle under a prickly bush, then glanced back at him and skirted around it instead. "Mind the thorns."

He sucked in his stomach, sidling between the bush and a tree. Past those, she ducked inside a short, round tunnel leading into a hill. He had to bend halfway over to fit through. The cut on his thigh, still bandaged, stung.

The tunnel led down into the foundations of the hill and then opened into a wide, cavernous room of stone and dirt. Along the wall, shelves displayed many things both uniform and not: seashells and tiny glass tubes in pretty rows, random objects like various sized jars, stacks of papers, and even a pile of leaves on the deep corner of a shelf.

The sound of the hollow hill seemed muted, more temperate, not quite so sharp on the highs and lows of footsteps and echoes.

Saida grinned and spread her arms wide. "Hello, everyone! I'm home!"

Alesio glanced from side to side. Nobody was there besides them.

The fox-woman strode over to one of the jars and held it up the ceiling, gazing at it. "I know, I know, it's been too long. I'm sorry. I got held up."

She's crazy, Alesio thought. *I should have known. All that talk about another world.* He rubbed at his head. *And I don't even know where I am.*

"I haven't forgotten about any of you." Saida wandered to the line of glass tubes and plucked one of them from their row. Alesio backed away, bending so he could fit back through the tunnel. *Maybe I can back out without her noticing. Maybe she won't even remember I'm here.*

"Him? Oh, he's just visiting." Saida glanced over her shoulder. Alesio froze, half bent over. "Where are you going?"

"I—I just need to—use a privy." That wasn't a lie.

"Oh!" She waved him on, still riveted by the glass tube. "The forest is yours. Go on."

I have no idea how to get there. I could wander around for days. "Uh, I might just head to Anthem, now." He swallowed. His throat seemed less sore, now. "I know you somehow helped us . . . travel . . . to the countryside to escape that monster, but I should really get back. Can you point me in the right direction?"

She paused and placed the glass tube back in its holder. She folded her hands in front of her. "I can't take you back yet. It's not safe."

"You don't have to come with me. But I should check on my father. He was hurt." *Because of me.*

The tall, pointed ears on top of her head never seemed to shift to human. He could interpret what some of her different ear angles meant, now. Upright and straight indicated alertness. Flat meant scared or angry. Half straight with little flickers implied uncertainty. She drifted closer to him, her ears flickering. "I saw your father, after the bad man, the strait's leader, dragged you off. I helped him to his home."

Alesio's mouth fell open. He closed it. "You were the one—? I *knew* he couldn't have gotten home by himself."

She curled her shoulders inward, her ears folding halfway down. What did that one mean? "Alesio, I don't know how to tell you this, but, um, we are not on Sound. We are in another place. This is Between, and you cannot return by yourself."

Alesio blinked. *Is she messing with me? She* seems *genuine. But she also seems a little insane.*

He shrugged, sliding on a smile. "Thanks, but I'll try anyway." He turned to leave.

"Saida!"

A fox-woman barreled through the tunnel. Because of his black eye, he didn't see her quite fast enough to gracefully avoid her, and he leapt to the side and almost fell. The cut on his thigh protested and he winced.

"What is this? You bring a . . . human here? Are you trying to give me a heart attack?" Her gaze flicked to Alesio, and she yipped. "Oh, he's right here!"

"Hello." Alesio gave a little wave, pitching his voice as calm and gentle as possible. He didn't want to startle any more skittish fox-people.

"Alesio, meet my mother, Falrie. Falrie, Alesio."

Falrie scuttled over to Saida, her nose pointed in the air. She had a lankier frame, and the lines on her muzzle seemed to show the age hollows of her cheekbones. Gray fur interspersed her orange stripes. "What were you thinking? It is one thing . . . you traipsing around the different worlds and putting yourself in harm's way, but to bring a human back . . . to the safety of Between? You endanger all of us!"

Different worlds? Were all the fox-people here insane?

Of course, he'd had that sensation of movement, like a sinking, or a floating. And he'd ended up somewhere new.

Wait. I'm not actually considering this, am I?

"I know I messed up." Saida crouched to Falrie's level. "I'm sorry. I had to."

"By the Senses. If you knew it was a mistake, why did you . . . do it? What kind of idiotic—"

Alesio held up his hands. "She brought me here to save me from the monster chasing us!"

Saida winced.

"The monster?" Falrie whirled to face Alesio. "What monster? She never tells me . . . anything."

Saida shook her head at Alesio, mouthing, "No," but Falrie scampered over to him, and he didn't seem to notice.

"He was big. So tall. And gray. And his hands, they were like—" he spread his arms. "This big!"

"Saida. What is this thing he's speaking of? This does not sound like an animal."

Saida curled her hands. "Someone that has followed me around the worlds." She hesitated, but she'd held the secret for too long, and she was tired, and in pain. "He . . . he holds that box you're all afraid of."

"The box! The box!" Falrie scuttled to the far end of the den like a red leaf in the wind. "And he can . . . teleport? Like a foxan? How can this be?"

"It's my fault," Saida said in a quiet, quiet voice.

Falrie whirled to face her. Alesio did, too, his eyes narrowed, and his jaw tensed, but she had to tell them.

"I—" She wet her lips and opened her locked mouth. The words flowed out of her, finally free. "I found him . . . Watthe . . . in another world. Under the ruins of Vision. It wasn't even another world, I didn't smell there better, or taste or hear anything better there. I guess I teleported to it. I wandered there for . . . I don't know how long. It was like a swamp, or like I was half-floating in a strange water. And then part of the land broke off, and *he* appeared in front of me. I even gave him his name. I said, 'What the!' and he repeated it like a baby, like he imprinted on me, and I ran away, but he must have followed me through the portal." She hung her head. "It's my fault he's around at all. I was too curious, like you always say. Explored where I . . . shouldn't have."

Alesio watched her with wide eyes. The angry, surging Sound magic around him had disappeared here in Between. At least his overgrowth had stopped hurting him, though he probably also felt strange, not producing magic at all.

"The Primal Plane," Falrie said. "You teleported to the Primal Plane."

"What is that?" Saida asked.

"Another place. The five worlds comprise the Sensory Plane, yes? Well, there is another Plane. The Primal, the place where raw magic flows from. Where *we*," she pointed at herself, "come from. The

Severing did not just isolate the five Sense worlds from each other. It cut everyone off from the Primal Plane. It's been almost a thousand years."

She'd stopped pausing between her words. Her eyes shimmered with unshed tears.

"How did I manage to teleport there, then?" Saida frowned.

Falrie shook her head as if water were in her ears. "You . . . you have made many transplants. They help tie the worlds together. Maybe you produced enough to support a portal connecting the two Planes, for a brief time. Enough for you to teleport there and back."

Saida shivered. "The whole place had a magic, and it was so overgrown, it was like everything there wanted to—to—"

"Consume? Eat you alive? Tear you apart?"

Saida nodded.

Falrie blinked, and the tears fell onto the dirt. "We felt that from the box. It fell from a portal in the sky, and that intense hunger sprang from it. None of us could open it or knew what it was. And then it sent out a signal of some kind, a wave, or a giant knife, that cut the Primal Plane away from the Sensory. It caused the Severing." She pawed at her ears. "Why do you think we have hidden here for so long?" She twisted towards Alesio, then rose on her hind legs. "And now you have brought this human here! We don't do this anymore! It's too risky!"

"You don't do what anymore?" Saida asked.

Falrie shut her mouth and landed back on all fours. "No, no." She milled around, twining between Saida's legs. "No . . . I must not speak of it."

"What aren't you telling me? Is there something else?"

"Can't, can't. I don't remember." Falrie fled the den in a flash of red.

Saida harrumphed and plopped on the ground. Fatigue weighed on her eyes and in her arms and legs. "Sometimes, I think she just doesn't want to answer questions."

"To be fair," Tricksy Stone said, "You kinda do the same thing."

"So, she thinks you can travel to other worlds, too," Alesio said.

She didn't have the energy to convince him. She yawned, and rotated her arm, wincing as it stretched her injuries. "Okay, Alesio. I know you don't believe me. Go ahead and look around. Pee on a bush. It'll take you a few hours at most to explore all Between." She curled up on the floor. "And while you do, I'm gonna sleep."

He backed out of the den. "I might do just that. Sleep well."

Darkness overcame her in just a few seconds.

ALESIO JOGGED west towards the hazy light, the vague brightness of a perhaps-sun shining through fog. According to the few travelers who had come through the Drinks De Capo, a forest lay to the east of Anthem. He hoped that by heading west, he'd find a road, and maybe even some travelers who could point him back to Anthem.

The trees dwindled after about ten minutes, becoming sparser, and gave way to dry shrubs, a bright, blue sky, and a long stretch of sand. Alesio shaded his eyes—well, his non-blackened eye—squinting at something green and growing not too far off. He started onto the sand but had to stop jogging from how it shifted under his feet. He panted after not too long, sweating in the sudden heat. He still wore his security guard uniform, and the cut on his thigh stung badly enough that he untied the sound cloth bandage to check on it. It was trickling blood again. If he kept trying to run, it wouldn't heal, so he begrudgingly slowed down.

What is this place? There's so much sand!

The shimmering of water tantalized him to continue. He hadn't drunk water in a while. He trudged on and made it to the edge of a lake, and the pounding heat cooled a bit. He bent and sniffed the water; it seemed fresh. He tasted a little, then realized how thirsty he was. He dunked his head in and drank. It was warm on the surface, but cooler a few inches down, and tasted wonderful. It soothed his raw throat. In fact, the soreness had gone down considerably.

After drinking his fill, he strode around the perimeter of the lake.

The land transformed from sand to lush greenery, squelching mud, and buzzing insects. He waved at a cloud of gnats.

Something isn't right. Sand changing right away to wet, spongy ground? The dry heat had moistened into a humidity that he had to drag into his lungs. Did the wilderness and temperature really change so fast outside of a city?

He didn't know. He'd never left Anthem before. And that strange, muffled feeling, like he had a tiny bit of cloth in his ear, hadn't left! He shook his head, plugged his nose, and left ear, and blew out a sharp breath.

He swayed, dizzy, his equilibrium disturbed, and he stumbled and almost fell in the lake to his left. Nothing changed.

Fine. It's fine. I'm sure it'll go away soon.

He continued around the lake and left it as he found a path, still heading west. A line of trees blanketed this side of the lake, and he squelched over there to escape the mud and the humidity.

The path led him under the cover of the trees, to chirping birds and firmer ground. He jogged again now that the path showed a clear way. The air cooled off and he breathed easier. He'd traveled for maybe an hour. The trail wound along some bushes, around a fallen log, past a large hill—

Wait.

He'd seen that hill before. It was the one Saida had called her den. He was back where he'd started.

Impossible!

He'd traveled in a straight line! He'd followed the brighter part of the sky to the west!

Just to be sure, he crept around the hill. There waited the same small tunnel entrance, and the thorn bushes she had warned him about. Her words echoed back to him: *It'll take you a few hours at most to explore all Between.*

Have I gone mad? He slumped down on a nearby fallen log, trying to stay calm. Rational. He must have gotten turned around. Maybe he'd gone east to start, following that bright light he'd assumed was the sun. That made more sense than the alternative, that he'd traversed a whole world in an hour.

That he was in another world altogether.

He breathed. In and out.

Rustling nearby. One of the fox-people peeked out at him from behind a tree. They ducked back behind when he jerked his head up.

"Hey," he said. "Can you tell me how to get to Anthem? Or even Flock?"

They crept out from behind the tree, ears flicking side to side. Parts of their fur seemed to have either fallen out or been rubbed off from their forehead, and something in how they moved seemed more animal-like than Saida, and the other fox-people he had seen on Anthem. They went so still every other step. Could they shift to a human like her?

"This is Between." The fox-person settled halfway between him and the safety of the tree, their tail curled around their paws. "There are no cities. There are no humans."

"Between *what?*"

They cocked their head, their ears straightening a bit. "The five worlds, of course." They padded a little closer. "Which world are you from? Why did you come here?"

"I didn't come on purpose." He kept his voice level and calm. "I'm from Anthem. The only world I know is Sound." *Might as well play along and get any information I can.*

"Oh. Sound." Their ears flickered. "I sort of remember that world. I think . . . I used to visit. People played lots of music. And sang. I think . . . I had a daughter there." They stared at him.

"Pell!" Another fox-person trotted up the path. He recognized her as Falrie, the one who had scolded Saida, with her speckled gray throughout the stripes in her fur and the lines on her snout.

The first one, Pell, ducked to the ground.

"What did I say about staying away . . . from the human?" Falrie narrowed her eyes at Alesio.

"Sorry, Falrie." Pell slunk away, his tail between his legs. Falrie followed.

"Wait!" Alesio called. "Please. Just—just tell me. How do I get back? I don't want to be here either. I need to get back to my—my world. My father needs me. I have things I need to do."

Falrie glanced over her shoulder and paused. "Saida will take you back as soon as she can. She can't right now, anyway. She must wait a day . . . before she can teleport again."

"Couldn't one of you take me?"

Falrie stiffened, and her ears flattened. "We foxans do not . . . leave Between. Saida should not, either, but does so on a regular basis, and her . . . recklessness landed you in this mess. She will clean up her own mistake." She sailed away into the forest, tail, and ears on high alert.

Alesio sighed and stood up. *I guess there's nothing for it but to try and get out by myself again.*

He circled the entire lake and trekked across the sandy heated place again. A few steeper hills rose in the north, where some snowdrifts lay, and after that, rolling grasslands led right back to the forest and the hill in the middle of it. At certain times, flashes of red fur and perked ears showed around a bush or bolting past a hill.

What word had Falrie used? Foxem? No . . . Foxan. Maybe other cities had different breeds, different kinds, where they could shift more of their bodies. Did that make Saida a fox-person, not a foxan?

After another hour, he collapsed in the grass field, coming to an impossible conclusion: either he was dreaming, or Saida and the other fox-people had told the truth: that he had arrived in another, tiny world, and he had no way of returning to Sound by himself.

SAIDA WOKE up with gummy eyes and soreness everywhere. She tried to stretch but stopped when the injuries on her shoulder, back, and collarbone cracked open, oozing blood. She plodded over to a water container and drank. *Ugh.* It was stale. Smacking dry lips, she set the container down and rubbed at her eyes.

"That human that teleported with you," Goosefeather said. "I hope he found a place to sleep."

"The human!" She jolted, glancing around. He wasn't there.

How long had she slept? She shambled outside, shifting to her foxan form to avoid her shoulders brushing against the tunnel walls. The hazy morning light had waned to late afternoon. The human had propped himself against the outside of the hill by the entrance. He'd unbuttoned his shirt down to the middle half of his chest, and her cheeks warmed while she tried not to stare at the dark brown muscles there. He must have dunked himself in the lake to try and clean his clothes, because they clung to him. He peered at her through one eye as she appeared; the other seemed to have swollen shut.

"Morning," he said. "Or evening, or whatever the sound it is in this place."

"You explored?"

"Oh, the first couple hours I explored. Then I fell asleep in the grass. Then I scoured every rock and tree in this forest and climbed over all the hills." He straightened. "No wonder you say such crazy things. I've gone crazy being here one day."

"Alesio—"

"The other fox-people—foxans—? I don't know what to call you all —say that you can take me back. Just you, apparently. You've had your little nap, and it's morning, so now it's time you did just that." He wiggled his fingers. "Sink us into the ground. Make a hole in the earth. Float through the air. Just take me back to Anthem. I'd like to change my clothes, and I need to see my father."

She swallowed and sat down next to him. "Alesio, it's too dangerous to go back to Sound right now. Watthe is still there. He found me so fast, and—and that reverend at the cathedral worships him."

"What? Lasrial does? How do you know?"

"I was at the cage match, and—" her throat closed at the memory of getting caught, of all those reaching hands.

"You were there?" His eyes widened. "Wait. Did you do that? That, that sinking feeling, in the match. It was the same as when—"

"You were trapped. I couldn't let that man hurt you."

He stared at her, his mouth hanging open. Her gaze trailed from his mouth down to his half-opened shirt, where the little curls of hair resembled the down feathers of a bird.

"Ahem," Tricksy Stone said.

She inhaled and tried again. "But making the portal gave me away. Somehow, Clef knew I could do that, and so he knew I was there. They caught me, and his humans took me to Lasrial. The reverend has a secret room where he worships Watthe, and then Watthe showed up."

"Clef and Lasrial? Working together, for the monster?" His brow furrowed. "That does make sense in a way. It would explain why Clef visited the cathedral the other day. And why he—" Alesio shuddered. "He was drawing the monster. Like he needed to see it when it wasn't around." He shook his head. "But why? Clef would rather swallow a sound-knife than be told what to do. Why would he do the bidding of that thing?"

"Power is attracted to power, isn't it?" She pulled on some grass and picked it into little green bits. "Maybe Clef worships Watthe too."

He rubbed at his left ear. "Clef doesn't even believe in the god of Sound. But maybe because he can see this monster, he respects it. Or wants to use it." He shivered. "He said to 'join us,' whatever that means. Do you know what that means?"

Saida worried at her lip with her teeth. "Maybe Watthe can teleport with them."

Alesio's one good eye widened. He dropped his head in his hands. "Sounddamn it."

"I don't know. I don't know what he can and can't do. He has *skin* now, which is somehow worse than when he was just smoke . . . but that's why I stayed so long in Sound, to try and warn you about the reverend, to stay away from him, because he worships Watthe. Now, though, Watthe could have a trap set up for both of us." She folded her hands in her lap, watching him out of the corner of her eye. "I can't take you back right away."

"My father is back there. He's hurt. And I have things to do."

"What things?"

"Does it matter? This is my life. You can't keep me prisoner." He swallowed. "Don't *you* hate being caged?"

She hunched over, staring at the verdant forest floor. "This is for your safety."

"My safety." Alesio went a little too still, like when he worked a shift at the cathedral. "You know, when I was five, my father and I almost starved on the streets. Clef offered us to join his faction in exchange for protection, and food, and water. My father refused. He said it was for our safety, but he was just scared of Clef."

He didn't breathe in between his sentences. He could hold his breath for an unsettling amount of time. Maybe that contributed to the potency of the magic he generated on Sound.

"Later that day, I left and begged Clef to let me join. He raised me to fight." He paused. "I'm used to giving things up to survive, to keep my dad alive. But I paid my debts to Clef, and I waited to live my life." His words steeped in silence for a few seconds, then he continued. "I'll wait for this, now, too, but I don't want to just pay, and wait, and pay, and wait for safety, and never live the life I paid and waited *for*. Do you understand?"

Saida's heart thumped like a caged thing in her ribs. "Yes," she whispered. "That would be a special kind of torture. I promise I'll take you back after things cool down on Anthem."

Alesio bowed his head. "How long?"

She considered. "A week or so. Then I'll teleport you into the nearby countryside on Sound. Not in the city, but somewhere close."

He stayed quiet for a few moments, and she stood up. "I'll get you some clothes to change into if you want. I'm sure I have something."

She trailed inside to her den, and he followed her. She dug into a pile of stuff in the corner, non-magical things she'd salvaged like the foldable water containers from Taste, or empty jars, or pieces of paper. "I know there's clothing in here somewhere. I wanted to wear something non-red. I can't change my fur or clothing color, so, I got curious, you know?" She was babbling to fill the silence.

"If you can teleport anywhere, why can't you just drop me off and come right back here?" His tone remained even and controlled.

"I can teleport just once a day." She set aside an assortment of different sized jars. "I don't know—I don't understand what Watthe can or can't do. Ah! Here it is."

She pulled out a short sleeved, light blue blouse and short tan pants from underneath a pile of paper. Holding them next to Alesio, she sucked in her lower lip. "Um. I'm not sure if they'll fit you very well. I think they're made for women."

"Better than wearing the same shirt for however long I'm here." He took them from her, his lips quirking into a smile. "Can you turn around while I change?"

Her whole body heated up.

"Oh!" She whirled around.

Clothes rustled behind her. "So, we stay here for a week?" he said. "What fun. I wonder, could I swim the lake a hundred times?"

She barked out a laugh. "Well . . . if you want to visit *other* worlds than Sound, you could just teleport with me to one. Just don't tell Falrie or she'll tie me to a tree for even suggesting it."

"You can turn around."

She did so slowly. His stocky chest strained the delicate indigo blouse, and his dark brown biceps swelled the short sleeves. She didn't dare glance down to see what the slim trousers did for him.

"Another world, huh?" He shrugged. "You know what? Why not. Might as well, right?"

Of course he didn't believe her. Not yet.

He would see soon enough. She needed to keep her promise to the people in Vision and find more transplants. She'd spent too long trying to trim the overgrowth in this human's throat; she'd have to focus on the other worlds, now, to have even a chance of saving Vision. Once she teleported him back to Sound, she'd ask him to sing straight into a seashell, and then she'd have all four transplants for Vision at the same time.

Along the way, watching him experience another world for the first time didn't sound so bad.

13

THE SALT-WILDS

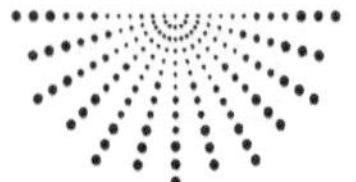

It rained that evening, so he slept inside Saida's den, even though the row of 'magic items' lining the walls unsettled him. Saida had set up a makeshift bed for him from a blanket she called 'Softdream,' and it did seem softer than anything he'd ever slept on. She slept on the pile of leaves she'd dumped on the floor, assuring him that she did so all the time.

The next morning, after he had washed himself and his cut from Brezeek in the lake, she led him on a short jaunt to the sandy, heated area. The bright light behind the fog in the sky did shine brighter, there. To give himself some sanity, he called that the sun in his head, though nothing seemed sure anymore. She looked like a little pack animal with the many pockets she grew stuffed full of various items. She carried two large containers of water, and she handed him another two containers and a belt to hook them to, along with a gray, washed-out rag. The containers were made of a strange material that squished when he held them, and he realized that they would fold down to almost nothing at all when they were empty.

They were going to 'teleport' again. That strange sinking sensation, and the absence of solidity. *By the Sound.* Alesio inhaled, working to steady his thoughts. At least the raw sores in his throat seemed somewhat soothed today by his long night's rest.

Saida sniffed around in the sand a little off the path. Alesio swallowed, anticipating the taste of bile.

"How do you do that, anyway?"

"Teleport?" She had a little bit of sand on her nose. She'd shifted to foxan, but still wore clothing; a reddish-tan set of shorts and red cut-off shirt. As she'd stated the day before, she always grew red clothes over her dark tan skin or red and tan fur. "I can sense where the portals are."

"How many are there?"

She scuffed her paw on the ground and stuck part of her tongue out. "Right now? About fifty or so for all the worlds."

"What? That's so many! How do you know which one to pick?"

"Portals move. They're kind of like . . . wandering gaps in between the worlds. They all open to random places unless I direct them to teleport me somewhere specific." She sighed. "There used to be a lot more portals. Three hundred, five hundred even. Each of the worlds are so big."

He squinted at the ground with one eye. The other remained firmly shut. The woman's shirt and pants she had lent him felt tight and restrictive, and he tugged the short sleeves down. "How specific can you get?"

"If I've been there before, I can direct them closer to where I want to go, like within a street's distance, instead of a mountain's distance."

"Oh." He frowned. "So, you can smell them? Or hear them?"

"Whichever world they connect to, they mimic that world's magic. So, if we were going to Scent, I would smell them."

"And . . . where are we going?"

She grinned at him, then lowered her nose to the sand again. The water containers in her pockets sloshed as she moved. "You'll see. This is going to be fun. Are you ready?"

He shivered. "Yes." A day or two. Then he'd demand that she take him back to Sound. She seemed absentminded; maybe she'd forget the week she had asked for and would take him back without any fuss.

His father would worry where he was. He'd have enough money for boarding at Mona's for another few weeks, but Alesio wanted to check to see how he was healing from that knife wound. He also hadn't told Mona that he needed to quit performing at her bar. And if Lasrial really did worship that monster, he didn't want Tak to work at St. Rina's any longer, either. The man might have prejudices against the poor, but Alesio still somewhat counted him as a friend. Even if Tak maybe didn't any longer.

Another part of him didn't want to return to Sound at all. What would he do about Clef's offer? The strait's leader had proven his point; Alesio fared better in cage matches than anywhere else in Anthem.

But he also didn't want to start that life again.

"Hold your breath." Saida leapt up and pounced nose-first into the sand.

The sand gave way under them like a large trap door, and it poured down with them, and he couldn't breathe, and he couldn't feel anything again for forty seconds.

He stumbled onto a flat white surface, just catching himself before he fell. He gulped in deep breaths.

Then he coughed, shocked at the strength of the salt in his mouth.

Saida shifted just her hands and tied a rag over her mouth and nose. "Drink some water. And pull the cloth up like this."

He guzzled water, trying to rid his mouth of the intensity of the taste. Even the water tasted heightened, he could parse out notes of sweet and stale and other, almost herb-like flavors; like he could taste what water had always tasted like but enhanced.

"Hey, hey, not too much," she said. "We're in the salt flats. We need those to last till we find a refill spot."

"This is your idea of fun?" He wiped his mouth and pulled the gray cloth she'd given him over his face.

She gestured outwards. "Just look at this. Look how bright and wide and beautiful it is. Welcome to Taste in the summer!"

He twisted to squint at where she had gestured. The sun shone bright, reflecting off a blanket of snow on the ground.

No . . . not snow. It shifted like sand underfoot, and it would have melted in the heat. He tasted . . .

Salt? All of this is salt? He blinked, staring at the expanse. A strong wind kicked up, and he couldn't hear the notes of music in the wind, like he could've in Anthem. Back home, he heard music in everything, in the dissonant chords of an angry crowd or the rhythm of people's footsteps.

Here, the high notes on the wind didn't ring, but even through the cloth he *could* taste the salt in the air, and other things like a hint of leather from Saida's belt, a far-off musk of dirt and soil, and past the strength of the salt flat taste; the taste of the summer wind and sky itself: a rushing, heady flavor like a sweet alcohol, warm and nutty.

"Holy Sound," Alesio said. "You aren't cra—I mean, um—you weren't lying!"

She shifted to her human form, twirling in a circle, and laughing. She adjusted the rag covering her mouth and nose as her snout receded into a nose. "I'm not crazy, either. Well, depending on who you talk to." She patted her pocket. "You stay out of this. Anyway, let's go. We need to find the overgrowth I'm tasting further south. And I want to show you more of the world." She traipsed off on human legs, gesturing for him to follow.

He wandered after her in a kind of daze, words like, *far, near, sweet, and salty* all shifting to mean different things in his head.

He was adorable.

He stared wide-eyed around at the expansive flats, tripping over the one random stone for probably several miles. He jumped, his hand covering his mouth over the cloth she'd given him. "Did I just taste that rock? By touching it?"

She grinned. "Just wait till we pass the city. We should taste it on the wind soon." She shaded her eyes, squinted at the horizon, and pointed at the small structures in the distance. "There."

"A city? How long till we get there?"

"We're not going inside." She plodded along, her steps kicking up little puffs of salt dust. "The overgrowth is far past the city, out in the salt-wilds where the people here don't usually travel. I picked this portal so we could pass the city, though."

They traveled on.

Her thoughts wandered. It had taken too long to teleport again, especially for Taste at forty seconds. Vision had taken fifty. Taste had drifted farther away, straining its magical tethers.

"It's good you noticed this time," Goosefeather said. "You usually forget to count the seconds."

They roamed through a few patches where the wind did not taste of salt, and even the brush of her boots on the ground evoked just the slightest flavor.

"Tricksy, has the magic faded here more since the last time I visited?"

"Are you talking to your magic?" Alesio asked from behind her. She nodded.

"Not as fast as Vision, but yes," Tricksy Stone said from her pouch. "This area used to be so intense, you'd need more than one cloth to keep out the salt."

By the Senses. How fast do I have to be to stop these worlds from ripping apart?

To distract herself from the problem, she stole glances back at Alesio. His stocky build filled out the clothing she'd given him in a way that couldn't be comfortable, but that she couldn't help but appreciate. The muscles in his arms rippled and his lips looked so soft. He swiveled every which way, trying to absorb the newness to his senses.

She blinked. "Al—Alesio?"

He bent his head towards her. "What?"

"Are you—do you have trouble hearing?"

He whirled, his face darkening, his lips thinning. "What? How do you know? Who told you that?"

"No one. I just noticed. You always . . ." she cocked her head to the right. "Do this."

"You can't tell anyone." His voice came swift and sharp. "No one. It's my only—it's the reason I'm good at fighting."

The wind stilled around them. Her mouth hung open, and the taste of salt piled on her tongue. She closed her lips. "Alesio. Who would I even tell?"

He brushed his hand through his hair. "Right. Right. Sorry." He cleared his throat. "It's just. I've kept it a secret my whole life. Clef was the only other one who ever figured it out."

She cocked her head. "How did he?"

"Remember that story I told you about when I almost starved at five years old, and Clef found my father and I?"

She nodded. He rubbed under his non-blackened eye, and jolted, probably at the taste of his own fingers.

"Well. He wouldn't have extended the offer at all if he hadn't seen what I could do. His cronies were roughing up a shopkeeper nearby, and a stray sound knife hit me in the ribs. Or, it would have, if it hadn't struck my left side, where I couldn't hear it, so it just dropped to the ground and fizzled." He shook his head. "Clef saw it happen and must have figured it out, and the potential for what I could do, because that's when he offered us protection." He clenched his jaw. "That's why he's so terrifying. He manipulates people and situations."

The wind picked up. They both tensed against the intensity of any exposed skin tasting the salt it brought.

"Well, you're in a different world. You don't have to worry about it. Sound powers don't work here." She gestured with curled fingers. "C'mon."

They traipsed on in silence for a while.

The reason I'm good at fighting. So, his hardness of hearing had protected Alesio his whole life. She couldn't help but wonder how difficult singing must be for him. *How does he generate such a powerful magic when he can't hear very well? Isn't Sound magic connected to hearing?*

Tricksy Stone jabbed her in her pocket. "Don't forget about the Palates. You told me to remind you whenever you teleport here."

Oh, right. She did not want a run-in with those creepy, white-cloaked rogues. After that she watched her surroundings better, rather than just Alesio.

They reached the edge of the city, the one-story structures clustering together like several small, connected villages. The taste of cinnamon, sugar, and crisp, baked bread wafted over them.

"Are you sure we can't go inside?" Alesio asked.

She lowered her cloth and stuck out her tongue. He did the same, and his eyes widened at the intensity. The first time she'd found the city, she'd lost her mind for a good ten minutes, just running in circles from the taste of sugar on the wind.

"I can't do another city right now," she said. "Taste is one of those worlds that doesn't like foxans. And I . . . I don't know what Watthe is capable of. If he can teleport or not. He would question the people in the city if he were here." She sighed. "It's too bad. Just like how everyone loves music in your city, the cities here love to cook, and bake, and make things to eat."

He licked his lips. What would they taste like?

Don't think about that.

"My mouth is watering so much," Alesio said. "I can taste—what is that?"

"It's called a cinnamon olo, a type of bread baked with layers of sugar and cream." She smiled. "Maybe, someday, I can bring you one on Sound."

"I'd like that. Please do that. That is the best thing I have ever tasted, and I'm not even eating it!"

She laughed. "C'mon. I don't have much self-control. I will eventually try to climb the walls."

"I'd be right there with you."

His words sent a shot of warmth through her like alcohol, trailing into her insides with unexpected fire. *With you . . . with you . .* .

She shook her head and led the way past the city, trotting at a faster pace, now. The overgrowth waited farther out, but they were getting closer. The sun shone bright at midday. As they traveled deeper into the salt-wilds, the white ground evened out even more, smoothed by the relentless wind. It seemed such an infinite plain that the world curved ahead of them.

"So, you can sense magic?" His tone was casual, yet a little hesitant. "Like, uh . . . like in the stories?"

"Not quite the same." She tugged one of her two water containers out and sipped the water, swirling it in her mouth. "Make sure to drink a little every once in a while."

He grabbed one of his containers and tipped it back, licking his lips. He didn't ask further, didn't push. She liked that about him, that he seemed to understand she would speak in her own time, on her own terms.

After about fifteen minutes, she said, "The stories of us on Sound are twisted. Earlier, you asked the difference between foxans, and fox-people. Well, I am a foxan, and so is Falrie, and those in Between. The ones on Sound, and the other worlds, are fox-people—descendants of foxans and humans."

"Of—of you?"

She laughed. "I've never coupled before, so no, I don't have descendants."

He blinked.

Did I really just say that? She coughed. "I'm just 300 or so years old. And Pell is like another parent, almost. And with humans, I just never, um, found anyone that I liked." Her face felt hot.

He blinked again.

"300 years old!"

Thank the Senses that's what he focused on. "You think I'm an old lady now, don't you?"

"It's hard to pin you down. Your age, I mean." He flushed. "There are times that you seem a lot younger. But also, you've seen so much, and you've traveled to all these places, it does seem like you've lived 300 years." He glanced down, avoiding another pebble. "I guess humans' lives seem tiny to yours."

She sighed, pulling her long braid away from her neck in the heat. The taste of sweat felt tacky in her mouth. "If the legends are true, humans used to live as long as foxans. A thousand years or more."

"I have a hard time believing that."

"Well. I hope you have a hard time believing the things humans say about fox-people. That they steal magic from people so they cannot harness their abilities. The stories are much the same here, on Taste, and on Scent. They all have similar versions of that myth." She paused. "It is not altogether . . . *untrue*."

She could almost taste his immediate distrust, flowing to her on the ever-present breeze.

"I do not steal peoples' magic. I trim the overgrowth. It's like trimming a tree; it helps the rest grow better, and healthier. And anyway, most of the magic I sense isn't the kind humans create, but the magic of the world. Like this." She shifted to her fox-form and nosed at a spot on the ground. "This patch of salt has absorbed some of the Taste magic from the city, some of the sugar, and it feels just a little out of place with the other salt. It's not strong enough for me to trim it, so I'm going to leave it there."

He furrowed his forehead, squinting at the patch of salt. "The fox-people, then, on Sound, do they do this, too?"

"Fox-people cannot shift, or teleport. Some of them can sense magics, though, and that is why the stories say they steal it."

"The bells!" He stared at her. "That's why you took the bells, to trim their magic?"

She nodded and shifted back to human, pressing her lips together. They were dry. She sipped her water, trying to wet her throat so the words would slip out easier. She'd never liked keeping secrets. She hated the way they churned in her chest.

Besides, maybe telling him would keep him at arm's length. She'd gotten so excited to show him the worlds, she hadn't stopped to think about how she could listen to him talk from morning to evening. She hadn't anticipated it would make her want to listen more.

"That's why—Alesio, that's why I followed you. On Sound, you have a powerful magic voice, but it's overgrown in your throat. Knowing now, about your half-hearing, it's even more amazing—"

He stepped away from her.

"It didn't work," she said. "Your magic didn't seem ready to make a transplant. Or more like it was blocked." His brow furrowed. "Don't worry, I don't uproot the full growth. I just trim it. It's better for the magic, that way. If it's overgrown for too long—"

"You understand why that doesn't sound great to me, don't you?"

She bowed her head.

"Look," Alesio said. "You showed me that portals are real. I believe in those now. So, I'm believing this, too, and by the Sound, you know that you can't do that to me, right? You're not going to—to take my voice when I'm sleeping?" His chest heaved, and the strength of his reaction surprised her. She'd elicited a strong reaction from him twice now in the same day.

"I won't take your voice." She turned away from the patch of sugar-salt, towards the vastness of the salt-wilds past the city. "I'll find another overgrowth from Sound that will work."

She turned towards the flavor of potent magic on the wind. She'd pinpointed the source: a solid rock of salt that, when the sunlight hit it just right at dusk, it cooled enough for the salt to resist melting in the mouth, long enough to savor. Salt rocks produced most of the overgrowths she'd found on Taste.

The best way to avoid something was to go towards something else. Tricksy Stone and Goosefeather had helped teach her that.

"You didn't have to push him away, though," Goosefeather said. "You did that on purpose."

<hr>

ALESIO FELT TERRIBLE. He'd freaked out on her, and she had swung away from him and trotted on, not saying a word to him for the past few hours except for small reminders to drink water and other short explanations.

But by the Sound! She'd made it sound so ominous! 'Trimming' his magic? How could she think that he'd be okay with that? He didn't know if he trusted her while he slept.

She'd said it was in his throat. And the monster Watthe had mentioned it, too: *You have overgrown magic in your throat.*

He rubbed at his neck. Was that why his throat had been so raw lately, because his magic had grown too much? What did that even mean? *I guess I can pay attention to what she does with the overgrown magic here. What happens to the magic that's left? And is that what's really happening, or is she just running around pretending to sense magic?* He couldn't deny any longer that she could definitely teleport, but he wasn't sure about the rest of her claims. He thought of how she'd talked to the things in her den and to her favorite items that she carried around with her.

She acted so . . . alien at times. She'd said she was 300 years old. The way she sometimes shifted part of her body to more animal, like her paw or nose, leaving the rest of her human. She could teleport, for Sound's sake!

"Try not to breathe," she said as they passed a pile of dried excrement. He was in the middle of filling his lungs already.

"Aww! Ugh! Oh!" He ripped down the rag and scraped at his tongue. This succeeded in letting more tainted air in. He held his breath.

She clamped her hand over her mouth and nose and motioned for them to jog. It took ten minutes for him to breathe without tasting dung. "That was the grossest thing—I mean, I've even eaten bugrat, and that tasted worse."

She didn't answer. She tasted the wind, pivoting to different directions, her bright red braid swinging around her calves.

"So, this magic you're sensing. Wouldn't a good-tasting dessert from the city have a stronger—"

"Shh!" She crouched, her eyes narrowing to slits, her tongue curling. "Get down! Lay flat!"

"What?" He dropped, testing the air with his tongue as she had. Sweat and salt and a strange, musky bitterness.

"Palates." She growled and flattened her ears. "Follow my lead, Alesio." She rolled on the ground, scooping salt all over herself, even rubbing it in her scalp. "Hurry!"

Something in her tone decided him, the urgency, the command. He coated himself in salt, rolling and rolling and massaging it into his skin, and his skin *tasted* it. A little got past the bandage on his leg and burned like fire, though it seemed to have scabbed over that morning when he'd washed in the lake. He fought not to cough, agitating the soreness in his throat. It felt like he had swallowed a tub full of salt, and his insides contracted.

What a strange world. What happens when I eat something? How potent would it be?

"Stop moving!" Saida peered out at the shining, lowering sun.

Then Alesio saw them. Their white cloaks camouflaged them against the white of the salt flats. But once he knew to watch, their movement gave them away. He stilled and controlled his breathing.

They glided closer, then farther, then closer again. They seemed confused, probably because their quarry had 'disappeared,' the taste of them cloaked by the ubiquitous salt. They milled about, maybe twenty or so of them—before veering off to the north. Saida waited a good ten minutes after they'd gone before she stood up.

"Who were those guys?" Alesio asked, shaking salt out of his restrictive pants. His whole body felt parched. He swigged some water, and the strength of the sweet herbs combined with the staleness of the liquid made him shiver.

"Cannibals." Saida snarled with foxan fangs.

Alesio started. "W-what?"

"Every year, Taste's city—which is made up of a lot of small villages clustered near each other—holds a contest to find those who harnesses Taste magic the best in their food. Each village nominates one person to represent them and spends a lot of money to support them and every year, it became more and more competitive. Everyone wanted something new, and unique, something they'd never tasted before." She chugged some water. "I guess, one year, a few rogue chefs decided to try something more of the ordinary than anyone expected. They used their magic to make food out of other humans."

Alesio gagged and bent over.

"Don't throw up. That would bring them right back here, the strength of stomach juice on the wind." Saida shook salt out of her fur.

"Anyway, the city banished them for their crimes, expecting them to die out on the salt flats. But they've found ways to live on."

"You mean—"

"They eat their own, when they can't find humans out traveling."

He swallowed the bile in his throat. "You came here, *knowing* that?"

She cocked her head. "Every world is dangerous, just in different ways." She motioned him to follow again. "C'mon. We need to distance ourselves from them so we can eat."

They rambled farther into the whiteness, leaving the city behind them altogether so that he felt that maybe he had died, and had gone to an afterlife of endless white and bright, bright sun.

After about an hour, Saida motioned for them to stop and dug in one of her pockets. She pulled out a cloth that she unwrapped, revealing a small loaf of bread and a handful of dark, purple berries. She handed him half the loaf and most of the berries and motioned them to sit. The taste of the food filled his mouth as he stared at it. His stomach growled. *I can't wait to try eating here!* He dumped the berries in his mouth.

"Not all at once—!" Saida clapped her hand over her face.

The berries exploded on his tongue like several tiny bombs. He jolted, and swallowed, and coughed, wheezing from how a sweet acid burned his tender, healing throat. Did he have tastebuds in his throat? Apparently.

Saida cackled, bending over, and slapping her knee. "I—your face —by the Senses!" She pantomimed drinking out of a cup. "Water! Drink your water!"

Still coughing, he guzzled from one of the containers she had given him. That helped wash away some of the intensity.

"People eat really slow, here," Saida said. "Sorry. I should have explained before." Little dimples on her cheeks appeared and disappeared as she tried to stop laughing.

"I was just so excited!" Alesio swallowed again, trying to recover from the blast to his mouth and throat. He regarded the half loaf she had given him with new respect. He worked on it little by little, copying how Saida nibbled at the edges of hers. The bits of oat and grain tasted stale, but also like parsley and basil and flour and salt, magnified to an intensity he had to process in his mind as well as his mouth. It was one of the best meals he'd ever eaten.

The wind picked up, whipping against his face. Saida was half-shifted, and the breeze streamed through the light fur on her human arms and legs and tugged at her long braid that morphed into a tail past her waist. It had a slight chill to it in the waning of the sun. Alesio gazed out at the vast expanse, that whiteness that went on and on. "How far does it go?"

"I don't know." Saida gazed in the same direction. "The worlds are huge, Alesio. I've only explored a fraction of each of them. And I've done this for almost two centuries. It took me about a hundred years to leave Between, but once I did, I never stopped wanting to discover new places."

"It's so . . . big," Alesio said. "It reminds me of when I first heard a performer from the Cadenza sing."

Saida nibbled on the remainder of her bread, lifting her eyebrows. "What do you mean?"

He struggled to speak.

Out of everyone he'd met, she might understand.

"I was four or five, maybe. Real young, young enough that sometimes I think I dreamed it up, before Clef discovered me. I'd gotten lost on the piper side of town, and I heard someone practicing in the back room of a fancy place. Their song was like those berries, and this view." He gestured at the brightness; at the unending ground he could taste through his knees. "Their voice —their magic, it broadened what I could see." He paused. "Later, I found out I'd stumbled on the practice room for the Cadenza. After that, it's all I ever wanted to do. All I ever wanted to be." He set the bread down and rubbed at his temples.

She scooted closer to him, just a little bit, and stared out alongside him in the same direction.

"And, when I saw you that day, in the garden . . ." he cleared his throat. "You *glowed*, and I heard that music from you, like when I was four. It seemed like—like—well, I didn't know it then, but maybe all the different world magics cling to you when you travel all over."

She blushed. Or not. It was hard to tell, with her reddish-brown skin. "I'm not sure what you saw or heard from me. But I do want to hear you perform at the Cadenza someday."

He gritted his teeth. "It's not possible. My father was right; big, pretty dreams should stay that way. As dreams."

The wind howled, now, picking up more, cooling the heat of the sun. "Why do you say that?"

"I was fired, Saida. I can't afford to sing at the pub anymore. And let's face it." He held his breath. "My half-hearing strengthens me in the cage matches and makes it difficult when I perform. I know where I fit the best."

"Oh." She rocked back a little, shivering. "You mean you'll do more of those fights?"

"Maybe. I don't know. I could also work in the factories, but Clef manipulates those, too. It wouldn't surprise me if he found a way to enlist me again, no matter what I try to do."

Saida licked the last bit of berry juice from her fingers and covered her mouth and nose with the cloth. "That's a shame. The worlds need every bit of magic possible, because, you know, all the people are dying out."

"What?"

Saida swept her arm to indicate the salt-wilds. "The worlds are all too empty. I've found at least five ancient city ruins in every world. Sound seems like the best off; it has two large cities, Flock and Anthem, quite near each other, and they even know about each other."

"There has to be more than two!" Alesio frowned. He'd never traveled outside of Anthem before. He'd focused on trying to reach the other half of the city he'd already lived in. But more people had to live on Sound than that.

"Maybe I just haven't found them." Saida rose and kicked the salt so that a large puff rose in the air. The wind picked it up and scattered it. "I've found at least one city in most worlds, and there's small, hidden villages here and there." She swallowed. "But, on Vision, I've just found one, tiny village. And even that one seems to be dying out."

Alesio's stomach dropped. "How? Why?"

She hugged her arms around herself, growing heavier fur on her body. The temperature had dropped fast as the sun hove to the shore of the horizon. "Vision's magic doesn't work for the most part, and it's somehow linked to the humans dying, and their shortened lifespans. I'm trying to stop it. The transplants help tie the worlds together and strengthen the world they end up in. But I can only do so much. I'm just one foxan. Falrie, Darrow, and Pell—you've seen how broken they are. They wouldn't last long outside Between. They can't help. But I— I—" She covered her face with her hands.

Alesio sucked in a breath. She had scared him earlier, but she didn't seem to have malicious intent. He didn't understand her magic or how it helped the worlds, but her willingness to try and make things better shone through. He wanted to do something for her, but he didn't want to frighten her with a hug or a touch.

He hummed a little tune, no words, just a melody his father used to hum to him when he was small.

Saida looked up, her ears flickering, her face streaked with salt and tears. Her shoulders relaxed, and she watched him with that wide-eyed awe that she had shown the first time he had sung in the garden.

"It's strange," she murmured. "Magic doesn't work outside its source world, not unless it's transplanted. But even so, your voice is so calming."

He blushed. At least it helped her. She'd seemed to live alone, except for her interactions with the other foxans, for many, many years. No wonder human interaction scared her.

He hummed for a bit longer, staring out at the lowering sun, tasting the salt in the heavy wind, the salt from her tears.

She jerked her head up. "It's there," she said. "The overgrowth. It's close."

14

A BILLION PHANTOM STARS

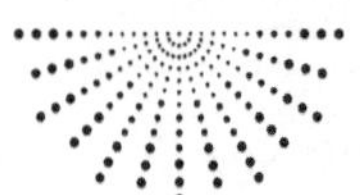

The sun lowered on the horizon, highlighting the curve of the world. The temperature dropped even more, and they shivered in the sudden chill, no longer a respite from the heat. Saida hunted the taste of the salt rock. Its magic had grown in the zenith of the failing light.

They reached it just as the sun dipped its toes on the skyline, a solid lump of salt on the smooth ground. Saida fumbled in her pocket for the paper she had brought with her, unfolding it, and smoothing out the creases as best she could. The overgrowth around the rock emanated for several feet around it, strong, ready for trimming, eager to blossom somewhere new.

Alesio hovered nearby, his dark brown face like an eclipse against the sunset. "Can I help?"

"Nope." She drank some water to generate some saliva in her dry mouth, then licked the paper all over on one side. The taste of old trees and pressed wood filled her mouth. Alesio grunted in surprise.

Saida pressed the wet paper down on the salt rock, careful not to shift it for a few seconds. She pulled it up along with a thin layer of salt, jiggling it a bit to let the extra shake off.

"That's it?" Alesio squinted at it. "I thought you would take the rock."

"Just a cutting big enough to transplant." She folded it and creased the edges of the paper together, then slid it into her pocket again. "Each of the worlds transfer magic in different ways. Seashells for Sound to hold echoes. Tubes for Scent to contain vapor. Jars for both Touch and Vision, to hold temperature and the image of something through a glass. Wet paper for Taste to preserve melting salt."

"The Taste one seems specific," Alesio said.

She frowned up at him.

"I mean, not in a bad way. Just that the other methods you use seem like it would work on more things."

She shrugged. "I don't create transplants from anything in the city. So, I don't need something that would gather a different kind of Taste magic."

"Oh. Huh."

The wind changed direction, and a familiar pungent taste flooded her mouth. Close. She tensed and whirled around.

The Palates had hidden themselves upwind, and they rose just a few feet away from them, their white hoods covering their eyes, but not their grinning mouths. Their skin matched their clothing, as they always covered up from the sun to ensure that their skin tone camouflaged them against the salt flats.

"Run!" Saida screamed.

They bolted.

A small bag sailed through the air and hit the ground. An orange dust spilled out onto the flats near their feet and the wind scattered it up into their faces.

"Don't breathe it!" Saida shouted to Alesio, covering her mouth and nose with the rag. Some dust had slipped in her mouth when she shouted, though, and now it coated the back of her throat. It held cinnamon's sweetness, but with more musk, that same taste that followed the Palates everywhere.

She coughed, her vision sparking up with stars, her limbs slow and useless. Ixor. The slowing spice.

Alesio had run ahead. He glanced back at her and slowed, even though she tried to wave him on to escape.

Can't teleport yet. Not till morning. Can't protect him.

One of the Palates snaked out a leg and tripped her as she faltered. She rolled and the world swirled, alternating between salt and darkening sky.

Alesio ran back. She coughed, again, her throat constricting. She pushed herself up on her knees, her legs trembling.

Alesio dodged a swing from one of the Palates then delivered a solid uppercut to their chin. They crumpled to the ground. She tried to gauge how many Palates had shown up, but their cloaks and skin blended in with the ground so she couldn't tell. Seven? Eight?

"Leave me!" She wheezed. "You can make it!"

He didn't answer. He held his breath, she realized, so the ixor wouldn't coat his mouth. *How long can he do that?*

Two of the white cloaked humans rushed him, and one threw another spice bag. The dust scattered everywhere, coloring the salt orange and red in the sunset's light. Alesio dashed towards the thrower, leapt up to avoid the tainted ground, and swept his leg in a roundhouse kick to their face so they stumbled and fell, groaning. Alesio landed on the other side of them. The other one swung at him with a clumsy punch at his nose. Alesio ducked and slammed his fist in their stomach, winding them so they gave an audible gasp. They didn't seem like trained fighters.

By the Senses. Saida scooped some of the ixor up in one hand and rose to her feet. *Maybe he does have a chance—*

Three more of them, like blurry, white shadows to Saida, rushed him, one on his left, on his bad eye side, and two on his right. The one on the left wielded a chef's knife. "Both sides!" She wheezed.

He pivoted, avoiding the knife. The others punched him, one in the nose and one in the chest. He staggered, blood spurting from his nose.

"Ales—Ales—" Saida tottered towards him.

One of the Palates snuck up behind her. She slumped against him on purpose. He caught her under her arms, and she twisted and reached up, smearing his face and lips with the ixor she'd grabbed. He coughed and released her, clawing at his mouth.

Saida whirled. Alesio had curled up on the ground while three Palates kicked at him. One raised a chef's knife over him. "No!" She rasped, a little louder, the drug grating in her throat. "You don't want him! He's—he's sick!"

They paused to stare at her. Alesio coughed on the ground.

"It's true!" She wet her lips, hobbling closer. "He's got the hindra . . . lio . . . sapphire disease!"

"Lying fur-mix," one of them said. Another two appeared out of the blank, flat ground.

"You sure you wanna risk that?" She waggled her fingers. "One chomp on the wrong guy, and you're dead. Bleh." She dropped her head to the side and stuck out her tongue. Tasting the wind to count the Palates.

Five. Five of them still fighting, seven altogether. A smaller group than the one they'd avoided earlier, maybe to split off in search.

One of them laid on the ground, out cold. The other that Alesio had kicked had picked himself back up, holding his head. One still hadn't shown himself; she'd pinpointed him to the left, watching the fight. The one behind her whose face she had smudged with the drug still fought his own mouth, gagging.

The one with the knife left Alesio's side, stalking towards her, his white cloak flapping in the bitter wind. "Run your mouth much more and we'll cut your tongue out first."

She stumbled. She'd recovered use of her legs, but they didn't need to know that. "If you . . . don't believe me," she struggled to speak through the ixor, "Try his blood that's on the wind. Doesn't it taste odd?"

They all paused for a half second. Salt, blood, and ixor all mixed strong in the air around them. "Bites, but it does seem off, Graff," one of the Palates near Alesio said. "Different."

Different world, different taste. She fought off a grin.

The Palate with the chef's knife, Graff, strode up to her. "Well, if we can't eat him, we'll just eat you faster." She tried to snap at him in her foxan form, but the ixor in her system seemed to slow her shifting, too, and she changed just her teeth in time. He dodged her jaws with ease. "Never tried one of your kind before. Probably taste like bugrat." He grabbed her chin, forcing her face this way and that, his tongue flicking in and out. Her blood ran cold, her limbs freezing up again.

His voice lowered, speaking as if he sampled a wine. "Hmmm. The skin tastes exotic. Different. Not like the poisoned one." He glanced at the other four Palates. "What do you all think? She doesn't have much meat on her."

"Better kill her now. She might steal your magic."

She spit in his face. "How'd you like that for exotic?"

He backhanded her and she tumbled to her knees. *Still so weak.* His hand tasted like blood and remnants of ixor.

Saida had bought him some time. They had kicked him over and over, and if he hadn't held his breath, he couldn't have functioned until inhaling again. But he still had his reserve.

He focused on the Palate woman closest to him, who had turned to watch Saida be her distracting self. He swept the cannibal's feet with his bare arm (ugh, it tasted like that drug, and sweat, and piss) and as she toppled, he grabbed her arm and bent it back so that it snapped when she fell. She screamed, writhing on the ground, and pulling away from him.

He cringed at the brutality of his instincts, and he felt pulled back there, back into the cage matches. Doing what he was made to do. His throat ached with the memory.

Different world. Same problem.

The other three jerked their attention back to him. He crouched. They overcame unsuspecting prey with that drug, and their camouflaged clothing and skin tone, and didn't seem to have real fighting experience. At the same time, he didn't relish a three on one fight. He needed to incapacitate them one at a time.

One of them rushed him, and he stabilized himself, keeping his center of gravity low, and waited till they tried to throw a punch. He grabbed their outstretched wrist and twisted his body side by side with theirs. Keeping hold of their arm and using their momentum against them, he lifted them onto his hip and slammed them down on the ground, knocking the wind out of them. He followed that up with an elbow to the face, breaking their nose in.

The other two had flanked him, one on each side, more cautious. The two he'd already brought down still screamed and rolled around on the ground. The one on his left swiped at his back, trying to punch where they'd already kicked him, and he almost didn't see it out of his limited vision. He leapt away just in time, releasing a small part of his stored breath to produce a sound-knife. Of course, nothing happened.

He had about a third of his stored air left before he would have to breathe that toxic dust they had scattered in the air.

A snicking sound on his right. The other Palate had brought out a filet knife. He slashed at Alesio, and he rotated to the side, letting it pass by, then snatched the guy's wrist and bent it back. The Palate cried out and released the knife, dropping to his knees. Alesio kneed the guy in the gut, and he curled over, fighting for breath. He'd adapted much of his fighting style to make people lose their air, but that didn't matter nearly as much on Taste.

"Two behind you!" Saida screamed.

He dropped to the ground. The one on his left had tried to punch him in the stomach again, and another Palate had tried to slice him with a cleaver from the other side. They must have watched him the whole time and had tried to surprise him.

Saida scrabbled backwards away from Graff. The other one she had incapacitated with the spice in his face wheezed and glared at her.

A thud, and a scream! They whirled towards Alesio, who slammed two to the ground in a matter of seconds. But she couldn't let these Palates attack him too.

Leaping up, nauseous and woozy from the sudden movement, she waved her arms. "Whoa, you two can't handle a fur-mix? I'mma run away now, hahahaha!"

She shifted into her mostly-foxan form, small and nimble, and dashed between them, taunting them with a flick of her tail against their cloaks. They grabbed at her, and she pulled her tail in to avoid them. She led them in a circle, taunting them at intervals to keep them from leaving to attack Alesio.

The one who watched from the shadows tried to surprise him. "Behind you!" She yelled.

Her followers turned their heads. She had regained most of her reflexes back, now, and she streaked between them once more, shifting to her smallest at the last quarter second so their grasping hands fell short. "Oh, almost!" She laughed.

Graff snarled and flung his chef knife at her. She flattened against the salted ground, and it whistled over her head, just catching the tip of her ear. "Good thing your aim is about as good as your cooking, it just misses the mark every time, huh?"

ALESIO ROLLED ON THE GROUND, snatched the filet knife that the other guy had dropped, and stabbed the one in the leg who kept trying to punch him. They cursed and fell back.

The one with the cleaver swung at him with a powerful overhand. Alesio held up the little knife to block the attack and the metal rang through his whole body so that he tasted metal and blood.

He swept his leg, trying to trip cleaver-man, but he didn't have the momentum to do it and he just kicked his ankle. Now he lay belly up, ripe for the cleaving. The Palate grinned and raised his weapon again.

Alesio hooked his leg around the guy's ankle, using it as an anchor, and swung himself around to get out of the way. He pushed on his elbow, leapt up, and wrapped his elbow around the guy's neck, pushing him in the same direction that he had already pulled and throwing him to the ground in one motion. He held the filet knife to the guy's throat. "Drop it!" He motioned to the cleaver.

The guy did, shuddering. Alesio rapped his temple with the hilt of the knife, and he collapsed.

He hadn't done so many flips and throws in a while. He could do so much more when he didn't fear a sudden sound knife slicing at him that hadn't existed before. More, but at the same time, less. Less possibility of killing someone on accident.

A yelp. He looked up. Two Palates remained, and one of them had just kicked Saida, who tumbled across the ground.

"Hey, sickos!" He fueled the shout with a tiny bit of air. "You see this?" He gestured at the moaning field of people around him in various stages of unconsciousness or injury. Their eyes widened, and he stepped closer. "You better run and take them with you, or I'll kill you all!"

They hesitated, swiveling back and forth from him to the curled-up Saida on the ground. He reinforced his stated plan by striding closer.

They gathered up their wounded and disappeared north, the shadows of their cloaks like ghosts in the swelling darkness.

Alesio ran over to Saida.

What if they broke her ribs with that kick?

"Saida!" He hovered his hands over her prone body. Just a few days ago she'd hissed at him for getting too close. But this was an emergency. He brushed her shoulder with his fingers. "Saida, I need you to—"

She shuddered and growled deep in her throat. He backed off and she rolled onto her side, panting. She didn't look wounded except for the bloody tip of her ear. Just an anxious wreck.

"They're gone, Saida. Let me help you."

Her eyes darted all around. He didn't know what to do, except the one thing that seemed to calm her. His voice.

He hadn't brought his mandolin to this world, but he didn't need it to sing.

I have heard the echo
Of a billion phantom stars,
A silhouette of harmony
Far away, a world apart

The sun slipped below the horizon. The stars above seemed different, and bigger, and *closer*. The wind stilled, and in that surreal moment, he tasted what perhaps was the night, the dark blue expanse above them, and the hypnotic twinkling of stars scattered like salt, mirroring the flats. He tasted something like discovery, fresh breath, and a cool mint flavor that fizzed on his tongue. Something bigger than any stomping, bloodthirsty crowd. And he was that little boy again, in awe of what he sensed but couldn't quite understand. He wondered if whoever had written the lyrics had known about the phantom stars from other worlds or knew about the foxans.

His voice trailed off into the night, and the wind picked up again, biting, and merciless without the sunlight to warm it. Saida inched closer to him, near enough to hold hands. Alesio's breath caught.

She breathed in and out full without any issues. No broken ribs, then. She wiped at her bloody ear, wrapping it in a cloth she pulled out of her pocket, then wavered to her feet. "I have till sunrise before I can teleport us. Let's get back to the city, or close to it, just in case they try and attack us with more Palates."

She looked back at him, then, with a kind of emotional half-shift in her face, half sweetly curious, half desperate fear, and in that moment, he knew both sides of her considered the possibility of him.

He hadn't seriously considered a relationship before. Singing had always been his first love. But now, he couldn't help but wonder how soft she would feel if he wrapped his arms around her, and how her lips might taste.

15

A PALE DRAUGHT

Watthe lurked in the shadows of the cathedral, on the sides of the pews, watching the service unfold. The people stared up at the new statue of Sound. Instead of a gold sheet rippling upwards to the ceiling like many small waves, a representation of him towered there, twenty feet high. The reverend had had the statue installed the day before.

Watthe stared at it, too, frowning. He had not asked for a statue of himself, but he did wonder what he could see from such a height.

"This is a vision." Lasrial swept his long robes in a dramatic fashion. "One that I've had of the Sound. He has spoken to me, and he says this is what he looks like. Do you hear me, worshippers?"

"We hear you," they chanted back, hanging on to the tradition they knew, to anything familiar in the suddenness of the new statue looming over them. They hunched in the pews as if frozen. The security man seemed to have the same condition, staring at the front like a rabbit in the eye of a hawk.

What would happen if he stepped out of the shadows, out into the open? Would all the people stare at him in the same way they did now at the statue, with such open fear, yet also adoration?

You like this too much, The Hunger said in Watthe's mind. *It is I who should be shown with such majesty.*

Humans are stupid, Watthe thought back, trying to soothe The Hunger. *They do not what to know fear. I am a messenger just. Your will is I follow.*

And yet, you have consumed more than I told you to, more of the Sensory worlds' magic, and you have made followers from these husks. You are not pure Primal Magic, anymore.

Watthe shifted in the shadows. *I intended not.*

The performer that had agreed to play today did not have the same level of magic as that human that had teleported with the foxan. They sang with a high-pitched, off-key sound. The people in the pews hunched down further, but they did not try to leave, perhaps because the human from the other side of town also stood on stage. Clef.

After the performance, the people hurried out as if pushed by a strong current. When the last of them had gone, Watthe stepped out into the light, striding over to his likeness, carved in gray stone. He'd grown, of course, with the magic he'd consumed as of late. But he stood just half as tall as the statue. The reverend had to have planned such a structure for several weeks, ever since Watthe had first appeared to him.

What would the foxan think if she saw him so tall? Would she be as enamored as these people?

Lasrial and Clef both came over to him, the reverend bowing low.

"Why do me worship, human?" Watthe asked. "This . . . giant statue is not what I've asked you of."

The reverend kept his head bent. He licked his lips. "You are my guide," he said. "Is it so wrong to have devotion to that which I see, to something with a face and arms? I want to share that devotion with my parishioners. I want to show you to them as the Sound, personified." He steepled his fingers. "They are not ready, of course, to know the real truth, that you are much more than just the Sound."

Watthe cocked his head. "You humans. Always someone to 'guide' you wanting. That which you do not understand adoring. It does not sense make."

One of the last parishioners moved towards the door, an older man with a cane. An urge overcame him, a strong hunger. He speared the man through the chest on his claws, draining his small magic within a few seconds, then filling him up with some of his essence.

The man slumped, then his skin and eyes grayed. Watthe could look through his eyes, now, if he chose to.

Lasrial and Clef stared at him, and Clef's eyes shone with that gleam of polished gray, the same gray as Watthe's body, and now this man's.

The Hunger tsked in his head. *Acting without my orders again. The human's magic is corrupting you! I desire pure, unmixed magic, foxan magic when I arrive!*

Watthe had no excuses. He'd desired the human's essence and had acted on it. The last part, however, did make him pause.

Why say you, 'when I arrive?' Are you not here already?

The Hunger did not answer.

The pendulum swung back and forth between that hollowness of smoke and the satisfaction of nothing, to the newness of his skin and the coolness of the marble of the floor underfoot.

Before the foxan had teleported away from Sound, he'd tasted some of her magic. It had fueled him and given him strength beyond anything he'd eaten. The human's essence had been a pale draught in comparison. Yet, the human had become a part of him and had stopped existing.

He didn't want her to stop existing. He didn't want her magic to disappear. Maybe he wouldn't need to drain her all at once, not consume her, but just sip at her strength. Savor it. She'd looked at him with fear, too, but what if he convinced her to gaze at him like this Lasrial did? Could he do that without eating her?

What would be the point? The Hunger growled in his mind.

To have constant power source. Then I would not fear weak. Or alone. These husks, they do bidding my, but they are extensions of me just.

You need fear nothing. You have me, and you need only concern yourself with my commands!

Clef stood unbending before him. "My contacts have not found the fur-mix in Anthem. I have them out in the country, but she's not back in Sound, so far as we know."

Watthe slammed his fist against the statue of himself. The gold reverberated, and Lasrial jumped. "Damn foxan slippery!"

Clef did not seem fazed by Watthe's outburst. He was Watthe's puppet, but he had a stronger will than most, and had seemed to regain some of his essence after Watthe had drained him of magic. "She is resourceful, I'll give her that. If you teleported us to more worlds, we could set up more searches."

"When we another transplant find," he said, "Then we will do."

They were hard to find, though, and once he ate them, they only took him to where they were linked to from the world they originated from. He had no way of knowing if the transplant's original world was where she had decided to flee to.

When Watthe had first met Clef, it seemed like the human had grasped something that he'd waited for a long time. He'd immediately asked to journey to another world. Now that Watthe had consumed Clef's magic, he understood the human's ambitions. He wanted to control. He wanted to expand his reach.

You are wanting, The Hunger said. *This is good. I have made you so. But you must consume the proper things, or you will corrupt yourself, and in turn, corrupt my feast of the Primal Plane.*

Watthe could not control his answering thought, and he wished his mind did not link to The Hunger all the time. *Does that mean, consume me you wish as well?*

Of course not, The Hunger said.

Clef gave a smooth smile. "There are some fur-mixes hiding in town. I know where a few are. If they can sense magic as you say, they could hunt the transplants for you."

"Why did you not say in the first?" Watthe spread his smile across his head. With this, he could find her sooner. Her magic was so potent, so *powerful.* With it to power him, he could do anything. If she were to look at him with adoration, he could do anything.

"You mean, if you *kill* her, you'd be able to do anything," The Hunger said out loud.

Lasrial hunched at the entity's voice, resonant through the whole cathedral.

"Of course." Watthe strode towards the main door. "Come, Clef. We hunt down these transplants."

"It's still morning, though," Lasrial said behind him. "The other humans aren't ready to see you in the daylight."

"Do not your 'guide,' question, reverend." He and Clef strode out of the cathedral, and Watthe reveled in the peoples' screams and in the glow of the daylight.

16

BIGGER, BRIGHTER PLACES

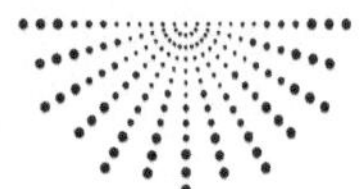

Saida hadn't slept much. She checked on the transplant, that page of half-melted salt she'd slipped in her pocket. Some of the salt had rubbed off during the fight, but the rest of them remained intact.

"I'm sorry," she whispered. "I promise I'll help you find a good home."

They sparkled in the morning light. She tucked them back away and stretched the kinks out of her back as she laid there. The blood on her ear had congealed overnight, she had some bruises from the kicks, and the taste of the slowing ixor lingered in the back of her throat. She still felt a bit slower than normal, but all she could think about was how hands could either grasp or hold, and what the difference was between them. How Alesio had stopped reaching for her when she had tensed and flattened her ears, and how he'd extended his voice instead.

He slept there, splayed on the salt flats, another rag she had given him as a partial pillow. Even in his sleep he breathed light. Controlled. What would it be like to sleep beside another person? To fully trust them, and for them to fully trust her?

"Sounds tricky," Tricksy Stone said.

"I think it sounds lovely," Goosefeather said. "She trusts *us*. Why not him?"

What am I thinking? She shook her head and yawned.

He stirred behind her. "Ah," he mumbled. "Your morning breath is, um. Potent."

She threw him a grin over her shoulder and hopped to her feet. "You ready to head back?"

He levered himself up to a sitting position, rubbing the sleep from his eyes, smacking his lips. "Water. Water, please."

She handed him her remaining container. He tipped it up and dribbled the rest into his mouth. "Ready."

Saida closed her eyes, the Taste magic of the portals returning to her tongue. She asked the nearest one to open the way to Between. It skittered up through the cracks of the ground, and she pointed the area out to Alesio. He hurried to the spot.

She leapt upwards and pounced as a foxan, and the ground parted before them.

They landed in the desert area of Between, streaming up through the sand like large fish breaching water. The vague brightness shone through the dawn fog, and Saida led the way to the forest for some shade and water from the creek. Alesio dunked his head in the cool water and guzzled for a long time.

"Oh," she said, when he came back up. "You drank half the creek!"

"What?" He blinked away water. "No, I didn't—hey!"

She giggled and took out the salt transplant from her pocket so it wouldn't get wet. She jumped in the water as her foxan self, saturating her fur and rolling around on her favorite grooved rock to wash the remaining salt away. She stood up, panting and grinning, padded towards Alesio, and shook water all over him.

"You are a menace." He brushed the water off his pretty, muscled arms. His water-spattered light blue shirt clung to him, contrasting with his dark brown skin. She missed hearing the silver-toned magic from his lips.

"Nice not to taste everything, huh?" She grabbed the transplant and trotted to the path that would lead to her den.

"By the Sound, yes." He yawned behind her. "Where does the water come from, anyway?"

She looked back over her shoulder. "The creek water?"

"The lake, the creek. Where does it come from? How does it stay clean?" He paused. "And how do all the foxans eat, when there's not a lot of land to live off of?"

Saida wound around the thorn bushes, then ducked into the entrance to the tunnel, giving herself time to ponder Alesio's question. "The water starts in a spring in the hills. As for our food, well. There are just three foxans besides me left, and they don't shift or teleport, so they don't need much food. So, the birds and the mice are enough for them."

She bounded into her den. "I'm home!"

"That didn't take very long," Rosewater said in their tube on the wall.

"Me first! Me first!" Crinkle Leaf Pile shouted. Saida laughed, shifted to human, gathered them in her arms, and jumped on them. They crinkled in their satisfying way, and their magic kept her wet fur from getting all twiggy and dirty.

"We missed you," Jar of Sky said in their breathy voice, and she took them from their place on the wall and gazed through them, at the sky they displayed from Vision.

"Saida," Goosefeather said. "Your human seems a bit, well, disconcerted."

She glanced over her shoulder at Alesio. He stared at her in that odd way, that showed he didn't understand. His black eye had turned greenish-yellow and had opened a little. She placed Jar of Sky back on the shelf. "Hmmm. Maybe . . . oh! Alesio, jump in the leaves!"

He waved his hands. "It's okay, really. It's fine."

"Alesio. Try it." She grinned. "It's fun."

He lowered himself onto Crinkle Leaf Pile. They crunched for him, and despite his reluctance, a smile spread across his face. He rose, then jumped, landing again, and laughed.

"They never lose their crunch. That's their magic! Leaf Pile's from Touch."

He frowned, rolling off Leaf Pile, and jumped again, with the same result. His mouth gaped. "It *is* magic!"

"Told you," Saida said. "It's too bad you can't hear them, you know. They're a right bunch of owl hoots and no mistake."

"I'm from a goose, you take that right back," Goosefeather said.

Alesio looked around as if to trying to hear her various magics. She patted Goosefeather in her pocket. "Now, who's ready to meet the new transplant?"

The den clamored and eddied and crunched in unison. She pulled out the paper she'd pressed onto the salt rock, the crystals on it half-melted from the wetness. At their most potent, as if inside a mouth. They shimmered and shone and puckered along the creases from Saida's original folds in the paper, creating unique patterns in the salt. "Where am I?" they asked.

"You're in Between," she said. "The place between all the worlds. You wanted to leave Taste, right?"

"I was wanting something new." Their voice popped like they fizzed in water. "I was ready."

"What do you want to be called?"

"My name is Effervescent," they said. The transplants usually knew their name right away.

"I'll take you to your new world soon, okay? In a few days."

"A few days?" Crinkle Leaf Pile said. "But you just got here!"

"I know, I know." Saida laid Effer on the shelf next to Jar of Sky. "But Vision's in trouble. I need to bring them as many transplants as I can so their magic—and their humans—don't disappear."

"Thank you," Tricksy Stone whispered, and she patted them in her pocket.

HER ITEMS *WERE* MAGICAL. He hadn't expected that, though maybe he should have at this point.

"Saida, why did you teleport here, instead of to Vision right away? Wouldn't that have been faster?"

Her ears flickered. "Oh, maybe. But it's good to check in on my friends. They help me, or I can get lost out in the worlds. I can forget."

"Forget?"

"Drift around. Little things distract me. I spend a lot of time in one world and forget about the others." She licked her paw, still wet from the creek. Though she'd rolled around in the leaves, none of them stuck to her, or him, for that matter. More proof of magic. "I'm pretty sure one time I stayed in one world for a whole three years. Leaf Pile was not happy with me." Saida licked the inside of her elbow, shifting it to foxan so she could reach that part. "I had to work extra hard that next year to create transplants for all the worlds, because I hadn't done anything for so long."

"What about your mother and father? Or the other one, Pell? Weren't they worried about you?"

She shrugged. "They forget too, if I take too long, you know? Or sometimes even if I'm right in front of them. I have to remind them who I am sometimes. But my friends here never forget." She smiled at the wall lined with magical objects.

She's so sounddamned lonely.

He'd planned on asking her to take him back to Sound, hoping that she had forgotten about Watthe, that her absentminded nature would let her previous timetable slip away. He hadn't known how close to the truth he had gotten while missing everything about her.

If he left now, would she remember him in a month? A year?

Falrie sailed inside the 'den,' as Saida called it.

"Daughter—" She saw Alesio and jumped high in the air. "A human! Why have you brought . . . a human here?"

Alesio opened his mouth, then closed it. Saida slumped and sighed.

"I'm from Sound," Alesio said. "She helped me get away from— from a bad person. I promise I won't stay long."

Falrie huffed. "Bringing a human in! It's dangerous! We don't do that anymore. Too . . . dangerous. There is a . . . hunger. It wants to consume us." Her eyes glazed a bit, and her legs trembled.

Saida sniffed and wiped at her cheeks. "Mother, you should go and lie down. You seem tired today."

"I will . . . not! You have brought this . . . human here, and I cannot rest until . . . we are alone. Until we are safe."

Alesio slung his mandolin from off his back. "Do you like music?"

Falrie's eyes darted to him. Before she could spring away, he plucked a soft, soothing melody, a piece without lyrics he used at the Drinks De Capo to transition from a fast-paced song to a slow one.

"Music," Falrie said. "I haven't heard music in . . . a long time." Her ears flickered.

Alesio played a little more, just a trickling of notes. He played as he always had, with the intent to harness magic and sway the listener. But here in Between, without magic, and his left ear somehow harder of hearing, he still loved sound and the act of performing. The soreness in his throat had almost completely gone away by now.

Falrie had closed her eyes, and a slight smile lifted her foxan cheeks. He sang a little, then, a little tune out of a folk tale to help babies sleep.

> *Rock, sweet one, rock and keep*
> *Your ears turned down*
> *To fall asleep*
> *Dream, sweet one, dream and hear*
> *Your mother's hands*
> *That hold you dear*

"My mother always said that was one of St Rina's favorites." Falrie's eyes had cleared.

Alesio smiled back. Then the name clicked, and his fingers slipped on the mandolin strings.

"St.—St. Rina?"

"One of the first foxans. A Guide of Sound," Falrie said.

"A guide?" Saida asked. "What do you mean, a guide?"

Falrie looked back and forth between Saida and Alesio as if surprised at the simplicity of the question. "The Guides. Before the Severing, legend tells of the Primal Plane growing the first foxans from its ground, the Guides, though humans often misinterpreted them as gods. They established permanent portals and escorted the humans back and forth between the Sensory worlds." She shook her head. "You should know this, Saida. Haven't I told you before?"

"Tricksy Stone," Saida whispered. "Has she told me this before?"

Alesio flicked his gaze to Saida. She mouthed the word 'no' as if in response to her own question.

Falrie shivered. Her eyes glazed back over. "Strange. There was . . . something I just said. What was it?"

Saida patted her mother's smaller foxan head. "You—you were going to go lie down. You said you were tired."

"Oh." Falrie sighed. "Maybe I am, a little." She narrowed her eyes at Alesio. "But don't forget. Take that human back . . . as soon as you can."

"Yes, Mother. I will."

Falrie exited the den, and Alesio swallowed a lump in his throat. He and Saida were quiet for a bit, waiting till the sound of her footpads against the dirt had faded. Saida had slumped over, watching where her mother had left.

He should return to Sound. His father waited for him, and the cage matches, since his chance at the Cadenza had been so thoroughly knifed. His father had a couple months' left of money boarding at Mona's pub. He'd like to talk to Tak again, try to smooth over and salvage the friendship. And traveling with Saida had its dangers. Cannibals! He shuddered.

But there were so many different starscapes that he had never seen, so many other magics he had never dreamed of. He could sing even without magic, and still, others seemed happy and even excited to listen. It seemed, outside of Sound, he could do more than just survive.

He chuckled, then, and Saida looked over at him, startled.

"St. Rina was a foxan!" He slapped his knee. "Can you imagine Lasrial's face if he knew?"

Saida snorted. Then they both laughed, and laughed, and Alesio wondered if the magical items laughed with them.

A day and a half had passed since he'd left Sound. His father rested at the Drinks De Capo with plenty of money. Alesio could stay with Saida a little while longer, to indulge the part of him that had always dreamed of brighter, shinier places.

"You know, experiencing another world sounds exciting. I'm ready to go with you again, whenever you like." He paused. "If you want to be my guide."

Saida raised her eyes up to him, her eyelashes shining with unshed tears. "I'd like that."

ALESIO SEEMED to settle into a new routine the next few days while they rested on Between. He swam in the lake in the mornings, traversed the whole space three times, slept for a while in the afternoon, then sang for the foxans in the evenings. They gathered around him, first Pell, then Saida's father, Darrow, slinking closer and closer. Falrie listened from a distance, though she continued to remind Saida to teleport Alesio back to his world as soon as possible.

She wished they could hear the magic of his voice, the true silver tenor as she had heard it on Sound, but of course they would not leave Between. Not yet at least.

On the morning of the third day, she blindfolded him and led him out to the forest a little way, before teleporting to Vision. She hadn't even had to ask Tricksy Stone what day it was, or how long she had been there. With him, she'd noticed each moment instead of drifting through them.

He'd seemed to enjoy Taste—besides the Palates, of course—and visiting somewhere new. She could understand that. She couldn't imagine having lived on just one world for her whole existence. She'd left Between the first time when she was in her 80's, or about eight years old in human time frame, then again when she turned 100, and hadn't stopped since. She would've compressed all her distractions inside herself, and she would've exploded into hundreds of Saida-bits.

So, she wanted to show off a little.

She untied his blindfold. His eyes widened—his black eye now mostly healed—and his mouth hung open, and he let out a little stream of breath like a heated teapot. A whistle. It sounded wistful, as if he had just found something he'd sought for a long, long time, and he had to release the breath in his lungs to breathe in the air of the new place.

They'd teleported at dawn. The portal had taken much longer to deposit them this time, fifty-five seconds, and she struggled to hold her breath in the limbo of the portal. Had Vision drifted too far for to reach?

Then they'd stumbled out of a tree, and the light of the purple sunrise threaded through the prairie grass countryside like a crosshatched painting, shining on some plots of land, and not others. The grass itself grew in patches, some on the ground, some as if on an invisible hill, or sideways on a non-existent building.

In many places, the trees grew upright with no strangeness, and the grass stayed on the ground. More and more of Vision had lost its chaotic beauty, becoming normal instead. Neutral.

Alesio, of course, didn't know what he missed. He stared around him at the strangeness that did exist, at the grass growing sideways.

She smiled. "Here, gravity can change. If your body moves somewhere that doesn't seem possible, just go with it. That's how things work around here."

"Gravity . . . changes?" He brushed his hand against a nearby piece of grass, growing sideways.

"Watch." She held her hands wide, striding towards that piece of grass. Her feet seemed to attract to the air, and she paced on a vertical line by Alesio's gaping face. The end of her braid tickled his cheek, and she grinned. "Now, to get back down, just walk the way you came. Or find a new path." She strode upward, into the sky, and after about ten steps, gravity shifted again, this time on a slight diagonal towards what Alesio considered the ground. "There isn't always a way to go where you want, though. So be careful." She rambled back over to him. "You okay there, Mr. Singer?"

"That's—that's—"

"It's another world, so it's got different rules." She patted him on the shoulder, where the short sleeves of his blue shirt ended. His chocolate brown pupils seemed to swirl in the magic of Vision, as if she could fall into the gravity of his eyes.

I just touched him!

Her hand heated up along with her cheeks. She backed a few feet away and cleared her throat. "Just follow me, and you'll be fine. We need to find where the transplant wants to go."

She roved along to the west, holding Effer out like a flag. They rippled in the slight breeze, absorbing the sights with much the same fascination as Alesio. "Feeling a pull anywhere?" She asked them after a few minutes.

"There're so many different things!" They crinkled a little. "So many trees! And birds! And grass!"

"You're used to the salt and the sky. There's a lot to like about Vision." She pointed towards one of the trees nearby, where the branches folded in confusing angles. "Look at that! Lots of different areas to wrap around!"

"No, no," Effer said. "I want a flat surface. Somewhere I can spread out."

Saida tapped her finger against her lips. "Okay, okay. Let me think." Flat places meant human-made things. She did not want to go back to the village, so that meant finding a ruin. She wandered about, trying to stick Effer on nearby changes of gravity, without success.

She led Alesio—who kept pointing at random things and saying "Whoa!"—up into the sky on a higher gravity shift where they could survey the nearby possibilities.

Far to the north, a tan line wove through a pink-pastel grassy field. The road to the village. Saida pointed south to another set of ruins she'd never visited before. "There! That'll have some flat surfaces."

They roamed towards it at a semi-quick pace.

"You're so focused," Tricksy Stone said. "You haven't gone quiet and stared for a day and a half at a patch of mushrooms. Or even forgotten what mushrooms were and asked me."

"Quiet, you'll distract her," Goosefeather said.

Saida shook her head. They'd traveled for a good long while, and Alesio had been quiet.

"What do you think?" She asked him.

"Everything is so different." He echoed Effervescent as if he had heard them speak. He swept his arm to indicate the tree growing overhead. "That tree bends upwards, but then some branches twist backwards, then sideways, and then that branch meets back up with the beginning of the trunk somehow . . . that's impossible."

"A different world means what's possible is different," Saida said.

His voice lowered almost to a mumble, as if he spoke to himself. "Just a few days ago, an old man I worked with seemed strange. He's from the piper side, but he's a good man. He wanted to work even when he didn't have to. I thought that was strange. Now this."

Saida tried laying Effer against a flat-ish rock. They flapped in protest. "Changing what you look at can do that."

He didn't respond. They rambled on until about mid-morning, and they reached the ruins. A shiver ran down Saida's spine. She had fallen into that other, twisted place, the place that Falrie had called The Primal Plane, while exploring one of these ancient cities on Vision.

She strode forward through the fear, up the crumbling old road slanting left, then right, a little off the ground. A large gear hovered at the entrance, rusted, and threaded with ivy.

"What's *that*?" Alesio asked.

"If the magic worked here, I could use the gear to change the direction of this road." Saida peered into the recesses of the tumbled down buildings. "It's probably supposed to move there." She pointed at the side of one of them, where the stonework of the road continued as if a giant had painted stones and veered off.

"But—but that's not where the gravity would go."

"That's the magic of Vision. It would've changed, too." Saida hopped over a hole in the road, pointing it out to him so he didn't fall as he swiveled his neck around like a weathervane. "Watch out."

He stepped over it, his larger stride spanning the distance with ease.

"How about here, Effer?" Saida laid them against the building they passed.

"I think, actually, I want a corner." Effer folded up a little along their original creases.

Saida lifted the transplant back up, sighing. "A corner? Okay, okay." She bit her lip, considering. "Well, there's lots of corners around here, so I'm sure we'll find something you'll like."

They meandered for a time, every so often trying another surface for the transplant. A few birds called overhead, flying along in strange paths, north, then upwards, then south, then west. The wind had stilled.

"It's so quiet, here," Alesio said. "You said that Sound has these ruins, too?"

"Well, yes. They don't look like this, of course, and the gravity is normal there. But yes."

"Will the. . ." he struggled to string his words together as he gazed at everything. "Will the magic on Sound start to leave, too?

They strolled on the side of the building now, maneuvering around crumbled bits of plaster and brick where the wall had begun to give way. She brushed her hand over a rusted windowsill. Not a good place for Effer. Too many grooves and little bumps of rotten wood along the surface. "I don't know. Maybe. Vision's magic used to work better. In some of these old ruins, the gravity might have jammed while pointing up, so you have to be careful you don't fall into the sky. It's not supposed to do that, but it's happened to me a few times the last few years. And one time, I fell, far, far down, without a road or a path to hold me."

"Where you found that—that monster."

"Actually," Effer said, "I think I want to try to wave in the wind, like a flag on a pole."

Saida brushed the stray hairs from her braid out of her face. Sweat trickled down her neck. "I need to sit for a minute." She plopped on the road spanning the gap between the sides of two buildings like a bridge. "Just . . . hold on, Effer."

He half-crouched beside her, like he still couldn't believe that he wouldn't fall. The sky stretched to their right and the ground to their left.

"Are you okay?" Alesio asked.

"Just . . . need to catch my breath."

He crouched a foot away. Too close, but also, somehow not close enough. The blueness of his shirt seemed bluer, here, a shade she hadn't known before. Her face warmed, and she wanted to inch her hand closer to his.

Fear has paralyzed us all, the fox-person from Sound's voice echoed in her mind. *You escape by moving a little at a time.*

"Saida, you seem anxious. Is it about that creature, Watthe?"

Watthe did induce panic, but the true monster was her traitorous heart beating in time with the rhythm of Alesio's silver-tenor voice, that sound that enticed her to inch closer. The sound of her name on his lips! She wished he would say it again.

He considered her a moment. Then he hummed the short melody to Gossamer God's chorus, as he had done back on Taste.

His singing voice draped over her like a warm blanket. Her pounding heart slowed and the prickling of her skin smoothed.

It's strange how the same thing can make me feel so safe, and so terrified, at the same time.

He stopped humming. After a few moments of silence, he spoke in a slow, steady voice. "You know, performing at the Cadenza was the biggest, most impressive feat I could imagine. When I was fired, though, I saw that I could never achieve something like that. I'm from the straits. I'm not fit for gold-lined walls and audiences that wear silk." He seemed about to say something else but stopped himself.

A swirl of dust roamed through the various gravities nearby, drifting like it couldn't figure out where it wanted to rest.

"I can understand not feeling like I belong," Saida said. "And like I'm not worth anything. People have shouted those things at me my whole life. But I don't believe those words, you know, what other people say, or my own head. Cause if I did, I would feel so bad all the time." Before she could overthink it, she drew Goosefeather out of her pocket. "Here. Hold them for a moment. They help me."

He didn't reach too fast towards her. He twirled Goosefeather between two fingers.

Panic swirled inside her that she didn't have her best friend in her possession, safe in her pocket, but she knew he would not harm them.

"Your voice is a gift," she said. "Your magic is what drew me to you in the first place. Whether you perform at a fancy music place or not, that doesn't change what you can do. What you were made to do." She hesitated. "Though, and I know I've said this, but the magic around you is so—so potent, so strong on Sound, that it hurts your throat. When you held your breath, sometimes I could tell you were also holding it back."

He smoothed a ruffled part of Goosefeather with his fingers.

"I'm not asking to trim your magic. I told you I wouldn't, and I mean that."

"That will make things more difficult," Tricksy Stone said. "For both of you."

I can find other overgrowths. I'm finding them faster and faster, with him around. Like you said.

Alesio smiled at her. "I trust you."

She scooted a tiny bit closer. He stilled in that way that meant he held his breath, where his whole body seemed controlled, every blink on purpose. He had his hand open beside her, palm up, Goosefeather held between two fingers and laying across it.

"I want to help you," he said. "I don't quite understand it, yet, but I don't want my world to lose its magic. I don't want people in Sound to die. My whole life, I've helped keep myself and my father alive. This is just a bigger way of doing that. Surviving, on a world scale." He paused. "What I was trying to say earlier is, the Cadenza seems . . . small to me, now, compared to all this. I want to help however I can. If you can trim my magic, and use it to help bring this world back, I want to do it."

Saida's vision swam, and blurred, and her throat closed like she'd inhaled some slowing ixor. She slipped her hand in Alesio's, on top of Goosefeather, letting it settle there like a bird in a nest. He did not move his palm or change position.

Effer rippled in the slight breeze and blew to the next building over, sticking to a cleaner part of the road. "Here," they said, before Saida could rise to chase them. "I choose here."

"Oh!" Saida didn't move from her place next to Alesio. "Why did you pick there?"

"I think I was just nervous," Effer said. "I just needed to get used to the new world. These angles. When the magic comes back, this road will revolve and face the sky. I like that."

"I'm happy for you." Saida smiled at Alesio. "That's wonderful."

17

AN AUDIENCE OF ONE

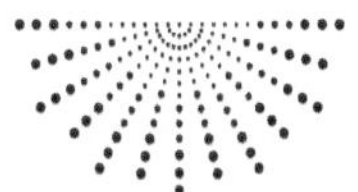

"I have a surprise for you."

Saida scampered up to him, her half-shifted braid-tail swinging against her calves. He could almost smell the mischievousness on her breath. And something else, something intoxicating, that same smell he'd noticed on Sound. On Scent, it made his head swim.

"Are you going to blindfold me? Or, no, wait. I guess you'd have to cover my nose?"

"You'll know when you see it." She skipped down the next hill on two legs. They traipsed through a forest, skirting a large mountain to their north. Smells wafted through the breeze so strong, so thick, it felt like he could touch them.

After Effervescent, that paper with the Taste magic, had transplanted, they'd teleported back to her den. They'd spent two more days for Saida to recharge her portal abilities and to spend a little time with Falrie, Darrow, and Pell, then had traveled to Scent today, hunting the next overgrowth.

She led him towards a bubbling stream that smelled chilly. "C'mon, get in!" She jumped.

He stepped back. "Is part of the surprise me freezing to death?"

"Aw, maybe! Please?" The fur on her now foxan form stuck up in little wet spikes. "It's s-s-super warm."

"You're not doing a great job of selling that. You sound like a bad corner singer."

She splashed him. He wiped the frigid water from his face and stepped towards the river, lowering his hands to the water. She swam farther away. He dipped his hands in, holding his breath, and dunked his head in, swimming towards her underwater. When he surfaced, he splashed her in a sneak attack.

"No fair!" She laughed and paddled away. "I wasn't ready!"

"That's the point!" He settled in the water. Oof. He *did* smell. He scrubbed himself and the feminine clothes she had given him. One of the sleeves had torn during his fight with the Palates, and parts of the trousers felt more stretched than they'd been before.

The fresh water smelled of moss and stones and the silt flowing along the bottom. Saida gave him some leaves to dry off with. Magic seemed to work a little different here than on Taste; the smell of something didn't seem at its strongest when he touched it, but instead a little away from it, like a cloud that wafted above the thing.

Saida steered him away from a bush with yellow ivy growing all over it. "That'll make you throw up. And if you don't throw up in time, it'll hurt like bee stings on the inside."

"Okay, yep. Let's go." He hurried away from it. "Where's the overgrown magic you're sensing? Do you know what it is, yet?"

She shook her head. "I found one a little bit ago, right before I met you." She glanced up at the mountain. "It was a big animal's yawn. But I would've had to get it while it was hibernating, and it's early spring now. I'll have to wait till next winter to trim that one." They crested another hill, and a village nestled down in the crux of the mountain and three knolls surrounding it. "The other overgrowth is down there." She flicked her ears halfway back. "Of course."

Her jaw clenched. He had growing suspicions about why she hated cities and humans, but he didn't want to press her.

He wanted to help her and help the magic of the worlds. He still wanted to check on his father, and Tak, but now more than that, he wanted to make sure that the world they lived in was safe. If he truly believed her about how the magic everywhere was fading—and he'd seen the evidence himself—then he couldn't just stand by and let that happen.

Besides, he didn't know if he wanted to rush back to Sound any more, to drop himself back into Clef's net, back into the grittiness of the straits, back into the everlasting tug-of-war that pulled him from one end of the town to the other.

"How many transplants do you usually find?" He asked, to distract her and himself. "Seems like we've found one after the other."

Saida cocked her head and patted her pocket. "I know, I know," she murmured.

She was talking to one of her 'friends,' those two magic items she always kept on her. She smiled at him. "I can't usually do it this fast. I think you help me concentrate." She roved on down the hill towards the village, and he followed. She trailed a scent, herself, something that reminded him of open skies, and fresh cut grass, and the mint of starlight over a field. It drew him after her like a perfume. "I was doing one a year for each world. So, five per year." She heaved a sigh. "But with Vision having this problem, I decided to try for one from each world all at once to really anchor it."

"What would happen if you weren't there to—to trim them, though?" Alesio frowned.

She paused. "Well, sometimes overgrowths can turn rotten, like stagnant water growing algae." She hopped over a stone, sailing through the air near the pink buds of a nearby tree. "One time, I found a network of mushrooms on Touch that had grown a powerful magic, and they were so frustrated by wanting to go somewhere else, they almost grew right over me! They were asking me to trim them, but they almost buried me alive, you know?" She stopped spinning. "Come and dance in this!"

Would that happen to me if she couldn't trim my magic? She said that she tried before, and it didn't work.

He hid his disquiet. "Is this part of the surprise?" He spun with her near the tree, in the magic he couldn't see. It didn't smell too strong. "Saida, I think this one's broken. Is it . . . dying?"

She shook her head and tugged on the edge of his sleeve with a human hand. She smelled of a subtle floral, now, and her other scents had softened, too. "Let's go."

She had less hesitation with every touch. At the same time, this served to confirm his suspicions over what had frightened her so much about humans in the first place. Some human had hurt her somehow, very badly.

He hoped that people couldn't smell anger here. He didn't want to scare her.

They reached the village outskirts, and Saida had shifted to her full human form. She folded her ears down and covered her head with a cloth. A few people working the fields shaded their eyes, watching them as they came closer.

"Hello." Saida bowed to the first two, an old woman and a young boy. They wore simple homespun clothes, and their faces were clean even though they worked in the dirt. "We are wandering entertainers, and we would love to perform for the village tonight!"

Alesio started, staring at Saida. She grinned at him.

The young boy jumped up and down. "A show? Really? Really?"

The grandmother pursed her lips, scanning them up and down. "Well," she said, her voice rough, "Smells like you're decent enough folk. Most countryfolk don't have any sense of what clean is." She lifted her pitchfork and pointed at the village. "Check in with Mother Rean."

They did so, and Mother Rean said she would love such clean and nice folk to perform for her village, though she did wrinkle her nose and mutter something about "pheromones." Cleanliness seemed to mean a great deal to these people.

Oh. Saida must have had them wash in the stream and spin around in that muted flower scent so the village would accept them. The people in the city all wore the same simplistic clothing, and they smelled of neutral things like clean linen or nothing at all.

It's like why people wear earplugs in Sound. On the piper side, at least. If he wore unwashed clothes it would be like slapping those around him in the face with sweaty socks.

They strode down a dirt street. Someone had raked it so that the lines still showed. Saida had her shoulders back and a smile on her face, but her eyes darted around like skittish fish.

"Saida, this is a wonderful surprise. I know how hard this must be for you, to be here."

She smiled at him, though she watched the people on the other side of the street. "Well, it's a little selfish for me, too. You're going to be my distraction. Someone here has the overgrowth on them." She wrinkled her nose, sniffing the air. "They're not producing it from themselves, like you do, but they're wearing it. While you're singing, I'm going to snag it." She licked her lips. "And. Well. I wanted to hear you sing again.'

A heat rose from his neck all the way to his cheeks. Several answers sprang to his lips:

"I gave that up."

"I promised I wouldn't sing anymore."

"I'm better at fighting."

But he had already sung for her back on the other world. And he knew, now. He'd never give up performing. He never could.

THAT NIGHT, the people of the village gathered under the light of several small fires, flickering like giant fireflies. The smoke emanated the scent of pine, fresh like a flute in a musical composition, and another wood smell that reminded him of a distinct bass line. They all waited for him to step onto the little raised part of the well that they had decided to use as a stage.

"What if I'm not any good at performing without magic, Saida?"

"What did I say to do when your head tells you terrible things?"

"Don't listen." He needed to control his air, or it would come out strained and pitchy. He felt like some newbie on the stage for the first time.

"That's right. Don't listen." She smiled at him; her shoulders hunched.

A man in the throng brushed past her, patting her shoulder as he did. She flinched. She breathed a little too fast, too shallow, and beads of sweat stood out on her reddish-brown skin, emanating an acrid scent. She feared close crowds more than anything, it seemed, and here she was trying to help *him*.

"Hey." The words streamed out before he could hold them back. "What happened to you? You seem scared of hands. I know someone hurt you." Her eyes darted to his, and the fear in them made his gut clench. "Saida. Who hurt you?"

"A human," she whispered. "His name was Carn."

Carn.

"Listen, Alesio. Your magic is strong. Your voice is strong. I think what happened to you—was—" Her breath hitched, and she tried to cover her mouth, but he saw it tremble. "No, Tricksy. I don't need to leave. I can stay. I can stay. Alesio, you had to listen so hard with just one ear all your life, that you made up for it tenfold."

"Saida—"

"You appreciate what you have, since you don't have much. You spin silver out of sawdust; you hear the song of Sound and translate it to your lips." She stared at him, at the lips she had mentioned, then the ashen tone of her face paled even more. "They're waiting."

She slipped away to the outside of the crowd. Out of his reach.

The crowd chattered louder. Alesio shoved his wrath down, forced a smile on his face, and spread his hands. He hopped up onto the little lip of the well, holding his mandolin with his fingers hovering over the strings.

"Welcome, one and all! We will be doing a few performances tonight. Who's ready for some song and dance?"

Cheering and clapping. Some of the children jumped up and down. The woodsmoke flared up as the citizens stoked the flames, per his request. Ambiance would help when his magic wouldn't. He started with a simple hum to warm up his voice, and to free his mind. The crowd quieted, and he began with "My Flute, My Love," fueling the vibrato needed for the chorus with the shaking in his hands, with the emotion of performing again, and the rage at the detail she had just told him.

Carn.

People cried in the front row. He spotted Saida in the back a few times, weaving through the audience. Searching for the overgrowth.

HE KNEW.

How did he know? She'd never told anyone except for Tricksy. "Did you tell him?" She hissed, fading to the back of the crowd.

"You know I don't talk to anyone besides you," Tricksy Stone said. "And I would never tell anyone, anyway! Maybe he's a mind reader!"

Saida slipped past a swaying human with their eyes closed. On the stage, Alesio poured out his dulcet voice like a misting summer rain, warm and light, yet hazy with questions, as if he wanted her to swirl and meet his eyes.

She didn't. She slipped around a few more humans and hunted the smell. With their eyes closed during this slower song, she could get close to them and sniff out where that savory, nutty scent originated from. Overgrowths weren't always powerful in the traditional sense. Sometimes the strongest magic stemmed from something small and overlooked.

Or hidden.

There. That lady! It came from the sleeves of her dress. Saida skulked over to her in the shadows of the swaying crowd.

ALESIO LIVENED things up with a quick tempo number, with lighthearted lyrics that talked of the favor of a ghost who blessed the silliest of their descendants. The crowd laughed.

They laughed!

He sang without fear of violence, he sang for the sheer joy of molding the sound through his lips into hovering silver bells, trembling and shimmering with a shivering delight. And the people below him closed their eyes, and their nostrils flared, and tears wet their faces. If his father could hear him now! Free of the straits, of cage matches and violence, free of drudgery at the factory, free to do what he was made to do!

Saida had given him this.

Saida, who found magic in the simplest of things. Saida, who whispered to the feather of a goose or to an interesting stone. Saida, with those tears in her eyes, glimmering like the salt-wilds at sun high, trying to reassure him while she had trembled and shook from fear from the touch of a man's hand.

He wanted to rip this Carn apart.

He searched for Saida again in the crowd, trying to reach her with his voice. She had disappeared. He wanted to sing for her, an audience of one.

She'd spoken to that magic rock. *"No, Tricksy. I don't need to leave. I can stay. I can stay."*

She'd had a choice to leave? Couldn't she teleport just once a day?

Then it clicked.

The magic items she carries must also work as emergency portals!

SAIDA FOUND her on the edge of the crowd, clapping along with the music. The woman hovered in the limbo of transition out of the body of a man. A yellow green stained the embroidery of her right sleeve, and a nutty, warm scent emitted from it.

I've smelled that somewhere before. Where?

She tried to sneak closer, but the woman turned towards her and waved. Had something given her away?

"You." The woman brushed her hand against her mouth to hide a smile. In foxan years, she might have been Saida's younger sister. "You're the one who came with that man up there. You like him?"

"What? No!"

A few other people nearby gave her startled glances at her exclamation. Saida swiveled to block their view of her face. "Why would you say that?"

"Your pheromones." The woman stopped smiling and held her stained sleeve up to her face as if to hide a smile. "I'm sorry. It's hard to control what you feel, isn't it?"

"Pheromones." Saida frowned. "You mean I'm still creating a scent? I tried to clean myself before I came to the village. Though, I know *he* still smells." She nodded at Alesio. She'd had him bathe in the neutral flowers to mask that invigorating scent of the ground after a rain, that sweet musk of soil. She'd had to stop herself from shoving her nose in his chest and breathing deep.

"How do you not know this? Have you never lived in a village?"

"Um, well, no, I've lived alone, mostly."

The woman's mouth opened in an 'o' and she paused too long. Saida shifted under her compassionate gaze.

"Well, here's how it is: when someone likes us, or when we like someone, everyone can smell it." The woman shrugged and folded her hands behind her back. "Makes some things easier, and other things more difficult."

She hoped Alesio couldn't smell it from her. And if he produced these pheromones, too, that meant . . .

Saida's cheeks heated up. Human skin was so frustrating, at times.

She maneuvered around to the woman's other side to smell her sleeves better, and to avoid the light from the nearby fire illuminating her sharp foxan chin. The nutty scent tantalized her again, and a memory flashed by.

She'd wandered for a few months in the wilds of Scent a few years ago. A crowd of humans had called her a dirty fur-mix and she hadn't stopped thinking about it. She'd laid under a tree, and it had had yellow green nuts on the ground around it that had smelled like this. The warm, savory smell had helped quiet the words those people had shouted at her.

"Oh." Saida decided her next words on impulse. "I can smell something on you, too. The crushed nut."

The woman pulled away from Saida and the nearby crowd, drawing into the shadows of the village. "Shh! We don't talk about the rala nut."

"Why not?"

The rala nut's magic reminded Saida of a barrier, though aimed inward instead of outward. It shielded the woman from thoughts of harming herself. The barrier worked so well it had overgrown, and now the magic wanted to help more people.

"Because it's—it's too strong," the woman said. "I shouldn't have to smell the rala nut to feel better. Why should I feel sad? Why should I hurt myself? There was no reason—"

"You've done well, though," Saida said. "Like you said, we can't always help how we feel. You must've pulled yourself through something terrible."

The woman stared at her.

"Look! He's doing another song!" Saida pointed at Alesio up in the front, clutching the tube in her other hand. The woman turned.

Saida swiped the tube through the Scent magic. She corked it and slid it back into her pocket, sneaking around another person on the audience's edge. Her gaze snagged on something clenched in another villager's hands as they swayed to the beat of the song.

A miniature statue of Watthe.

"Lady?" The woman poked her head, searching for Saida. Saida ducked and scurried away into the shadows.

"You've been a great audience! Now, everyone, hold your partner's hand," Alesio said. "Let's all take a few minutes and appreciate them. Look into their eyes. I've taught it to you, so you all know the words, now. Feel free to sing along." He began "My Flute, My Love" in a slower rhythm, a gentler pace.

When the crowd had paired up and their voices rose above his, their eyes all closed, he hopped off the lip of the well that had served as his stage.

He searched for Saida. He wanted to hold her, to comfort her. He didn't know if she would let him, but he wanted to at least try. Had she used one of her magic items to teleport in her terror, and left him alone?

He wouldn't have blamed her for doing so. People did what they had to, to survive.

A flash of red on the outside of the crowd. A red cloth-covered head. He maneuvered through the swaying, singing people towards the spot.

"Alesio." A man stepped in front of him. "Clef says hello."

Alesio tensed. "Who are you? How do you know—"

"We all serve a bigger purpose, now." The man's eyes gleamed a strange, glossy gray. "A higher power connects us all." He clenched something in his fist, a figurine of some kind. "A god who can give you anything you want, yes?"

"What do *you* want?"

The man bowed his head. "I am merely one of the Consumed. But if you could find it in your ability to convince your friend to stay here a few days, you might find yourself in a good position. In line to perform at this—this Cadensia, yes?"

Alesio crouched on instinct, ready to fight. *The Consumed? What is that?* "How do you know about the Cadenza? How do you know Clef's name?"

"Please." The man bowed lower. "I do not wish to alarm. We can all leave with what we want."

"Go shit yourself."

The man flinched. Perhaps that translated to a more vulgar curse here, on Scent. "I see."

Alesio shouldered past the man. He had to find Saida. They needed to run. He ducked and wove through the slow dancing couples.

"Over here," her voice hissed from farther into the darkness of the town. He snuck over to it, holding his breath by force of habit in tense situations. Saving it in case of a fight.

She huddled against the side of a building. "Thank the Senses, Alesio. We need to leave. Now. While everyone's distracted."

"Couldn't agree more. You get the—the thing, then?"

"Just barely." She peeked around the side of the building.

He hesitated. "Someone approached me. They seemed strange. They called themself 'one of The Consumed.' And they knew Clef's name!"

"What? How?"

"I don't know."

Someone shouted behind them in the crowd. They bolted towards the edge of the village, and she reached for his hand. "Someone had a statue of Watthe," she said in a small voice. "The kind humans make to represent the gods."

"That's . . . he's not, though, right?"

They rushed on in the darkness. Her fear smelled sharp and acrid, mixed with the fresh mint and open fields of her natural scent. "I don't know. Maybe—Maybe he is, in a way. I don't understand how he's gathering people like this. It's been how long?" She paused, as if listening. "A few weeks? Maybe he does have a godlike higher power."

"Should we teleport now?"

"I can't yet. We have to wait till sunrise, remember?"

So, she saves those portals for when things get really *dangerous?*

Why hadn't she used them on Taste with the Palates, then? He would classify that time as 'really dangerous.'

They fled further into the countryside.

"Saida. The magic items you carry around. They're portals, aren't they?"

"Oh." She released his hand. "Well. Sort of." She clutched at her pockets. "They're more like my friends. They help me. They remind me of things. If I use them to teleport, they'll disappear. Their magic will stop. I'll stop hearing them."

"But they can save your life. That's what's most important." Her reflective eyes did not meet his in the dark. "You need to know that. You know that, right? Even when it's hard, and it'll cost something else. The important thing is to stay alive."

The image of his father ignoring Clef's outstretched hand flashed through his mind like someone had flung a sound knife at him.

She nodded but didn't speak. Anger welled up inside him, sudden and fierce. *What's more important to her? Her magic, or her life?*

They found shelter under the overhang of a cliff, and she did not speak. They laid down to try and sleep.

Neither of them slept.

18

ANTICIPATING THE WAVE

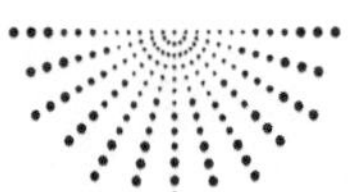

"I just want to check on something," Saida told Alesio.

She left him at her den, loped up to the hilly region of Between, and curled up in a foxan ball in the lee of a large, grassy mound. Time passed.

"You can't avoid him forever," Goosefeather said.

"Since when are you the one that tells me what to do?" Saida glared at them.

"Since you've gotten better at hunting overgrowths," Tricksy said. "When you're around him, you're more focused. You admitted it."

She groomed a tangle in her fur. It was true. In two weeks, she'd acquired two transplants *and* placed one into Vision. And all she could think about was the soothing embrace of his voice.

Why?

"You've drifted for a long time, alone," Goosefeather said. "You need to reconnect with real people. He's the first person you've trusted after Carn."

Carn.

Carn, with his hopeful smile, and his rope with the knot that tightened even when she shifted to the smallest version of herself. She couldn't let herself be caught.

One more transplant, she promised herself. *Then Alesio goes back to Sound.*

When she trudged down from the hills to the den in the afternoon, his voice resonated towards her like the calling of a bell. She found him outside the den with the other foxans gathered around him in a circle.

He looked up at her, his face bright, and held up a seashell between two fingers. "I don't know if it worked, but I tried singing into it for you."

"Alesio." Her heart swelled. She cupped her palms, and he dropped it in her hands without touching her. No magic emanated from it, of course.

He smiled. "If you've taken care of the magic in all the worlds for 300 years, I figure you know what you're doing. Like I said, I trust you." He raised his eyebrows. "So . . . did it work?"

"I—" she swallowed. "No. I'm sorry. You would have to sing on Sound, where your magic would be active. I promise we'll go there soon."

"So, where are we heading tomorrow?" Alesio gestured to the outside. He moved slower and languid, as if afraid of startling her. "Are we taking the Scent transplant to Vision?"

With him, she worked so much quicker. She needed to obtain the four transplants as fast as possible, so she could teleport him back to Sound and leave his luring voice behind.

"Touch," she said. "We're going to Touch."

They dove down, down, down into the lake, for a minute and three seconds, till Saida almost lost her breath, and Alesio struggled to swim beside her. She'd never had to wait so long before, even for Vision. Saida hated to think what that meant for her transplant quota.

Finally, the portal opened, and they washed out into ankle deep water, surrounded by an endless, shallow sea of freshwater.

Saida released Alesio's hand the second they tumbled into the new world. She wiped her eyes and shook herself.

Touch. The world that she avoided more than any other, even more than Vision.

The air clung to her, as did the drops of water, the magic of the world acting like humidity. She shuddered and shifted to more of her foxan self, except she still stood on two legs, as the fur on her legs and arms would keep out some of the sensitivity instead of bare skin.

Alesio gasped in deep breaths of air, then straightened, staring around him, sticking his legs in and out of the water, marching in place. "Amazing. It's like—like every hair on my skin can feel!"

"It gets old fast." Saida brushed the Scent transplant's tube in her pocket, who had named themself Rally. She should have left them in her den, but she'd been distracted. She shaded her eyes from the sun overhead, reflecting on the water. "We'll need to find the nearest shelter. I'm not sure when the next Wave will come, but from the water level, I'd guess today or tomorrow."

"Wave? This place has waves?" The water around their ankles lay smooth like glass, and when they moved, the ensuing ripples traveled far out of sight.

"One massive Wave." She pointed to the east. "It happens once a week and drowns everyone not inside a shelter."

"By the Sound!" Alesio folded his dark brown arms around himself, then his eyes widened. He must have felt the intense sensitivity of his skin. "And it could be today? That's just our luck."

"It's not luck. It's more because of the overgrowth we're searching for. I've done another like it before. It appears the day of the Wave."

He shivered and reached down to touch his boots. "My feet. They're tingling. Is that normal?"

"I don't know. I don't know what new humans might feel, here."

Wait.

A tiny magic rose from Alesio's boots. It vibrated through the air.

She blinked. Her mouth dropped open. "That's—that's not possible—!"

"What? What is it? Is something wrong?" He hiked his knee out of the water and hopped a few times.

She trailed closer. "There's one explanation."

"An explanation would be nice right now! You're freaking me out!"

"Your ancestors came from both Touch and Sound." She reached and touched his leg, and a small quiver ran through her paw. Magic.

It seemed happy, here. It didn't need trimming. She traveled her gaze up to Alesio's confused face. "You have a magic around you right now, Alesio. You're harnessing Touch magic."

His eyes widened. "What?"

"It explains everything." She covered her face with one paw. "Why didn't I think of it sooner? Magic is stronger when it's mixed! That, and your diligence to sing with a half-deaf ear? That's how you're so powerful!"

He stared around at Touch. "My ancestors? Lived here?"

"One of them, at least. You probably you have more ancestors on Sound since that's where you ended up. This is incredible!"

"What can I do with it?" He reached down and touched the water, then shivered.

"Lots of things. Pottery. Coral carving. Stonework. Water, of course. Anything that requires touch, people can enhance it with magic." People had visited her in the underground cavern. They'd begged her to confirm that they could harness Taste magic, and to tell them how powerful they were.

He straightened, narrowing his eyes at her, his lips pressing into a thin line. After a few seconds, he asked, "What's the overgrowth's direction?"

"That way." She pointed northwest. "Let's go."

They sloshed through the still water, picking their feet up and out of it as much as they could to avoid its drag. Her top layer of fur wicked away much of the moisture, but once the water seeped through to her skin, it tended to weigh her down.

Once, the water nearby darkened from a teal to a midnight blue-black, and Saida led them around that area. It marked a sudden drop into a deep, underwater cavern.

"How deep?" Alesio asked, gazing back at it.

"The darker the water, the deeper it goes." She paused. "That one? Very deep."

They traveled on into the afternoon. On Touch and Taste, the worlds with almost no landmarks, sometimes it felt like the terrain rolled so that she slogged the same spot over and over.

"You know," Alesio said, after a long quiet had stretched between them, "It makes sense. Sometimes when I would sing, my feet and my bad ear tingled. I didn't just hear the music; it was like I could *feel* it."

Saida didn't respond. The magic drew her on, becoming stronger. A dark spot on the horizon appeared, and as they neared it, it solidified into an isthmus. A few people floated out on the water, too far away to see their faces. About fifty or so circular pods dotted the thin piece of land like eggs lined up in a henhouse.

"What are those?" Alesio shaded his eyes. The sun sank into the west, shining in their faces.

"Houses." Saida bared her fangs and sloshed on, leading them around the isthmus.

"So, we'd be safe there? If the Wave came?"

She opened her mouth again, trying to explain. Then closed it. Carn had lived on an island. This spit of land was little more than a sandbar, but, if necessary, they could shelter there.

On the other side of the narrow strip of land, a young boy drifted in a flotation suit, a thin, all-over lining with air between the skin and the suit fabric. He aimed a slingshot at birds in the sky. He jolted, squinting at Saida, his eyes a strange, lustrous gray. Saida cocked her head at him. He had something in his hands.

A coral slingshot, carved to resemble Watthe.

She shuddered. The boy paddled away from them, back towards the other floating humans from the village.

"Talk to Alesio," Goosefeather said.

Saida opened her mouth. "I—"

He turned to her, smiling, his face a mosaic of reassurance, his posture open and inviting. He wrung out water from the bottom of his tight shirt that had splashed on him at one point.

She wanted to tell him. She did.

"We can't shelter there, unless it's a last resort." She worked the words out like stones lodged in her throat. "This is one of the worlds that thinks of foxans as . . . as good luck charms."

"Oh," Alesio said. "And that's a bad thing?"

Saida trudged on, pointing at another dark blue spot up ahead. "Also, that boy had a carving of Watthe. I don't know how that's possible, but he did." She shook her head. "Let's go around. Come on."

She sensed his question building behind her, like the Wave, growing more and more enormous the longer she tried to run from it. The water flowed around their ankles, and she found herself wishing that she had another pair of pants to cover herself from the touch of water and air. Of course, the touch of cloth would rasp and grate even worse on the skin.

"How do people stand it?" Alesio muttered behind her. "My feet hurt so bad."

"They don't stand much, here. Or travel at all. People spend most of their time floating outside their pods for relief from the heat of the sun, and the wind, and the air. When you're submerged, you don't feel as much. Look." She pulled her leg out of the water, winced, and shifted so that her fur receded. Her paw morphed to a human foot, and her leg thickened to the size of a human's.

Angry red splotches, like a rash, marked her reddish-brown legs. None showed on the tops of her feet, but then she angled them up. Red covered the bottoms of her feet, as bright as her hair in human form.

"Just from the sand and the rocks?" Alesio peered at the transparent, shallow sea.

"We're a little more sensitive than the locals." Saida shrugged and shifted back to her foxan leg and footpaw, then lowered it back down into the water. "We're not used to it like they are. Once you return to Sound, you might have to spend a few days with rags in your ears. Everything will be very loud to you."

"Tell him," Goosefeather whispered.

Alesio shifted his weight from foot to foot. "About that. Saida, I—I don't know."

"About what?" She pointed out a tiny bit of blue to avoid, a fissure in the sea floor. They went around it.

"If I want to go back. I mean, I want to sing you your transplant on Sound. But. I—I like traveling. Seeing new places." He paused. "Being with you."

She tensed.

"Tell him," Goosefeather said. "It's time. You know it's time. He needs to understand."

"I met him here." Saida stopped.

On her left, Alesio frowned and looked over at her.

She clenched her fists. "Not here as in right here. I mean here on Touch. I was young, naive, and curious. So curious about humans. I strolled right up to him." She trembled, and the air, her saturated fur, and the tacky dryness of her mouth all conspired against her, overwhelming her. "The pods are just the above ground safe places. People here also live below ground in caves, where they control how much water gets in with their magic. He chained me to a post in a cave for a long time."

Alesio's chocolate brown eyes had darkened to almost black, and he'd gone very, very still. The water around him did not ripple.

The words poured out from her. "He and the other people of the village thought of me as their 'good luck charm.' Gave me the best food and water they had. They kept me on a leash when they let me out and asked me to hunt down people who could use magic. But Carn adored me and visited me the most. He wouldn't stop petting me. It hurt so much, here on Touch, to be petted for hours . . . he said he loved me. He expected me to love him back." She shuddered. "Goosefeather thinks I was gone five years or so."

"Why didn't you . . ." Alesio's voice was low and more of a growl.

"Teleport?" She let out a laughing sob. "Because I thought I did love him. There were moments where he seemed different. Sometimes, he would bring me out to watch the sunrise as it came over the water horizon line, and he would tell me I was beautiful and bright like that,

that before I came into his life, he hadn't known what light was. And I . . . I liked hearing that. Like a fool." She bowed her head. "But then he would bring be back in the caves and chain me up again. I didn't even know, and he didn't either, then, but I'm not capable of love. I can't stand the way it hurts people. How it cages people to stay when they don't want to." She twisted her hands, digging the tips of her claws into her palms. It felt like fire.

"How did you escape?"

He seemed to become more and more of a statue with each question he asked. She swallowed. "Goosefeather. I found them when one the villagers asked me to hunt down some magic one day. I found them; a feather from a Dawncloud Goose. Goosefeather convinced me that I needed to leave. I heard a voice in the magic for the first time. They said that this man's love was bad for me." She drew Goosefeather out and laid them against her cheek, and their touch soothed her irritated skin. "They saved me. They picked the lock on the cage. And after that, other magics talked to me, too. I'd never heard them before. But they all helped me. They stopped me from being alone."

"*You* did all that," Goosefeather said. "You and me. One and the same."

"Is this Carn still alive?" He gazed out at the endless sea, crouching a little, his fist clenched.

Something inside her warmed, even though his posture scared her a little. She liked the idea of him getting angry enough to protect her. To stop others from hurting her.

"He followed me out here, into the sea-wilds. Humans don't come out this far. I teleported right as the Wave hit." She paused. "I don't like visiting Touch, even to create transplants." A slight wind picked up and they both curled their shoulders at its tug. Ripples spread across the expanse of water.

Saida tensed. "That's the sign. The Wave is coming today. In a few hours. We need to go."

ALESIO CURLED and uncurled his hands, irritating his palms. Saida's story had made him so sounddamned *angry.*

What kind of sick bastard tortures someone like that?

She'd shifted to mostly human, splashing with more urgency around the blue pools of water, leading faster. The breeze misted with seawater. The rash showed up on her arms and legs, now, and on his, from all the splashing.

Her pointed ears swiveled back and forth on top of her head, on high alert. She had shifted from the most vulnerable he'd ever seen her back to competent guide on the watch for danger.

I still don't understand why she didn't just teleport to escape! How could she think a relationship like that was love?

Why had she told him such a dark and vulnerable thing? He'd spilled his secrets to her with a certain amount of trepidation, but this thing in her past had shattered her. She'd closed herself off from humans. She feared human touch. Why would she have peeled back such a wound for him?

A line she'd said echoed in his mind. *"I'm not capable of love."*

She'd been warning him.

"There!" She pointed at a dark spot on the sea ahead, more to the north. "A shelter!"

They dashed towards it, spattering water everywhere. The wind picked up a little, and Alesio scanned the east horizon.

No giant wave yet.

They hopped over a foot-wide fissure of deep blue. After maybe six minutes, they neared the shelter. The builders had shaped it like an elongated teardrop, maybe twenty feet long. It reached eight feet high at the rounded end. *It's lower at the end where the wave comes from. So that the water doesn't rip out the structure? But why make it so long?*

Saida skidded to a halt and pointed at it. "You slide it open from the top. Get inside and pull the cover back over you."

"What? You're not coming?"

"I have to find the overgrowth before the Wave hits." She closed her eyes as if concentrating.

"You mean you're not sure if you'll get back here in time?"

"I don't know." Saida's voice sounded small. "I just want you safe."

"I'm not leaving you by yourself!" He marched away from the shelter back to her side. "What are we looking for?"

She licked her lips. "Okay. Okay, I don't have time to convince you. It's a pale patch of water, in the middle of a deep blue-black pool. I've done one like this before."

He followed her, scanning the nearby pools, more of them tinted the deepest blue-black than before. *Pale water. Like white? Like foam?*

The wind misted harder and the temperature chilled. Gooseflesh puckered his bare arms and the back of his neck. Hot and cold affected him more here, too, it seemed. Saida's reddish-brown face looked as if she had shifted to her foxan self with bright red fur.

Something white flashed out of the corner of his eye. He pivoted on his heel.

"There!" He pointed at a patch of pale blue water, drifting in the center of a large pool of the blackest blue.

They raced over to it. "What is it?" Alesio asked, holding his breath.

"It's magic water." She panted, her tongue sticking out of her mouth a little.

What would it feel like to kiss in the Touch world?

Alesio chased the random thought from his head. Now was not the time or place. And Saida didn't seem ready for a relationship even if she wanted one. Carn had traumatized her so that she believed closeness with humans led to harm and fear.

He wished Carn were still alive, so he could kill him.

". . . anticipates the wave," Saida was saying, "And changes its weight. It rises to the surface of the pool so it can ride the wave."

She lowered herself into the pool, her legs and torso disappearing below the dark water. He shuddered. How deep did that fissure go?

Saida kept her head above the water. Alesio had never needed to learn how to swim, and his experience with the lake did not give him any incentive to figure that out now.

She paddled to the middle of the large pool. Alesio couldn't reach her with just a jump if she needed him, and that made him nervous. Saida pushed one of her hands through the patch of pale blue water, and part of it clumped into small globules like beads on a necklace and clung to her fingers.

The misting of the air grew stronger, stinging through his tight-fitted shirt, now. Alesio glanced back.

Was that a cliff in the distance?

Not a cliff. A wave.

It stretched far and wide, so high it rose above the clouds.

<hr>

THE BEADS of the pale water magic had clung to her fingers, but then seemed to change their mind and trickled off, sinking below her. Saida stuck her head under the water, reaching for it. She'd trimmed magic here with just her touch, before, but now she wished she had brought along a jar to help contain it. She'd forgotten in her rush.

The water patch bobbed further down, into the recesses of the fissure, where the water deepened into black. She raked the water with her hands to swim down. She didn't have time—

The globules of water looped around her wrist, then changed their weight and yanked her down!

She struggled against them, trying to pull them off with her other hand, but they had a stronger magic than she'd expected. Much stronger. The skin on her wrist felt rubbed raw.

"Take me somewhere," they seemed to say. She had a harder time hearing magics before she trimmed them, but it happened from time to time. "Somewhere new."

"I can do that," She thought at them, hoping her words would reach them. *"But you have to want to leave! And please, let me go!"*

They tightened around her wrist, pulling her farther down. She sensed, now, how their globules snaked all the way down to the bottom of the cavern, hundreds of feet below. They became heavier, and she sank faster.

It whispered, *"You* are somewhere new."

Their nature had twisted. Their overgrowth had gone on for too long. They wanted to drown her, they wanted to consume her magic. Just like the swanseize, Watthe, and the whole of the Primal Plane.

A disturbance beside her. Someone had jumped in above her.

Alesio!

The water magic paused. She sensed their interest in the human, another energy source.

No! No! she wanted to scream at Alesio. *Get away!*

The magic sent a tendril upwards, a different one than that had a hold of her, brushing past her. A few seconds later, a shock shuddered through them, and they released their hold on her wrist. She paddled upwards, not questioning the good fortune, and she met Alesio halfway up.

He gathered her up and shoved her towards the surface. His brief touch felt like it burned her, with her skin so irritated already.

She burst from the water, gasping for breath.

The Wave rolled towards them, so high it seemed close. They had maybe half an hour.

Alesio hadn't surfaced. Had the malicious overgrowth dragged him down?

Rally tugged on the fabric in her pocket. "Here," they said. "I want to go here."

"You're supposed to transplant to Vision." She stuck her head under the water, trying to catch a glimpse of Alesio. Nothing but pitch darkness met her straining eyes. *"Besides,"* she thought to them, *"There's already a powerful overgrowth here."*

"I can help. I know I can help."

No sign of Alesio.

He can hold his breath!

But he didn't have experience with the terror of not being able to breathe if he needed to. This fissure went deep.

"I'll go here," Rally said. *"I can find him. I can help."*

In desperation, Saida lifted her head out of the water, yanked out the tube, and uncorked it. The Scent magic wafted down into the fissure, the calming smell of the rala nut. After a few seconds, a patch of the water magic floated up to them, as if curious.

The two merged, the white beads of water turning a yellow green. A ropy stream of yellow green water rose from the pool, then another, and another. They took the shape of a tree, ever flowing. The hostility and hunger had disappeared.

Transplants could merge . . . with each other?

"Your human, as promised," the new, merged magic said in a serene voice.

Alesio bobbed to the surface and flowed into one of the water branches, which deposited him out of the pool and into the floor of the shallow sea, limp and sodden.

She rushed over to him, propping his head up to get it above water level, not caring about how touching him both terrified and exhilarated her. He coughed and vomited up some water.

"Alesio!" She pressed on his stomach, and he vomited up some more, then rolled over, gasping for breath. "Alesio, you shouldn't have jumped in after me!"

The water at her feet rumbled. Spray stung her face and she winced. She didn't want to look behind her, but she did.

The Wave loomed.

The humans on Touch called it the Summit Wave. It stretched like a giant wall, horizon to horizon. And its height! She craned her neck and still couldn't see the top; it vanished as it crested through the overcast sky.

They had twenty minutes, maybe, before it hit.

Could they dash to the shelter in twenty minutes? She didn't know. Hunting the overgrowth had distracted her and she hadn't noted the distance.

Frustration competed for her attention. *I lost the Scent transplant, and now I can't take this one either. I'm back down to just one.*

Alesio coughed and hauled himself to his knees with all the energy of a waterlogged bell-bug. She bent to help him stand. *No time to complain. We need to run.* The water level had risen to her knees.

The sounds of a bustling city rose. Human merchants hawking wares. Squeaking carts.

Where is that coming from? What is that?

A portal opened in front of them, above the fissure.

What? I didn't—

Watthe stepped through.

HE HAD GROWN to the height of a tall tree and had to duck through the portal. His fingers had lengthened to as long as her foxan form, sharp and curving from his hand like scimitars. His form had changed to a more substantial, yet still wavering gray; his jaw split open to reveal the rows of teeth through his cheek. The water just level lapped over his clawed feet. He gazed at Saida, holding the box like an afterthought between two of those huge claws.

"Run!" Goosefeather screamed.

"Use me!" Tricksy said. "Don't let him catch you! He'll kill you!"

If she used either of them to teleport, she would lose them.

Beside her, Alesio coughed up some more water, struggling to stand. She moved in front of Alesio, holding her trembling hands wide. "You want me?" She poked her chin at Watthe. "Go ahead! But let him get to the shelter!"

"Saida, no!" Alesio coughed, then retched on the ground again. He must have swallowed a lot of water.

Watthe reached out. His giant, sharp finger-claws curled around her torso. She winced. In Touch, his gray fingers flash-burned her skin like freezing rain.

Something in his touch told her that if he held her too close, for too long, she would lose all sense of herself.

The wind sprayed them with a torrent of cold and rain, now, the headwind from the Summit Wave. It lashed her skin like whips. She trembled. Watthe was sipping at her magic. She had no strength, not even to shift and try to escape by being smaller.

"I don't want to eat." Watthe looked down at the box. "At least, not all at once. What if god I *am*? Then I don't have you to listen to."

A voice resounded from the box, and its raised design of tangled knots moved faster and seemed more substantial, like real worms.

The sound reverberated through their feet. "Don't be a fool. I am your god! I say you must eat her now! She will not stay at your side like a pet!"

"She could learn as I have!"

Silence reigned for a moment, except for the wind and the sleet. Her energy drained faster. Her eyes drooped.

Alesio lunged forward, Touch magic vibrating and sparking between his fingers, water knives forming in his hands. He stabbed both of Watthe's legs, and Watthe roared, throwing his head back.

He must've done that to the water overgrowth when it dragged me down!

Watthe bent down and sliced at Alesio, who ducked just in time, rolling under the waves and out of sight.

"No!" Saida said. "Stop!"

Alesio lunged out of the water, his fingers sparking again.

"Alesio, run! Get to the shelter!" She tilted her head up at Watthe, reaching up to him, trying to divert his attention. His eyes flicked to her. "How did you find me?" Saida forced the words out. "How are you—teleporting?

"I am warning you." In Watthe's other hand, the box's twisting mass lifted like a nest of disturbed snakes. Even with the headwind from the Summit Wave whipping the water to waves, its voice reverberated in their feet and up their legs. "Do not say anything. Do not tell her—"

"I will tell her." Watthe seemed to steady, unaffected now from Alesio's water knives. "I want to tell her everything, I find." He watched Alesio, who waited off to the side as if torn between helping Saida and escaping the approaching Wave. "Saida. I have your transplants. I find and eat them, and from the world they started, their magic takes me to." He gave her an approximation of a grin, those gray lips widening much too far into his cheeks.

"W-what? No!" *My transplants? Eaten?*

Everything connected in her head. *The worlds are losing magic because of Watthe eating transplants. And I'm the one who let him loose.*

Falrie's voice echoed in her ears. *"There is a hunger that wants to consume us . . ."*

"The transplants disappear," he said. The now-shrieking wind, the spray, the dull roar of the wave, and her crushing fatigue, all blurred his words. "It makes difficult for finding you. I cannot on portals every day depend, as you able to can. How do you do that? Everything you, fascinates me—"

"Stop talking to her!" Parts of the box's raised 'pattern' uncoiled and wrapped onto Watthe's other arm, pricking at him with sharp bits of metal. Shadow substance trickled down his arm.

Alesio screamed, "Use your portals, Saida!"

She opened her mouth to say she couldn't, but she had no strength to speak.

Watthe ripped his arm from the box's grasping tendrils, though he still held onto it. "No! I will stop not!" He curled his finger-claws around Saida's middle tighter, and she opened her mouth to scream, but the drain on her energy sapped her strength to a whimper.

Memories of Carn flooded through her. Her skin burned like she'd been set on fire.

"I like she has this wild magic. I do not want to disappear it. I want to sure it does not stop being."

"I am your god—" the box said.

"No! You are not now the most powerful! I've consumed twelve portals, and each time, I in power grow. I become more real with shape. You do not command me."

"Saida! If you don't use them now, we're both dead!" Alesio shouted. "And you! Watthe! Look behind you!"

Watthe seemed to consider the Summit Wave for the first time. It loomed so close. So high. The water level slapped at Alesio's thighs, now, vicious and foaming. *We're not making it back. Not enough time!*

"Use me!" Goosefeather cried out.

"Me!" Tricksy Stone said. "Saida! We're just pieces of you—"

"No!" Saida shouted. "No, I can't use either of you! You're the only ones I can love!"

Watthe curled her close to his body. Parts of his gray skin reached out and latched onto her like hundreds of fingers, and under that skin, the smoke and void of his original form waited.

She shuddered, her mind splintering back to Carn, to that cave he'd kept her in.

Watthe's long, long legs traversed through the high waves. "You taste wild. So free," Watthe said. "Potent. I will you save up."

"Let her go!" Alesio cursed, following, but slower. "Saida! Sounddamn it!"

Watthe headed to the shelter, running at the Wave. The rain and mist hit her skin with such force it felt like running into a wave of sound knives. She felt out of her mind. Pulled in opposing directions. She couldn't hear Goosefeather, or Tricksy Stone.

Alesio's head bobbed just above the surface behind them, falling behind.

"Watthe!" Saida screamed. "Save him!"

"Why? No. No. I do not."

"Please! He's important to me!"

"Don't listen to her!" the box reached a tendril out, this time to prick at Watthe's face.

Watthe glared at the box, then stuffed it into his chest. Gray fingers formed there and grabbed it, sucking it inside, then he swept Alesio up in his massive claw.

He carried both her and Alesio, the water now up to his waist, dashing into the cutting wind and spray. He reached the shelter, slid the cover open, and stuffed them inside.

"Stay." Watthe peered in at her, staying outside the shelter. He couldn't fit inside. He pulled the cover closed.

The Summit Wave hit like a thousand rumbles of thunder.

19

ALL FOR NOTHING

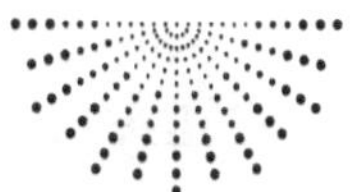

The Wave slammed against the shelter like a thousand orchestras, roaring and crashing and booming. But whoever had built the structure must have known how to shape it so that the water streamed over it and didn't pluck it out of its moorings.

Alesio wheezed on his knees, his breath rasping in his burning throat. Beside him, Saida lay limp on the shelter floor.

That monster had folded her body against his, and she'd sort of . . . half vanished, as if into a void. Alesio knew that feeling. He remembered how the monster had enveloped him. How it had *tasted* him. He'd felt exhausted after a few seconds. She lay there, bedraggled, half-shifted, her sharp foxan chin and cheeks sallow instead of their usual reddish-brown. Her chest rose and fell in shallow breaths. But she breathed.

Alesio sagged down onto his side. How long would the Wave last?

An hour passed. Maybe two. His eyes weighed heavy. His thoughts slowed into impressions.

She'd screamed something. *"No, I can't use you! You're the only ones I can love!"*

More time passed. He rolled over on his back beside her. His eyes fluttered. It hurt to breathe. So, so much, more so on Touch.

227

The Wave lasted and lasted.

Would they run out of air? The structure's length, twenty feet or so, must have been built to keep as much air in as possible.

His eyes closed.

HE WOKE to the sound of water lapping against the outside of the shelter, and Saida opening the cover in her human form, letting in fresh air. He rubbed his eyes and they burned at his touch. His throat felt like a grater had passed over it.

"Oh, everything hurts." He rose with a groan. "Saida, are you ready—"

She stared out at the water. It lapped a few inches high, the lowest point after the Summit Wave. Alesio followed her gaze.

Watthe stood out there like a tree, head bowed, his long, long arms lengthened beside him and bracing with further support. He held the black box in one giant clawed hand.

Saida closed her eyes. "Come on. Come on, please—"

Her eyes snapped open, and she pointed at a spot past the monster. "The portal will come up there."

They crept through the shallow water, trying to keep quiet and not ripple the water.

Watthe's eyes opened.

"Run!" Saida yelled. She shifted to foxan.

They dashed through the water, throwing up spray. The huge monster struggled to rip his legs out of the ground. They ran past him, and the portal met them, and they fell through the ground together.

They teleported to the lake of Between, just under the surface after a minute and ten seconds. They broke through at the same time, gasping, and Alesio breathed for the first time without it feeling like sound knives in his throat.

Saida flopped onto the bank and crawled over to a rock to lean against. Her face was expressionless, but her eyes seemed like they belonged to a dead person. "My transplants. He ate them—he's eating them—it was all for nothing."

Alesio hauled himself out of the lake. Pell dashed off, he assumed to fetch Falrie.

The events of the day before crashed in on him. The overgrowth in the fissure that had become the water tree. Almost drowning. The terror of the monster.

How Saida had refused to help herself, or him. The relentless, unending Summit Wave.

Something huge rose in his chest, like a swelling tide, that same anger that had emerged whenever Clef had forced him to fight, the need for violence. He struggled to hold it back.

He dragged himself up, wavering on his feet. Everything seemed distant, and he had trouble concentrating on moving his legs. He staggered past Saida, not even sure where he was going. He needed time to think. To process.

After a few minutes of lumbering into the small, forested area of Between, he stopped and leaned against a tree, exhausted. His skin remained a fiery, irritated red.

Why didn't she use her portals to save us?

Well, he knew why. She thought of her magic items as her friends. They helped her cope with what had happened to her. What that bastard Carn had done to her. Of course she hadn't wanted to use them. She'd said that if she did, she would stop hearing their voices.

But, sounddamn it—!

Darrow, Pell, and Falrie appeared a few yards away, panting.

"What happened?" Darrow asked, while Falrie loped towards the lake.

"Watthe showed up." Alesio rubbed his eyes. "We barely escaped. Not even the Summit Wave managed to kill him."

Pell's mouth gaped. "The Summit . . . Wave. I remember . . . it."

"And the box spoke. I thought at first it was like Saida's magics that only she can hear. But I heard it speak."

Darrow crouched, whining, his ears flattening. "The box!"

"What did it say?" Pell asked.

"It's more what Watthe said *to* it. He's been eating the transplants. That's how he's traveled to the different worlds, I guess. The magic teleports him to the world where they originated from."

Darrow bared his teeth. "Senses damn it all."

He swallowed. All Saida's work, down the gullet of that monster. Strengthening him.

Alesio was just a cage match fighter from a gritty city. He hadn't signed on to deal with terrifying shadow creatures that could wring his energy out like a dishcloth.

He swallowed. His head throbbed, and his ears felt like he had stuffed them with cotton, as it always did here in the neutral Between.

Behind him, Saida talked to Falrie, stepping into the forest, her voice halting. "He can—suspend people inside. It's like a floating nothing. He's the hunger you were all talking about."

Alesio had been willing to sacrifice himself for her.

That knowledge terrified him, that he would give himself up for another person. His whole life, he'd focused on surviving, on keeping himself and his father alive, and now he'd found someone he would've thrown all that away for. She was like a complicated song come to life, full of frolicking tempos and intricate harmonies of fear and curiosity. She'd opened his eyes to a much bigger life.

But she had the same issue as his father, of not valuing her own life enough to fight for it.

Words formed in his throat like knives. He turned and faced her, his voice low. "Saida. Why didn't you use your emergency portals?"

She tensed, her mouth dropping open. Beside her, Falrie frowned at him, flicking her tail this way and that.

"You said you would. Back on Scent, you agreed to use them if you were in danger."

Her lips moved, but no sound came out.

"You could have teleported us anytime Watthe chased us. Anytime that Wave came at us. But you chose not to."

Her face paled. "I can't lose them."

"So, you would rather us both die?" Fear moved his lips. It came out as anger, but he shook with the terror of what she'd rather lose.

Saida shrank down into her smallest form. She clutched at her pockets.

Falrie stepped between them. "Stop it, human." She growled, showing her teeth. "Stop it, you're not helping."

He gave a bitter laugh. "Is it helping to let her play pretend, to get so attached to magic things, she believes they are more important than her own life?"

The older foxan hesitated, then glanced at Saida, her ears flickering.

"Do you remember what I said about my father?" Alesio stepped past Falrie. Saida had frozen there on the little path next to a tree. He strained to keep his voice from rising. "How he was ready to starve in the streets just so we didn't have to live under Clef's boot in the future? He wouldn't have survived to see that future."

He stopped before crowding her against the tree, his fists clenched. She flattened her ears, curling her tail between her legs, not looking at him.

"You do what you have to, to keep yourself and the person you love alive. Love isn't about cages, or about someone forcing you to love them back. That's selfishness. Love, *real* love, is about helping the other person because you want to. Because you care about them, and that's all that matters. I was ready to die, for you. I've never—I've never felt that for anyone." He unclenched his hands and lifted them, trembling, hovering near her downturned face. His voice cracked. "But—you don't even love *yourself.*"

Saida's eyes widened, and she looked up at him.

His voice lowered into a growl as he tried to control it and failed. "I've tried to help you this whole time. I traveled to different worlds with you. I fought for you. I almost drowned for you. I care about you. Maybe you don't want to care about me, and that's fine." He inhaled a quivering breath. "But I can't keep caring for you, not if you don't care enough to save yourself. I can't—I can't do that. Not again."

She stared at him; her ears slumped.

He stepped away from her, his hands shaking. "Tomorrow morning, when you get your sounddamned portal back, teleport me to Sound."

He stalked away towards the forest.

2 0

TO ESCAPE A LOVE

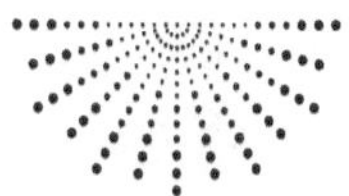

Saida dropped Alesio off outside of Anthem and, as he became re-accustomed to the loudness of even just the outskirts, holding his hands over his ears and closing his eyes, she darted down a dirt path away from the city. She both hoped for, and dreaded, him chasing after her.

He didn't.

She couldn't teleport back right away, of course, so she loped out to the surrounding countryside. A farmer had lined up his hay bales, and she dug into one, fashioning a small haven in the yellow itchy stuff. She tucked herself into a ball, wrapping her tail around herself, and tried to sleep, but she couldn't. It wasn't even midmorning.

She tried to block out Alesio's words. How he'd loomed over her, his words sharp as sound knives. She curled herself tighter, farther into her momentary safety.

"He had a right to be angry," Tricksy Stone said.

"I know," Saida said.

"But not in how he showed it," Goosefeather said.

The day passed. The hay rustled in the biting wind, that late fall wind that smelled of snow. The farmer harvested crops in his field but didn't approach the hay bales. A few flurries drifted down.

"Saida," Tricksy Stone said. "We need to talk."

"We've helped you for a long time," Goosefeather said. "But we're not helping you anymore, are we?"

She clapped her paws over her pockets. "I don't want to hear this. No. Not right now."

"Saida—"

She focused on Watthe. Could he follow her here? If he found a Sound transplant, he could. He'd said he used her transplants as portals, and she'd planted a few Sound-based ones on Touch over the years. A merged portal of Touch and Scent had appeared in front of him.

He wouldn't know she'd teleported here, right? Or could he?

"You need to listen to us," Goosefeather said.

"But you're saying I shouldn't listen to you, right? That's what you're saying—that I shouldn't be able to hear you at all. Well, I'll take that advice for now."

"Saida—!"

The worshippers. They must have communicated with Watthe somehow. The reverend had called to him in the chapel, and he had emerged from the portal. That kid on Touch had had a slingshot carved like Watthe, and he had shown up later that day.

How far had his influence gone? How had he gathered so many followers? Did even this farmer know of him? Would he whip out a carved figure and call Watthe down in the middle of the field?

So, what if he did?

She'd lost Alesio. She couldn't save Vision, not when Watthe had consumed her transplants like she could eat a dozen cinnamon olos. If she produced more, she'd just fuel his appetite and he'd become even stronger. The worlds would lose their magic, and those overgrowths would grow even more tangled and angry, all of them behaving like the water magic on Touch, or the swanseize, or the Primal Plane itself. Vision and Sound and the rest of the worlds would wither and drift far away, and even if she could travel to them, the humans would have all died, and Scent's pine trees would lose that richness, and Taste's salt-wilds wouldn't taste of anything more potent than normal salt.

And then, eventually, they'd drift so far away, she'd never reach them again.

How did I not figure this out? The transplant on Vision had vanished at the fountain, the one before Winter Lightning. She'd forgotten about that until now. Watthe must have consumed it. Had he eaten Winter Lightning now, too? What about Effervescent? Or Saltfall?

She slept around midday, tossing, and turning. She woke and slept and woke again. The snow thickened and fell faster.

"Hey! Get outta there!"

She jolted awake. The farmer glared at her, pitchfork in hand, and she shot away, dodging a jab with those big tines.

"And don't come back! Stay away from my chickens!"

Would this human summon Watthe? She panted, her tongue lolling out, dashing through the fields, leaving footprints in the layer of snow. Across a road. Into another field that the farmer hadn't harvested yet, hiding in the beanstalks. They rustled around her, their dry leaves whispering about the cold, telling on her to the farmer. The farmer kept shouting, and she kept running.

This is better for both of us. I put him in too much danger. And he was right. I can't love him the way he deserves. I'm just not built that way.

Pain sliced through her mind then, like a knife cutting up her thoughts and memories. She bowed her head and kept running.

She found cover in a hollow tree and stayed under there, shivering, listening to the insects puttering along through their different worlds of leaves and fallen trees and rocks and leaving their tiny tracks behind them.

Hours passed, and she drifted in and out of consciousness. The sun rose, and she shivered in her tree, and fatigue plagued her still. She hadn't slept well, though she'd tried for a while now. She tried to drift off again and woke up in the late afternoon.

She cleaned the snow from her fur. She liked grooming, sometimes, rather than shifting and drying off. She liked the routine of it, and how fresh her fur felt after, and her tail fluffed just a little more.

What had she been doing? Why was she out in the cold?

Saltfall. She locked on that name. She could check on Saltfall, here on Sound. She needed something to focus on, or she'd lose days here, or months.

She padded along the country road. Sound. She was in Sound. She could tell because the birds sang louder where the magic worked, but only in small, sparse areas, maybe for a few yards every hundred yards or so. She trotted past a line of hay bales on someone's farm, hiding from the farmer who seemed irritable for some reason, pitching hay over his shoulder with vehemence.

Past the farm, the sound of falling snow caught her ear, a dreamy, gentle sound that generated an overgrowth. She fumbled in her pockets for a seashell but came up empty.

Why had she journeyed to Sound without any seashells? How odd. She'd have to come back for it later.

Saltfall. I need to check on them.

The echo of urgency hurried her steps, and she cantered towards the city with easy foxan strides. She snuck along the outskirts, dodging burning fires in streets, and avoiding all the humans. Humans would capture her and shove her in a cage.

A silver sound, like the purest bell ever rung, shivered in her ears. A powerful overgrowth, but one she should avoid. *Dangerous.*

She'd come here for Saltfall, not whatever that was. She crept along an abandoned house next to a broken-down fence, hopping the fence whenever humans walked past on either side. She found the underpass, where the rain of salt fell from the curved ceiling, and hesitated. A horde of children sometimes played here, but the road was empty.

"Saltfall?" She stalked forward, keeping low as her foxan self. No answering patter of salt greeted her. She stopped just outside the entryway to the underpass, peering upwards at the ceiling.

A gash in the stone showed where something had ripped Saltfall out, leaving what looked like a giant maw of broken teeth.

Saida gasped and backed up, her tail between her legs. Her skittering claws echoed through the underpass like a thousand spiders. She whirled to flee.

A fox-person crouched on the side of the dirt road, watching her. She yipped in surprise.

"It's gone," the fox-person said. The pattern of the stripes on their cheek seemed familiar. "The monster came and—and just—" they hunched their shoulders inward and stared at the ground.

"Have we met?" Saida asked.

The fox-person jerked their head back up. They narrowed their eyes. "Are you pulling my tail?"

"W-what?"

"You took the singer away. Now he's back, and he's no different. You didn't help his magic, the way you said you would."

The word 'singer' made Saida shiver all over. Her friends pounded on her mind, trying to reach her thoughts, to tell her their thoughts, no, *her* thoughts that she'd shut out, but she didn't let them inside her mind. Not right now. She couldn't listen right now.

"And now," the fox-person strode closer to Saida, their bright eyes reflecting in the light of dusk, "The clefs roam the streets along with the worshippers of St. Rina's. They know we can track magic. How do they know that? If they capture us, they force us to guide them to magic. They have strange eyes. Their chests have big wounds, but still they walk. One of us, they had tortured, and forced them to show the monster this salt magic. Then the monster ate both my friend, and the salt magic—!"

Saida clapped her paws over her ears. They rang with a horrible, discordant sound, the sound of pain in the fox-person's voice. She ran away, then, calling a portal, the closest one she could find. They all seemed far away and moved so slow.

The fox-person did not chase her. The portal wobbled up through the cracks in the ground between the worlds.

Where should she teleport? Vision! She should check if—if Effervescent was still there!

The portal opened, and Saida stumbled through. The way between the worlds lasted for more than a minute and a half, and she gasped for breath on the other side, falling to her knees on the dusty road in the setting summer sun on Vision.

The shock of the temperature difference, the influx of air in her lungs, and whatever she'd run from—what had she run from? —made her tremble for several minutes before she could stand. She shifted to human, no longer needing the warmth of fur, and shortened her clothing to shorts and a crop top in the heat.

Her body relaxed. Everything was fine. She'd teleported here to check on one of her magics.

The long shadows of grass growing up the side of a different gravity waved in the subtle breeze. She ran her fingers through it as she ambled along, feeling it tug her to walk sideways. Not enough for trimming, though. It stopped, after a few steps, and gravity oriented itself on the side back to neutral, and her hand dropped.

She peered up into the sky again. No trees grew on the horizontal line, no clouds scudded up and down instead of overhead along a variant force. Most everything here seemed too normal, neutral, almost like Between. Had she forgotten Vision's transplant for the year?

The transplant. Winter Lightning. She'd come to check on them. She'd placed them in the human village. How far away was that? She shaded her eyes, squinting into the fading light. Ruins to the east, ruins to the west. Had she visited any of those before? She couldn't remember. Maybe Tricksy Stone would know, but she hesitated to talk to them right now. She'd shut them out for some reason.

The gravity shifted upwards, and she twirled on a broken-down brick road that guided her up, up, and up. How like a cloud she coasted into the lavender sunset. The wind picked up stronger up here, and almost blew her higher, past where the road ended but the gravity did not. She clutched at the brick so that she did not fall up into the sky. The wind gust passed, and she laughed a little from the exhilaration, but hurried back down just in case it got stronger.

The sun dipped below the horizon, and the shadows elongated, and dusk approached. A few bats fluttered from a tree growing in the normal direction, and she watched them as they dipped and squeaked, hunting insects. She mimicked their motions as a foxan, wheeling and diving along the ground, pouncing onto pebbles and clumps of dirt and flinging them into the air. She laughed, and laughed, and the night passed in what seemed like moments.

She curled up in the chill of a gray dawn and woke again to grass tickling her nose, and the warmth of the sun high overhead. She blinked and stretched and licked her lips. Hunger and thirst vied for her attention. She should hunt now. Yes! That sounded nice.

The day opened before her without a plan, without a schedule, just a nice, drifting day full of meandering hours . . .

"—aida!"

Tricksy Stone's voice pierced her thoughts like a blinding shaft of sunlight through clouds. She stopped. Her head hurt again, and she pressed her fingers to her temples.

"Saida, listen to us!" Goosefeather said.

"No. No." The pain reverberated through her whole body. She froze and tears leaked down her cheeks.

Goosefeather continued, "You found someone to connect with. You don't need us anymore—"

She ran, summoning a teleport, blocking out their voice again. She couldn't listen to this. She couldn't. Where could she travel to escape her own thoughts? Between? No, wait, she'd come to visit the transplants she'd already placed. She could check on one of them in the other worlds. Taste. She had some there.

"You would be safest on Between! You must—"

She called a portal and asked it to send her to Taste. It struggled up through the fissures of the world, then stopped halfway as if tired.

"C'mon, c'mon!" She pulled it towards her, willed it upwards, and it burst open in front of her, half-formed, half of it mixed with the dirt and grass and brick of the road like a whirling vortex. She plunged into it, holding her breath, and the portal lasted for what seemed like well over two minutes. She lost her breath at some point and writhed in the void of the portal, that long hallway between the worlds, until it spit her back out again.

She convulsed on the salt flats, gasping in deep breaths. She did not taste the salt on her tongue or the pebbles she rolled around on.

At some point she sat up again. She needed water, and she

followed a faded taste of it on the small breeze. She didn't find the small pond until later that morning, and she gulped it down, tasting the silt, sand, and the salt that had settled at the bottom of it as if she had bitten into a sand-salt dune. She coughed but drank more. It was still water.

She wandered. For how long, she did not know. At some point she neared the city, or rather, the many small villages that connected to make up the city. She stared at it, considering, her mouth watering for the taste of cinnamon olos loose in the air. She'd have to avoid the people, but it might be worth it, considering the state of her stomach.

Saida slipped up to the edge of the wooden palisade surrounding the city and prowled the edge, searching for an entrance that did not involve the main gate. She didn't find any side doors or breaks in the wall, and after a few hours, she returned to the main gate. She grew her clothes out of her fur, covering her body with a plain shirt, trousers, and soft boots, and a hood and high collar, of course, as always to hide her foxan chin. A few humans went in and out with small wagons, pulling blocks of salt they had harvested out on the flats. It didn't seem like they checked people' ears like they did in—in Anthem—

Why did her head hurt so much? She clutched at it.

"Hey, you!" One of the guards at the gate shouted at her. "You coming in or not?"

She swallowed and nodded, walking over. The guards surveyed her and pursed their lips. Salt and dirt spattered the clothes she had grown, which tasted of sweat and grime. Their gray-eyed gaze lingered on her hooded face. She held her breath.

"Alright, you're good." One of them gestured for her to pass through the gate. She slunk through before they could peruse her further and followed the taste of cinnamon.

A hundred lovely tastes pulled her in as many directions. Apple pie, and something with chocolate and peaches over to her left, and a savory soup full of chicken and parsley and another spice she did not know—!

She had no money, let alone Taste-based currency, but that didn't mean she couldn't find something. The olo taste emanated from a humble shop with blue shutters, and she snuck around behind it to check the dumpster. She found three half-eaten cinnamon treats, and she couldn't stuff them in her mouth fast enough. On a world where taste reigned, the humans threw away many things that would have claimed a spot in a fancy restaurant anywhere else. She clambered out of the dumpster, licking her fingers.

A musty and strong taste made her duck instinctively. A bag landed near her and spilled out an orange dust. She clamped her mouth shut on a half breath.

Ixor!

She bolted out of the alley into the main street, trying not to breathe, not daring to glance back for fear of slowing down or running into something.

How had the Palates snuck into town?

Someone appeared in front of her holding a bag of ixor.

Clef!

Wait, why did that name pop up in her head?

His eyes had that same polished gray as the guard at the gate. That seemed important for some reason.

She skidded and dashed to the left towards a bread shop and shoved past a few people trying to exit. Screams erupted, and startled shouts from those in the shop as she scrambled past them, searching for a back exit, her hood fallen around her shoulders.

"Was that a fur-mix?"

"It's the Palates! Run!"

She guessed that Clef had run inside the shop. She snatched a dishtowel off one of the counters and held it over her face, daring to inhale a quick breath and running pell-mell towards the back door.

Another cloud of orange dust billowed around her, and her eyes watered with the intensity. Some of it clung to the dishcloth, and she had to breathe a bit in. All around her, people fell to the floor, their limbs slowed, their bodies not reacting to their wishes to run. Except for a Palate, not Clef, who jumped in front of the back door, wearing a mask, reaching out for her.

She shifted her fingers for claws and raked at his grasping hands.

He yelled, holding one hand with the other. She leapt onto the shop counter, then onto his head, clawing at his mask and tearing the little straps that held it in place. It fell to the ground, and he screamed, flailing, catching her arm and digging into her skin with his fingers. His touch tasted like rancid, rotting flesh.

She tried to yank away from the cannibal, but he was much bigger than her and her reaction time had slowed.

Footsteps behind her made her tense. The Palate holding her flicked his gaze away from her. She used that moment to shift the rest of the way and bite the arm that held her, gagging at the taste.

The Palate screamed and flung her across the shop, past Clef, and she landed full foxan, feet splayed out. She careened out the front door and around the corner.

Something grabbed her shoulder. She bent her neck around to bite but registered reflective eyes and the pattern of stripes on the person's cheek and stopped herself. The fox-person pulled her through a tiny door in the wall of the bread shop and pulled it shut behind them.

"Where are you?" Outside, Clef's voice was smooth and calm. His footsteps passed the tiny side door's entrance. Saida tried not to breathe. Her legs trembled, threatening to give out. His footsteps paced back to the bread shop's door. "You cannot hide from him forever. Everyone will worship in the end."

All around, huge bags surrounded them like a wall. It was a storage space for the bread shop. The taste of flour floated strong in the air and covered everything like a thick dust, keeping them hidden.

"He is the god of the Planes! We will all become a part of him, and he a part of us! We are The Consumed!"

Saida fought to keep her shallow breaths from squeaking and giving them away. Her head pounded. Her mouth was so dry. *Who is he talking about? Why do I know his name?*

Another voice pounded on the walls in her mind. "Saida! Please! Remember!"

Remember what?

Footsteps took off down the street, and at least three more people followed if she guessed right. She and the fox-person waited in that hidden place for several minutes. There was a touch on her shoulder, and the fox-person led her away through a sliding wall on the other side of the storage space. A secret way.

She'd slunk through places like these before.

She shook that thought away, but the sounds of her friends' voices increased, loud enough for her to acknowledge.

"Thank you," she whispered to the fox-person in the dark.

They did not stop ahead of her, but guided her through the sliding partition, and into the back of another storage space, this one filled with barrels of what tasted like fermenting wine. They maneuvered around the barrels in pitch darkness, using their senses of what tasted closer, and came to another sliding wall leading to the outside. Saida had to squint for several seconds from the brightness of the sun, dark spots prickling her vision. The fox-person gestured at a tree in the backyard of the shop with long, overhanging branches, a wonderful hiding spot until the night descended to conceal her.

"Thank you," Saida said again.

"We rise like dough." The fox-person punched their fist into an imaginary mound of dough, then lifted their hands. "We do not stay down."

Another fox-person's words echoed in her mind, from another world, and another time that she'd segmented away into a different part of herself.

Fear has paralyzed us all. The trick is to not let it keep hold of you. You escape by moving a little at a time.

Saida blinked. In the light of the sun, the fox-person's pattern showed clear. Pell's pattern. Three stripes down the nose, and red-brown fur on the person's arms and legs.

Saida's mouth opened and closed, and then the fox-person had gone.

Pell. How had she forgotten about Pell, and her promise that she would find his descendent? That she would bring them all out of Between? Why had she . . .

"Saida," Goosefeather's voice sounded far away. "Listen. Please listen."

Her head hurt so much. But she needed to hear what her friends had to say. She couldn't let whatever it was keep hold of her.

"Saida, you *know* we don't speak. You made friends when you were afraid of everyone else. But we are just parts of you, different things you tell yourself."

She bowed her head and tucked her tail. She wanted to deny it. She wanted to go on pretending, as she had for so long.

How long?

"Two hundred years," Tricksy Stone whispered, that part of herself that remembered, that had never forgotten, that she had boxed up, and caged, and shoved into a magical stone. She slipped them out of her pocket, and they shifted in the slight way that they could. The magic was real, and responded to her, but they'd never had a voice beyond her own.

Alesio.

The events she had repressed crashed like a flood, like the Summit Wave. Alesio, singing to her on Taste when she was scared. Alesio's surprise at the gravity on Vision. Alesio, leaving, because she refused to love herself, and couldn't handle being loved, again; she was much too fragmented to remember how. She remembered Watthe and how he'd destroyed Saltfall, and perhaps all the other transplants she had placed. She remembered all the worlds were fading, drifting farther apart, far enough that soon she'd be trapped on one of them forever.

She had lost Alesio. He wanted nothing more to do with her.

". . . go to Between," Goosefeather said. "You're safest there. Oh, by the Senses, she's still listening to me. Tricksy, she's listening!"

Between. The one place Watthe couldn't reach, with no transplants to take him there. Besides, she had to see her mother and father. She had to tell Pell that she had found his descendent. She would stay there with them.

She slunk over to the tree with the overhanging branches and remained there, shivering. Clef and his initiates of Palates did not return. Maybe the city guards had taken care of the Palates.

She teleported to Between as the sun rose the next morning.

21

LIKE BIRDS, WE ALL TAKE WING

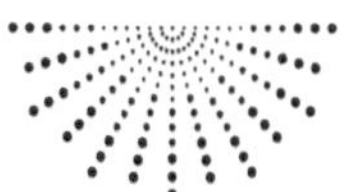

She rose from the desert sand in Between, and everything seemed quiet, the nearby lake not even quivering with a breeze.

She'd almost passed out, waiting for the portal to deposit her. She struggled to catch her breath. The currents of space had carried the worlds too far apart to teleport again.

She would have to stay here forever. Trapped.

I'll have plenty of time to think about that later.

After she caught her breath, she trotted away from the desert area and into the forest. The birds huddled in their nests when they should've chirped. A light dusting of snow lay over the underbrush and on the sides of the trees.

Large, clawed footprints marred the snow.

"No," Saida whispered. "How?"

Between didn't have any transplants!

"How?"

"I've consumed twelve of these portals, and each time, I grow in power." Watthe's words from the encounter on Touch echoed back to her.

Her mind dulled and her breathing sharpened. *No. NO!*

Her body responded, leaping forward with the quick, flashing

245

stride of the foxan. Drops of blood and scraps of fur showed here and there on the path.

A sob escaped the cage of her throat. She slowed for a half second, then ran on, blinking back burning tears, searching, and not searching for her mother. Would searching for a thing prove it to be so?

Saida tried to call out, though it bubbled out as a half-whimper, "Falrie! Falrie?"

Silence in the hush of the forest.

She bounded towards her den, a growing realization in her chest. She leaped over the fallen log, ran between the two thorn bushes.

Something had widened the tunnel to her den. Slash marks showed everywhere.

She raced inside, though Goosefeather and Tricksy Stone shouted at her to stop, to turn around, to run away—!

Rosewater and Jar of Sky lay smashed on the floor with other tubes and jars, seashells crushed, Leaf Pile shredded into fragments. Watthe crouched to fit inside the den, taller than he'd been on Touch.

"Hello, Saida."

She couldn't breathe.

He regarded her with a cocked head, waiting for her to respond to his greeting. Next to him, she felt like a bell-bug.

"Did you kill any foxans?"

He opened his palm over the shelves littered with shards of glass and shells. His long, clawed hands had grown as large as her whole body. He shrugged. "They scurried when saw they me. Out with those portals zipping they make."

They left Between?

Of course. They did what they had to do to survive.

She surveyed the wreckage, her chest refusing to let air in, though her mouth gaped. "I thought—I thought you didn't listen to that box anymore."

He laughed, and his smile stretched up to his eyes, the teeth creeping up into his cheeks. He gestured at the box, which he had set on one of the empty shelves he'd left on the wall. "I don't. I my own make decisions. And I decided that foxan magic very good tastes, better than humans much. In this, I agree with the box."

Her body shuddered, coming off the shock. She tried not to let herself crumble. Tears flowed down her foxan cheeks. *My fault. This is all my fault.*

Watthe snaked an arm behind her as large as a tree trunk, closing off the bottom of the widened tunnel. "I can almost anywhere now teleport, after all that magic eaten. But I don't you eat. I saw the way you with that human were. By his side staying."

"Watthe!" The box said. "It was I that separated the Planes! I who caused the Severing! I am but a fragment of what is coming, a fragment of The Hunger! If you do not eat her now, I will not spare you in my cravings!"

Something changed in the air when it said, 'The Hunger.' The ground vibrated, then the reverberations traveled up her leg, and into her bones. Greed. Craving. An insatiable want, a concentrated and otherworldly—or rather, other-*planar,* hunger. Watthe had always seemed hungry, as had the Primal Plane, but this . . .

There is a hunger that wants to consume us.

Falrie and the other foxans had mentioned the box years ago, before she'd ever told them about Watthe. Did that mean that the box posed the most danger between the two?

"Wh-what do you mean?" She asked the box, her voice thick in her ears. "What is coming for us? What are you?"

Watthe scooped her from behind with his hand, throwing her off balance. She stumbled, her vision blurry with tears. He held her in his palm like a mouse. His gray skin lifted away from him in hundreds of hands, enveloping her. Underneath, that smoke and hollowness waited.

"Do not waste your time with The Hunger," Watthe said. "I do not serve this box any longer, and neither you should."

"Why do you keep holding it, then?" Saida asked.

Watthe looked confused.

"I am *not* the god of your Planes!'" The Hunger's voice vibrated the ground again so that the loose dirt in the den created small dust clouds. "I'm not just from another place, I *am* another place. I am above your comprehension—"

"Why stay with that puny human? When I am tall and powerful?" Watthe held Saida closer to his giant face.

She swallowed. "Because I—I want to."

"How do I make you want to stay with me? He squeezed her tighter, pinioning her back legs. "I would only you every so often taste. I would not you kill."

She tried to shift to escape the hands. The innate magic that allowed her to shift filtered down the hundreds of gray fingers attached to her, then into his giant, smoking palm. She shuddered.

He smiled. "Mm. Magic. That is what do you will. You use magic, and I taste it will. Yes. This is good."

She raked her front claws into the leeching fingers. He screamed, and the void released her for a moment. She leapt to the ground of the den.

"Why did you do that?" He slammed his arm down in front of her, as large as a tree trunk, still covered in gray skin. She leapt over his arm.

"It's time," Tricksy Stone said.

"One of us," Goosefeather said.

Saida dashed through the widened tunnel. *He's eaten so much. He's grown too big to leave the den.* She would hide in the hills. She would—

A portal opened outside the den, as tall as the tallest tree. Watthe strode through, grinning that unhinged smile. "I told you. I can *anywhere* portal now. Anytime."

"Saida," Goosefeather said.

"I know," Saida said.

Fear has paralyzed us all, the fox-person from Sound had said. *The trick is to not let it keep hold of you. You escape by moving a little at a time.*

And the other fox-person, the one who had helped her on Taste, punching her fist into her hand. *We rise like dough.*

Alesio, humming the tune to "Gossamer God" to soothe her when she shook with fear. *It's important to do what you have to, to survive.*

She slipped Dawnsky Goosefeather out, brushing them one last time. "Take me to Sound," she mouthed. "Unlock a door for me, just once more. Somewhere in the city."

She dropped Goosefeather. A portal opened a foot in front of her, just big enough for a foxan and small enough that she hoped Watthe couldn't tell where she headed. She leapt through and he roared behind her.

She lost one of her two best friends in all of the worlds, as they gave feathers for her to fly.

22
WHAT WE HOLD ONTO

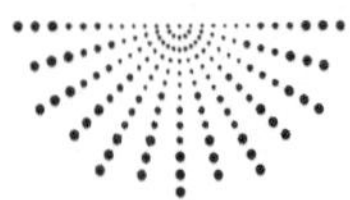

Saida slumped by the dumpster in the alley, numb, gripping the empty pocket where Goosefeather used to stay.

Gone.

Why did her mind hover around that? She should feel something, not this floating detachment that contemplated the grime on the bottom half of the buildings and not summoning a single tear.

Watthe had said the foxans had teleported away. They had violated their cardinal rule of staying in Between. Where would they have escaped to?

Her mind wandered.

Without her den, without the comforting presence of Alesio, she had nothing to hold onto except for Tricksy Stone. She found herself staring at the Drinks De Capo in the familiar alleyway. She could not let anyone see her face, even more so, now. Who knew how many people had joined Watthe's new religion? Part of the . . . what had Clef called them? The Consumed?

Anthem did seem quiet. The town did not trumpet at her. The bars did not blare. No corner singers vied for her attention, advertising the latest news. The humans all skulked with their heads down, even on the piper side, with fancy cloths stuck in their ears.

250

She watched for any that had gray, polished irises with that strange gleam.

She wandered.

But she remembered.

She hid in the back alley behind the Cadenza. When had she drifted all the way here? Distracted. She was so restless. But she couldn't—she shouldn't—make any more transplants, and she couldn't save Vision, or any of the worlds, for they would all die out without transplants to anchor their magic together. They'd faded for decades, now, and she'd tried so hard to bind the worlds closer, but now none of it mattered.

Watthe would find her. She had come to terms with that. He could teleport as many times as he wanted, and his extreme power allowed him to travel even though the worlds had drifted so far apart. He would cycle through the worlds to find her, or sooner or later, one of his worshippers would spot her, and summon him somehow.

We will all become a part of him, and he will become a part of us.

She had run out of places to run to. Goosefeather had only been able to reach Sound because they were a stronger transplant, the same as Tricksy Stone. Except for Alesio, they'd been the strongest magics she'd ever found.

She couldn't run from the truth anymore, either. After Carn, she had fragmented into different voices, different desires. Parts of her wanted to love and be loved, and parts of her wanted freedom, and parts of her wanted to forget. So, she'd given Goosefeather their name, and then had found Tricksy Stone ten years later. She'd magicked parts of herself into them so someone would travel with her. Herself, in pieces.

She remembered. She'd invested in Goosefeather the part of her that wanted to love, to reach out, to try again after cages and grasping hands and huddling in a ball. She'd named them her friend, because what else would she call someone who wanted the best for her even when she pushed them away?

Could she still love now that they were gone? Would she still have that part of her when she had used them?

"Let me help," Tricksy said.

She gazed up at the Cadenza, at that great, huge pipe organ sanctuary where Alesio aspired to perform. Four security guards patrolled nearby. She padded on silent paws behind a line of manicured bushes, climbed a trail of ivy up to a second-floor window, fiddled with the catch (Goosefeather could have helped with that) got it open, and dropped down into a marble hallway, behind a statue of the Sound.

She meandered through the vaulted marble hallway; her claws retracted to avoid clicking on the ground. She felt like she wafted through a dream.

A woman with a guitar strode past, and Saida flattened against the wall. After a little bit, she followed.

Around a corner, the human presented a slip of paper to a guard at a doorway. The guard opened the door and while he turned his back, Saida slipped in before he could close it.

The woman sauntered onto a stage in front of a massive velvet curtain. Saida scurried behind it. The lady performed a piece to what seemed an empty audience, except for a few people at the front with notebooks and ink pens. Her voice resonated, but she didn't have as powerful a magic as Alesio, not enough to trim. She bowed and left the stage.

Saida tied a cloth around her ears, shifted to human, and tried to stride like she belonged out on the stage. The lights shone bright, and she lowered her face to keep it somewhat concealed. The three people out in the audience squinted at her.

"Hello," she said. "I'm here as a scout for a singer."

One of them rose, a man with a red silk shirt and matching pants. "You don't look like any of our scouts. How did you get in here?"

Another shouted, "Guard!"

"Change for me," she whispered to Tricksy Stone. "A gemstone, please. A big one."

They hesitated. "Are you sure? I could be your next escape route from Watthe. I could try and teleport you to another world, though I don't know if I could reach them for much longer."

"He will find me anyway, someday. I want this for Alesio, before it's too late. Please." She lifted them from her pocket, her hands shaking.

They morphed and shifted to resemble a massive gemstone, lifting into the air like a low chandelier in her hands, floating as if creating their own gravity. The light danced on them, and hundreds of shafts of light streamed out into the rows of seats.

The people in the audience gasped. The guard they'd shouted for gasped, too.

"Wait," the man in red silk said. The guard didn't move.

"I'm proud of you." Tricksy Stone's voice faded in her head, or maybe it merged with her thoughts. "You've come so far. I'm glad we *were together, for a little while.*"

You've helped me so much. I want to hold on to you forever, Saida thought.

"*You helped yourself through something hard. You created my voice, and Goosefeather's, to listen to in the dark, but now, it's best to let me go. Become whole again. No more walls between your thoughts. Let me do this for you.*"

"Goodbye," she whispered.

The judges stared at the transplant. She must have kept them waiting for a little bit.

"The singer is very good." She still held out her hands as if proffering Tricksy Stone, though they floated a few feet above her. "He's had to work much too hard to get your attention. Send out one of those slips of paper for an Alesio who performed at the Drinks De Capo. Do that, right now, and I will hand this over."

They whispered among themselves, a heated but short conversation. One by one, they came up and touched the transplant, exclaiming, and reassured themselves that the floating giant gemstone was real.

Tricksy Stone was no trick; when they transplanted, they had merged with the Sound magic. The acoustics of the Cadenza lifted them into the air, the angles and cut of them spiraling and shifting, beaming out different streaks of light, some in different colors. But they could no longer become anything other than a gemstone. And she couldn't hear them anymore.

A seed of an idea formed in her mind. She could do one last thing to help the worlds. She had tracked the notion by instinct, sensing the opportunity the way she hunted overgrowths.

Watthe dealt with loneliness just like she did. Like she had, before she'd found Alesio. The monster searched for someone to stay by his side.

"Deal," the man in red silk said.

ALESIO DUCKED his head as he entered the Bow and Heart, a violin store on the piper side. The woman behind the counter jerked her head up, then scanned his face. He paused in the doorway to check if a fist-sized wound showed on her person, or if an unnatural gray glazed her eyes. If she had a wound, she'd covered it. Narrowed brown irises met his.

"Welcome to the Bow and Heart." Her voice had a rote tone, that of a practiced phrase that had lost all meaning for the speaker. "Can I help you?"

"Looking for work." Alesio stepped away from the door, resisting the urge to massage his neck. His throat had started to ache again in the past few days, and now he knew why. "I'll sweep floors and dust the instruments. Anything."

He'd tried so many places, traveled to so many different stores, the museum, the post, the upper crust news corners. But Anthem had shut down in the past week. Even Mona's pub remained silent at the prime ten o'clock time slot, a few straggling in for the drinks they couldn't go without.

The cut of money that Clef had passed him all those worlds ago still lasted, but it would run out within the next month or so. Mona had given him the benefit of the doubt after he'd disappeared, and had cared for his father, making sure his wound didn't get infected and keeping him fed and housed. But with the way things seemed to be heading, and the whispers in the streets, even Mona had said she would need to shut down the pub in the next few days. "Till things blow over," she had said, but she had swiped the dishcloth across the bar with a quiet resignation.

"We're not hiring." The Bow and Heart store clerk's shoulders had a tense cast.

"*No one's* hiring."

The woman barked a laugh, then lowered her voice. "Course not. Not with that rogue reverend and his cult roaming everywhere. You'd think the Cadenza would do something about it!"

Her voice held such a dissonance of restrained panic that Alesio almost winced. He stepped closer, also keeping his voice down. This shopkeeper seemed more willing to talk about the state of the city than others he had spoken to today. "Have you known anyone that changed?"

She pressed her hand to her mouth. "My sister. She attended St. Rina's, and afterwards, she wouldn't stop talking about how she wanted me to go, too, saying it would change my life."

"But you didn't go."

She shook her head, closing her eyes for a moment. "She . . . had a hole in her neck."

Alesio jolted, his eyes widening.

The woman stared through him, not seeing him. "It was like someone had punched her. It was that big, fist sized. She'd covered it with a scarf, but there was this whistling sound from her neck as the wind blew, and the fabric moved, and I saw it. She didn't even notice." She refocused on Alesio, her lips trembling. "No, I didn't go. I'm not *insane.*"

"I'm sorry. That was a stupid question."

She turned away, wiping at her eyes with her sleeve.

Lasrial had apparently replaced the statue of the god of Sound with a giant stone monster, and he'd held services where, some people said, the actual monster had appeared: an entity as tall as the cathedral, with too long arms and claws. People everywhere whispered of a monster that killed but kept the victims' bodies walking and talking and spreading the news of their 'conversion.'

"Did your sister mention anything about a security guard there? Someone named Tak?" He swallowed. "He's my friend. I haven't heard from him."

New suspicion wrinkled the corners of her mouth. "She didn't mention anyone. But if he worked there, well, best you stop looking."

Alesio slumped.

What if I can't find anything, even in the straits? By the Senses. I wouldn't be surprised if everyone stops using notes for money soon if no one can work.

All this trekking around the city held a pale echo of traveling with Saida, of experiencing new places, other worlds. His dream of singing at the Cadenza seemed minor compared to that golden night in Scent, where he had sung for that small village, and they had enjoyed it for the pureness of loving something, not for anything else.

He couldn't return to the cage matches either. Clef had thrown his lot in with Watthe, for one, but Alesio would have refused to go down that path again anyway. He just couldn't, not after knowing how much more he could do with his life.

If he didn't find anything in the next few days, maybe he could slip out of town and try to survive in the sound-wilds with his father. He could learn to live off the land. Saida had done it, hadn't she?

The shopkeeper eyed him for a few moments with that frown, then she sighed and wrapped her arms around herself. "She did call herself something. She said she was one of 'The Consumed.'" Her voice thickened, and she blinked and wiped at her eyes. "Has the whole city gone mad? A piper reverend letting the strait's leader run his services? A monster that controls dead people? This is all happening so fast." She gestured at the store. "I'm thinking I'll move to Flock. Get away while I still can. Maybe there'll be a work opening for you here soon, after all."

"Thank you for talking to me," Alesio said. "Everyone's so afraid, it's hard to know how bad things are, or where it's safe."

"Nowhere." The shopkeeper shook her head. "Maybe out in the country. Somewhere far away from here."

That's truer than you know.

"I'm sorry about your sister. Good luck with getting out."

He slipped outside, his footsteps ringing like alarm bells in the unnatural quiet of Anthem's empty streets.

———

ALESIO HELPED PROP up his father on the small bed with a dingy pillow. He still had some trouble standing and sitting, but Mona had told Alesio that his stab wound had not bled for two weeks.

"Where's that young woman at?" His father asked. "The secret one. Shouldn't she come around soon?"

Alesio sighed. "I told you. She's a foxan. It's not safe for her here."

I can't think about her.

It all seemed like a dream, now, those different worlds she had shown him. The freedom to live, to thrive in a new place. To sing to just one person, and have it mean so much. A beautiful, impossible dream.

"Well. I must say, all those stories about fox-people stealing are true."

Alesio wheeled and glared at his father. "What? Why would you say that? She saved your life!"

His father chuckled. "She stole your heart right quick, didn't she?"

Alesio let out a slow breath and massaged his neck. He laid the one thin blanket from the room over his father's legs. "I'm going to make some food. Some tea."

"Have you sung at the pub yet?"

"I'm trying to find work at another place uptown. There's not a lot of options."

"Cause of that new cult running around?"

Alesio paused. His father didn't know as much about the recent events in Anthem, having remained in the pub since Alesio had had him carried there. "I was gone for all of two weeks, and it's like everyone went insane!"

His father chuckled. "Now that you've visited 'other worlds,' you know all about how this one works?"

Alesio rolled his eyes. His father believed he'd taken a hallucinatory drug in the past few weeks and had scolded him for it at first. Now he just joked about it.

"You should sing at the pub tonight."

"Dad."

"What?" His father grinned at him, those milky white eyes squinting at him. The whiteness of them had spread to cover most of his pupils. Sometimes he bumped into things when he walked, so Alesio had moved the one chair and the dresser to the same wall, to keep as much open space as possible.

"Mona's closing the pub because of everything." Alesio paused. "Why are you acting so strange? When I used to say anything about performing, I might as well have told you I was singing for the moon."

His father plumped the pillow behind him again. "She talked some sense into me, I'll have you know. The fur—ahem, the foxan. You know what she said to me? 'If he loves doing something, that's another way to make sure he's safe. In his own mind.'"

"Dad—"

"Sssk! Let me finish." He sighed. "I thought about that. I thought about how you love to sing, and about how I never attended any of your performances. Sounddamn it, I never thought I was putting you in danger by *not* going."

Alesio's mouth gaped. "You really—you'd really come and listen?"

A knock at the door made them both turn their heads. A pompous voice issued from the other side. "Summons for an Alesio."

Alesio frowned and opened the door. A man wearing a silk pantsuit and vest leaned against the wall, bent over a little and panting. He held out a gold-trimmed piece of paper. Alesio bent to check the man's eyes for that tell-tale gray. The man had blue eyes, so Alesio took the paper. It read:

"This notice hereby summons Alesio, he who performs at the Drinks De

Capo, to the Cadenza for an audition. Please come as soon as possible, preferably when you receive this message."

Alesio's knees had buckled, and he held onto the chair. The paper trembled in his hands.

"What is it, son?"

"Is—is this a trick?" Alesio asked the piper.

The piper straightened his collar and gave a little cough. "It most certainly is not."

Alesio held out the paper to his father, tears streaming down his face. His throat ached. *I guess it does still matter to me. Even after everything. Even with the threat of dead people roaming the streets.*

"Do you want to come and hear me audition at the Cadenza?"

His father's milky eyes widened. He swung his legs off the bed, hobbled over, and clapped Alesio on the shoulder. "Let's go."

THE CADENZA ROSE ABOVE THEM, not quite as tall as the wave on Touch. His escort ushered him and his father through the doors. The security guard gave their rough straits clothing an up and down scan but bowed as they went through. A summons to the Cadenza seemed to forgive even poverty.

Or is it because they have no one who feels safe to leave their houses to perform?

They had crept through the streets, their piper escort starting and stopping every few minutes and glancing over his shoulder with the same manner that someone from the straits might have done—except the escort was a lot more conspicuous about it. One of The Consumed had appeared a block away, and the escort had dashed down a side street with all the surreptitiousness of a startled rabbit. When they reached the Cadenza, a glossy sheen of sweat covered his bald head.

This all seemed too good to be true. They had to be desperate for performers, or even attendees, at this point. Alesio's mouth twisted, and he almost reached out to tap the piper's shoulders. Then they stepped through the front door.

The inside glowed with sound; the walls were crafted for acoustics and amplifying harmonies. Even the hallway had a vaulted ceiling.

Alesio stared. He stopped himself from dropping low to the ground, crouching, ready for a fight.

He didn't belong here.

He rounded on the escort. "Why was I invited?" he asked, his teeth clenched. "Why me? I'm a *straiter*."

"Alesio," his father said under his breath.

"No. I want to know." The ache in his throat intensified. "Am I just anyone off the street? The first performer that said yes to even leaving their house?"

The piper wiped at the sweat on his forehead with a silk embroidered cloth. "Good sir. I am just an escort. I was told to bring you, and I have."

Alesio frowned, the anger waiting.

His father whispered in his ear, "To earn their true favor, you'd have to be rich. If anything, this has forced them to give you a fair shake."

The escort glanced back and forth between them.

The last time Alesio had allowed his anger to run free, he had perpetrated violence with his words. And for just a half moment, he felt something surrounding him—maybe that magic Saida had talked about—like hundreds of sound-knives pointed at him, cutting him whenever he breathed too deep.

Your voice sounds like it's suffering, she had said once, in the cathedral garden.

He breathed in, and out, and restrained the violence, that ball of condensed ache and anger in his throat. When she had said that to him, a beam of sunlight had spilled down, and her eyes had reflected it. She'd looked like a section cut out of a red-dawn sky.

The escort cleared his throat. Alesio blinked, and the Cadenza's golden, arched ceilings, and the piper's gleaming head, and his father's intent eyes all came back into focus.

"Alright," Alesio said.

The piper escort waved another attendant over. He gestured to Alesio's father. "Would you seat this gentleman in the theatre, please?"

The second person bowed. "Of course. Right this way, sir."

"Wait," Alesio said. "I want him with me."

Watthe still lurked out there, and those strange followers Lasrial had gathered. He didn't want his father to leave his sight.

His father waved to Alesio and whispered, "Go on."

"Sir?" The escort said.

Alesio shook off the nerves as best he could and followed the escort, tiptoeing, hesitant to disturb the hallowed hush of the place. The mandolin slung over his shoulder seemed rustic and plain. He clutched the folded slip of paper in his hand. Should he have folded it? He tried to wipe off any sweat with his shirt, but that just smudged it with some dirt.

The escort let out a muffled cough, wiping at their forehead again. He had led Alesio to a side door, with a guard in front of it.

"Your invitation," The guard said.

Alesio handed it over, trying not to let it tremble. The guard unfolded it, then glanced at the escort, who nodded.

The guard opened the door, and Alesio drifted through like a ghost, holding his breath. What would his magic look like, now, that he had tried to hold back the sharpness that wanted to dart from his lips? The soreness in his throat had lessened, just a bit.

A velvet curtain waited, and beyond that, the stage. It hit him, then. He was here. At the Cadenza. Auditioning so he could perform in front of thousands of adoring fans. Well, maybe not thousands. Not until they figured out what to do about The Consumed. But. *But.* He was here.

And his father was, too.

The lights shone so bright. He could just make out the people in the front row. Something bright shone above him, casting streams of purple and red, then yellow and orange. It shone like the sun in the dark room, and he had to look away.

He was shaking. What if he messed up again, right here? He would never have another chance like this! A sudden summons, without a scout to vouch for him? It didn't happen for people like him! Musicians from the straits lived their whole lives performing for apathetic curbside crowds and the raucous audiences of seedy bars.

Wait.

I've already performed in better places.

That night on Scent, when all the people he'd sung for had seemed so happy. Or when Saida had trembled and shook after the Palates' attack, and he had sung for her about the stars, and had tasted the night sky above him.

"What are you going to sing for us?" One of them asked, a man in a red silk ensemble.

"Dear Flute, Dear Love."

It was one of his best. But he had another reason, something that he'd hidden away until now. He wanted to sing it for her. He wanted to give her a voice, to show that he understood what she'd meant, when she'd said she couldn't lose her friends.

"Whenever you're ready."

He unslung his mandolin and breathed for a moment, his fingers hovering over the strings. They steadied. Thankfully, he'd had the presence of mind to tune it before heading out of Mona's pub.

I am trapped inside this flute,
And live my life rolled like a scroll,
But he unwraps my prison cell
When he takes me out to hold

I sing for him whenever
He presses his lips to me
The people, they all love him
When I sing his melody

He does not know my name,
Or that I used to have dark eyes,
But his sweet whispers, they do echo

Through my narrow, too-close skies

I wish that I could tell him
Of my feelings when he plays,
But I have no lips for speaking,
So, I will love from far away

Tears streamed down his cheeks. He wiped his face and bowed. *I was so horrible to her. I tried to hurt her with what I said. If I had been on Sound, my magic could have attacked her, like the water magic did on Touch.*

"That was . . . well done," one of the judges said, a dark-haired man with a mustache.

The next, a man in red silk, looked over at the other two, rose, and bowed. "I vote that you have passed this audition, Alesio." He sniffed and dabbed his eye.

The last also stood up. "Welcome to the Cadenza."

From somewhere out in the dark of the theatre, Alesio's father shouted. "That's my son!"

Alesio let out a half-sob, half-laugh.

"I say he performs next week!" The man in red silk said.

"Well," the third said, "We might have to re-think our performance schedule. Considering everything. The authorities have not given us an answer about when the streets will clear of this riffraff." He sniffed. "Disgraceful work."

"Incompetence." The man in red nodded.

"Oh, and you should know," the one with the mustache said. "A friend of yours alerted us to your talent. You have her to thank for this audition."

"What? Who?"

"Yes, I had no idea that such ability existed in the straits!" The third man tapped his pen against his chin. "Perhaps we should have our scouts go there more often. Especially with our current situation."

"Our bellringer Hestafon still won't answer?" The man in red asked.

The third shook his head. "Neither will Lotes or Istasian. And I'm not sure if the guests themselves will—" he coughed, then glanced at Alesio. "We can talk about it later."

"What friend?" Alesio asked again.

"We didn't get her name," the mustached man said. "But she was very persuasive."

Saida is still here? But it's not safe! Watthe's followers are everywhere! Why didn't she go back to Between?

Wait. How did she get me this audition?

The light in the room changed from purple and red to a cool blue and silver, something easier to look up at. Alesio tilted his head up.

A glowing, ever-changing gemstone floated above the stage. As large as it had grown, he recognized it as Saida's magical rock.

She gave up one of the only friends she knew how to love.

"Thank you, sirs." Alesio's lips formed the words, and he heard himself say them, but his brain didn't process what he had said till a few seconds later. "I need to leave." He ran off stage, leaving the judges gaping.

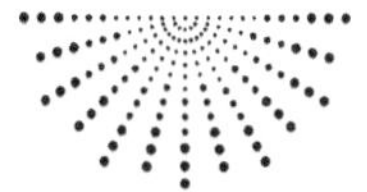

23

TO CATCH A FOXAN

lesio's father squinted milky eyes as he emerged from the auditorium. "Alesio!" He called across the Cadenza foyer, the sound loud in the vaulted ceiling. He rushed over. "Alesio, you did so well—wait. What's wrong?"

Alesio ran his hand through his hair. "Saida's in trouble. That gem they had in there, the big, bright one? That was hers." His voice cracked. "It was very special to her."

By the Sound . . . I told her to do that. I told her to make a sacrifice to prove she could love. But I didn't mean for me!

"Well, I could see why," His father said. "It was as big as my head!"

Right. Who would believe that someone kept a giant gemstone for reasons other than money?

"Son. I need to tell you something." His father shifted his weight on one leg, then the other. His voice resonated in the space.

Guards stood at the doors to the auditorium, but they didn't move to usher Alesio and his father away. Was it because Alesio was an official performer for the Cadenza, now?

"Alesio." His father laid a hand on his shoulder. "I know I've been hard on you over the years. I've made mistakes and I've called them advice." He took a deep breath. "But I want you to know, that when I refused Clef's help, all those years ago, I did it because I was trying to protect you in the best way I knew how. I was trying to protect your future. But because of that, I ignored what you needed in the moment. I was so wrapped up in saving you from what could have been, I didn't realize we were both starving. In more ways than one."

A lump stuck in Alesio's throat. He couldn't swallow it, and it hurt. His father hadn't whispered those words, and they resounded through the Cadenza, bouncing off the walls, leaping to the highest part of the ceiling. The guards straightened, their throats bobbing up and down. One of them scrubbed at their eyes.

Tears streamed down his own cheek for the second time in ten minutes and plopped on the floor. *Plop. Plip plop.*

He'd shouted at Saida. He'd screamed at her for not caring enough to rescue herself, for not trying to survive.

But he hadn't really been talking to *her*.

"Dad." Alesio cleared his throat. "Thank you. I guess . . . I got mad at you so much because I was scared. Not just that you would die, but I was afraid you would rather die than—than be with me if I chose the wrong thing. I was afraid you would just stop trying."

Something in him sighed when he said those words, as if he'd let a bird out of a cage from his chest.

His father pulled him in for a hug. "I'm not going anywhere. Are you kidding? My boy's a Cadenza performer! I'm pretty sure I get special seats!" He pounded Alesio's back a few times, and Alesio let out a choked laugh.

At the doors leading to the auditorium, the guards wiped at their eyes with their shoulders, then straightened again, then had to wipe again.

Alesio and his father straightened, both clearing their throats and wiping at their own tears tickling their cheeks.

"So, the fur—" Alesio's father paused. "The woman, gave that gem up for you?" He thumbed back at the auditorium.

Alesio nodded.

"Sound*damn*, son! So, she did come back! I told you she would!"

She was supposed to go back to Between. She was supposed to stay there!

Then it hit him.

She forgot.

"Dad, I have to go to her. I have to find her. But it's not safe out there, now. I don't want you leaving the Cadenza."

"I can make it back to the pub just fine."

Alesio looked up at the guards watching them, then said a bit louder, "Is it alright if he stays here for a few hours? Because of the freaks running around? I promise I'll come back."

One of the guards stepped forward, his eyes a clear blue. Alesio cocked his head. He'd seen a picture of the man before.

"Alesio?" The guard asked.

Alesio blinked. "How do you know my name?"

"Tak, my husband, talks about you sometimes. You worked together at St. Rina's."

Talks. "Is he alright?"

Estro nodded. "He . . . came back after a service last week, and said he couldn't go back, that a monster had taken over the church."

Alesio slumped in relief. *Thank the Sound.*

"He's afraid to leave the house," Estro said. "He keeps talking about how the monster took over the parishioners, and controls them, somehow."

Saida could already have faced the same fate.

"Dad," Alesio said. "This is why I need you to stay here. Just like you tried to protect me all those times, it's my turn now, okay? *You have to stay here.* Lock the doors."

Alesio's father opened his mouth, then closed it. "Alright. But what are you planning to do? If that monster is out there killing people, and changing them into something else, then what could you do against it?"

Estro, the other guard, and his father all looked at him. He inhaled deep and stored the air in his lungs.

Something in him had loosened when he'd confessed to his father. Something had unfolded in his throat like a flower that wanted to bloom, easing the ache. Something powerful.

"I'm going to fight it."

Lots of people milled around St. Rina's cathedral, almost like they patrolled it. Saida had known the secret ways of the fox-people without Tricksy Stone's help. That made her feel both alone and relieved, but it had allowed her to sneak closer. She huddled under the thick bushes on the outside of the cathedral's garden, watching a strange scene unfold. The people moved in random ways. They paced without patterns, at a slant down the street, then a straight line back, then perhaps in a small circle. They all displayed huge, gaping wounds in various places, and their gray eyes matched the gray gleam of Watthe's skin. She couldn't help but think he saw everything they did. They all had a thinness to their frames and had shriveled skin. They did not generate any Sound magic.

The Consumed, Clef had called them. Watthe seemed to have absorbed their magics. Sucked them as dry as leaves in the fall.

Am I really doing this?

She had no other choice. It was this or wait for him to find her. At least she could go in with the hope of doing things on her terms and change the flow of Watthe's—or The Hunger's—plan for the worlds.

She ducked out from under the bushes and strode up to the cathedral's main doors. Shifted in her human form. Her ears uncovered.

Alesio crept through the streets towards St. Rina's, both dread and desperate hope warring for room in his chest.

People peered out from behind curtains, watching with pale, drawn faces that spoke of staying inside for a while now, too afraid to leave their houses. What had happened at the hostels in the straits? Those rooms of stacked beds, where the people packed in to just have a place to sleep? Had they emptied out? Did people still work the factories?

Thank the Sound he'd gotten his father out of there before Saida had teleported Alesio away. The whole city had sunk into a kind of hypnotized waiting period, as the people tried to wait out the dead roving the streets.

A Consumed in a silk pantsuit lumbered down the middle of the road ahead. His chest displayed a hole the size of a fist which he hadn't bothered to cover up with a new vest.

Alesio hid behind a shop door left open, swinging a bit on its hinges. He still had about seven blocks till he reached St. Rina's. If she'd been caught, it seemed that was where she'd be taken.

The man stopped and stood unmoving for several agonizing seconds before continuing, sometimes straight, sometimes at an angle towards the right or left. A few times he whirled and marched the other way.

Alesio didn't have time for this. He needed to find Saida before Watthe killed her. The power burned in his throat, that power that wanted to be set free, that wanted to help.

He formulated a small dagger of sound and let it fly. A javelin emerged from his throat and stabbed the Consumed in the heart. The dead man fell over and didn't move.

Holy Sound! That was way more powerful than I've ever done before! Alesio clapped a hand over his mouth. Still, the power roiled there, past his throat now, pushing up against his soft palate and his clenched teeth. Trying to find an outlet.

Throwing caution away, he dashed down the street, watching for any Consumed that might get in his way. Six blocks away, two Consumed appeared, and he tried to measure his sound even smaller to produce knives, yet spear-lengths catapulted out from him, poleaxing the two before they even detected his presence. They dropped.

At five and a half blocks, five ran towards him. He sang them down, though the last two got a bit too close for his liking.

Four blocks. Ten or twelve. He couldn't kill them all—was kill the right term? —not before they swarmed him. They all had the hole in their chest, or their neck, or their head, even. None of them seemed to care about hiding it.

He sent a thin line of horizontal sound at them, like a trip wire, slicing through their knees. They all fell like so many snipped flowers, and something gripped him in his heart.

Three and a half blocks, and they came at him in waves, now, their feet pounding the rhythm of the dead with no rests in between. He sang out more wires, with no time for individual knives or spears or swords, just sending out sharp lines of violence.

Two and a half blocks. Fifty or more blocked his way. They threw themselves at him with no regard for anything, the holes in their chests filled with that gleaming gray matter. He didn't know how long his newfound magic strength would hold out, but he couldn't have them leaping at him from the sides.

He hated this. He hated using his voice like this. But it didn't feel wrong, like it had in the cage matches. They were already dead. He just sang their requiem.

He prayed Saida's face didn't appear in the hordes.

Two blocks.

The waves of Consumed reversed like an outgoing tide, hundreds of them dashing towards St. Rina's.

Hold on, Saida! I'm coming!

ONE OF THE CONSUMED, a man with long, gray hair, turned Saida's way and ceased all motion. He pointed at her and screeched without words. The others all spun towards her as one entity might, and chills ran down her spine. They all screeched.

She kept walking. She couldn't save the Sense worlds with transplants any longer, so instead, she would trap Watthe using his own desire to capture her. She would trap them both, as far away from the rest of the worlds as she could. Back on the Primal Plane.

If she had to be caged, she'd prefer it if she walked inside her prison on her own terms.

The Consumed followed her, gathering behind her, leaving the way open to the cathedral, herding her. She strode through the giant front doors, and there Lasrial waited, his arms crossed in his robes, his eyes that same gray as all the others.

She tilted her chin up. "Summon Watthe."

Lasrial glared. "You're such an annoying little shit-mix."

One of The Consumed grabbed Saida from behind. She tensed, every muscle in her body protesting. *Trapped, oh, Senses, I can't—*

No. I can do this.

"Bring her in here!" Lasrial strode to the front of the cathedral.

They surged, propelling her forward, and poured in after her, filling the pews and the whole space with packed gray bodies, gray eyes, and gaping wounds.

The old monolith that had depicted the god of Sound, that giant golden wave, had been replaced by a rough but giant statue of Watthe, the head brushing the high, domed ceiling of the cathedral. Saida gasped.

Lasrial knelt in front of Watthe's statue. "Oh, great god of the Planes! I have captured what you seek. I send my voice out across the worlds, pleading for you to hear me! See through my eyes!"

The reverend's eyes gleamed brighter. Then a wind rushed through the cathedral, and a portal opened from the statue itself.

The real Watthe stepped through. He had grown larger, almost too tall for the cathedral. He crushed the front pews under his feet. He still carried the box called The Hunger. That surprised her. She hoped it wouldn't change how he reacted to her plan.

Saida breathed in and out, trying to copy how Alesio stayed calm in difficult situations. "Watthe. I've thought about your offer."

The creature lowered his head down to hers. The gray skin stretched over his face shone bright. "Saida." His voice rumbled like thunder in an endless sky. "I missed. Your magic, it's tasted the strongest I've ever. I want to stay you. I want . . . you to stay with me. I want you to worship me. You do this. I decided."

He wanted the twisted kind of love that Carn had shown her.

That isn't love, Alesio's voice echoed in her thoughts. *Love isn't about cages, or about someone forcing you to love them back. That's selfishness.*

Love, real love, is about helping the other person because you want to. Because you care about them, and that's all that matters.

She loved the worlds. She loved the foxans. She loved Alesio.

She *could* love using the kind of love that Alesio had told her about. She wanted to help them and make things better for all of them.

Saida licked her lips. "I have one condition."

Watthe lowered his oversized, sharpened fingers, his hand large enough to hold ten of her at once. "Go on."

"We go back to where we started. That place below Vision. I will be your worshipper. And we stay there. Together."

"The Primal Plane," Watthe said.

She had no idea if this trap would work, but if the different Sensory worlds had drifted so far apart that she could no longer reach them, the Primal Plane must have drifted much, much farther. She hoped to all the Senses that teleporting there would drain the transplants' magic he had consumed all at once. Once there, he would have no transplants to eat and power his portals.

She could trap him there with her.

Of course, he'd grown so big and powerful he might still be able to teleport after, especially if he ate her. But she had to try. She had to save the Sense worlds before Watthe consumed every bit of magic everywhere.

"No!" The Hunger thrashed in Watthe's arms, the solidity of the box writhing like a mass of worms. "She is dangerous! You cannot take her there!"

"Oh, Great One!" Lasrial said. "Please! Do not listen to this fur-mix! You are god, you are not bound by the wishes of half-animals! You make your own choices!"

Watthe reached out and speared Lasrial through the chest with one of his giant claws.

The reverend looked down at the claw through his chest, then melted into a pile of gray sludge. What used to be the reverend oozed around Watthe's claw and joined with it.

Saida covered her mouth, trying not to throw up.

"I do not listen *anyone's* wishes but to mine!" St. Rina's stained-glass windows cracked from the thunder of his voice. "And wish I to be with her!"

"Saida! Saida!"

Alesio's voice reverberated through Saida's body like a shock from Winter Lightning. She pivoted. He had pushed through the press of The Consumed by creating a bubble around himself of sharpened sound, which none of them could pass without slicing themselves in two. His magic soared around him, more potent and powerful than anything she'd ever witnessed.

"Remember what I said!" Alesio shouted. "The important thing is to survive! Remember? To love yourself?" He clenched his fists, his stocky chest heaving. "I never meant for you to sacrifice *yourself!*"

He couldn't be here. He'd almost died, and it had been her fault for not using the magic in her pocket.

She'd known that Tricksy Stone and Goosefeather didn't really speak to her, that they were just extensions of her thoughts she'd placed on objects. She'd *known* that, and yet she hadn't been able to let them go to save a real life.

"Run, Alesio! I swear, I don't have either of the transplants left to save you!" Saida twisted around. "Watthe, if you kill him, the deal is *off!*"

Watthe narrowed his huge eyes at Alesio. "Your magic is much, human, but you are too late. She has promised stay to."

Alesio sang a giant spear at Watthe's torso, but the creature vanished through a teleport and reappeared a few inches away.

Watthe extended his claw and curled it around Saida's middle. The gray skin of his arm peeled away and formed into smaller gray hands, hundreds of fingers extending and locking her in place. Underneath his skin, that void-like smoke waited, too close, and the fatigue overtook her. Her eyelids fluttered.

"Human, do no more. I will her hurt if you do."

He raised her to his face, to the top of the cathedral ceiling. She tried to twist her neck around to look back at Alesio, but she couldn't move inside of Watthe's suspension.

Watthe pointed at the main doors. Another portal opened.

Through its yawning oval, a tangle of trees and vines showed. The Primal Plane.

Watthe strode past Alesio and through the portal in two steps.

"Do not leave us!" The Consumed cried out. They crowded through the portal after him.

The giant oval of the portal showed St. Rina's, the smashed pews, and Alesio on the other side, still with that Sound magic protecting him, staring after her and Watthe. The Consumed streamed around him into the Primal Plane like water around a rock.

The portal closed, but slowly, the size keeping it open longer than Saida's portals.

"Saida!"" Alesio held out a seashell, and he sang his next few words to the tune of "My Flute, My Love."

> *I'm coming with you,*
> *Because I love you*

His tenor voice swirled like a silver thread, winding inside the shell, trimming his magic, and creating a transplant.

He jumped through the portal.

"No!" Saida screamed. "No, no!"

24

THE PRIMAL PLANE

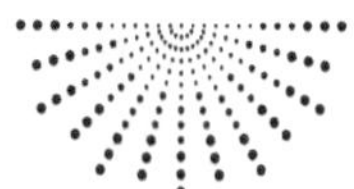

The air was thick and fetid in the Primal Plane. Saida wheezed just to fill her lungs.

Trees grew massive and twisted, here, curling like vines, and vines wrapped around them the size of normal trees. The ground squelched as Watthe traipsed further in. Behind them, Alesio had to pull himself out of one area where he sank up to his knees in the suspended spaces of smoking matter. The huge portal hadn't yet closed behind him. The crowd of The Consumed streamed through.

"Go back!" Saida's voice had weakened to a hoarse whisper.

Alesio would be trapped here, forever. She didn't have the power to open a portal all the way back to the Sensory worlds. He would never perform at the Cadenza. He'd never see his father again.

Or Watthe might just eat him once he'd finished with her.

The giant stopped and raised her to his face, holding her with two fingers curled. One of them dug into her torso.

"Your magic is water in a desert." He breathed in, and she slumped, her energy depleting. He grew larger, now standing above even the trees here, his fingers the size of the vines. The Consumed swarmed around him like ants protecting their queen, their heads reaching the lower half of his legs.

Not good! Not good!

Alesio shouted something, dashing towards them, though Watthe had strode a fair distance in mere seconds.

Watthe reached inside his chest and pulled out something, something tiny in between two fingers. The box.

Watthe tossed it to the side, tipped his head back, and roared to the smoke-filled sky. "See me, Primal Plane! Tremble! I god am! This box nothing equals, it commands me, nor you!"

He set Saida on the branch of a tree. "I can't all of you taste, or you'll disappear." He rubbed his palms together where she had stood, then pressed them to his face, inhaling, and growing again, apparently from the remnants of her magic. "I have make you to last. I have make sure you to stay."

You're the only one I can love.

Saida managed to swallow, her limbs trembling. She clutched the branch with a shaky grip to keep from falling.

Under her palms, the branch seethed with hunger and anger. It burned the skin on her hands. No, not just the branch. The whole place felt angry, and fermented, and hungry.

Watthe buckled. Something had sliced his legs off at the knee with a humming wire of sound. He hissed, glancing back at Alesio.

"Pesky human!" He speared his claws through five of The Consumed milling at his feet like a skewer. They melted into the gray substance of Watthe's skin and oozed into his body, creating new legs all in about a second.

Alesio sent another sound-wire, but Watthe dodged it by teleporting. "You want me to pain her?" He gestured at Saida trembling in the tree. "I spare you once more. For her. Then I will kill you."

Alesio hesitated, glaring at Watthe.

"Saida!"

Saida jerked in shock. Was that Falrie's voice?

Below her, the foxan woman waded through the muck and the shadows in human form. She grabbed Alesio's hand and boosted him up to the tree Saida stood on. "Alesio, give her the seashell! Saida, transplant it now! I'm too out of practice!"

The surprise of Falrie's entrance slowed Saida's understanding for a moment. Then comprehension hit her.

The entire Primal Plane was an overgrowth. If another transplant merged with them, like how the twisted water magic on Touch had merged with the transplant from Scent, the magic could realign.

"You're not near her getting!" Watthe raised his arm to swat Alesio out of the tree.

"No!" Saida gasped.

Her father and Pell appeared behind Watthe. They must have run through the huge portal Watthe had summoned before it closed.

"Falrie!" Darrow shouted. "Falrie, I remembered! And so did Pell! As soon as we left Between, it all came back—oh, by the Senses, there he is!"

"I feared you all off," Watthe said. "Now, you come to me. You are here to worship your god?"

"Worship?" Pell said. "You *are* crazy!"

Alesio scrambled up the tree towards Saida, reaching for her hand, lurching a little on the insubstantial nature of the Primal Plane foliage. Their fingers brushed just out of reach.

Watthe teleported the twenty feet to the two foxans, snatched Pell, and snapped his neck.

"Pell!" Saida cried out in a dry whisper. "No!"

"Grab this!" Alesio had clambered up to the next highest branch. He passed her the seashell.

"Where do you want to go?" She asked the transplant, trying not to sob.

She couldn't hear their voice. They'd never had voices. But she still understood their feelings. This place scared them.

"I know," Saida said. "But please. This could be a wonderful place.

She searched for her mother. Falrie stared at Pell broken on the ground. Darrow knelt next to her; his shoulders slumped. Everything had happened so fast.

"Falrie," Saida called, her voice wavering. "Are you sure this will work?"

"Yes! I remember!" Falrie raised her head. "The Primal Plane is the source of all magic!"

What? Saida didn't understand what her mother meant.

"What about you?" Watthe asked Darrow. "Will you worship me?"

Saida's father glared up at the creature, tears streaming down his face. Falrie stepped in front of him, her paws outstretched.

On the ground below, Alesio sang two sharp notes, and two sound-spears whistled through the air and buried themselves in Watthe's neck.

Alesio whooped. "Yeah! All magic means Sound magic, monster! You feel that?"

Watthe hissed and whirled towards Alesio.

AFTER SINGING INTO THE SEASHELL, a new power felt like it had unlocked inside him; as if, after the overwhelming pressure had eased in his throat, he'd noticed what had been there all along.

Touch magic as well as Sound magic.

It vibrated through his boots and into his feet, up his legs, and through his half-deaf left ear. Tingling, tingling, tingling!

Not sure what would happen, he unslung his mandolin, and the tips of his fingers vibrated on the strings. He strummed loud, trying to direct the magic as he did when he fought in the cage matches, but focusing on how it *felt.*

A wave seemed to travel from his fingers down his feet, then a line of wood spikes appeared all the way down the tree. More erupted through the mire, stabbing upward and through Watthe's reformed feet.

"You will die, human!" Watthe roared.

"Sounddamn!" Alesio grinned. "I've been waiting for this fight!"

Watthe stopped moving for a moment, and the wood spikes disappeared into his body.

Oh. Oh, no. He can just absorb the magic?

Watthe expelled a heavy breath. He'd done that a few times, now, and he'd always done it right before he teleported. Alesio jumped down from the tree.

Watthe teleported and swung his claws where Alesio had been. Alesio landed in the ankle-deep weird smoke in a crouch and let loose a barrage of sound swords angled at Watthe's neck. If he could slice his head off, maybe it would hurt the monster too much to absorb. The swords dug into his torso instead.

"Sounddamn it. Bastard is stupid tall."

"You!" Watthe stomped with his massive foot, trying to smash Alesio. He rolled out of the way awkwardly with his mandolin. The foot squelched down like part of a mountain had fallen, right onto the hidden line of spikes Alesio had left from touching the half-sludge, half-void ground. The monster screamed again, then paused to pull the magic up through his feet.

Falrie shouted more things in the background to Saida. ". . . the Primal Plane is supposed to flow to the Sensory Plane! That's why this place is so angry and inflamed, and why the Sensory worlds' magic is dying! If the seashell transplants here, it could reconnect the Primal to the Sensory! It could undo the Severing!"

Watthe raised his other foot to stomp. Alesio had rolled into a deeper part of the shadows and smoke and stuck there, suspended inside it.

Darrow ran next to Alesio and yanked him out.

Watthe roared in anger and let loose another heavy breath.

"He's teleporting! Split up!" Alesio zigzagged to the left, Darrow to the right.

"Where do you want to go? Here?" Saida held the seashell up to one of the smoking vines, and it didn't seem to like that. "Okay, what about here?" She knelt and smoothed a part of the ground. The seashell's magic recoiled in her hand.

If what Falrie shouted was true, Saida hadn't caused the worlds' magic to fade. A small relief.

But it would be her fault if this transplant wouldn't take root! She held them up to the shadowy vine wrapped around the branch. "Here?"

No, not there.

ALESIO DODGED another swipe from those long, sharp finger-claws. He and Darrow knew to dash whenever Watthe breathed, avoiding those spearing claws.

"He just regrows everything! Or absorbs your magic!" Darrow said. "How can we kill him?"

"Let me try something." Alesio ducked and bought some time with another quick wire of Sound magic, slicing off Watthe at the torso, revealing the smoke and shadow underneath the gray skin. While the monster screamed and grabbed more of his followers to shore up his body, Alesio concentrated.

He located the energy inside his lungs, the Sound magic of his held breath. He breathed the full ball of energy out, and though *he* couldn't see it, Darrow watched his lips, his eyes wide. Accessing his magic felt easier after he'd sung into the seashell and he could do it with more precision.

Keeping it there, he focused on the energy in his fingers, his feet, and the tingling in his left ear. Gathering the Touch magic into another floating ball, he molded that one with the Sound magic, mixing them together. He couldn't see anything, but he could hear it. Could feel it, shape it in his hands.

"You have *two* magics?" Darrow's mouth gaped.

"I don't know what I'm doing yet," Alesio said. "But this seems powerful, right?"

Watthe teleported and raked at them with his claws from a few feet away.

Alesio flung the ball of mixed magic at him. It hit him in the thigh and his whole body stopped as if stunned by the fusion of power, his arms flung wide, one leg in the air. An invisible tangle of wires sliced his leg, up his torso, across his waist, and other ways all in the space of a moment. Watthe fell in gray outlined pieces, sinking into the strange shadow-mud of the Primal Plane.

"Did that—did that work?" Alesio huffed. He'd used the rest of his saved breath to do that.

The hundreds of Consumed all screeched and dove down after the pieces, immersing themselves.

Something rose from the depths. A lump. Bigger than before. A bulge the size of St. Rina's cathedral itself.

Sounddamn it! He just absorbed that, too! Along with the rest of his followers!

"Run!" Alesio said.

He and Darrow scattered to the left and right.

A gray-skinned, even larger Watthe burst back out of the void ground, shrieking with such primeval rage, Alesio had to cover his ears. *Thank the Senses that thing cannot use Sound magic. But how in all the worlds am I supposed to stop it?*

"Stop screaming like a child!" That black box had risen to the surface from where Watthe had tossed it, spreading outward into a mass of seeking tendrils. The Hunger. "That's nothing compared to what will happen if you don't stop *her*! Watthe, stop your pet from uniting the Planes!"

"Come on, come on, please," Saida said.

They didn't *like* the tree hollow, though. They wanted to transplant somewhere like a stage, somewhere grand to match the grand declaration of love that had created them.

"You will ruin my fermented Plane!" The Hunger thrashed in the sludge, its slick, metallic tendrils reaching towards her. "It is almost ready! I am on my way to consume it! I will not let you plant this magic!"

Could that work?

Saida raced towards the box's tendrils, gripping the seashell in one hand.

Before she could get more than five steps, Watthe teleported and scooped her up in his giant, clawed hand. "Stop throwing your magic annoying at me," he said to Alesio. "You could hit her! You could kill her! I kill her won't, but I hurt her will if you send that me again at!"

"You are a selfish, monstrous bastard!" Alesio shouted.

The skin, that horrible touch of hundreds of fingers, reached out and latched onto her once more like a swarm of leeches, reminding her of how The Hunger writhed and twisted.

Saida floated once again. She shivered, more of her energy draining out of her, and slumped. Watthe closed his eyes and grew upwards, towering over her friends like a mountain. "She is my source of power. With her magic, I can do anything!"

What about him? She asked the seashell. She couldn't hear their voice to ask their name. *He's from the Primal Plane.*

Her thoughts scrambled. *Wait, what if it just makes him stronger? What if he just eats them like he did the other transplants?*

She missed the other voices helping her in her head. She missed Tricksy Stone's sarcasm, and Goosefeather's reassurances. Maybe they would've known what to do.

But she'd always had those voices. They *were* her.

"The human's magic is strong," Tricksy Stone's voice sounded in her head.

No. Not Tricksy's voice. *Her* voice. The part of her that knew things. It sounded different from the Tricksy Stone she'd listened to for so long, maybe because she heard herself clearer. *"They are two magics already mixed. Two threads, already combined."*

The seashell vibrated with such power, it felt like she held the Summit Wave in her hand. Sound and Touch magic from Alesio, merged into one transplant.

"When they transplant, you know what happens," Goosefeather's voice —no, that part of her that was kind to herself, said. *"How they change things for the better."*

Maybe. Maybe this will work. If it doesn't, I don't know what else to do.

"Here?" She asked the transplant. "He speaks very grand. And he's from this Plane. He used to be a part of it." She recalled how when she had first met him, the ground had swelled, and he had oozed out of it like pus from an infection.

The transplant considered her words, then seemed to nod.

Saida let it roll out of her hand and it landed on Watthe's giant palm, then swirled inside like a silver thread.

Watthe's gray flesh burned and began to melt wherever the thread touched. He shuddered. He spasmed. The transplant grew, and grew, branching down through the skin, and into the smoke, and Watthe shrank as if in tandem.

The silver thread shot upwards, growing, growing like a flash of lightning up into the sky.

Alesio's tenor voice reverberated from above, and all around them, as if thunder had started to sing, replaying his words to Saida.

I'm coming with you
Because I love you

"What is this?" Watthe fell to his knees. The silver thread touched the ground, and something like an electric shock flashed through it.

"No!" The Hunger screamed. "No! I told you this would happen! I told you that you had to kill and eat the foxans! *All* of them!"

Watthe shrank again, faster. He dropped Saida, and she fell, still quite a long way to the ground. Alesio caught her by the shoulders.

"NO!" Watthe screamed. The silver thread, now more of a rope, twisted inside of him, inside the floating void of his body, merging with him. He wasn't absorbing the magic and using it, it was changing him into a transplant and binding him to one place.

All around them, the shadowy sludge of the ground turned a different color and texture, less void-like, less hollow, and wetter. The trees and the vines seemed to untwist themselves, and the sky overhead brightened, as if a sun had appeared behind clouds.

"What is happening?" Alesio asked.

Falrie and Darrow had tears flowing down their cheeks. "This is how it used to be, little autumn leaf," her father said.

"Saida," Falrie said. "We're from here. We are . . . living parts of raw magic, from the Primal Plane! Do you see?" She pointed at Watthe.

His body had shrunk further down, even more than the first time he had pulled himself out of the smoking shadows of this place. He had a tail. And pointed ears. His body was still gray, and his fingers were still sharp, but she recognized the enlarged, grotesque claws.

"He—he's a foxan?"

"A twisted, angry one," Falrie said. "When it's connected to the Sensory Plane, the Primal Plane creates new foxans to keep our race going." She wiped at her eyes, tears streaming down her face. She regarded Watthe. The silver thread worked their way through his body, snaking through him, tying him over and over to a nearby tree. "And, apparently, when the Primal Plane has no outlet to the Sensory, it crafts distorted, overgrown foxans."

"I told you!" The Hunger shrilled. "I told you to stop her! I needed to keep the Planes severed! I needed the Primal Plane to ferment! Now it's all ruined! You've ruined everything!"

Watthe tried to stand, now the same size as the rest of them, but the silver thread whipped around him, and pulled him against the tree tighter. Transplanted.

Saida swallowed. "Does that mean all foxans are sort of like transplants? Primal magic waiting to bind with another magic and stay in one place?"

Falrie frowned. "Well . . . when we are ready to die, yes. We put down roots in a world and bind with another magic type. We become part of it." She pointed at Watthe. "We forced him to do so when the sheer power of the seashell's mixed magic transplanted to him."

"Saida." The silver thread wound around Watthe's chest. "Why do to me this? You promised staying. You promised love."

Saida shivered. His words were so like Carn's. Accusing and laced with lies. Alesio stepped towards him, but she held out her hand. "Wait, Alesio. Let me do this."

Alesio clenched his jaw but nodded, his brown eyes darkening to almost black like they had when he'd found out about Carn.

She waded through the thinning smoke over to Watthe. He tried to reach for her with those grasping, grasping hands, but he couldn't extend his claws. "I promised I would stay. I never promised to love you."

He flinched.

"And you don't love me. Love doesn't force anyone to do anything." She glanced over her shoulder at Alesio. At Falrie, and Darrow. "Love cares for the other person."

Alesio smiled at her.

"You are liar." The thread worked through Watthe's neck now, as if sewing him up. "You lied me to. You led me here. You said you worship. This is worship? This is love? I hate, you fur-mix! You're—"

The silver thread closed his mouth, and he merged with it, then, as a transplant of Sound, Touch, and Primal magic.

"Well, that's one way to stop him from talking." Alesio crossed his arms beside her. "I was about to stick a sound-knife there. But that works, too."

Saida shuddered.

"Hey. He's gone. He can't hurt you anymore." As always, he did not reach out to her, but let her know she could come to him.

"Do you think your magic—the sound of your voice—" she hiccupped. "Do you think that love, real love, will reach him? Since he merged—with it?"

"Oh, Saida."

She buried her head in Alesio's chest, and he wrapped his arms around her. His voice felt safe, like her den. Precious, like her magic friends.

Around them, the Primal Plane continued to change.

25

HOW TO BE HELD

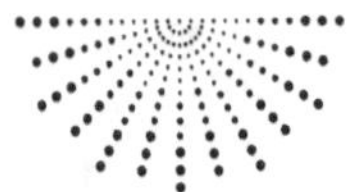

1 YEAR LATER

"What did you name this one?" Saida asked, brushing her fingers over the transplant Falrie had trimmed from Taste. Saida had ferried aliberries over to Taste a few months before, and the bakers and chefs had all gone mad for the new fruit. An old man had baked an aliberry muffin to thank the foxans, and Falrie had taken a paper rubbing from it.

Falrie smiled. "I think it likes 'Purple Sugar,' but I could be wrong. You're the expert at this kind of thing."

"Oh!" Saida grinned. "Purple Sugar is wonderful!"

Falrie shrugged, her ears folding at the tips and her human cheeks blushing. Saida handed the paper transplant back to her, and Falrie placed it with the four other transplants on the pedestal.

Each of them originated from the other sensory worlds, and one from the Primal Plane. It seemed that, when working together, the transplants settled down with more ease. They were happier together.

"It's happening," Saida said. "Look!"

The different magics swirled around each other, twisting like ribbons. They merged, shimmering, and flattened out into a large portal on the pedestal.

The crowd of people behind them clapped and cheered, dancing in the street. This was the second permanent portal that Saida and the other foxans had helped to craft on Vision. Falrie and Darrow bowed, fending off those few who tried to raise their hands in worship.

"We are not gods," Falrie said, after the hubbub had died down a bit, while a line began to form. "We are *guides*. We do not lead you to the afterlife, we lead you to see what life you can live. We help you acclimate to the new senses you will experience." She spread her arms in human form, the prepared speech flowing from her like a song on Sound. She'd practiced with Saida many times so she wouldn't stumble on her words or run away in fear.

Saida placed a hand on her shoulder, anyway.

Falrie continued, "When the Great Alesio's voice worked to reconnect the Primal and Sensory Planes, the magic in the worlds began to work again. Your gravity, your gears, your houses, your trees, all of them began to move as they should. Your bodies grew healthy. On this world and others, raw magic flowed from the Primal Plane to the Sensory and supported more life." She smiled. "Now, who here wants to find out what Scent is like?"

Screams and cheers erupted. Saida wiped tears from her eyes.

Falrie and the other foxans had remembered many things once they had gone back to their birthplace in the Primal Plane. One of them was how to create permanent portals, which helped direct and balance the flow of magics between the worlds now that more poured in from the Primal Plane.

It would take a while to trim all the necessary transplants, but they planned to fashion five permanent portals for each world: four to travel to the other Sensory worlds, and one to the Primal Plane. The overgrowths had also flourished, making it easier to find and trim them.

They had a lot of work to do, but she didn't have to do it alone anymore. She had her parents to help, and humans, too, on the worlds. Falrie and Darrow had reunited with Pell's descendent on Taste, a fox-person named Naya, and Naya had helped many of the other fox-people come forward and emerge from their safe passages and hideaways across the worlds.

Many humans, of course, remained wary and hateful towards foxans and fox-people. But the discrimination had started to fade in cities where they built permanent portals and the humans traveled to different worlds. The more places and differences people saw, the more they seemed to change and accept in their personal worldviews. Tak and his husband, Estro, had been two of the forerunners of that change, traveling with the foxans and fox-people to help the humans see there was nothing to fear in diversity.

Tener, a tiny newborn foxan, romped among the people of Vision. Unwary. Innocent. Without fear. Tener had developed straight from the healthy areas of the Primal Plane, rising from the ground like a bird hatching from an egg. This had proved that the magic from the Primal Plane was strong and ready to flow.

Falrie had explained that every foxan was a living, sentient transplant from the Primal Plane, and that eventually choosing a world to transplant to was how they died, in their way. But they affected whatever world they chose, binding the Planes and the worlds closer.

"Where did the first foxans transplant to?" She had asked Falrie one night. "Where did St. Rina end up?" They had gazed out at Scent at the top of the mountain, where Saida had found Winter Lightning. The darkness of night had outlined the stars with such precision, she imagined she could make out the framework of another world's constellations. Perhaps Sound's.

Falrie chuckled. "Do you want to guess?"

Saida pondered, chewing on her lip as a human, then gasped. "The cathedral? The St. Rina's cathedral?"

"You guessed it." Falrie raised her human hand to the sky. "She is the building, the magical part of it, anyway." She glanced over at Saida. "Have you gone to see Tricksy Stone?"

Saida nodded. They revolved, as always, in the Cadenza on Sound, one of the few magics humans could see. They had originated from Vision, after all. "But I couldn't hear their voice. I can hear some of the magics still, sometimes. But not theirs."

Falrie had sighed and gazed up at the faint tracings of far-off stars, behind the bright, close ones. "I am sorry for what you had to give up. But I am also grateful that you did, or neither of us would be standing here right now."

Saida blinked, bringing herself back to the present. Falrie guided the first set of ten humans to Scent, where a delegation of humans on the other side waited to receive them. Darrow would lead the next group in fifteen minutes.

Saida, though, had other things to do today. She teleported to the Primal Plane.

The bluest of skies waited for her. Scents swirled around in little clouds. A bush that grew upside down, but without a path of gravity to tend to it. It had a fermented shadow smeared on it.

The Primal Plane was the source of all Sense magic: raw, unfiltered, and wild. Where the sludge and shadow remained, so did some of the blockage, stopping Primal magic from flowing to the Sensory Plane.

She slipped out another transplant that she had hunted earlier in the week, the yawn of the hibernating swanseize, whispered to them about how they could thrive in the bush, and uncorked the tube they swirled inside.

They floated upwards and settled on the bush, connecting to the Primal magic like another thread joining a rope. The shadow-smoke dissipated on the bush, and the gravity shifted, letting Saida trot upwards as a foxan, into the sky.

She gazed out over the vast expanse. The shadows still existed in many places.

The Primal Plane had reabsorbed Watthe into the tree. He had vanished—though The Hunger remained, wedged in a stubborn area of that smoking shadow, that shifting mass of worm-like tendrils. A kind of strange barrier pushed away any foxan who tried to near it.

It shifted, seeming to sense her. "I've teleported from far away, much farther than you simple beings could comprehend! The box I sent is just a single brick from the world of my body! I will arrive soon!"

"Why are you still coming, if we ruined your meal?" Saida shouted back down. She'd asked a version of this question before.

"I've teleported from far away, much farther than you simple beings could comprehend!" It repeated the rest of its diatribe.

Falrie, Saida, and Darrow prepared for the threat, though they didn't know how to stop a power from a place they'd never seen.

Its grasping tendrils still reminded her of Watthe. *It's almost like . . . it's an older form of Watthe. If it's telling the truth, it ate everything from wherever it came from.*

They still found The Consumed sometimes, in some worlds, wandering the countryside, or stuck in abandoned houses on Sound, though fewer of them surprised them as time went on.

They hadn't found Clef, and that frustrated Alesio perhaps more than anything, nowadays. Saida hoped he had just died somewhere on Taste after her run-in with him and the Palates, but she also now knew the danger of ignoring something because she feared the possibilities.

Saida poured a little bit of water on the bush, playing Alesio's voice in her head. His voice soothed her when nothing else did. She didn't have to be alone and cut off, from others or herself, anymore. And that helped her not be as afraid.

***

ALESIO INHALED A DEEP BREATH, gazing out over the crowd that had gathered. He found his father's face at the front, wearing that threadbare shirt he refused to throw away, the lines on his face somehow still shaded with grime — but he smiled up at Alesio.

It had taken a little over four months to convince his father to go through the permanent portal to visit another world. Now, his father passed through it at least once a week, marveling at the cakes on Taste, and at the smell of rain on Scent.

In this model of the Cadenza built on Touch, Alesio sang a dedication song, the song they had asked him to sing as the Voice of Reconnection: his official title.

He was famous—what he had always wanted. Throughout the worlds, when the Planes had reconnected, everyone had heard his voice, and the words he had said to Saida. But now that it had happened, he no longer felt like singing for the masses was as important as singing for those that mattered to him. He sought out Tak, and his husband, Estro, holding hands near a group of straiters.

Performing, as well, had become easier, without the rawness in his throat. When he had sang into the seashell, it had taken all of that, and now, when he performed, he felt lighter. Free, with no strings of fate pulling him down.

The trimming hadn't taken his magic away at all; it had cleared space for it to fly.

He sang the updated lyrics he had worked on for "Gossamer God," which he had renamed to "Just a Teleport Away."

Have you heard the singing
Of another world's stars?
A transplant of harmony
Just a teleport apart?

Just a teleport away,
Come reconnect your souls,
Just a teleport away,
There's more wonder you can hold

The footpaths of the foxans,
That constellation street,
It guides us to higher heights,
Where we thought we couldn't reach

Have you touched
The velvet of the starlight?
Can you taste
The silver in its words?

> *The scent of the mint-fresh*
> *Sky at night*
> *Lifts us, like*
> *The gravity of birds*

His father clapped, and Saida grinned. The cheering crowd faded to the back of Alesio's mind, and he yelled, "It's time to dance!"

Saida leapt up on the stage. He had time for nothing else than to spread his arms before she dashed to fold herself around him.

HER HEART FLUTTERED in her chest like a caged and restless thing.

No. Not caged. More like a bird winging for the sky, striving ever upwards.

No. Not restless, or unfocused. More like anticipation.

He stood so close. On Touch, his breath on her face, his arms around her, felt like nestling into her favorite place.

She'd learned. This was the way she liked to be held.

www.ingramcontent.com/pod-product-compliance
Lightning Source LLC
Chambersburg PA
CBHW061222310726
48971CB00007B/1915